THE HAYSTACK

THE HAYSTACK

BRANDON CALVILLO

MASTERLESS
P R E S S

www.masterlesspress.com

Masterless Press
www.masterlesspress.com

The Haystack
Copyright © 2021 by Brandon Calvillo
Cover design by Jeffrey Nguyen

First Masterless Press print edition: October 2021

Printed in the United States of America

ISBN: 978-1-7350801-6-1 (print)
ISBN: 978-1-7350801-7-8 (ebook)

CONTENTS

Brad's Story

Chapter 1

When you look back on your life, there always seems to be one significant memory that stands out as the moment things really started to change. For me, it was this one day back when I was 11. Or maybe 10. Somewhere around there.

It was raining out, so I was just hanging out in my room and playing that old handheld ring toss water game when my oldest brother, Glenn, walked in, his blue eyes wide with excitement.

"What?" I asked, pumping the button as the rings swirled around.

"We found porn."

"Porn?"

"Yeah, in Dad's room. Follow me."

Whatever porn was, I wasn't sure that I was ready to look at it, but the seriousness in his eyes made me worry that this was too important to miss out on. I followed him down to the basement, where our middle brother, Johnny, was standing outside of Dad's room nervously raking his fingers through his brown hair. Our father had been sleeping there for around a month while Mom still stayed in the room upstairs.

"You gotta be quiet," Johnny whispered. "I don't know if he's in there or not."

"What are we doing?" I asked.

"Just be quiet!" Johnny demanded, sticking a bobby pin into the doorknob's lock.

He spent, like, 20 seconds twisting and fiddling with the thing, but the lock wouldn't give. I got the impression that he didn't know what he was doing.

"Give me that!" Glenn whispered loudly, snatching the hairpin from his hand.

Maybe ten seconds after he took over, the lock clicked. Scowling at Johnny, Glenn slowly opened the door. "Wait here," he whispered before tiptoeing into the dark room.

Johnny's head hung, and he stared at the floor looking all crushed. Knowing him, he'd probably told Glenn he knew how to pick a lock so he could seem tougher and more useful than our big brother made him out to be.

Moments later, Glenn emerged with a dirty old cardboard box that seemed pretty heavy by the way he carried it. When we got upstairs to the living room, Glenn set it down then pulled out two VHS tapes, gazing at them all wide-eyed like he'd just found the Holy Grail. "Porno," he said in awe.

"It's video of people fucking?" Johnny said like he was unsure.

Now, I'd said that word many times before—"Fuck you," "Fuck off"—but I'd never used it as a verb. Or thought about people fucking. What did that even look like?

I had to know.

"Put it in the VCR!" I said.

Glenn popped it in and hit play. The video opened in a gym. The picture was shitty, like in a straight to TV movie you immediately know isn't worth watching. The camera panned to a woman doing crunches shortly after. She was awfully pretty, and wearing a very low-cut shirt and a skirt. Her skin glistened with sweat. That's when something began to happen. Things *down below* began to feel... different. This sort of thing had happened randomly before, but never while just looking at a woman. I wasn't grossed out by girls at my school nor did I hate them, but I found it hard to talk to them, and I figured most of them didn't want to talk to me either. But this woman was different. She had boobs bigger than anything I've ever seen, thick legs, and a round butt. None of those things had mattered to me before, but they certainly did in that moment.

Then this guy with a gross mustache and veiny muscles walked in. The next thing I know, his pants are down and she was doing things to him that made no sense to me. I mean, it didn't make sense, but it sort of made perfect sense.

"Go outside!" I said to Johnny.

"What? Why?" he asked.

"Dad should be home any minute now. Go be lookouts while I watch."

"What?! That's not fair!" Glenn yelled.

"Just give me five minutes," I begged. "After five minutes, I'll switch places with one of you. Please."

Glenn stared me down for a moment before eventually getting up and leaving with Johnny on his tail.

I turned up the volume and watched curiously as the man and woman wrestled and mashed their naked bodies together. Sometimes she was on top of him, sometimes he was on top of her, but the thrusting motions were the same. They both made sounds like they were in pain, the woman especially, but they kept at it.

I was losing my mind. I'd never been so focused on anything before, and I certainly didn't want it to end. But then Glenn and Johnny came running back into the house.

"Mom's pulling up!" Glenn yelled.

In a panic, I ejected the tape and threw it in the box with the others. Then I ran it down to Dad's room, threw it behind his mini-fridge, and slammed his door behind me. Johnny and Glenn's bedroom doors slammed as I bolted for the stairs, panting. Before

I could clear the foyer, the front door swung open and Mom saw me standing there like a possum who just spotted a coyote.

"Hi," she said, brushing her dirty-blonde hair out of her face.

"Hi," I replied as calmly as I could.

"Where are your brothers?"

"I don't know."

Her blue eyes studied me for a moment. "Everything okay?"

I nodded and then raced upstairs to my room.

Later that day, I was playing FIFA when Dad came into my room—something he never did unless something was wrong.

My always stern, Mexican father sat on the other end of my bed and his brown eyes stared into mine. Back then, he was stocky and his black hair was just starting to grey a bit on the sides. "Who broke into my room?"

"What do you mean?" I asked, looking away from his gaze.

"My door was open when I got home, and I know I locked it before I left. Your brothers both denied breaking in, so either you tell me the truth or all of you are going to get shit."

Imagining the sting of his belt lashing me over and over made me shudder. If it came to that again, I hoped that Mom would hear my cries and intervene for once, giving me a chance to escape while they screamed at each other.

"Johnny did it!" I blurted out.

Dad straightened his posture. "So you're telling me your brothers are liars?"

I nodded. "Johnny told us to keep it a secret."

"What did he take?"

"A few cans of Coke," I said, hoping that would make his punishment less brutal.

The springs groaned as Dad leaned closer. "Are you telling me the truth?"

"Yes," I said. I had lied before, but never like this. Probably because I'd never been in this much trouble.

Dad slowly rose and left. Seconds after he knocked on Johnny's door, the screams started, followed by the clap of a belt lashing bare ass. A single tear rolled down my cheek as I sat in the quiet listening to the punishment all three of us should've been enduring.

Chapter 2

Our home in Placentia, California was this giant brown house that sort of looked like a creepy old barn from the outside, the kind that kids in scary movies walk by and make up urban legends about. Since home wasn't far from school, Glenn used to walk us there and back when Dad couldn't drive us. But now that Glenn was in middle school, Johnny and I no longer had a chaperone. We did, however, have Johnny's friend Michael meet up with us.

The two of them would usually exchange Pokémon cards while I watched in silence. Johnny was always good at making friends while I never made any of my own. I was a shy chubby kid who barely said two words during most days at school, even at lunch when I would sit with Johnny and his friends. I just had nothing to say. I'd just listen to Johnny make everyone cackle with his jokes, like I was trying to live through him.

When Johnny stayed home sick, I had to walk to school alone. Those were the days I felt most vulnerable. Johnny was the shield I could hide behind from the other kids. Without him it always felt like the wolves could attack at any second, even though they never did.

There was really only one actual wolf, this kid Terry Evans. He wasn't known for being the "school bully" because he only directed all his anger at me, and it started out of nowhere.

One day, not long after Johnny took a beating for breaking into dad's room, I was walking home from school and heard a voice yell out, "Fat ass! Hey, fat ass!" Since I was the only one around who fit that description, I turned around and saw a large black-haired kid wearing a crusty black jacket, sizing me up as he approached.

"I don't like you," he said.

"Why?" I asked.

"Because you're fat. Fat fucks make me sick!"

"Oh, okay… Just don't look at me then…"

"Well, that's fucking impossible—you're too huge to avoid!" As soon as I turned to walk away, Terry grabbed my backpack and dragged me to the ground.

"Don't turn your back on me. Who do you think you are?"

"Hey!" a woman's voice cried from afar. It was a teacher named Mrs. Loretti who came charging through the crowd. "Knock that off right now!" she yelled as she walked closer. "Help him up."

Terry shook his head.

"You want me to call the principal?"

"I don't give a shit," Terry spat.

With wide eyes, Mrs. Loretti pointed back toward the school. "Principal's office, now!"

Terry sneered at me as he started toward the school.

"Do I go, too?" I asked.

"No," Loretti said. "If he ever does this to you again, you tell me or one of the other teachers. Okay?"

With a nod, I left the school grounds. When I got the feeling that I was being followed, I ran the entire three blocks back home. Wheezing, I opened the front door, slammed it shut behind me, locked it, and trudged upstairs. When I got to my room, I found Johnny playing video games on my bed.

"I thought you were sick," I said.

His blue eyes gleamed. "Nah, I faked it. I poured a bunch of Fruity Pebbles in the toilet and told Mom I threw them up."

I wanted to tell him to get out of my room, but since I still felt guilty about ratting on him a few nights before, I headed back downstairs and kept lookout for him. And the second I saw Dad pulling into the driveway a bit later, I hurried back upstairs.

"Dad's here! Get back in bed," I said.

Johnny turned off the game and ran back to his room.

Right after the front door closed, Dad marched right upstairs and checked Johnny's room. Then I heard his footsteps approaching my door before he opened it and poked his head in.

"Was Johnny in bed when you came home?" he asked.

"Yeah," I said.

Dad shut the door without another word.

Knowing that I had lied to make sure Johnny didn't suffer any more of Dad's rage made the guilt in my gut diminish, for a moment, only for it to return the next second. Lying to make myself feel better about another lie? It felt like I was lying constantly. But I had to. The truth usually led to pain.

Everyone must be lying all the time, I thought. How else could anyone get through the day?

The look that Terry gave me as he walked to the principal's office popped into my mind when I woke up the next morning. I knew what that look meant. It meant going to school would be suicide. But telling Mom and Dad I'd probably get beat up wouldn't do any good. School could literally be a giant woodchipper and they'd still make me walk in.

It was 6:10 A.M., so I knew everyone was still asleep. Taking a page from Johnny's book, I crept downstairs to the kitchen, opened the cupboard, grabbed the Fruity Pebbles, and snuck back upstairs to the bathroom. I put a handful of cereal into my mouth, then chewed them for a while before spitting them in the toilet. Chew, spit, repeat. When the toilet looked like a Leprechaun shat in it, I returned the box back in the cupboard then laid in bed until I heard Mom calling out for me. And when I didn't respond, she came into my room.

"What's wrong?" she asked.

"I puked," I said.

"Where?"

"The bathroom."

She left, and when she returned, she gave me a sympathetic look. "Okay, you can stay home. No video games. Just rest. Got it?"

She brought me a Sprite and a sleeve of Saltines then kissed me on the head before leaving for work. My mom was nicer to me than my brothers, probably because I made the least amount of noise. It was occurring to me that that's all parents wanted, less noise. I tried not to take advantage of my mother's faith in me, but sometimes I couldn't help it.

I spent the majority of the day playing video games. And when the clock struck 3:00 P.M., I hopped back in bed. First through the front door was Johnny.

He barged into my room and smirked. "Are there any Fruity Pebbles left?"

"Enough for a bowl."

"Alright."

"Johnny," I said, "please don't tell anyone."

"I won't have to. I know you'll end up cracking," he said.

"No I won't!"

"Sure," he said as he walked out.

What if they find out? A voice in my head asked. *Will Mom be angry? Will she tell Dad? And what will Dad do? The belt? Worse? What's worse than the belt? I have to tell them everything. Because if they find out through someone else, I'm dead.*

"Boys! I'm home!" Mom yelled out as she usually did. The old wooden steps creaked louder and louder as she walked upstairs.

Do I tell her now? How do I tell her? Do I just blurt it out?

My mom finally walked into my room with a warm smile on her face. "Hey, honey," she said, kissing me on the forehead. "How are you feeling? Any better?"

My heart raced as she looked me over with those caring, concerned eyes. I didn't want to see her smile fade away. Now wasn't the time to confess.

"I'm feeling better, yeah," I said.

"Good! Did you throw up again?"

"No, just that one time."

"Did you eat?"

"Yes."

"Good, well, I'm going to work in my room. Just call out if you need anything." She kissed my forehead again. "I love you."

"I love you too."

Ironically, I felt sick after she left. Telling her that I loved her was the only truth that came out of my mouth. But how could I lie to someone I loved? Maybe because if I told her the truth she'd be hurt, and I didn't want to hurt someone I loved.

Then I thought, *I just lied so easily to her and I'm only in elementary school, does that mean that she's lied to me? She must have, she'd had to. Who else has lied to me? My teachers? What about? Something huge? Have they been telling me that the Earth is round when there's really no Earth at all? What reason do I have to believe anything that anyone tells me, when I know that anyone can lie?*

My heart started racing again, and I felt nauseous. Part of me wished that I had just gone to school and let Terry beat my ass. That would've been painful, but at least that pain was guaranteed to go away in time.

Chapter 3

During dinner that night, I didn't say a word, which was typical for me. But on this evening, I was silent for a reason that only Johnny was aware off. Occasionally, he'd glance over at me, like he was just waiting for me to crack.

As I took small bites of my chicken, Dad rambled on about his day and all the people he hated who made his job harder.

"Then we had this delivery," Dad said. "Ten boxes of laptops. But that bastard George was late *again*, so I had to carry the boxes in myself! I'm the manager, for fuck's sake!"

Mom didn't like when Dad cursed in front of us, but every time she brought it up, they'd wind up fighting. I think she'd succumbed to the idea that having us grow up with filthy minds was better than having our childhoods tarnished by memories of them arguing all the time.

"That's too bad," Mom said. "George'll get fired soon, I know it."

"Doesn't matter. If he does, he'll probably get replaced by someone equally as lazy. They just have to stop hiring Italians."

Mom raised a hand. "Francisco, don't."

"What? It's true! Every Italian we've hired we ended up firing!"

"It's not because they're *Italian*," Mom spat. "You can't stereotype people like that!"

"Stereotype? What are you talking about?"

That argument went on for a while. Like most fights, it didn't get any worse than mild shouting. The *real* fights were saved for nighttime in their bedroom. Those were bad enough to wake the ghosts in the attic. At first, those screaming matches were hard to sleep to. But eventually, it became like rainfall.

This is just what it's like to be married, I thought. *When you fall in love, you get married and have kids and fight all the time. That's just what you do.*

After dinner, I helped Dad clean the dishes. He'd wash a plate, then hand it to me to dry. This was the only real time I ever had alone time with him. Some days he'd ask how school was or if I was talking to any girls, but most days we said nothing at all to each other.

"So," he said as he handed me a wet plate, "your mom tells me you stayed home today."

My heart skipped a long beat. *This is it… But how would he know? Johnny must have told him, that slimy bastard.* I could already feel the belt on my ass.

"Yeah," I said, wiping the plate with the rag.

"You feeling any better?"

"Yeah."

"You gotta go to school. You don't want to be a dishwasher for the rest of your life, do you?" he asked as he handed me another plate.

"No."

"Well, what *do* you wanna do?"

"I don't know."

"What do you like doing?"

"Watching movies. Maybe I'll make those when I'm older."

"That's a pipe dream, Brad. You'll just end up washing dishes in East LA with a bunch of Mexicans. Don't you want to get married? Have kids? How are you gonna do that making six bucks an hour?"

I didn't know what to say, so I just put the dry dish in the pile of plates to the side as he washed another one.

"You have to start thinking of things like this. When I was your age, I was cutting off chickens' heads on your grandfather's farm. That hard work got me to where I am today. Your mom doesn't understand that, but I paid for this house, understand?"

He went back to scrubbing the dish, more vigorously than before. Sometimes it felt like the only times he wanted to talk were to complain about Mom and how angry he was with her. I wondered if I'd be using my own son as a confessional one day. I hoped not.

After drying all the dishes, I went back upstairs and played more Halo. I enjoyed it because I imagined the people who I was killing were people I didn't like. Lately, I was imagining almost every bad guy to be Terry.

Out of nowhere, Mom opened my door. "Time for bed. Are you feeling any better?"

Okay, I thought. *End of the line. You either confess right now or bury this and never talk about it again. There's no going back, this is it. What're you going to do? The Truth. I'm going to tell The Truth.*

"Yeah, much better," I said.

"That's good, honey. Love you." She kissed my forehead and left the room.

Usually, I'd turn my game right back on after she left, but not tonight. I couldn't. The sour feeling in my stomach made it hard to do much of anything, let alone something that goes against her wishes. Instead, I brushed my teeth, cut off the lights, and went to bed, counting the stippling of the popcorn ceiling to help me fall asleep.

I was about an hour into counting when I heard shouting coming from my parents' room. It was even louder than usual that night. They both sounded... angrier.

Dad was doing most of the shouting, and my mom was crying. That worried me because she'd never really cried in the middle of a fight before. She'd yell, but never cry. It was odd, and as upsetting as it was to hear her sobbing, I figured it was just a new sound that'd become a part of my bedtime soundtrack.

The next morning, Johnny looked exhausted on our walk to school.

"Did you hear that shit last night?" he asked. "Sounded like someone was being stabbed."

"That's not funny!" I hollered. "Don't joke about stuff like that!"

"Don't be such a pussy! If you can't joke about stuff, you'll never make friends."

That comment hit me like a punch in the gut and shook me so bad that my pace slowed. If that was the kind of stuff people laughed at, then maybe I didn't want to make friends. Maybe I'd just stay in my room and play video games every day until I got my own house. Then I'd lock all the doors, buy a giant TV, and watch all the porn I wanted.

But how do people do it? How does anyone get a house, a TV, and all of that?

My parents gave me all those things, but how'd they get it? I mean, I knew they were gone every day at their jobs while I had to go to school and sit in a room all day listening to some old person telling me things I didn't care to know. I didn't see how school was going to teach me how to get the house or the TV, but I didn't seem to have a choice.

As I watched a squirrel run up a tree with an acorn in its mouth, I thought, *the bastard didn't have to learn math to eat that acorn, why do I have to go to school to live my life?*

Johnny and I walked back home that day in silence like we did most days. But unlike most days, we found Glenn sitting in fetal position on the curb outside of the house, his eyes wide with fear.

"What's going on?" Johnny asked.

"Someone broke into the house!" Glenn said with a tremor in his voice. "All the doors were open when I walked inside! All the cupboards too!"

"Bullshit!" Johnny said.

"You think I'm kidding?" Glenn yelled as he stood. "Go inside and see for yourself!"

"Fine! I will!" Johnny yelled.

I stood there wide-eyed, hands trembling, watching Johnny as he entered the house. A minute later, he poked his head out the front door.

"Glenn, are you high? All the doors are shut!"

"That doesn't make sense," Glenn said.

"See for yourself."

Johnny ducked back inside and Glenn followed him in. Being the coward I was, I just stood at the bottom of the stoop for a while, waiting for someone to tell me it was safe to go inside. And when no screams sounded off in the house in the seconds that followed, I decide it was better to be with my brothers than standing outside alone.

"Every single one of these were open!" Glenn said from the kitchen. "I swear!"

When I peeked around the corner, I found Johnny grabbing a soda from the fridge. "Sure they were," Johnny said, cracking open his drink.

"Johnny, I'm telling you—" That's when whatever sound I heard shut him up. "Is that... music?"

"Sounds like..." Johnny's words trailed off as he looked around, his head tilted to track the sound. "Sounds like it's coming from the basement." He looked at Glenn.

Glenn looked at me.

"Is Dad home?" I finally piped up.

"No… pretty sure he's at work," Glenn whispered.

Without another word, Glenn crept toward the music, and we followed close behind him. What sounded like opera music got louder with each step down the basement stairs. Glenn looked back at us for some sort of reassurance, but Johnny and I just stared back at him. Slowly, Glenn reached for the doorknob, his hand trembling as he inched closer to it.

Right as he grabbed the knob, the music just stopped.

Glenn looked back at us all wide-eyed and confused.

Before anyone could say a word, a door upstairs slammed shut. Never have I felt more connected to my brothers than I did in that moment. Fear can do that sometimes—it can bring people together.

We all ran at the same time, Glenn hitting the stairs first with Johnny right on his heels. At the top of the steps, the crucifix that hung above the entrance to the kitchen had fallen to the floor and smashed into two pieces. That was the sign we all needed to get the hell out of there.

The three of us raced out of the house and gathered on the sidewalk outside.

"We have to move out!" Glenn yelled. "This place is haunted!"

"Fuck that," Johnny said, trying to reestablish his tough-guy attitude. "I hate moving. Even if this place *is* haunted, there's no way I'm moving again."

My brothers and I sat on the curb arguing and freaking out for an hour before Mom pulled into the driveway. Glenn told her what happened, but she wasn't having it. She just marched past us, and we followed her into the house. Without a word, she picked up the broken crucifix and put it on the counter as if it was just a normal thing instead of a sign of a poltergeist that we all knew it was.

"Boys," she said, an unnerving seriousness in her voice, "when your dad gets home, we're going to have a family meeting."

"Mom, there's *ghosts* in this house!" Glenn exclaimed. "We have to move out!"

"Glenn, did you hear what I said?" she snapped.

Glenn's posture went rigid and he just nodded.

Mom walked upstairs to her room and slammed the door.

We all looked at each other.

"That was weird," Johnny whispered. "She never yells at us like that."

"Maybe she's possessed!" Glenn shouted through a whisper.

"Shut up!"

Glenn and Johnny started arguing about ghosts and possession while I slipped out into the backyard. Ghosts or not, I didn't want to be in that house until Dad got home. So I laid down in the grass and looked up at the orange tree until I spotted one that wasn't small and green. After plucking the big, ripe orange, I stood there peeling it while staring at Mom's bedroom window. She was just walking back and forth in there on the phone. Even from where I was standing, I could tell she was upset, I could tell she was crying.

Mom didn't stop pacing the room until she hung up the phone. That's when she just randomly stood in front of her window looking at the orange tree. I was right beneath it, but she didn't seem to notice me. She just stared blankly in my direction with this dead look in her red and puffy eyes for almost a full minute before she suddenly walked away.

Maybe Glenn was right, I thought, popping the last piece of orange into my mouth. *Maybe she is possessed. Maybe not by a ghost, but maybe a demon, or something worse. But what's worse than a demon?*

Around six that evening, Dad walked in the house then immediately walked upstairs to Mom's room. They were in there for almost half an hour, not screaming their heads off, but speaking calmly to each other. Of all the odd things that happened today, that was the strangest.

Then her door opened suddenly. "Family meeting!" Mom called. "Downstairs."

Everyone gathered in the living room. Mom and Dad sat side-by-side in the two armchairs. Glenn, Johnny, and I sat on the big couch across from them. A long silence hung over the room.

"Boys," Dad finally said, "you know your mom and I love each other very much. And we love you very much." He looked at each of us one by one. "We're, uh… we're a family. We're always going to be a family." Out of nowhere, Dad looked down at his hands then started crying silently.

I'd never seen my father cry before. Until then, I didn't think it was something he could physically do. But there he was, crying in silence, streams of tears rolling down his cheeks.

Mom looked at us with red, teary eyes. "Your father and I are getting a divorce," she said calmly, like she'd been rehearsing that line over and over.

"What?" Glenn croaked.

In that moment, the world felt like it stopped spinning. I knew what divorce meant because most of the kids at my school had parents who'd gone through it. But I had no idea why it happened. I mean, my parents fought, but wasn't that just what parents do? They ate dinner and, after we went to bed, they yelled at each other. It'd been that way for as long as I could remember, so it just seemed like things were supposed to be that way.

"Now…" Mom choked out. "What happens now is… we're going to be moving out of this house and getting our own apartments. Some days you'll stay with me and some days you'll stay with Dad."

"Why are you doing this?" Glenn shouted. "Why do you guys have to do this?"

"Glenn—" Mom said.

"No, fuck this!" Glenn said. He jumped up and stormed up the stairs.

Mom and Dad didn't try to go after him. They just sat there, looking down at the ground, humiliated. Empty.

I looked over to see how Johnny was taking in all of this, and found him just staring at our crying parents. He didn't seem angry or sad. Just… indifferent. Then, after a few moments, he just got up and wrapped his arms around Mom, hugging her tightly. As though he'd become an emotional sponge, the longer he held her the more he started crying along with her.

Unsure of what else to do, I got up and walked over to Dad, opening my arms to him.

"No, it's okay," he said. "Go to your mother."

I followed his orders like I usually did, walking over and wrapping my arms around Mom. We held each other for a while as Dad stared at the ground in silence.

Out of nowhere, he rose from the chair and walked upstairs.

That night as I laid in bed, I heard nothing. No yelling from Dad. No crying from Mom. Just an eerie, unsettling silence.

I didn't sleep that night. I was too scared.

Chapter 4

The month following that divorce announcement was a stressful, confusing blur filled with uncertainty. One day we were all living under the same roof and the next, Mom had moved to a condo in Placentia, leaving us in our old house with Dad. And before we even had time to adjust to Mom living away from us and having to go from spending the week with Dad to spending the week with her, Dad told us he'd found a new apartment in Corona and that we needed to pack up our rooms.

While I packed up, I tried to imagine what Dad's apartment would be like. Mom's place was nice and expensive looking, with three bedrooms and a pool in the courtyard, so I figured Dad's apartment would look about the same as hers, if not better.

Once everything that I owned was packed into cardboard boxes, I carried them into the moving van. Dad, Johnny, and Glenn were doing the same, so making trips in and out of the house was a bit chaotic.

It was a long day, and I felt like I didn't stop sweating until the last box was in and we all finally piled into the moving van.

"Any of you want to say anything?" Dad asked as we all stared out the window at our now empty house.

There wasn't a single peep in the car.

What was there to say? It was just a house—a bunch of wood that we lived inside of. It didn't speak, it didn't know we even existed.

As Dad drove away, my brothers and I didn't stop staring at our home until it disappeared behind a row of houses. That's when

Glenn started to sniffle a bit.

"I asked if you wanted to say something, Glenn," Dad said.

Glenn turned back to the window, fuming silently.

Corona was around 20 miles away from everything—our school, Johnny's friends, Mom's place in Placentia. When Glenn asked why he was moving so far away, Dad responded, "This place is for rich people. Too expensive. How many Mexicans you see living here who aren't mowing lawns or maids for people who look like your mom?" Dad had a really good job, so I knew deep down the reason he moved so far away had nothing to do with money.

It took almost an hour before we finally rode past the WELCOME TO CORONA sign. None of us had ever been here before, so this drive through town was our first tour. I had heard someone on TV say that first impressions were everything, and my first impression of Corona was about as awful as one could be. Every corner had a rundown liquor store, several cops sped by with their lights flashing, and there were hobos on every block.

"This is it," Dad said, turning into an apartment complex.

What do you mean this is it? This place is as rundown as the rest of the neighborhood...

The buildings were a brownish white, the grass surrounding the place was all dry and blotched with dead patches, and the people on the various balconies who were smoking or drinking looked like zombies.

"We have to live with these people?" I asked, staring at the neighbors who were watching us with indifference as we carried our boxes to our new home.

"No, they all live in their own apartments," Dad said.

"I don't have to talk to them, do I?"

"No, Brad. Don't talk to anyone unless I talk to them first and tell you it's okay."

The second we walked into the apartment, I got really bummed out. The apartment had this shitty brown carpet with what looked like oil stains all over it. One of the kitchen lights was out and the other was flickering on and off.

"Goddammit," Dad said, looking up at the lights. "The manager said these would be fixed by now!" Shaking his head and grumbling, he led us past the kitchen to an open door. "Alright boys, here's your room."

"Like, a room for all three of us?" Glenn asked. "We don't get our own rooms like at Mom's?"

"I'm sleeping on the couch to give you boys a room, so be grateful," Dad said sternly. "Now, I'm going to call the manager, so put your boxes in there then keep unloading the van."

The room we carried our boxes into was bigger than I'd expected—filthier too. It was stuffy and had black scratches on the walls. When I looked out the one tiny window to check the view, all I saw was the wall to another apartment.

On the way out of the apartment, Glenn and I jumped when Dad suddenly began screaming on the phone about the blown and flickering lights.

"Can you believe this place?" Glenn said as he climbed into the moving van. "It's a shithole!"

"It's not so bad," I said as though I believed it. "There's a video store right down the street."

"Pssh. Mom has Netflix."

It took a few trips, but eventually we got the van unloaded and got to unpacking. It wasn't until me and my brothers started trying to fit all of our crap into one room that we realized one big room still wasn't big enough for all of us. Not only was there no space for all of our stuff, but there were only two beds. And since I was the youngest, Dad said I had to sleep on the floor. That's the way it always was. Glenn always got first pick, Johnny got second, and I always got the scraps, whatever they were. Sometimes I wondered if they were just treated better than me because they all had blue eyes like Mom and I was the only hazel-eyed brother. I mean, it couldn't just be my age, it had to be something else…

That night, it was impossible to sleep. How could I? The floor was itchy and just smelled so terrible it was impossible to ignore. In the middle of the night, I got up and walked out to the bathroom, staring at Dad who was sleeping on the couch snoring loud enough to wake the neighbors. After taking a piss, I went back to my spot on the floor, and that's when I realized what the carpet smell reminded me of.

Piss… that's what this floor smells like… Piss and mold…

Every time it felt like I was about to doze off, something that sounded like either fireworks or gunshots outside broke the silence. A few minutes after the loud popping stopped, I heard what sounded like an older couple fighting on the balcony next door.

"What do you want from me?" the man yelled.

"I just want things to go back to the way they were!" the woman shrieked.

"Well maybe you shouldn't have fucked him! This is your fault, *bitch*!"

This is what I'm going to have to get used to, I thought. *Gunshots and yelling neighbors.*

Strangely enough, the arguing, as loud as it was, is what helped me relax enough to fall asleep.

The weekend marked the end of our first week at Dad's. Dad packed us in the car then hit the freeway, driving in silence the entire way. There was an anger in his silence; I could tell by the look on my brothers' faces that they felt it too.

Along the way, Dad stopped at a diner. After we finished our pancakes and eggs, the waitress asked if we wanted anything else.

"Can I get an ice cream sundae?" I asked.

"You're kidding, right?" Glenn asked, smirking. "For breakfast? You just had pancakes!"

"Dad? Can I?"

"Go ahead," Dad said. "Boys, do you want one?"

Glenn and Johnny looked at each other, then shook their heads.

"One ice cream sundae coming up!" the waitress said.

"You're going to become a fat fuck if you keep eating like that!" Johnny said.

"Yeah, and pretty soon you'll have bigger tits than the waitress's!" Glenn laughed.

"Hey!" Dad yelled, shutting them up quick. "Leave your brother alone! He can eat whatever he wants!"

My dad wrapped his arm around me and shot my brothers an angry look.

For once, I was getting special treatment and I didn't know why. I didn't care, I just accepted it.

Mom was waiting for us in the parking lot when we pulled in to her complex. When she approached the car, she completely ignored Dad, greeting us with hugs and kisses before grabbing our stuff from the trunk.

Dad just sat in the driver's seat, scowling. "Sam!" he yelled out, causing my mom to turn around. "Come here for a second."

Mom looked at Glenn. "You know where to go. Take your brothers."

My brothers and I had barely taken ten steps away from the car before our parents began shouting at each other the way they always had. For some reason, I'd thought the divorce would've put out the flames of anger between them, but all the separation seemed to do was give their bitterness time to soak in gasoline.

I didn't realize how good this place smelled the last time we came here, I thought when we walked into Mom's apartment. *And why does it seem so much bigger?*

Paintings hung on the spotless living room walls. The floors were hardwood and clean enough to eat off of. The grass out back was bright green and decorated with healthy flowers around the edges. Just being here was enough to put me in a good mood.

Mom and Glenn each had their own rooms while Johnny and I were stuck sharing one. It wasn't all bad, though. He and I had our own beds so I didn't have to sleep on the floor. The second I walked into the upstairs room, I smiled at the sight of the bed. And when I sat on the edge of it and felt how soft it was, I wanted to nap immediately.

When I got back downstairs, I found Glenn sitting at a desk with a brand-new computer sitting on it.

"Holy shit! Is the internet hooked up?" Johnny asked.

"It sure is," Glenn said, clicking around a web page.

"Make sure to take off the child restrictions," Johnny demanded.

"Already did."

The door opened behind us and we all turned to see Mom stepping into the house with red and puffy eyes—a normal sight that followed any interaction with Dad.

She wiped the snot off her nose and quickly composed herself. "What do you guys want for dinner?" she asked with a smile like nothing was wrong.

Chinese takeout was what we settled on. During dinner, Mom asked about our week, but then she started asking all of these questions like she really only seemed to be interested in talking about Dad.

"What does his apartment look like?" she asked.

"Small and dirty," I said.

"Has he brought any girls over to the house? Or introduced you to anyone?"

"No, not at all," Johnny answered.

Questions like that kept coming until dinner was over.

Later that evening, Mom came into our room to say goodnight. "How do you guys like the place?" she asked.

"It's nice, I like it a lot," Johnny said.

"Good. I want you guys to feel at home here. I know things have been hard for you, but it'll get better. Pretty soon this will all start to feel normal," she said with a smile.

After that, she kissed us each goodnight and shut the door.

"Pretty soon this will all start to feel normal..." That sentence lingered with me for a while after she left.

Dad was an hour away, and we wouldn't be able to see him for a week. And now we'd have to live in this place and pretend like it was home only to go back to Dad's and do the exact same thing there. How was this normal? How could this ever feel normal?

I couldn't take how quiet it was at Mom's place at night. Trying to fall asleep without hearing people argue was just too weird. But I didn't want to hear strangers fighting like at Dad's, I wanted to hear my parents shouting on the other side of my wall.

As sad as it was, I realized I'd rather hear shouting between two people I loved than any of the new alternatives.

The new route to school that Johnny and I had to walk went right by a grocery store, so that Monday morning we stopped in for breakfast. I got a chocolate donut, a bag of cherry sour balls, and a Coke.

"Dude, you gotta stop eating like that, Brad. No girl will want to talk to you." Johnny sipped his black coffee.

"I don't care! Why would I even want girls to talk to me?"

"You'll find out eventually…" he said as we cut down the shortcut through the store's back alleyway that led right to the back of our school.

I pointed at a small broken tent sitting next to a dumpster. "Is someone camping in there?"

"Yeah, a bum. They say he snatches kids up if they walk through here at night."

"Bullshit!"

"That's just what I heard. Who knows if it's true."

I spent most of first period trying to imagine what the child-snatching bum looked like, smelled like, talked like. A man with a scar over his right eye and the nose of a witch is what I pictured. Maybe he had burnt skin and no teeth too. Or maybe he had no skin at all. Or maybe he looked totally normal.

How does someone even become homeless?

I figured maybe his parents got divorced too and he couldn't handle going from house to house, so he ran away from it all, got a tent, and lived in that alley since he was a kid.

Maybe that's what will end up happening to me. Maybe I'll get a tent next to his. Then some other kid from a broken home will get a tent and move in right next to us.

I imagined that happening over and over for decades until that alleyway turned into a piece of crap apartment complex like Dad's—a complex filled with people who were either forgotten by everyone or who really wanted to be forgotten like me.

I just sat there in class thinking about one day running into the bum during one of our walks to and from school and asking him how he ended up living there. In the off chance I never ran into him, I had to know how he ended up living that life. So I took a piece of paper out of my binder and wrote a note that read: HI. WHAT'S YOUR NAME? Then I folded it up and put it in my backpack.

After school, Johnny and I cut through that same alley again, and as we passed the tent, I started walking towards it.

"What the hell, Brad!"

"Hold on one sec," I whispered, picking up a chunk of loose concrete along the way.

"What're you doing? Get away from there!"

"It's okay. Just relax."

I removed the note from my bag then set it on the pavement next to the front flap, placing a concrete chunk on top as a paperweight with a pen beside it.

Johnny scowled at me. "What the fuck was that? You leaving him a love letter?"

"Shut up and mind your own business!"

The next morning Johnny woke up with the flu or something, so I had to walk to school alone. I took our usual route and even detoured down the alleyway alone, as scary as it was. As I passed the tent, I saw that my note was sitting a few feet from where I'd left it.

Did he write back? I pushed the concrete paperweight aside and unfolded the note.

My eyes widened when I saw the name LEONARD scribbled underneath what I wrote.

I looked back and forth in a panic. *What if he's here right now watching me? What if this note was left here as a trap?*

I shoved the note in my pocket and ran the rest of the way to school with my heart pounding like it was going to explode out of my chest.

The library is usually where I spent my lunch period when Johnny was out sick, so that's where I headed when the lunch bell rang that day. It was either that or sit by myself at a lunch table, something no kid would do if they could avoid it. Anyone unfortunate enough to find themselves alone at a table just wound up getting stared at. School isn't like the movies. If you sit alone, some random kid doesn't see you sitting by your lonesome and ask to join you. Nope, in real life, it was best to be alone in isolation instead of where everyone could see you being a loser.

So I parked myself at one of three computers in the library and looked at the poorly scribbled name on the note.

I wonder if he'd write me back if I asked him something else. I had a million questions, but I settled on one.

WHY DO YOU LIVE IN A TENT? I wrote below where he scribbled his name.

The next day, Johnny was feeling better, so I had to deal with him giving me shit when I stopped at the alleyway tent to pick up the note I'd left yesterday.

"Wait, you're still writing to that bum?" Johnny laughed. "Are you fucking nuts?"

"He's been writing back! I found out his name's Leonard."

"Who cares? What, are you trying to become friends with him? He's crazy."

Ignoring Johnny, I opened the note and found a poorly written answer to my last question.

WHAT DO YOU CARE?"

"What does it say?" Johnny asked.

I showed him the response.

"See! Even he wants to know why you're asking him a bunch of questions…"

Chapter 5

Despite having a ton of questions that I wanted to ask Leonard, I didn't write back to him following his cold response. Part of the reason is that it was clear he didn't really want to talk. The other reason was because I had a nightmare that I was placing another note by his tent and a burnt hand came out and grabbed mine.

That dream scared me so bad that I woke up in a cold sweat. *Maybe Johnny was right…* I thought, sitting up in bed that night. *Maybe this whole thing would lead to something terrible.*

The nightmare shook me so bad, I convinced Johnny we had to take a different route to school.

That following Friday, Johnny was going on about going to the high school football game, something I'd never get invited to. He and his friends would always go then he'd come back home bragging about how many girls he'd flirted with.

"I'm going to get so many numbers tonight," Johnny said on the way back from school that Friday.

"You don't even have a cell phone," I said.

"Yeah, but when I get one, it's going to be game over!"

Right before it was time for him to leave for the game, I was just watching TV on the couch and Johnny was over by the door tying his shoes. That's when Mom walked by and glanced at me with this pitiful look.

"Johnny, I want you to take Brad with you tonight," she said.

Johnny looked up at her like she'd just asked him to stick his hand in a deep frier. "What? Why?"

"Because he's your brother and you never spend any time with him, that's why!"

"Well, Glenn doesn't spend any time with me!" Johnny protested.

"Jonathan, either you take him or you're not going! I want you back by 10. No later."

Even though I often pretended that I didn't care about going to the football games with Johnny, part of me always wanted to go. And I wanted to be excited about going that night, but I could tell by how quiet Johnny was during the walk that he didn't want me there. I mean, of course he was ticked off. Mom *made* him take me, it's not like he invited me to tag along himself.

The entire ten-minute walk there, Johnny just dragged his feet and stared at the ground in silence. I never quite figured out why he didn't like me hanging out with him and his friends. I always thought that being quiet and keeping to myself made me easier to be around, but it seemed like my presence alone was a natural repellent for most people.

The second Michael spotted Johnny coming up the bleachers, he smiled and waved. Then he saw me trailing behind him and his expression changed. "Hey, Brad... You decided to come too?" he asked flatly.

"My mom made me bring him," Johnny groaned.

"Oh, okay... But I only saved one spot. Had I known Brad was coming—"

"It's fine," Johnny interrupted. "Brad, go sit down there in the front row."

Sulking, I walked down the bleachers and found a spot on the very bottom row, the place no one wanted to sit because the players on the sidelines made it impossible to see the field.

Being at the game wasn't as fun as I'd thought it'd be. Every so often, the audience would either holler, cheer, shout, or boo while I just sat there not reacting at all. It also didn't help that I was alone.

Occasionally, I'd look up to where Johnny was to see if he was as into it as everyone else or as bored as me. At one point, I saw him and Michael talking to two girls. Michael had said something that made the girls laugh. Then Johnny said something and the girls just awkwardly looked down at their nails. When Michael started talking again, the girls looked over at him and they were all smiles again. That's when Johnny looked back at the game like he'd given up on trying to talk to them altogether.

Around the fourth quarter, I had to piss so I went looking for a porta potty. I wound up wandering to the back of the school and couldn't find a single place to go. I mean, I could've gone in the bushes, but I didn't like to do that at night. I'd always been afraid that a raccoon would hop out of nowhere and sink its teeth into my dick. I'd rather piss my pants than risk being known as the kid who got his dick bitten off by a raccoon.

The further I walked, the quieter it got and the more my bladder hurt. The next thing I know, I'd wandered all the way over to a sidewalk next to school. That's when I saw the alley.

As long as no one sees me and I can see at least a few feet in front of me, I should be fine, I thought, creeping into the alley.

When I got behind the dumpster I unzipped and did my business. And right as I zipped my fly back up, I heard a noise.

"What're you doing back here?" a gravelly voice spoke.

My heart sank into my stomach. When I spun around, I found a shadowy figure in the middle of the alley. He didn't move, and neither did I. My hands trembled and my heart jackhammered in my chest.

Should I run? What if I run and he takes that as a challenge to chase me?

"I asked you a question!" the man growled.

"I'm just taking a shortcut to get home, sir," I said, my voice cracking.

"So, you piss in *my home* on the way to yours?!" the figure stalked towards me.

"I—I'm sorry?"

An old man wearing a big green torn-up coat with badges on it emerged from the shadows. His skin was leathery like my mom's purse, and his nose was massive and speckled with boils. His beard was bushy. The hair on his head was long and gray, clumped together with grease. One of his bright blue eyes was bloodshot and puffy while the other was white with a few bulging veins.

"What's your name?" he asked, glaring.

I was too scared to speak, too busy preparing myself for him to pounce on me.

"Where you off to, boy?"

"Sir, please… I just want to go home."

His glazed-over eyes burned into mine. "You can stop lookin' at me like that, I'm not gonna hurt ya," he said, looking at the ground.

Something about his slumped posture and defeated expression reminded me of how I felt after my brothers would pick on me when I was younger. Hell, I still felt that way when they ganged up on me, but I hid it from them because I thought that's what you did when you got older. But here was this frightening old man who suddenly looked like a scared lost dog.

"You know," he said with a newfound tenderness in his voice, "I used to live around here. Believe it or not, I used to have a house only a few blocks away. I had a wife. A daughter. A job. All of it—everything I could want and everything they told me I needed. Then I started seeing things. Things no one else could see. Horrible things, things most people could only see in their nightmares. Creatures. Demons."

The man kept looking at the ground as he spoke. "These things," he continued, "they kept following me wherever I went. I tried convincing myself they weren't real, but I'd always catch them out from the corner of my eye. Then they started talking to me, you see. Telling me disgusting things. My wife told me to see someone—to take something to make it stop. My doctor gave me pills, so I took 'em. For a while the demons stayed away, but they came back. The doctors gave me different pills, but they all stop working eventually. I couldn't pay for the house, so my wife took my daughter and left. Now all I got is the demons telling me I'm no good. Telling me they'll eventually kill me. So I live wherever I can, until they do."

Whatever fear I'd felt earlier had almost completely dissipated. "Do you see anything right now?" I asked.

He looked up at me with bulging eyes and nodded. "They're all around you. Two behind you and one at each side of you."

I looked around nervously. "Do they scare you?"

"No. What scares me is I don't know if you're real or they are."

"They're not real. I am."

A twisted smirk crept across his face. "Funny, they're telling me the exact same thing about you…"

Beads of sweat formed on my forehead as the fear returned. *If he thinks I'm a demon, what's stopping him from lunging at me? What if he has a knife?*

Suddenly, the man sat down on the pavement, turned his head away from me, and covered his ear with his hand. "It's okay, Leonard," he said to himself. "If they wanted to hurt you, they would've by now. They're all talk. They're all talk! They're not going to hurt you! They're all talk!"

As soon as he started shouting, I ran out of the alley. I didn't look back to see if he was chasing me, I just kept running, even after his shouts faded. Every house I passed around the corner had their lights off. The only light I had was from the stars above and a few streetlights in the distance.

After looking back and realizing I wasn't being chased, I stopped to catch my breath. That's when it hit me. *That guy was the same Leonard I was writing to…* The sound of an audience erupting in applause snapped me out of my trance. *The football game.*

Still panting, I walked in the direction of the game, looking over my shoulder every time I thought I heard footsteps. There was never anyone there, except for the one time I saw a dog walker. Night or day, these sidewalks always seemed to be empty.

By the time I found my way to the back of the school and started climbing the gate to the football field, my legs were sore. As I got closer to the field, everyone was filing out from the bleachers into the parking lot.

After weaving through the crowd in search of my brother for several minutes, I eventually found him standing by a tree at the edge of the lot, watching Michael walking away with the girls he was charming earlier.

The second Johnny spotted me in the corner of his eye, he glared at me. He didn't even ask where I went. Even though he didn't say anything, I just knew he was pissed at me because he somehow blamed me for not lucking out with those girls.

Chapter 6

By the time I was in eighth grade, I'd gotten used to the whole bouncing back and forth between Mom and Dad's places. Well, maybe not *used* to it, but I sort of developed a new routine to help me cope with it. Basically, on the weekends and every day after school, I'd lay in bed all day and only leave the room whenever I got hungry. Then I'd go back into the room and do it all again until I zonked out.

No matter whose house I was at, both parents would give me crap for my new lifestyle, mainly because they didn't like what it was doing to my body. My stomach plumped out with each passing month, cheeks had gotten so big that I could see them in my peripheries, and, like my brothers had warned, I had essentially grown a significant pair of breasts just like the girls in my grade.

I didn't care about any of this though. There were a lot of other boys at school who looked identical to me, so I figured that puberty was just a luck of the draw and that certain boys developed differently than others. Some grew taller, their arms got muscular, their chests more toned, and they grew hair in places you wouldn't expect. Meanwhile some stayed the same height, and the only things that grew were their stomachs.

Johnny was in high school during my eighth-grade year, meaning whenever some asshole would yell, "Hey, fat ass!" or something along those lines, there was no one left to make them stop. Not having him around also meant I never had anyone to sit with. At the beginning of the year, I really tried sitting in the cafeteria with everyone else, but sitting alone at a table on the outskirts of the lunchroom while watching everyone else socialize and laugh started to sting too much. So, after a few months, I decided to go back to spending my lunch break in the library like I used to do when Johnny was sick.

My first day of going to the library for lunch, I walked in and went right up to the librarian's desk. The woman with frizzy red hair and thick-rimmed glasses was back there scribbling something on a piece of paper. It wasn't until I was right in front of her desk that I noticed she had freckles from her forehead all the way down to these large breasts that looked like they were ready to pop out of her gray blouse. I didn't look away until I realized her piercing green eyes were staring into mine.

"Yes? Can I help you?" she whispered in a southern drawl.

"Uh, I was… uh…" I stammered in embarrassment from being caught.

She placed her pointer finger against her mouth, and I shut right up. "Do you need help finding a book?"

"No. I was, uh… just hoping I could eat my lunch here?" I whispered.

She stared at me with those green eyes for a moment then pointed her pencil at a table in the back of the library. "Don't make a mess. If you do, clean it up," she whispered. "And absolutely no eating at the computers."

With a nod, I staggered off with my tray toward the back of the room. That's when realized I wasn't the only loner who wanted to hide out here. The other library-lunch kids were chubby like me or they were deathly skinny. Even though everyone in the library probably weren't the types to pick on anyone, none of them ever made contact with each other or with me.

The table the librarian pointed out to me already had a kid sitting there. He was this thin boy who was chewing with his mouth out, smacking and breathing super heavy.

I sat a chair away, eating my lasagna as quietly as possible, looking up every now and then to stare at the librarian. Part of me hoped she'd catch me looking and lock eyes with me again.

"She's hot, isn't she?" the boy beside me spoke.

I looked over at the skinny kid right as he was stuffing his face with fries like he was trying to see how many he could fit. "Yeah. Yeah, she is," I whispered. "What's her name?"

"Miss Reynolds," the boy said. "Not *missus*. That means she doesn't have a husband."

"So?"

"So that means she's fair game, dude."

"Fair game for what?"

"Fucking, obviously."

I chuckled, looking back and forth between him and Miss Reynolds. *There's no way a physically mature woman would go for some scrawny eighth grader,* I thought.

"Have you ever even done that?" I asked.

"Yep. Twice."

My eyes widened. "And you think you could do that with her?"

The boy stopped eating and looked me right in the eye. His face was gaunt, but well structured. His brilliant blue eyes scanned me like he was trying to read my mind.

"How many girls have you fucked?" he asked, intensely staring at me without blinking.

I didn't know what to say. There weren't very many boys at school with girlfriends. The only eighth grader I'd ever known to hook up with a girl was Michael. Before he went to high school, he told us he had been with two girls. The only reason I believed him was because Johnny vouched for him. My brother said he had heard it happen once while spending the night at his house. Also, when the other boys would ask Michael about what it was like, he provided the kinds of details you couldn't make up. It made

Michael cooler in our eyes, like he had accomplished some unimaginable feat.

And because this scrawny kid before me had done it with a girl when I hadn't, I felt inferior.

"One girl," I finally answered.

"When?"

"Last year at my friend's house."

"She go to this school?"

"No. She was a friend of a friend visiting town for a couple days. We were all spending the night at our mutual friend's house when it happened. My buddy heard the whole thing. I'd say ask him about it, but he's in high school now."

The boy stared at me, red veins bulging across his eyes like a live polygraph test.

I stared right back, knowing that if I looked away he'd know it was all bullshit.

Without blinking, the boy popped another fry into his mouth. "I'm Travis, by the way."

"I'm Brad."

As I took another bite of lasagna, I glanced over at Ms. Reynolds again. After I'd ogled her for a few moments, she looked right at me. I quickly averted my gaze and tried to play it cool.

Travis snickered. "You're a funny guy, Brad," he said, smirking.

Something about how he smiled told me that he knew I was lying about having sex. I didn't care that he knew because he didn't seem to care that I lied. I made him laugh and, for that, he liked having me sitting there with him.

For once, it finally felt like I was making a friend.

Things changed since I met Travis. He and I would meet up after the lunch bell then go to the library to eat. Some days we'd talk, and some days we just ate in silence, stealing glances at Ms. Reynolds.

One day, Travis opened up to me about his life as an only child in Chicago.

"My mom was a therapist and my dad was a firefighter," he told me at lunch that day. "She hated his job because she thought it was too dangerous, especially for someone with a family. Dad would always say that he'd rather save lives than protect his own. He had a lot of balls, my dad. But Mom didn't think so. She just thought that was selfish."

"Your mom just didn't get it, that's all," I said.

"No, she was right. See, we all moved to New York when I was 11, and my parents kept their same jobs." Travis turned to me with this serious look. "That was 2001… Dad's need to be selfless cost us everything on September 11th…"

I didn't know what to say.

"My mom was at home with me when the first plane hit," Travis said. "I don't remember most of it, only that she was crying a lot and telling me to go to my room. I told her I didn't want to. I begged her to tell me what was going on. She said Dad ran into the first tower to save the people who were trapped. Then the second plane hit and both towers collapsed. We didn't hear anything until the next day when some policeman came by to tell us he was dead." Travis had stopped eating and just stared off into nothing. "After that, my mom sort of lost her mind. She kept it together just long enough to move us out to Orange County, but once we got here, she completely lost her shit. She got sent to the looney bin in Santa Ana a few months later, and I've been living with my aunt in Placentia ever since."

I stared at him for a while in silence. "Shit, dude, I'm… I'm so sorry."

"Eh, it's alright. That's just how things are."

He and I didn't talk the rest of lunch. And he didn't look down at his food once like he usually did, he just stared ahead at nothing the whole time.

A week after that, Travis started walking home with me after school. Not long after that, he invited me over to his aunt's house to hang out. We'd pretty much just sit around and play Call of Duty and Guitar Hero on his Xbox. I got pretty good at Guitar Hero, but I sucked at Call of Duty—Travis was a beast at that game, probably because all he did on weekends was play online. Sometimes, he'd even play all night and well into the day.

The crazy thing was, all Travis did was play games yet he still somehow had a 4.0 GPA. He didn't even act smart, or at least act the way I thought smart people were supposed to act. All he talked about was video games, movies, and girls—not science or things he learned at school. However, he did tell me that when he got to high school, he was going to take mainly honors classes.

Being quick-witted is how he showcased his intelligence. Quick wit and the ability to make anyone he talked to laugh their asses off is what made him popular at school. That and the fact that he was a smooth talker. When we'd walk home together, there'd always be at least four or five people who'd warmly greet him, or shout out his name from a car. He'd always play it cool when that happened.

It didn't make sense why someone as smart, funny, and charming as him would hang out with me. I wasn't funny, and I was nowhere near smart. I barely had a 2.6 GPA, which was painfully below average. It would've been more exciting if I was a full-blown idiot. And to top it all off, I had all the charm of a dog staring right into your eyes as it took a shit on your shoes.

"You seem to have a lot of friends," I said to Travis on the way home one day. "So why do you eat in the library?"

"I don't have friends," he said as he pressed the button at the crosswalk. "Why would you think that?"

"Because everybody's nice to you, even the popular kids."

"Yeah, but I wouldn't call any of them my *friends*. They're more acquaintances than anything else."

"What's the difference?"

"Okay, so, everyone is forced to go to school, right?"

I nodded.

"If you really think about it, we're all just random kids who live nearby who are forced to be in the same space for five days a week. Sure, I make kids laugh and I know their names, but I don't *actually* know any of them. Interacting with people I don't really want to hang out with just makes them an acquaintance to me. It's all circumstantial."

"Why don't you want to know them?"

"Because most people are pretty damn boring, I guess."

That blew my mind. If he thought most people were boring, what did he think of me? Was I just an acquaintance like all the others? Was he just hanging out with me out of pity?

"Well, look who it is," spoke a voice that sent shivers down my spine.

Standing right in front of us was Terry Evans, my old bully. I hadn't seen Terry since elementary school, and I'd forgotten about him entirely. But there he was, standing five feet away from us looking taller and bulkier than I remembered him, his giant gut popping out of his tragically tight shirt. There were deep scars on his cheeks and the rest of his face was riddled with bright-red pimples, and dark red scabs. It seemed like puberty had hit him like a grenade.

"It's the pussy!" Terry spat through his retainer, glaring at me with wide, fiery eyes. "The kid who got me expelled!" Then he looked over at Travis, sizing him up. "And look what we got here, his queer fuckbuddy!"

Travis looked over at me, chuckling. "Is this some sort of prank of yours, Brad?"

"No," I croaked.

"Oh, so this guy's for real then?" Travis said, turning to Terry. "You're serious? I find it hard to believe that you're some kind of badass."

Terry slowly walked up to Travis and got right in his face. "And who the fuck are you, huh? Other than this loser's boyfriend."

Travis didn't move, he didn't break eye contact, he just smirked. "Yeah, that's totally right. And we fuck all the time! Nonstop, really. Like, his ass is basically like the container you put that retainer in every night, but for my dick."

Terry grimaced. "Ugh, that's fucking gross!"

"What's gross to you is beautiful to us," Travis said. "Not that you'd know what beautiful is. Looks like you've broken every mirror you've stared into."

My jaw hung. How could Travis not be scared of someone of Terry's size? Somehow Travis was basically laughing in his face. And there I was, frozen in fear, trying to work up the nerve to take a punch for Travis so he could run away. The last thing I wanted was him getting beat up for me.

Terry grabbed Travis by his shirt then raised his fist. Then wham! Travis punched him in the face while Terry's fist was still cocked back.

Tears welled up in Terry's eyes as he grabbed his blood-gushing nose. And as he backed away, I saw fear in his eyes. "Fuck!" Terry honked. "What's wrong with you?! You fucking broke my nose!"

"You better get to the ER then. I think there's one that way," Travis said, hooking a thumb over his shoulder. "I'd hurry, though. I hear there's a major artery in your nose that'll make you bleed to death if it isn't professionally treated."

Terry's eyes widened then he ran past us without a word.

Travis watched him run off, then looked over at me. "Alright, so I'll ask again… Who was that guy?"

"He used to pick on me in elementary school," I said. "His name's Terry Evans."

"Ah! You know what? That's the kid who got transferred to my old middle school before I started going to Yorba Linda Middle! Thought he looked familiar."

"You knew him?"

"Nah," Travis said. "Kids talked about him though. Word around school was that he had a screw loose—some sort of personality disorder, I think. He'd lash out and threaten teachers all the time, but never actually made a move. Now I see why; he's all talk. Most guys like him are." Travis started walking again, and I hurried alongside him. "By the way, Brad, I'd never do something like that for an acquaintance."

Chapter 7

With Travis by my side, eighth grade flew by. Seriously, it was the fastest year of school ever. Having Travis around gave me an outlet for all of the bad and good thoughts I've kept to myself forever. Travis not only heard what I had to say, he related to every ounce of madness I spoke to him.

A few months before the summer, I failed a science test and started freaking out over the fear of being held back a grade.

When I vented to Travis about that at lunch, he let out a half-laugh. "What are you worried about?" he asked. "Worst case scenario is you drop out. I'm pretty sure you can do that when you're 16 if your parents are cool with it. Isn't that what you want anyway?"

"My parents would *never* let me drop out. And if I did, I'd feel like an idiot."

"Why?"

"Because only idiots don't finish school."

"Dude, have you seen how many fucking idiots there are in the world? A lot. And guess what? Most of them graduate high school. Hell, a lot of them even go to college."

"So?" I asked. "What's your point?"

"Dropping out or failing school doesn't mean you're dumb. It means you're lazy or careless, but not dumb."

"Okay, then I'm lazy or careless. That sucks too."

"Look, they're just not teaching you anything you wanna learn. That's why you couldn't remember what was on that study guide, because you didn't give a shit what you were reading."

"Makes sense… You scared about high school?" I asked.

"No, why would I be? That's when we start going to parties and having some *real* fun."

After that conversation, I tried not to worry as much and talked myself into looking forward to making it to high school.

By the summer after graduating eighth grade, having divorced parents and bouncing between two homes was starting to feel more normal, at least to me. Even after all that time apart, Mom and Dad still seemed fairly bitter toward one another. When one would drop us off at the other's apartment, there would be no talking and barely any eye contact.

Things with Mom had changed a bit. She had stopped asking us how Dad was doing around the time she started bringing other men to her place. She'd introduce each of them to us as her "new friend," like we didn't know what *boyfriend* meant. There was a Peter, a Derrick, a Nathan, and two Stevens. Each one of them only came around for about three weeks before they stopped coming over. And after each ended *relationship,* Mom would sob in her room for a couple days before a new guy came into the picture.

The most recent "friend" Mom brought over was named Mac. He was a tall, burly man with a military haircut and a country twang. Mac was one of the few "friends" my mom brought over who broke the three-week curse, and he actually seemed interested in talking to us unlike the rest. He'd ask us questions about school and crack jokes that were funny half the time.

One summer night, Mom asked us if we wanted to go see some animated movie called *Cars* with her and Mac. Johnny and I said yes, but Glenn refused.

"C'mon, Glenn," Mom said. "He really wants to hang out with you guys."

"Well, I don't wanna hang out with him!" Glenn barked.

"Mac's just trying to be your friend."

"I don't need another goddamn friend!" Glenn ran upstairs to his room and slammed his door.

"Glenn!" my mom called out, chasing him upstairs.

"What a pussy," Johnny said after listening to them argue for a bit. He then sat down at the family computer and logged into his Myspace page.

"Woah," I said, staring at his 97 friends. "How do you have that many friends?"

"Because everyone at school has a profile, and everyone asks everyone to be their friend. Sometimes people I've never even talked to send me friend requests, dude. There's this one girl at school who has 3,000 friends."

"Seriously?"

"Yeah, she's like a famous person on campus. Everyone wants to be in her Top 8 friends."

"What's that?"

"Eight people you choose to be seen on your profile, so everyone knows they're your *best* friends. Most of the time it's bullshit, though. It's like a status thing. One kid said he'd give me 30 bucks to be in my Top 8, and I never even met him before."

"Did you end up doing it?"

"I made it 100."

"Holy shit!"

That's when Mom came down the stairs wiping tears from her eyes. "Come on, boys, it's just going to be the three of us.

The entire ride to the theater, Mom didn't talk about what happened with Glenn.

Mac grinned at us after him and Mom were done hugging. "Hey, boys! Where's Glenn?"

"Oh, he's got a terrible cold," Mom said, pretending to be all enthusiastic. Johnny and I knew her well enough by now to know when she was putting on a show. "He couldn't make it, but he really wanted to."

The theater for *Cars* was jam-packed, so we couldn't all sit together. Johnny and I sat next to each other near the middle while Mom and Mac sat two rows in front of us. The entire movie, Mac had his arm wrapped around her and, whenever something funny happened, they'd laugh louder than the children in the theater. It was weird to see Mom laughing with a guy. I never really saw her laugh with Dad or any of her new boyfriends. Mac seemed to bring out a new side of her, one that was filled with joy instead of anger—glee instead of pain. Seeing her like this made me wonder if there was ever a time before I was born where Dad brought out those exact same feelings.

Johnny nudged me when he saw me staring down at them. "I give it two months, tops," he whispered, shoveling a handful of popcorn in his mouth.

In the parking lot after the movie, Mac kissed Mom on the cheek, shook both of our hands, then we went our separate ways. And on the walk back to our car, Mom was giddier than a kid who just inherited Disneyland. Hell, from the time we left the theater right up until we finished packing up to go to Dad's, she was in a great mood. That is, until Glenn brought his bags out to the car with an attitude, not making eye contact with any of us as he tossed his crap in the trunk.

The entire drive to Dad's was filled with awkward silence. And when we pulled up to his place, Glenn climbed out of the car, grabbed his bags, then stormed off to the apartment without so much as looking at Mom. Mom tried to hide how hurt she was while she helped us with our bags and said goodbye to us but, after watching her holding back tears for years following arguments with dad, I knew she was on the verge of breaking down. I knew she'd cry the whole way home.

"What did you really think of Mac?" Johnny asked as we walked side by side to Dad's place. "No bullshit."

"I liked him," I said, staring at the ground.

"Well, I got a bad feeling about him. I don't know why, just something in my gut telling me he's bad news waiting to happen."

"Mom seems happy, though."

"I know, and that's what scares me."

Dad was standing in the living room curling two 40-pound dumbbells when we walked in. He was so focused on his reps, he didn't acknowledge us, he just stared at the wall ahead like he was in a trance.

"Hey, Dad," Johnny said, shutting the door behind us.

Dad didn't respond, he just kept doing curls like we weren't even there. Johnny and I exchanged looks then we turned back to Dad right as he set his weights down. And even though he was done with his set, he still didn't respond. He just walked to the kitchen without looking at us, filled a cup with sink water, chugged it, then slammed the glass on the counter. After that, he marched right back over to the dumbbells and started curling again.

My heart started racing. *Something's not right,* I thought, picking up my bag and hurrying into our room, where Glenn was lying on the bed all curled up, facing the wall.

"What's going on with Dad?" I whispered.

He didn't respond.

Johnny rolled his eyes when he walked in the room. "Okay, Glenn, what's up?" he snapped, tossing his bag in the corner. "Did you say something to him? Because he's acting like... well, he's acting the way you've been acting all day..."

Glenn didn't reply at first. After a few moments, he just rolled over onto his back and stared at the ceiling. "I told him about

Mom's date and how you guys went to the movies with him," he said.

"What? Why the fuck would you do that?"

Glenn rolled back over and faced the wall.

With a growl, Johnny dumped all the clothes out of his bag then started throwing them into the closet.

Now that I knew what was wrong with Dad, I figured it'd be better to be in the living room with him than with Johnny while he was raging out. When I saw Dad sitting on the couch staring at the carpet with tears rolling down his cheeks, I froze at the end of the hallway. Even though I'd seen my father cry when he told us they were getting divorced, I still wasn't used to seeing him go from a macho, influential figure to this sniveling, unrecognizable man.

With a sniffle, Dad looked up at me, something like shame in his bloodshot eyes, like he was upset that I had witnessed him during another moment of weakness. Unexpectedly, he just started crying harder.

That's when I sat beside him and hugged him tightly.

Just like that, he stopped crying, like he'd suddenly realized that he needed to be strong because it wasn't a son's job to comfort a father. Then, after a loud snort, he placed a hand on my head then we sat there like that for a little while.

"Okay," he huffed. Then he rose from the couch and wiped away his tears on the way to the kitchen. "What do you want for dinner, mijo?"

"I'm not really hungry," I said, watching him rifle through the fridge.

He stared at me for a moment, then reached inside the fridge and pulled out a steak. "I'll make you some carne asada," he said, ripping the plastic off.

The grilled beef my father cooked for me that night is still hands down the best carne asada he has ever made.

Chapter 8

On the first day of ninth grade, Mom actually drove me to school for the first time in forever. It's not like she took off time from work to take me or anything though—she just happened to take the day off to go to a wedding with Mac, because she loved weddings too much to miss even one.

At that point, her and Mac had been dating for four months. She had become so obsessed with him that she didn't even talk about her day when she came home, she'd just talk about Mac. And as soon as she did, Glenn would storm off to his room. Mom didn't care about my brother's reaction to Mac anymore; she was too in love for that.

Seeing all of the kids hanging out in front of El Dorado High was a bit overwhelming.

"So, you ready to start your high school career?" Mom asked excitedly, almost like she was the one going instead of me.

"Not really… There's a lot of kids out there," I said, still staring out the window.

"It's okay. They're probably just as scared as you are."

"I'm not scared. Just… I don't know what to expect because I don't know any of them."

"Don't worry, honey. You'll be fine."

"What if I won't?"

"You're too young to be that pessimistic. Think of it as the start to a new journey. Who knows who you'll meet here or what'll happen? Just try to have fun, okay?"

"I'll try," I said, climbing out of the car.

When I was about halfway to the bustling campus, Mom pulled out of her spot behind me, shouting, "Have fun, sweety! Love you!"

She always seemed to save the loudest and cringiest displays of affection when there were tons of people around. Any other day, that would've embarrassed me, but the dread I felt as I trudged toward the concrete prison where I'd be serving a four-year sentence overshadowed that.

A lot of the younger-looking students I passed on my trek across the courtyard were short and stocky, baby-faced kids with acne who looked lost and nervous. In other words, they looked just like me, minus the extra 80 pounds I had on most of them. And then there were the towering figures who were laughing and smiling with their friends. Some guys were muscular. Some had facial hair. The girls were developed like the overly mature teens they cast in movies. The only way I could distinguish the upperclassmen from the teachers was to check for backpacks, full beards, and formal attire.

From the middle of the courtyard, I spotted the cafeteria, which was next to the admin offices. Right outside of the lunchroom was the senior quad, the place where the twelfth graders ate their lunch at special cement tables that my brothers told me to avoid. Smack dab in the center of the courtyard, there were rows upon rows of bleachers—that's where the rest of us were supposed to hang out at. Beyond all of that were these identical long buildings where the classrooms grouped together.

Like a lot of other nervous freshmen, I walked through the courtyard holding the straps of my backpack while staring at the ground. It's not like I was any more scared of being judged for walking around alone in high school than I was in middle school, it was more so that not looking up from the floor kept me from finding out if there really were hundreds of eyes on me like I imagined.

Johnny and I are in the same school again, and I've got Travis here with me. All I've got to do is stick with them and I won't have to walk around like this forever.

Johnny and Travis were supposed to meet me at the bleachers, but when I got there, they were nowhere to be found. Instead of wandering around, I took a seat and looked around for them. Beside me, there was a pack of kids laughing at something the one guy was showing them on his cell phone.

Oh yeah, I could just text them instead of sitting around looking like a lost puppy, I thought, pulling out the phone Mom had just bought me that summer. It was just a cheap flip phone, not the fancy T-Mobile Sidekick with a full keyboard and internet that Travis had had since last year. When I opened my address book, I shook my head. Travis's was the only one of the five numbers that wasn't a member of my immediate family.

With the sun beating down on me, I sat there on that hot metal bleacher for what felt like forever, obsessively flipping my phone open every few seconds only to find zero new messages.

At the sound of the bell, I knew there was no chance either of them would show, so I shoved my phone in my pocket, picked up my backpack, and followed the flock of kids to the back of the school where my algebra class was.

The room I strolled into hardly looked like a class. It had white cement walls with splotches of dirt and old pencil marks etched on them, and there were these fluorescent lights that made the classroom feel like a hospital ER waiting room. Bland was the only word to describe it.

At least the classrooms in middle school had character, I thought, taking a seat.

At my old school, our classes were decorated with corny educational posters with sayings like, "**COME TO THE NERD SIDE, WE HAVE PI**" or "**110 PERCENT OF MATH STUDENTS DOUBT THEY WILL EVER NEED MATH.**"

I never thought I'd ever miss those stupid posters…

The only thing written on the whiteboard was: **MR. MARTINEZ.** My eyes wandered from the board to where our teacher was sitting behind his desk writing away, paying no mind to the kids who were finally starting to file into the classroom. His head was down, so all I could really see was that he was tan and his dark hair was slicked back with gel. Then, the second the bell rang, the tall man stood, adjusting the dress shirt he had tucked into his pants as he walked straight over to the whiteboard. Without addressing the class, he started writing something in red marker.

"Seven hundred and twenty days," he said, stepping aside and pointing to the number he'd just written. "That's how many days you're going to be spending at El Dorado High. You'll have 720 days to figure out what you want to do with your life and who you want to be before you leave here. Now, that may sound like more than enough time to do all that, but time flies the older you get. With the snap of a finger, you'll be out into the real world as adults. You're young now, so enjoy your time here, but don't get lazy. Be idiots, but idiots with a plan. You understand?"

The only sounds were a few chairs creaking and someone in the back coughing.

Martinez shook his head. "Alright… open your textbooks to page three."

Biology class was about the same as algebra. Ceramics, however, got a little intense. When our teacher Mrs. Barzeloni caught this guy using his cell phone, she marched over to him and smacked it right out of his hands. Everyone gasped when it cracked against the floor. The teacher glared at him with zero remorse as he ran over to his broken phone and picked it up like it was a hurt hamster.

"You bitch!" he shrieked with fury in his eyes. "Look what you did! You can't do that, bitch!"

The kids gasped and clamored.

Barzeloni sneered. "I can do whatever I want," she said in a cold, raspy voice. "This is my classroom. As I've said at the start of class, there is to be no phone use while you're in here. *You* are a student in my classroom, and you are expected to follow the rules."

Out of nowhere, the kid started crying and ran for the door. Of course a few students snickered at him.

A few minutes after he ran out crying, the bell rang, so I headed down the hall and ducked into the bathroom so I could check my phone.

"Finally," I whispered when I saw a text from Johnny.

Johnny: Mike and I got there late. Going to bleachers now.

After texting Travis where to meet me, I hurried out to find my brother.

Eventually, I found Mike and Johnny sitting mid-way up the bleachers with two girls.

"Brady Boy!" Mike said with a wave. "Girls, this is Brad. He's Johnny's little brother. Brad, this is Morgan." He pointed to the brunette. "And this is Kylie." He pointed to the girl with long black hair.

Morgan kept talking to Johnny like I didn't exist. But Kylie, on the other hand, looked over at me with these bright green eyes that popped due to the contrast of her dark eyeshadow. And when her gaze met mine, she smiled and waved.

I waved back shyly, trying not to cheese too hard. But all I wanted to do was smile, because her acknowledging me in that moment was worth more than gold.

"Yo, Brad," Travis said as he climbed the bleachers. He and I shook hands. "What's up, dudes. I'm Travis!"

In a few minutes, he'd gone from a stranger to talking with them like he'd known them for years. Hell, he even had the group laughing a few times. Meanwhile, I silently spectated, trying to figure out how Travis seemed to get more sociable over the summer while I still came off like a kid who spent the last ten years in a bunker by myself...

A pit formed in my gut when the fourth period bell sounded off, because that meant it was time for gym, the class I'd been dreading all day. It wasn't the physical activity that I feared, it was the part where I had to change in the locker room with the other boys. Like my brothers, many of the guys around me seemed to be growing taller, leaner, and more muscular while I just kept gaining weight. It didn't make sense because whenever I looked around to see what all of the skinny kids were consuming during break or lunch, they seemed to be stuffing their faces with the same junk I ate and chasing it with the same sugary sodas I drank. Yet, for whatever reason, they looked like teens from a Disney surfer movie while I looked like Shrek.

Everyone met in the gym. Then, after a roll call, Mr. Peterson told us to hit the locker rooms.

Before I dared take off my clothes, I scanned the locker room to make sure no one was staring at me. A few lockers down, there was a kid who happened to be looking in my direction, and when my gaze met his, I froze like a deer in headlights. What began as a confused look on that kid's face quickly turned into an angry glare, probably because I was just awkwardly staring at him still. The boy tapped the shoulder of the shorter guy beside him then whispered something. As soon as the shorter kid looked my way, he pointed and laughed maniacally.

My gut twisted and my heart jackhammered in my chest as I grabbed my gym clothes and ran for the exit. Even after I left the locker room, I could still hear that asshole laughing.

I only had five minutes to get dressed and meet the coach outside so I ducked into the nearest bathroom and used the stall as my private changing room. It was a struggle changing in the bathroom stall, mainly because I had to keep my clothes from falling on the gross floor or into the toilet. Once I got my white shirt and black gym shorts on, I piled all my school clothes in my arms and ran back into the locker room only to find out everyone had already left.

By the time I ran out to the field, my class was already in the middle of running laps around the track.

Mr. Peterson looked up from his stopwatch when he saw me in the corner of his eyes. "Castillo, already acting up on the first day, are ya?"

"No sir," I wheezed. "I… I've had a stomach problem the past week so I was in the bathroom…"

"Uh-huh… Excuses are like toilets—everyone uses them and they're usually full of shit. I want sweat, not excuses, boy. So get out there, now!"

I quickly hobbled over to the track and fell in line behind a few stragglers. I struggled to keep up with them, but after a minute, I had fallen behind. On the other side of the track, I watched the kids at the front of the pack walk off the track and take a seat in the grass beside Mr. Peterson. The longer I ran, the fewer kids there were ahead of me. The next thing I know, I'm the only person running and Mr. Peterson was glaring at me, along with the forty kids in my class.

"We're waiting for you, Castillo!" Peterson yelled.

I started sprinting like I had never done before. My heart was pounding so loudly, I could barely hear myself wheeze. Just about halfway, my legs were going numb and my muscles felt like someone set them on fire. By the time I rounded the curve on the homestretch, I was drenched. And when I finally got to the finish line, I collapsed to my knees and doubled over, panting like a dog.

"Alright class, let's head to the gym," Peterson said. "Castillo, make sure to keep up this time."

Keep up? I can't even stand right now, I thought, gasping for air as I watched my class leave me behind.

"Seven-hundred-twenty days," Martinez's voice echoed in my mind. *How am I going to survive another 719 days of this?*

Walking to lunch after gym was a struggle. And if my day wasn't already bad enough, right as I went to pay for my apple sauce, meatloaf, and potato wedges, the lunch lady sneezed all over my food. Then she just handed me my change and stared at me all annoyed like I'm the one who did something wrong...

I dumped the entire tray of food into the first trashcan I passed on the way to the courtyard.

"Where's your lunch?" Travis asked as I sat down next to him on the bleachers.

"Lunch lady sneezed on it," I said. "Can I have your pretzels?"

"Ah shit, hate when that happens. Yeah, here."

I ripped open the bag of pretzels and shoved a handful into my mouth.

"So, how's your first day going?" Michael asked me.

"It's okay. Pretty boring," I said, trying to play it cool.

"Just wait till you go to the party Friday night. Then you'll see what this is really all about..."

"What party?" Travis asked.

"Kylie's parents are going away on a business trip, so she's inviting a bunch of people over."

"Brad and I are invited, I'm assuming?" Travis asked.

"Yeah, of course!" Mike said with a nod.

"Uh… what're you doing?" Johnny barked at Michael.

"What? Kylie asked me to. She said she wanted a ton of people there, remember?"

"Yeah, but not—" Johnny side-eyed me, then back at Michael. "Look, it's gonna be hard enough for *me* to get outta the house Friday night. I can't get caught the first party of the year."

Mike snorted. "And you're not going to! Jesus, take that tampon outta your vagina, Johnny, and man up!"

Michael and Travis cracked up.

Johnny's face went beet red then he put his food down and stormed off.

"Don't worry about your brother," Mike said to me. "He just has a hard-on for Kylie. That's why he's acting all fucking weird."

"What?" Travis said, draping an arm over my shoulders. "He's afraid Brad is gonna steal her away from him?"

Mike absolutely lost it.

At the start of fifth period history, a potbellied, gray-haired man who was barely a hair taller than five feet walked out from behind his desk.

"Now," he said with a nasally tone, his thick, twirly mustache covering his upper lip, "By now, I know you're all probably like my toast this morning… burnt out." He paused with a gap-toothed smile like he was expecting a laugh, but all he got was someone clearing their throat. "Alrighty then… Well, my name is Mr. Sanders and—"

A loud beep from the intercom interrupted him.

"Good afternoon, students. This is Principal Schwartz. In the next minute, we are going to perform a fire drill. When you hear the alarm, please form a single-file line and maintain an orderly fashion as you follow your teacher to the football field behind the school. Thank you."

Everyone began exchanging looks.

"A fire drill on the first day of school?" some girl behind me said as commotion broke out across the class.

The second the eardrum-shattering alarm blared, everyone jumped and there was a cacophony of groans.

"Okay, students!" Sanders yelled over the alarm, wincing like the rest of us. "Form a line and follow me!"

Our history teacher led us into the hall where we, like other single-file lines pouring out of the other classes, joined the mass migration of students towards the exit. The entire time we were being herded to the fence at the back of the field, I kept my head on a swivel, searching for a familiar face among the 1,500 students spreading out across the grass.

"What the hell's going on?" some dude said.

"I dunno…" a girl responded. "Who has a freaking fire drill the first day of school?!"

"I'm not complaining," another girl added, "I'd rather be outside anyway."

Back in middle school, most fire drills ended in five minutes. But we wound up standing outside for thirty minutes. A bunch of kids around me had begun sitting in the grass, and I was just about to do the same.

"Hey," a girl's voice spoke right as I was about to sit down.

Whoever it was, I doubted they were talking to me, but I turned around anyway out of curiosity. And the second I saw Kylie walking towards me, my cheeks got warm and my heart started racing.

"Hey," I said in a deeper voice than usual.

She flashed me a wicked grin, like she enjoyed the fact that she made me all flustered.

"You hear anything about why we're out here?" she asked.

"Nope. Pretty sure it's just a fire drill."

She smiled. "Aw, you believe everything you hear? How cute!"

Just hearing her say "cute" must have sent all of the blood straight to my head because my face went from hot to feverish.

"So, are you coming to my party on Friday?" she asked.

"What? Oh, right. Yeah, I'll probably go …"

"Why probably?"

"I don't know. I'll have homework to do."

"So will everyone else… Just come! It'll be fun! Here." Kylie looked around then handed me her cell phone. "Put your number in there. And hurry, I saw, like, five phones get confiscated today."

"Yeah, okay!" I punched in those numbers fast like I was button mashing an arcade fighting game.

Right as I handed her the phone, the intercom beeped and the teachers started rallying the kids to return to class.

"Bye, Brad," Kylie said cheerily as she hurried back over to her class.

There was something off about her, I thought, watching her disappear into the crowd. *If a girl as pretty as her is willingly talking to me, there's got to be something wrong with her…*

Not long after we returned to class, the intercom beeped once more. "Good afternoon, students," the principal began. "Now that we're received the all clear, I wanted to announce the reason for the abnormally long fire drill before the rumor mill gets going. Sometime around the end of lunch, a student called the office claiming that there was a bomb hidden somewhere on campus."

Everyone in class exchanged looks with those around them, muttering quietly until their whispers became full-blown uproar.

That's when Mr. Sanders shushed us.

Principal Schwartz continued. "Please be advised that the threat was, in fact, determined to be a prank as no bombs were found by the SWAT team who swept the entire campus. So please remain calm and enjoy the rest of your day!"

Right as the noticeably disturbed Mr. Sanders opened his mouth to speak to us, the bell rang yet again and class was over.

On the way to my last class, there was a weird vibe in the halls and out in the courtyard. Everyone seemed eerily quiet and had this mix of dread and paranoia plastered on their faces.

When I felt my phone buzz in my pocket, I urgently pulled it out to see what Travis or my brothers had to say. Except it wasn't any of them, it was an unknown number…

(Unknown): WTF! A bomb threat?! Told you don't believe everything you hear. Also, hey it's Kylie :).

Just like that, my entire mood changed. I felt dizzy, in a good way. I felt alive, for once.

There were hundreds of worried and scared faces all around me, and there I was walking across the campus smiling like a lunatic.

Chapter 9

At lunch the next day, Johnny and Mike were going back and forth about the different rumors they'd heard around school surrounding the bomb scare.

"I heard there was a bomb but the principal just lied that SWAT didn't find one so we wouldn't panic," Johnny said.

"You know what I heard?" Travis asked as he took a seat beside me on the bleachers. "This kid in science class told me that his buddy heard from his mom who works in the office that the kid who called in the bomb threat is a kid from school."

"Makes sense," Johnny said like he knew it all along. "It's not like terrorists would blow up a random school in Placentia..."

"Who do you guys think it is?" Travis asked with a mouth full of tuna sandwich, scanning the kids below us.

"Hell if I know," Mike mumbled, "but it's always the quiet ones who do stuff like that."

Travis turned to me. "You know... Brad's pretty quiet. Maybe we should tip the cops off before he blows the place up!"

Everyone laughed.

I forced a smile. "What? I could never do something like that! I'm such an idiot that I'd probably wind up blowing my dick off while trying to make the damn thing!" Of course, that would be my response. I never really defended myself when I was the butt of Travis's jokes, I usually smiled and made fun of myself.

Mike cracked up.

Travis doubled over and laughed so hard that he sprayed bits of tuna sandwich on the girls sitting on the bleachers below us.

Three of the girls turned around, and they all looked pissed off and grossed out.

"Ew! Are you fucking kidding me!" one girl screamed.

"Sorry," Travis said, wiping his mouth. "Blame my buddy here for making me lose my shit while I was chewing." He bumped me with his elbow.

The girls rose from their seats, flashing us looks of disgust before storming off.

"Asshole!" one of them yelled.

That made Travis and Mike howl with laughter.

"Holy shit," Mike said between laughs.

"Brad," Travis said, "that joke was so good it inadvertently made half the cheerleading team hate us! Good shit, dude!"

"Who knew Brady-boy had it in him?"

Damn did it feel good making people laugh for once. Usually people laughed at me, not at something I said. Sure, they were laughing because I'd made fun of myself, but it didn't feel as bad since it wasn't someone else insulting me jokingly. I realized in that moment that all I had to do was crack jokes on myself before someone had the opportunity, and then I'd be the funny guy. Making fun of myself for laughs made as much sense to me as trying to understand how water stayed in clouds, but if that's what kept people from making fun of me, that's all I needed to know.

At the end of the day that Friday, me and Travis met up with Johnny and Mike out by our usual spot, then the guys got right to talking about how psyched they were for Kylie's party, like they hadn't spent all lunch talking about it.

A few yards past the edge of the courtyard, a group of kids raced by us, almost knocking me over. Me and the guys just froze in our tracks then watched them join a horde of kids flocking towards the football field.

We all exchanged looks.

"You think they're running from another bomb?" I asked.

Travis shrugged.

"Yo, they're beating the shit out of each other!" some guy near the football field shouted to a group of kids near us.

Johnny and Mike smirked at each other then ran toward the crowd.

"Dude, come on!" Travis said, chasing after them.

Even though my instincts told me to run away from danger, I tagged right along with him. If I didn't, I know I'd lose his respect.

The four of us pushed our way through the wall of kids. Right as I sidestepped through a gap with a view of the scene, I watched as this tall blonde kid with a swollen eye and a bloody nose punched this stocky Hispanic kid in the gut. The Mexican guy had blood all over his white tank top and on his blue jeans, but it didn't look like he was bleeding, so I figured he was the one winning.

When the blonde dude grabbed his opponent and slammed him on the ground, the crowd went nuts. The kids who weren't recording the fight cheered and started instigating the fight, shouting things like:

"Kick his *fucking head in*!"

"He's not bleeding yet, *you pussy*!"

"*Yeah, make him bleed!*"

Everyone in the crowd was in this wild-eyed, bared teeth frenzy—every single one of them looked desperate to see more blood and pain, desperate in the way my brothers and I were to watch porn way back when. Seeing them like that was more disturbing than the actual fight.

I can't believe these kids are going to grow up and become lawyers, judges, policemen, doctors one day, I thought.

A collective roar of cheers erupted from the circle of spectators when the blonde kid got on top of the Hispanic kid and started beating his face in. I swear the pummeling went on for nearly a minute until Mr. Sanders barged through the crowd and ripped the blonde kid off of the kid I was convinced was about to die.

"Break it up! Break it up!" Sanders shouted.

"Let me go!" the blonde kid yelled while shrugging off the teacher. "The beaner started it!"

The Mexican kid got up and just ran up to the blonde kid then he cracked him square in the jaw with an uppercut.

A harmonized "OOOOOOH!" rumbled through the crowd as the blonde kid went unconscious and slumped in Mr. Sanders's arms like a ragdoll.

At that exact moment, the school police officer pushed through the crowd and grabbed the victor by the arms and cuffed him.

"Who's a bitch now, white boy?!" the Hispanic kid yelled over his shoulder as the cop hauled him off through the disbanding crowd.

"That was fucking wild!" Travis said as we started back towards our route. "Finally, something exciting happened around here for once!"

"Was the bomb threat not exciting enough for ya?" I asked.

"Dude, a fight trumps a bomb threat any day of the week. Now, if they'd actually found a bomb, that'd be a different story."

"Exactly," Johnny chimed in.

"Man, I hope the kids from Esperanza show up to Kylie's tonight!" Mike said, pumping his fist. "That's a guaranteed fight right there!"

For some reason I couldn't quite figure out, Esperanza was our rival school. I don't know if it was because their football team was better than ours or if something happened between our two schools years ago, but everyone hated them. Hell, even some of our teachers couldn't stand them. Whatever the case was, all I needed to know was that Esperanza High was a threat to my life. At least, that's what Johnny made it seem like. He told me once that, if I ever saw a kid from that school walking the streets, I should either walk faster or prep for a fight.

It was around 8:00 that night when Mom called us down for dinner. Right as I was getting up from bed, my phone buzzed with a text.

Kylie: Hey! Party's at 10, in case you forgot :)

I didn't reply. I couldn't yet. I hadn't asked Mom about the party yet, and neither had Johnny.

"So," Mom said, setting a plate of spaghetti and meatballs before me as I took my seat. "I was thinking we could get a DVD from Blockbuster and have a movie night tonight. How's that sound, boys?"

"Can't. I have homework," Glenn said coldly while pushing meatballs around with his fork like he'd suddenly lost his appetite.

She frowned and just shook her head. She knew damn well that Glenn happened to be busy only whenever she wanted to do something with us. Any other time, he was in his room doing nothing, unless he was at the gym working out.

"What about you, boys?" she asked with a hopeful smile.

Johnny glanced at me with this worried look. "Uh, actually," he said, turning back to Mom. "I told Mike I was gonna go over to his place tonight."

Mom's smile instantly faded. This was the fourth week in a row where my brothers shot down her plans to spend time with us. For nearly a month, it had just been me and Mom doing stuff together on weekends. And because I was the only one who spent time with her lately, I was the only one who knew her and Mac hadn't spoken to each other for a few weeks.

"I don't understand," Mom said to me a week ago on the way to the grocery store. I could tell by her voice she was on the verge of tears. *"Everything was going great and now it's like I don't exist… What's wrong with people? How do you just cut someone out of your life so quickly for no reason at all? It's just wrong."*

When Mom looked at me that night with those pitiful eyes, I already knew there was no way I could ask her to go out with Johnny without feeling super guilty for the next month…

She smiled warmly at me from across the dinner table. "Looks like it's just gonna be you and me tonight, Brad!"

"Okay," I said, forcing a smile to hide how bummed I was about the party I spent all week psyching myself up for.

The movie I got stuck watching with Mom was about a man who went off to fight in a war and started writing letters to his wife back at home. That's about all I knew because I was daydreaming about the party and missing the chance to spend time with Kylie more than anything.

Right as the movie was ending, my phone buzzed on my lap.

Kylie: Hey, are you here?? I sent you the address, right?

Me: Yeah, you did, but I'm not there yet.

Kylie: Are u even still coming??

Me: I dunno yet.

Kylie: WHY!?

Me: My Mom made me do chores and my homework.

Kylie: Bummer :(:(

Me: I might come later though.

Kylie: OK! just text me if u decide to. Would be cool to see u :)

Why can't I just be a heartless bastard like Johnny and Glenn? I set my phone down and looked over at Mom, watching her wipe a tear from her cheek as the movie faded to credits.

Mom sniffled as she turned to me. "I think I'm gonna go to bed, honey," she said, wiping another tear away. "I'm sorry I can't watch your movie with you, but I'm just... really tired."

"It's okay, we can watch it tomorrow," I said.

She kissed me goodnight then walked upstairs.

I sat there waiting until she stopped walking around. Then I crept up the stairs and looked under her door. The lights were off, so I snuck back downstairs, my heart hammering in my chest.

With one foot out the front door, I looked up to the top of the stairs one last time to make sure Mom wasn't there. The coast was clear, so I shut the door quietly behind me and stepped into the night.

Chapter 10

I didn't need to look at the addresses of the houses on that block to know I was getting close to Kylie's—the voices in the distance and the faint bumping of music gave that away. Also, since hers was the only house on the street with lights on and kids with red cups standing in front of the window, I knew I was walking towards the right place.

I raised my hand to knock on the door then froze.

Wait, will anyone even hear me if I knock? Do I just walk in?

No, everyone would look at you like you're weird. They'd think, "Who the hell is this kid? Why's he here? Who's he with? Where's his friends? Maybe he doesn't have any. Maybe he's just a fat fucking loser who's here to stand in the corner and watch us like a weirdo. He's weak. Kill him!"

Right as I was backing away, the door suddenly opened and two tall, spaced-out boys with red eyes stared down at me.

Of course, I just stood there blinking at them like a freak.

"You comin' in?" the brown-haired guy slurred.

I nodded.

"Right on!" he said, stepping outside while still holding the door open for me.

"Best we leave before they show up," the blonde one said to the guy holding the door.

When I heard that, I froze in the doorway.

"You pussy," brown hair spat.

"You wanna stay and see what happens then?" blondie asked.

"Nah, my wrist is still jacked up from practice last week. But if it wasn't, I'd stay and kick some ass."

Before I could even process what their conversation meant, someone shouted. "Brady Boy!" When I turned around, I saw Mike stumbling toward me, spilling whatever was in his red cup all over the floor. "This is great!" he said, putting his arm around my shoulders. "I didn't know you were gonna show up! What the fuck you doin' standing out here? Come inside, you creep!"

Michael pulled me into the house and, even though he was right beside me with his arm around me, I couldn't hear a damn thing he was saying as he led me through crowds of insanely loud clusters of kids.

Somehow, he and I bumped past and squeezed our way through a bunch of kids without pissing any of them off.

"You want something to drink?" he yelled into my ear.

"Huh? Oh, yeah sure!" I yelled back.

Thankfully, the kitchen wasn't as packed as the rest of the house. When we got to the fridge, Mike released me then yanked open the door with dramatic flair.

"Here you go, bro!" he said, shoving a bottle of beer into my chest.

"Beer?"

"What? Yeah! Duh!"

"Oh," I said, "I thought you meant like water."

"Brady Boy, you're fucking hilarious, man! Here, take it."

I grabbed the ice-cold bottle then just stood there staring at the piss-colored liquid inside. I'd barely had a chance to finish reading the label when he snatched it away from me and popped off the cap with the bottle opener he'd just grabbed off the counter.

After prying the cap off his beer, he raised his bottle to me. "Here's to getting fucking wild tonight, Brady Boy!" He clinked my bottle then started chugging like his life depended on it.

Before I ever drank or ate something new, I always gave it a sniff. The second I smelled that drink, it made me wince. *This doesn't smell like something someone would want to drink.*

When I saw that Mike was nearly done with his beer already, I started chugging mine, because the last thing I wanted was for him to think I was a bitch for not following suit. The beverage fizzed in my mouth and down my throat like crisp soda, but it tasted more like bitter sparkling water than Sprite or ginger ale. After guzzling to about halfway, I hiccupped then wound up inhaling the beer. That's when I started coughing like I'd just drowned.

"Whoa! Slow down!" Mike said. "You gotta pace yourself! Come on, let's go upstairs!"

Michael led me back through the crowd, taking a swig of beer then jumping up and down to the music as we weaved through clusters of kids. When we got to the top of the stairs, I stared at the line of people standing against the wall. It wasn't until I saw a sobbing girl with her face buried in the toilet that I realized what everyone was waiting for.

This is hell, I thought as I watched the girl hurl into the toilet as her friends held her hair back.

Near the end of the hall, Mike shoved open the door ahead like a SWAT officer trying to catch someone in the act. When it crashed into the wall, everyone in the room jumped and a few kids screamed.

"What the *fuck*, Michael?" a girl shouted.

"What?" he asked as he strolled inside the red-and-green-lit room.

"You opened the door like a fucking cop, that's what!"

I stood in the doorway and stared at all of the celebrity posters hanging on the walls. When the two kids in the middle of the room moved out of the way for Mike, I spotted my lunch crew. Travis was sitting on the couch with a half-empty beer. Johnny was on the other side of the couch talking to Kylie.

"Hey!" Travis shouted from the couch, grinning harder than I'd ever seen him grin before. "Johnny said you weren't gonna show!"

The second Johnny heard that, he turned away from Kylie then gave me a death glare as soon as our eyes met.

Kylie's face, however, lit up like a kid who just got a puppy for Christmas. "Oh my gawd, you made it!" she squealed, springing off the couch. Her heels clacked against the wood floor as she stumbled towards me like a zombie, her arms wide open.

There's no way she's about to hug me, I thought, my heart racing.

Sure enough, she wrapped her arms around me as soon as she was in range. "I'm so—" she burped between her words— "so happy you're here, Brad!" The smell from her belch burned my nose.

"Yeah, me too," I said as calmly as possible.

"Hey, come here… I wanna show you something!" Kylie grabbed my hand then pulled me out of the room.

She dragged me past the bathroom where the one girl was still puking up everything she'd eaten that night, then she tugged me left down a hall where there were photos of Kylie all along the wall. There was one of her as a newborn, then one of her as a toddler on a swing, one in a Halloween costume, and a few current ones. Her mom was in a bunch of the photos, but I didn't see one with her father in any of them.

I wonder if her parents split up too…

As we approached a door at the end of the hall, she looked over her shoulder at me, smirking mischievously. "Come on in," she whispered, opening the door and pulling me into the dark room.

Everything went pitch black when she shut the door behind us. Then, with a flick of the switch, the lamp in the corner bathed the room in a warm light.

There was something in the way Kylie smiled as she crept towards me that made me nervous, so I quickly broke eye contact with her and pointed at the first thing I saw. "Is that your mom in this picture?" I asked, my voice cracking.

"Yup, yup! This is her bedroom."

"Are we—are we allowed to be in here?"

Kylie just giggled and kept getting closer.

For every step she took towards me, I inched back toward the wall a little. "So, uh—uh…" I stammered. "We should probably get back to the room with the others, huh? I told Travis I'd—"

"You're really cute, you know that?" She was so close that I felt each hot breath between her words against my neck.

Something isn't right, I thought, looking everywhere but her eyes. *Why is she acting like she's missing half her brain? There's no reason someone like her should be getting this close to me of all people…*

"What?" she asked. Her smile faded. "Don't you… don't you like me?" she asked so plainly it threw me off guard.

Unsure of how to respond, I just stared blankly at her.

She took a few steps backward, her bottom lip quivering. "Don't you think I'm pretty?" She plopped down on the bed all pouty and dejected looking.

I didn't know what to say. I never knew what to say, especially to someone like her.

After that long pause, Kylie's eyes welled up with tears. Then she blinked, sending beads of salty water tinged with black eyeshadow rolling down her cheeks.

My gut churned with guilt. *You did that to her, Brad. You were too chickenshit to speak your mind and now you hurt the feelings of the one girl who was ever friendly to you…*

All I wanted to do was make everything right, but I didn't know how to do it. I didn't think there was anything I could do now that she was sobbing with her face buried in her hands, not when I was the one who ruined her night.

Suddenly, the bedroom door swung open and Mike burst into the room, panting. "Kylie! There's a huge fight downstairs. Some kids from Esperanza showed up!"

Kylie just sat there in a trance staring at the palms of her hands.

Michael looked back and forth between the two of us like he was trying to deduce what happened.

A second later, Johnny appeared behind Mike and took one look at Kylie before glaring at me with a fury the likes of which I'd never seen.

"Brad, what did you do?" Johnny shouted, bumping past Mike.

"Nothing!" I yelled back.

The way Johnny looked at me when he got in my face, I was sure he was going to punch me. I was so sure that I preemptively flinched and squeezed my eyes shut. Instead of the clap of his fist against my cheek, all I heard was screams and yelling from downstairs accompanied by the sounds of glass shattering and what sounded like chairs being thrown into walls. That's when I opened my eyes and saw Johnny storming out of the room.

"Johnny, what're you doing!" Michael shouted, chasing after him.

Kylie didn't budge. She just sat there all spaced out like the commotion and pandemonium downstairs was nothing more than rainfall beating against the roof.

I thought about saying sorry to her but, instead, I just crept out of the room and followed Johnny.

I froze at the bottom of the steps when I saw the army of kids circling the six dudes beating the shit out of each other. All I could make out over the bodies blocking my view were three Hispanic kids exchanging blows with three white kids. From the looks of it, it was a one-on-one fight.

It wasn't until I pushed my way to the front of the crowd that I realized Johnny and Travis were two of the three white kids. The third guy, who was choking the life out of an Esperanza High kid, was some random dude with red hair and freckles. When Johnny swung his opponent around to my side of the crowd, my eyes widened in horror at just how much blood was gushing out of my brother's nose.

"Johnny, don't!" Michael shouted as Johnny charged the kid he'd just shoved.

As the Hispanic kid stumbled back, Johnny hit him with the mother of all uppercuts that made the kid go limp and crash onto to the hardwood floor like a sack of bricks.

The crowd let out one harmonious, "*ooooohhhhh!*"

Now that Johnny was in the clear, I looked over to Travis. "Holy shit," I gasped when I saw him.

Travis was mounted by his opponent and the guy was wailing on him, slipping through Travis's guard and repeatedly punching his already swollen face.

I watched as Johnny snatched a bottle from a guy in the crowd across from me and swung it down on the Hispanic kid's head like a club. The damn thing exploded into a million tiny shards that clattered against floor as the Hispanic kid collapsed onto Travis.

Thunderous cheers and applause erupted throughout the house. Johnny didn't even react to it at all. He just used his sleeve to wipe the blood from his nose while extending his other hand to Travis. After being hoisted up, Travis followed my brother to the gap in the parting crowd, staring down at the guy Johnny had knocked out who was now squirming and struggling to get up.

"Stay down, bitch!" Travis said, stomping on the side of the Mexican kid's knee.

Even though I could see the kid screaming, I couldn't hear him over the roars of the crowd. By the time I looked up, Travis and Johnny were pushing through the crowd, leaving the redheaded boy to fight the final Esperanza opponent on his own.

As Michael and I followed the winners out of the house, all I could hear was the bloodthirsty crowd cheering on the last fighter from our school.

Chapter 11

"The fuck's the matter with you?" Michael shouted as we caught up to Travis and Johnny a few houses down from Kylie's.

Travis lit a cigarette then spun around to face me and Mike. "I think a better question is what the fuck's the matter with *you*?" A deranged, drunken smile stretched across his bruised face as his eyes darted back and forth between us.

"You realize cops are probably on the way and you two look like you just left a fight club, right?" Michael asked.

"Well, then we follow the first rule of *Fight Club*," he said, taking a puff of the cigarette.

"This isn't funny, Travis! You guys could go to jail for—"

"Relax already! Look, first off, nobody in that house is gonna call the cops. If any cops show, it'll be a noise complaint from one of the neighbors or something. And if they *do* show, then the Esperanza kids will be the ones who get locked up. You really think anyone in that house will sell us out and defend them?"

Michael scowled at Travis, but said nothing. It was always hard to argue against Travis's logic. He had this way of convincing you something was true with his conviction alone. And if you dared question him, he'd make you feel dumb for it by calling you names or using that belittling tone adults used to talk to a four-year-old. After Travis spent all week making Mike seem like an idiot, I get why he didn't argue any further.

"Maybe get out of here just in case the cops do show up and decide to stop us," I said, trying to defuse the situation.

"Obviously. That's why we're going to Travis's house," Johnny groaned. "His house is the closest and his aunt's not home."

"That okay with you, Brady?" Travis asked. "Down for a little slumber party?"

Either I go home and risk waking Mom, which means I'd have to fess up where I've been, or I go to Travis's and pretend like I just went out for a walk after I get home tomorrow, I thought.

I nodded. "I'm cool with that."

Travis smiled at me, then looked over to Michael with a shit-eating grin. "See, sometimes it's best to leave the ideas to the men."

Right as Travis started walking away, Michael spun Travis around and punched him right in his already bruised eye.

Travis stumbled backward, roaring a cry of pain into the night sky like a werewolf's howl. Then he smirked at Michael, like he wanted to let him know he'd just dug his own grave.

"What the fuck is wrong with you, Mike?" Johnny shouted, shoving him.

"Me? What's wrong with *me*?" Michael yelled back, poking his chest with a thumb. "That psycho is giving me shit and you're asking what's wrong with *me*? You know what? *Fuck* this shit!" Michael turned around and started walking away.

"Dude, where are you going?" Johnny shouted.

Mike just kept walking.

"I tell you what," Travis said, holding his eye, "it's a good thing he punches like a bitch and not like a Mexican." He smirked.

As Travis and Johnny started walking away, I just stood there, unsure of whom to follow.

"What're you doin', Brady?" Travis shouted as I watched the darkness swallow Mike near the end of the block. "C'mon!"

I took a deep breath, let it out nice and slow, then jogged down the street to catch up with them.

"Are you absolutely sure your aunt's not home?" Johnny asked for the twelfth time as we approached the house.

After struggling with the lock, Travis pushed open his front door so hard, it crashed into the wall and rattled the windows. Then, in a dramatic fashion, he poked his head inside with his hand cupped behind his ear. "You hear that, Johnny?" he said, grinning. "Quiet. You know why? Because, like I told you, no one is home…" Shaking his head, he marched inside.

While Johnny and I flopped down on the plastic-covered couch and armchair, Travis click on the lights then veered off into the kitchen. The fridge slammed shut a few moments later then he rejoined us with three beers in hand. For the next ten minutes, we sat around downing beer while he and my brother recapped the fight. The entire time they talked, Travis seemed so unhinged, in a giddy maniacal sort of way.

"And when you smashed that bottle over his head!" Travis hollered. "If they aren't in the hospital for a week, those pussies will probably go back to Esperanza telling everyone that they won."

"You think they're going to want revenge?" Johnny asked.

"Exactly why we need to start driving everywhere—walking home now's gonna make us targets. We gotta keep our eyes open from now on." Travis shook his can then stood up. "I'll get us another round.

It went on like that for the rest of the night. Every time we got close to finishing a beer, Travis grabbed three more. And even though I thought it tasted like carbonated piss, I kept drinking them. I drank every single ounce because I felt like I had to— because it made me feel more like a man, like I was on the same level as Travis and Johnny, even though I hadn't beaten anyone half to death.

The room started to spin after my third can, and I felt like I was getting close to puking my guts out like that girl at the party earlier. My skin felt kind of numb too, and my head felt heavy. Aside from the fact that Travis and Johnny stumbled to the bathroom and kitchen, the way they were all smiley and laughing told me they were fine.

Maybe Travis poisoned my beer, I thought, laying against the armrest and sprawling out across the couch. *Maybe he's trying to take me out so he can replace me as Johnny's younger brother.*

"Hey, you alright there, Brady?" Travis asked. For some reason, his voice sounded really muffled, like I was underwater.

I was too busy focusing on the swinging pendulum of the brown grandfather clock in the corner. For whatever reason, I felt as long as I focused on the pendulum and nothing else, it would keep the room from spinning.

"You okay, Brad?" Johnny asked. When I didn't respond, he huffed. "Shit… I think I gotta call my mom so she can—"

"No!" I groaned. "I'm fine. Just dizzy. Just let me rest."

"You sure?" Johnny asked.

I nodded.

Johnny sighed. "Maybe we should stay down here with him in case he pukes and drowns in his sleep or something," he said to Travis.

"Dude, he'll be fine," Travis said. "C'mon, let's go chill in my room so he can rest."

I didn't even look at them as they left the room, I was too entranced by the swinging pendulum.

The stairs groaned. The floorboards creaked above. While I could just barely hear their muffled voices upstairs, the *clink-clunk* of the pendulum pretty much drowned them out. It wasn't long after that when the room stopped spinning and my eyelids started feeling too heavy to keep open.

Not only did I wake up with a banging headache the next day, but something that smelled like hot skunk was so thick in the air, my nose burned.

"Johnny?" I called as I started up the stairs. "Travis?"

No response.

With each step towards Travis's room, the smell grew stronger. And the second I opened his door, the skunk odor smacked me in the nose like a bare-ass fart to the face, instantly sending me into a coughing fit as I covered my nose with my shirt. Inside, Johnny was sleeping with his arm dangling off the edge of the bed, and Travis was sprawled out across a furry rug on the floor with some sort of transparent glass tube beside him.

I crept across the room and picked up the object. There were some black, burnt leaves of some kind packed into the smaller piece near the base and, in the bottom of the main tube, there was dirty water with bits of ash and charred leaves swirling around in it. It took one quick sniff to let me know that the object in my hand was the source of the skunk smell, and it was so pungent, I started coughing and nearly dropped the heavy thing on Travis's head.

Travis stirred and peeked at me through his swollen, reddened eye. When he saw what I was holding over him, he smirked mischievously at me. "Need help with that, Brady?" he muttered in a raspy voice.

"What is this?" I asked.

"There's no way you've never seen a bong before," he said.

I shrugged.

"Not even in a movie?"

Out of nowhere, Johnny reached over and snatched it away from me. "What're you doing up here?" he yelled as he sat up in bed. "Why didn't you knock?"

"I called you guys—" A creaking from somewhere in the house shut me right up, then my head snapped toward the hallway.

"Is that the front door?" Johnny whispered as he perked up.

That's when we heard keys rattling.

Johnny looked at Travis, his bloodshot eyes wide with fear.

Travis let out a big yawn and stretched out his arms like nothing was wrong and he was just chilling on a lawn chair on a warm summer's day.

"Travis?" a woman yelled from downstairs.

"Yeah, up here," Travis said casually.

The woman stomped her way up the stairs.

Johnny ran to the closet then buried the bong in the laundry.

Travis just sat there smirking. "What are you doing, John?"

Johnny looked around in a panic, grabbed a Febreze bottle on the floor beside the laundry basket, then started spraying the room with mists that smelled of old roses.

Right as Johnny tossed the Febreze in the closet, Travis's aunt appeared in the doorway. The second she sniffed the air, her wrinkled, freckled face scrunched up.

"What were you boys doing in here?" she asked. Of all the times I came over here, that's probably the most I'd ever heard her say. She'd asked my name once, and she'd ask if I was hungry if I was still here when she got home from work but, other than that, she never seemed to care to get to know me.

"Nuh—nothing, ma'am!" Johnny muttered, his voice wavering. "We were just leaving!"

She looked down at Travis, who was in the middle of another big yawn. "*Travis*," she said in the stern voice Mom used whenever we were in trouble, "what were you boys doing in here? And what happened to your face?"

"Isn't it obvious?" Travis said coolly. "I was getting high, Joan. On *weed*, if you couldn't tell from the smell. You know, marijuana.

Devil's lettuce." He pointed at Johnny. "Oh, and that's Johnny, Brad's brother. Rest assured, neither of them took part in any smoking. Brad actually tried to stop me, but I did it anyway." He cocked a thumb at the bruises on his face. "And *these* are battle scars. You see, me and Johnny had to defend ourselves last night, like men do."

Joan scowled at him, her baggy eyes twitching.

Travis somehow seemed completely unfazed that his aunt was growing more and more pissed by the second.

Travis's ability to never let anything bother him was something I admired. The way he could take whatever life threw at him and let it roll off his back was a gift I wish I had. But that's not what he seemed to be doing these last twenty-four hours. It seemed like he'd been deliberately causing trouble and relishing in seeing me, Johnny, and Mike squirm.

Joan took a deep breath. "I got a call from Newport Academy," she said.

The smug look on Travis's face vanished in the blink of an eye.

"Your mom's done with her treatment," Joan continued. "I'm picking her up on Monday."

The look on his face in that moment—he looked like a confused, scared, and vulnerable child, not the beer drinking brawler I saw last night.

Travis's aunt left without another word and Travis just sat there, his eyes darting around like two flies trapped in a hot car.

"You alright, man?" Johnny asked after Joan's door slammed.

Travis inhaled deeply. "I'm fine, just go. I'll call you later."

"You sure?"

"Yes!" he snapped. "Get out of here!"

Johnny and I exchanged looks then headed out the door.

Chapter 12

"We should just tell Mom the truth," I said to Johnny during the early morning walk home from Travis's, scratching at the mosquito bite that I got at some point the previous night.

"Are you kidding me? Hell no!"

"So how do you plan on explaining your face?"

Johnny pondered it for a quarter of a block in silence then pulled out a balled-up bill from his pocket. "I've got an idea," he said, showing me the ten dollars he'd just uncrumpled. "When we get to the 7/11, I want you to go in and spend every single dollar on Slurpees, candy, or whatever you want. Then, go home without me."

"Wait, what about you?"

"I'm gonna hang back for a while and come up with an excuse. When Mom asks where you've been, all you have to do is just tell her you woke up then went to get something to eat. Don't tell her you were with me, and definitely don't mention going out last night." Johnny checked the time on his phone. "It's only 9:30. She doesn't work today so she's probably still asleep. Has she tried calling you?"

I checked my phone. "Crap, she called five minutes ago!"

"That's fine," Johnny said. "That means she probably just woke up. Let's hurry."

I popped in 7/11, grabbed a bag of chips and a cherry Slurpee, then me and Johnny just started hauling ass. Three-quarters of the way to Mom's neighborhood, I was panting for dear life. Not only were my legs burning like that day on the track, there was also a cramp flaring in my side.

Halfway through the complex, Johnny stopped to do whatever he was planning, but I kept running until a thought popped into my head.

Wait, if you burst through the door all sweaty and panting, Mom's going to know you sprinted back home, then she's going to ask why you ran home if you were just out for a leisurely stroll to get some snacks… Shit, okay. I should probably catch my breath and cool off a bit so I don't have to come up with another lie, especially when Johnny didn't even tell me what he was going to say.

Around the corner from Mom's place, there was this fig tree with a nice patch of shade under it, so that's where I decided to take a quick break. I set my drink and chips on the ground, then I doubled over with my hands on my knees, panting for dear life. I remained in that position until my wheezing stopped almost a minute later. Even though I wasn't breathing hard anymore, I was still sweating my ass off, so I stood there a bit longer sucking down that delicious, ice-cold cherry Slurpee until I cooled off.

When I walked through the front door, the house was quiet the way it was on most mornings. That is, until Mom's toilet flushed above me. To play it like everything was normal, I parked myself at the computer, put the password in, then opened up the browser. The first page to pop up was Myspace and, to my surprise, Johnny was still signed in.

I had a profile of my own, but I only had three friends on it—Johnny, Michael, and Travis—so the only posts I saw were from them. But Johnny had 97 friends, which meant I had access to a big chunk of our school's feed.

I scrolled down to check the bulletins, which was where your friends would write little paragraphs about themselves, their thoughts, their crushes, or whatever. The first bulletin was titled

"**HOLY SHIT WHAT HAPPENED LAST NIGHT!?!**" Of course, I clicked on that right away.

The post read: *WTF! That party was INSANE! It was already a crazy night… but then that BRAWL?! Once the cops showed up, I DIPPED!! Did anyone stay long enough to see what happened to the kids from Esperanza? They were still knocked out on the floor when I bolted.*

Someone named Julie commented on the post: *I KNOW, RIGHT?! I could've sworn those kids were dead, but as soon the cops pulled up with the sirens on, 2 of them got up and bolted out the back door. They left the other guy who got hit with the bottle on the ground LOL. Pretty sure he was dead…*

Charlie replied to Julie's comment with: *Yeah, I figured they'd run after the cops showed up. That night was 2 CRAZY for me! Never going to one of Kylie's parties again lol*

Kylie, I thought, *what happened to Kylie after I left?* Part of me wanted to text her, but I was too embarrassed after what I did to her. Instead, I just scrolled down to the next comment.

"Where's Johnny?" Mom said out of nowhere, startling me so bad that I jumped and spun around like she caught me watching porn. She didn't look angry or anything, just confused. And I guess the circles under her eyes were darker than normal, but that's about it.

"Not sure," I said. "I went to 7/11 to get something to eat. Just got back."

She scanned my face. "I didn't hear you leave." Her tone was more accusatory than surprised or concerned.

My heart thumped away in my chest like I had just got done sprinting.

As I opened my mouth to speak, the front door's knob rattled and clicked. Johnny limped through the door, one hand rubbing his swollen eye like he just got beat up all over again or something. He groaned all the way to the couch and looked over at Mom like he was waiting for her to ask what happened.

She crossed her arms over her wrinkled white shirt. "Where were you last night?"

"Huh?" Johnny groaned. "You know I was at Michael's…"

"Then what happened to you?"

"I got jumped by three Mexican kids on the way home just now. All I had was the 10 dollars you gave me, so they kicked the shit outta me."

Mom didn't look at all worried. In fact, she looked annoyed with him, pissed even. Suddenly, she turned to me, but she didn't say a word. It was almost like she knew we were both lying and she was giving me one last chance to come clean. And when I said nothing, she sighed in disappointment then turned back to my brother who was dramatically groaning and squirming on the couch. "Michael's mom called," she said flatly.

Just like that, Johnny cut the theatrics.

"He told her about the fight last night, and the party. All of it." Mom said through clenched teeth, looking over her shoulder at me. "*All. Of. It.*"

My heart skipped one long beat.

She redirected her glare back to Johnny. "You want to guess why I'm angry with you, Johnny?"

Johnny just held her gaze.

With a sigh, Mom reached into her pocket then tossed a small bag of weed and a pipe on the table in front of him.

Her eyes welled with tears. "Do you have any idea how bad it scares me to know that you're screwing around with this stuff?" she asked, her voice strained from holding back tears. "Do you have any idea where *this* leads? Because you know I do."

We both knew well.

Not long after the divorce, Mom tried to help us through the split by telling us what it was like for her growing up in a household back in the 70s with parents who chose to fight nonstop instead of ending things. Her parents would have screaming matches at the dinner table every time they caught each other cheating. Sometimes, arguments were so bad, Mom sat there and heard her parents threaten each other with violence.

Instead of divorcing, they chose to abuse different vices to cope with their crumbling marriage and deteriorating mental health. Grandma Mary calmed her nerves by smoking weed, because *"that's what they did in the 70s,"* as Mom put it. Grandpa Edward's means of escape, however, was a handle of liquor and a three-pack-a-day smoking habit. All he'd do was get drunk and yell at Grandma for being a drugged-out hippie who was unfit to raise a child, and he'd do that right in front of Mom like she wasn't even there.

Whenever Mary reached her breaking point, she'd randomly go missing for days on end. Back then, there were only landlines so Mom had no way to reach her and see if she was okay—she just had to wait for her mother to call the house or come back home. More often than not, Mary would call sometime after nightfall one to three days later and Mom would be the one to pick up. Each call was usually the same—Mary would answer with labored breathing then tell her in a slur of mumbled words which stranger's house or shitty motel she woke up in that night. After that, Mom would take her father's car and go pick her up, and Edward never knew because he was usually passed out drunk by eight o'clock every night.

This was so routine for Mom that she got in the habit of grabbing a book and reading next to the kitchen phone from the time her father went to sleep until midnight. That went on until the night Mom found Grandma dying of a heroin overdose in some rundown motel room.

I always thought that was a pretty messed-up story to tell your kids, but I get why she told us. She told us to scare us. At least, I think that's why, because I know I was absolutely too terrified to even dare think about doing drugs after hearing all of that.

Clearly, Johnny didn't get the moral of the story because there he was, sitting before Mom with the bloodshot eyes of a stoner who'd spent all night drinking.

"Do you have anything to say for yourself?" Mom asked.

Johnny just looked down at his hands and picked at a hangnail.

After a few moments of silence, Mom snatched the weed off the table, stormed into the kitchen, and threw it in the trash. "Your dad's on his way," she said to Johnny, still staring at the garbage as if she was in a trance. "Go upstairs and pack up your stuff. All of it."

Johnny's eyes went wide and his body went rigid as stone. He just sat there all zoned out and quiet like that for a few beats, processing the hidden threat in Mom's words. Then, with a deep breath and a loud huff of a sigh, he rose from the couch and sulked his way to the stairs.

That's when Mom turned to me and stared at me with disappointment in her bloodshot eyes. "I expected better from you, Brad," she said softly. "Really, I did. The only reason I'm not furious with you is because Mike said you had no part in the drinking or the fight."

Thanks for having my back, Mike, I thought.

"But that doesn't mean you're not in trouble…" she said flatly. After that, she headed for the stairs.

I sat there like a statue until Mom's door slammed shut above, then I doubled over and buried my face in my palms. *Oh God, what's my punishment going to be? And why is Johnny the only one going to*

Dad's? Mom said to pack all of his stuff… does that mean he's never coming back here? The stress of it all made my headache worse.

Not knowing how else to cope, I just turned back to the computer and went back on Myspace to read the rest of the posts about what else happened after I left Kylie's.

Maybe fifteen minutes later, there was a knock on the door, so I got up to answer it. When I pulled the door open, Dad was standing there with the most pissed look I'd ever seen.

"Where's Johnny?" he almost growled.

On cue, Johnny jogged down the staircase with a large duffel bag in hand. As he walked by, he paused and glanced at me with this pitiful, defeated look. "See you at school tomorrow," he said flatly.

"Yeah, see ya tomorrow I guess…" I whispered, flashing him a half-smile.

After he walked out the house, Dad gave me a warm hug then left.

As I watched them climb into the car, I suddenly became overcome with this unnerving dread. *This is it, isn't it? Not only am I going to only get to see my dad twice a month, but now I can only see my brother at school and every other weekend?*

"Fuck this…" I whispered to myself, my eyes burning.

Chapter 13

That rest of that first weekend without Johnny was horrible. Per usual, Glenn was locked up like a hermit in his room, and he didn't even find out that our brother moved out until dinner that Sunday night. Meanwhile, Mom basically took a page out of Glenn's book because she spent the rest of Saturday and most of Sunday up in her room weeping. Minus the hours I spent watching TV or playing videogames alone, the house was just freakishly quiet.

This is what I'm going to have to get used to now, I thought, staring at Johnny's empty bed that Sunday night after dinner.

"Get used to it," I whispered to myself as I laid down in bed. Those four words seemed to be something I've been reciting in my head my whole life, a mantra that was synonymous with being sucked into a black hole.

Get used to your parents arguing all the time.
Get used to your parents living apart.
Get used to sleeping on the floor at Dad's.
Get used to Glenn being antisocial.
Get used to being a fat fuck even though everyone else is skinny.
Get used to having no friends.
Get used to going to a new school.

As soon as Mom dropped me off at school that Monday, I hit send on the text to Johnny that I drafted at the last light before campus.

Me: Hey just got to school. Where are you?

While I waited for him to text me back, I meandered over to the courtyard to see if I could find him in the usual spot, my phone clutched in my hand so I didn't miss the vibration. When I got to the bleachers, I didn't see him or the rest of the group, but I did see a few kids from the party. Last Friday, they were a bunch of smiley, loud drunk kids who turned into a bunch of raving maniacs high on bloodlust when the fight broke out. But there they were that Monday morning all back to normal, sitting around all dead-eyed and bored-looking, probably counting the days until they can get drunk and unleash the beast again. Now that I'd seen that side of those kids, I couldn't look at any of them the same way again.

After walking around the courtyard for a few minutes like an idiot, I opened my phone to check and see if I somehow missed Johnny's text. Of course, there were no new messages. As I debated between texting again or calling him, my eyes wandered down to the message below our conversation.

Kylie… She hadn't texted me since before the party. I wonder if she's still upset with me… I wonder if she's okay after what happened.

I did another lap around the courtyard, checked the area by the cafeteria, then I walked around the outskirts of campus and I still couldn't find anyone.

Are they all playing hooky or something?

When I began seeing a bunch of kids migrating to the classrooms, I checked my phone. There was five minutes to the bell and my bladder was full, so I hurried over to the boy's bathroom on the way to the building where my first class was—one of the restrooms no one really used.

As soon as I walked in, I inhaled a lung full of something that smelled like hot skunk, almost like I was back in Travis's weed-scented room all over again. A plume of smoke rose up from overtop the stall beside my urinal right as I started pissing.

A guy in the stall coughed his lungs out.

A girl giggled right after that. Something about that little laugh was familiar to me, but I couldn't figure out why.

"Shit, the bell rings soon," the girl whispered.

I stopped peeing mid-stream when I realized whose voice that was. *Kylie?* Then I heard something that sounded like glass scraping together followed by the flush of a toilet and a backpack zipping open.

"Give it to me," a voice that sounded like Travis's said. A backpack zipped closed after that.

When the stall opened, I looked down as though that'd stop them from recognizing me.

"Brad?" Travis asked.

After zipping up my fly, I turned and saw him, Johnny, and Kylie staring at me with bloodshot, half-open eyes. Travis looked like he didn't have a care in the world. Kylie looked absolutely embarrassed. After an awkward staring contest, she looked down, and just bolted past me.

Johnny hurried off behind Kylie with terror in his eyes. "Don't you fucking tell Mom about this!" he said as he passed, sounding half-scared and half-threatening.

Travis studied my face with those glassy, reddened eyes of his. In that moment, he seemed so vacant and distant, like he was miles away but his zombified body was still in that school bathroom. For some reason, he felt like a completely different guy—a far cry from the charismatic warrior I spent Friday night with. Something told me that wasn't just because he was high out of his mind either.

"You doing alright?" I asked.

"Of course. Why you asking?" Travis turned on the sink and splashed his face with water.

"I dunno… When we left your house the other day you seemed… upset."

Travis went from aggressively drying his face to frozen like a statue in the blink of an eye. Then, as if he'd suddenly regained control of his body, he crumpled up the paper towel, chucked it in the trash, then faced me and stared at me with this coldness I'd never seen in him before. "I don't know what the fuck you're talking about." Just like that, he turned away and stormed out of the bathroom.

He looked like Travis and sounded like Travis, but that wasn't him, I thought, staring worriedly at myself in the mirror while I washed my hands. *Johnny, Kylie—none of them seemed like themselves… Did they seem off because they were stoned or is there something else going on?*

Every class that day dragged. Even though it was only the second week, school was already starting to feel daunting, like those long stretches of desert we'd have to suffer through when Dad used to take us on Las Vegas road trips.

Following the third period bell, I headed over to the courtyard and sat at the bench were me, Johnny, Travis, and Michael had met up every day last week. After a few minutes of sitting there alone, it was clear that none of them were going to show up. *Johnny and Travis are probably getting high again,* I thought, hopelessly staring into the crowd of kids before me… *And Mike… I'm not even sure if he's here today…* I hadn't seen Michael since that the altercation outside of Kylie's Friday, but it made sense why he wasn't around.

So, there I was, sitting there all alone during break right in the middle of a sea of students, sweating my ass off because I chose to wear a jacket as some sort of futile means of hiding my fat from the world. Without my friends around to be my armor, the insecurity and low self-esteem I thought would never return came rushing back all at once. It felt like everyone in the courtyard was staring at me. Every time I looked up and saw someone laughing with their friends, I imagined they were all laughing at me. Then these phantom voices starting going back and forth in my head as clear as day, like I was sitting right beside them and not a few yards away.

"Look at that fat fuck by himself!"

Laughter.

"What a fucking loser!"

"I know, right? He's wearing a jacket in 90-degree weather! Who does he think he's fooling? It's not like we can't see that massive gut bulging through the fabric!"

More phantom laughs.

"His own brother doesn't even wanna sit with him! His own fucking brother!"

My chest suddenly felt like it was filled with hot coals and my heart throttled like a startled jackrabbit. I looked down at my trembling hands, and beads of sweat dripped off my head, dotting the pavement below like rain.

This wouldn't be happening if Johnny and Travis were here, I thought as I began to hyperventilate.

That's when the bell rang.

I got up and hurried to gym with my head down, like it was the first day of school all over again. Just like I did every day since last Monday, I grabbed my gym clothes from the locker room then ducked into the boy's bathroom to change. After shutting the stall door, I removed my shirt then looked down at the blob of fat around my abdomen that blocked my view of my feet. I shook my hips side to side, just to watch the fat jiggle around.

I began picturing all the other slim guys with their sharp jawlines, their visible cheekbones, their flat chests and lean stomachs, guys who spent their days laughing and living their lives without a care in the world—who spent their breaks and lunches eating whatever they wanted without worrying about gaining weight.

Why me? I looked up to the fluorescent light above the stall. *Why oh great and powerful God would you grant all the other boys desirable bodies that allow them to have the confidence required to get girls and to make friends? What could I have possibly done in my short life that was so terrible that you made me like this? I kept to myself. I didn't bother a soul. I followed the rules more than my brothers, and all they do is act like assholes, but you didn't make them fat! At least the few times that I lied, I felt remorse afterwards! So why? Why was I cursed to look like this? Why do I have to be this pathetic kid who can't seem to think or act like everyone else?*

Is this because my parents split and Dad stopped taking us to church? Is this because I didn't pray to you every night, like my old priest hammered into us?

I thought of kneeling on the piss-stained tiles, closing my eyes, cupping my hands, and pleading with God for something— anything to change. And as I looked down at my hands, I stared at the mosquito bite on my arm from the other night.

If a mosquito flew over this graffiti-sprayed stall door right now and smelled my sweaty ass, it wouldn't put its little legs together and beg me for blood. No, it would fly down here and take from me what it wants until I swatted it, because a mosquito just does what it has to do to get what it wants, just like everything else in nature.

That's when it hit me…

I'm more pathetic than a bug…

My blood boiled with rage as I walked out to the track for our weekly one-mile run. Barely five seconds after I joined the pack of students near the cones that marked the starting line, Mr. Peterson yelled, "Go!" and I just started running faster than I ever had in my entire life, blowing past several guys who started at the front of the pack. They all turned and looked at me in shock as I overtook them one by one. Soon I was sprinting alongside the most athletic boys in class. I could feel their stares—their judgement. That's when the phantom voices I heard in my head during break returned, mocking me.

"Look at that fat fuck!" a voice echoed in my mind.

"What a fucking *loser!*"

Keep going, Brad. You're halfway, just keep looking forward.

"His own brother doesn't even wanna sit with him! His own fucking brother!" another voice taunted.

Another wave of anger washed over me, then it felt like a surge of adrenaline pumped through my veins and purged my body of the pain and fatigue that was setting in. That's when I pushed myself harder, running faster than before like there was a lion chasing me.

This is it, I thought, focusing on Mr. Peterson, who was less than 100 feet away. *This is the homestretch!* The next thing I knew, I was passing him and the starting cones.

I slowed myself to a stop only to collapse onto my hands and knees in the grass beside our coach, wheezing and panting for dear life until I had the strength to maneuver into a sitting position. As I watched the kids who originally led the pack approach the finish line, I noticed Mr. Peterson was staring at me in disbelief. The other runners slowed to slow walk as they passed Peterson, all of them staring at me the same way the teacher was.

I stared right back at them, not one shred of fear or nervousness in my mind for once, no voices in my head telling me to avoid eye contact this time.

"Uh, alright, students," Peterson finally said. "Let's head to the gym for… weight training."

I didn't get up right away. I just sat there for a bit, staring at the green field with brown patches ahead. As a cool breeze washed over me and cooled my sweat-drenched body down, it felt like every dreadful thought I'd had for the day was washed away. All the anxiety I felt about getting through the rest of the day was gone. For once, I felt… elation. And, just as suddenly as the breeze came and went, so too did the brief moment of happiness.

Chapter 14

As expected, when I walked up to the bleachers with my lunch later that day, Travis, Johnny, and Kylie where nowhere to be found. Even though I had a hunch that they wouldn't show again, I still sat at our usual spot and waited for them before eating, staring at the soggy calzone with its blackened edges that oozed spaghetti sauce into the crinkled plastic wrap.

The longer I stared at that calzone, the more grossed out I became. *What is this shit they're feeding us? This is basically overcooked garbage that'd make a stray dog puke…* I then picked up the bag of Flaming Hot Cheetos and looked at the nutrition information and all the crap in the ingredients. That's when it hit me. *I've been eating filth like this my whole life.* It occurred to me that the only difference between the school calzone and all the other fast food, chips, and sweets that I adored so much was that those other things had slightly better packaging that tricked people like me into thinking it was of a better quality than our shit school lunch.

My gaze wandered from my lunch to my pregnant-looking belly that spilled out over my jeans. Suddenly, I wasn't just disgusted with my food, I was disgusted with myself.

"Hey! Brad!" Johnny called right as I dumped all my food in the trashcan.

When I turned around, I found my brother standing there with Travis and Kylie.

"Where you going?" Johnny asked.

"Where've you been?" I asked.

Johnny looked over at Travis, whose eyelids were at half-mast. Then, as though I hadn't even asked a question, he just zoned out and followed Travis to the bleachers.

Kylie wasn't even in the same universe as us. She was just standing there feverishly ripping open the plastic on her burrito, and when she finally got it open, she chomped into it like a rabid coyote.

Something about seeing her all high like that again made me lose interest in her. I no longer felt curious to get to know her or find out why she seemed so broken. *That's probably for the best,* I thought as I walked away. *I just want to be alone.*

As soon as I reached the grass at the edge of the courtyard, I broke into a jog, the soreness in my legs from today's run burning like hell. And then I just started sprinting until the cacophony of chattering behind me faded into nothing but the sounds of my heavy breathing. I ran all the way to the track, dropped my backpack, and started sprinting. Halfway through the run, the ache in my body turned to numbness. At the end of the lap, I sat in the grass with my eyes closed, listening to my heartbeat while I tried to catch my breath, waiting for that dizzy euphoria from earlier to set in again.

As my heart throttled down to a steady, even beat, the euphoric high returned. For a few minutes, I was free of all my troubles and paranoia—I was completely at peace. Then the fucking bell rang, yanking me right back into reality. Just like that, I was angry all over again. On the way to class, it dawned on me that the anger would always be there, but at least I had learned how to control it.

Chapter 15

At the end of the second week of school, I pretty much walked right into Mom's house, dropped off my backpack in my room, then walked down the hall and knocked on Glenn's door, something I never did.

A few seconds later, my now six-foot-one brother opened the door looking extremely perplexed, his hair a disheveled mess. It was crazy how much he was starting to look like Dad. "Oh, hey, Brad... What's up?"

My gaze flicked down from his eyes to his broad chest then to his toned arms. "I... uh... I want to start working out with you."

Glenn cocked his head slightly. "Wait, really?"

"Yes," I said.

"Why?"

"Why's there gotta be a reason?"

"It's just kinda random, I guess. Are you trying to impress a girl or something?"

"No."

"Alright, well you'll need to get a membership at my gym."

"And how much is that?" I asked.

"If you don't have any money to your name, expensive."

"I just want to run. That's all I wanna do."

He snickered. "You don't need a gym for that."

"I know. All I've been doing is running around the field at lunch every day."

"Wait, you're skipping lunch?"

"Yeah."

"Have you eaten since breakfast?" he asked, concern in his eyes.

"Yeah." That was a lie.

"Well, if running's all you wanna do, then—"

"But I want to go to the gym with you, maybe try some other exercises and stuff while I'm there."

"Oh, yeah, sure. But you'll have to ask Mom for a membership then."

There's no way she'll say no to that, I thought, walking back to my room. For as long as I could remember, my parents had been trying to talk me into playing every sport on the planet, their way of sneakily getting me to engage in some kind physical activity. *"It'd be fun!"* That's what Mom said after signing me up for baseball, football, soccer, and swimming lessons against my will back in middle school. Thankfully, none of those lasted, mainly due to my parents' busy schedules and the costs associated with them.

When I heard Mom come home a few hours later, I ran right downstairs and asked her.

"Oh, honey, of course!" Mom said with unbridled glee. "I'm so proud of you!" She gave me the money right there and then.

That evening just after 6:00, I cruised with Glenn in his truck to the gym, windows up and A/C blasting. The radio wasn't on because he was on the phone with his buddy Terrance, so I had no choice but to eavesdrop on their conversation. Apparently, Terrance was deathly afraid of sitting on public toilets and Glenn was making fun of him for this one time where he left school to race home for the bathroom only to end up shitting his pants mid-drive.

"Man, well I really hope you get your shit together before it happens again!" Glenn cracked up, and Terrance laughed so hard, I could hear him from the passenger seat.

I turned to the window so Glenn didn't see me smirking, not like it was a secret or anything.

This is how friends are supposed to be, I thought, thinking back to the squabble that happened between Johnny, Glenn, and Mike after Kylie's party. It felt nice hearing friends digging into each other without arguing and fighting after.

"Alright, dude, I'll catch ya later," Glenn said, closing his phone and returning it to the cupholder as he pulled up to the red light. When the car came to a stop, he stared at me for a bit like he was thinking of something to say. "So... how's school?" he asked, the lively tone he spoke to Terrance with now absent from his voice.

I shrugged. "It's school," I said just as flatly as he spoke.

"Freshman year's a cunt and a half, dude. It's like stepping into really slow quicksand that you know will take four years to completely swallow you whole."

It was in that moment that I had an epiphany. *The tone we speak to each other with... it's like we were total strangers.*

Essentially, that's what we were.

The most I ever said to him was, *"Dinner is ready!"* Then he'd come downstairs, grab his food, and take it back to his room.

And then, if I was sitting on the couch watching TV when he was going out, he'd tell me, *"I'll be back later!"*

Other than that, he was either always locked in his room when we were at Mom's, driving his truck down to Orange County from Dad's apartment to see his friends whom I never once met, waiting tables at Lupe's, or at the gym. The guy never seemed to stop moving when he left his room. He always had something to do, someone to see, or something to achieve. I just figured that was his way of distracting himself and coping with the madness that was the past couple years.

"The worst part is," Glenn continued, "the second you get swallowed up by the quicksand, it spits you back out, then you have to figure out how to walk all over again in the world as an *adult*. And, news flash: there's no class in high school that prepares you for adulthood."

"Yeah," I said. "School sucks."

"Glenn!" this jacked, six-foot-tall bald guy wearing a black polo shirt one size too small said as soon as we entered the gym. His nametag read: OSCAR. "My man! What we hitting today?"

The two dapped each other. "Biceps and back today." He then explained my situation to him before leaving for the weight room.

Oscar led me to his desk and, a few short minutes later, he set me up with the gym check-in code and we finalized my membership paperwork. After that, he gave me a tour of the place, starting with the first level, where all the cardio equipment was. Then we went down to the weight room, which looked like a barely renovated basement. Brown drywall peeked through the chips in the white painted walls, and there were rusted pipes zigzagging above us. It was there that I saw Glenn lifting on the bench press.

During the entire tour, Oscar kept trying to sell me on some training package where, "*for just $100 a session*," he could give me the results I wanted and then some. His impersonal, scripted pitch left me feeling annoyed, probably because he wouldn't stop talking and kept calling me Brody. And he put on this fake smile the entire time. The whole thing felt like a weirdly polite robbery.

"Well just consider it, Brody," Oscar said. His Grinch-like grin seemed more disturbing the longer the tour went on. "A personal trainer would be really good for you. My desk is just over there. It was Brody, right?"

"Sure," I said through a sigh. At that point, I would've gone by any name so long as it meant escaping Oscar.

I headed right back up to the cardio level after that. There were a bunch of older people hogging the treadmills, but I managed to find one in the back row near the corner near this 70-year-old guy. It took a few seconds to get it started and find a good speed to jog to, but once I did, I got into rhythm and watched the subtitled news on the wall-mounted TVs to pass the time. There was a story about a father of five who murdered his family then killed himself. Then there was something about an E. coli outbreak in romaine lettuce. Then there was a segment on a new cell phone called the iPhone that Apple had unveiled at a recent press conference. The thing was so high-tech, it was just one big touch screen with no physical keys, all for $499 dollars. It was set to launch in the summer, and tech analysts were predicting it would bomb harder than some device I'd never heard of called the Newton.

After a while, I went into a trance, staring through the TV more so than actually watching it. When my head started to spin, I looked down at the elliptical and my jaw dropped when I saw the timer. It had somehow been over 40 minutes and I had burned around 600 calories.

The second I stopped jogging, pain flared in my thighs and my legs felt too weak to stand on, then I got so dizzy that I almost fell as I limped my way downstairs to wait for Glenn to get done.

Mom was in the kitchen making dinner when we got back home.

"Going to do my homework," Glenn said as soon as he walked in.

"Alright!" Mom said, turning to me with a smile. "Jesus, look at you!" she said, referring to my soaked shirt and the greasy brown hair still clung to my sweaty forehead. "Must've been a workout from hell!"

"Yeah, pretty much. What're we having?" I asked.

"Steaks with Caesar salad."

I sat at the computer until Mom called upstairs to Glenn that dinner was ready. To my surprise, he didn't grab a plate and retreat to his room like he did every other day, he actually pulled up a chair and sat at the table.

Mom looked over at me like a talking purple gorilla had just joined us.

I glanced back at her just as bewildered.

Glenn looked up from his steak at us and chuckled. "What? You guys seen a ghost or something?"

Mom smirked. "Or something," she said.

For the first time in years, Glenn and Mom struck up a real conversation over dinner. The way she asked him about school, his friends, other personal matters, one would think he'd been away at college for the last three years.

There was no vitriol or tension that night. The three of us even shared a few laughs. It'd been so long since we had that kind of effortless warmth between us, I forgot what it was like, especially after the last few weeks.

I knew good things didn't last, so I just relished it for as long as I could while I ate every bit of my steak and salad.

Chapter 16

Running during lunch and hitting the gym with Glenn every day at six became a routine part of my day after that first gym session. Sure, I was back to being a loner at school again, but I didn't care. As long as I had those two things to look forward to, I didn't need friends or Johnny's company to make it through the day anymore. All I had to do was endure six classes and a few hours of homework, then I was off to spend some quality time with Glenn at the only place I liked being at. And even though having something to look forward to made classes drag, somehow time flew by and, before I knew it, three months had come and gone.

Just like every Monday since I began training, I finished our weekly lap before everyone else did, and Mr. Peterson nodded at me like he was more impressed than usual.

"Well, I'll be damned, Castillo," Peterson said to me right as I reached my gym locker. "Looks like you lost 10 or 15 pounds. This class seems like it's doing some good for ya, huh?"

I nodded.

He wasn't far off. I'd weighed myself on Mom's scale the other night and I was 179 pounds—that was down from my initial weight of 192 pounds.

People are starting to notice, I thought, turning to the mirror at the end of the row of lockers. The fat under my chin was gone and my cheekbones were slightly visible. On top of that, I no longer had red marks around my waist whenever I took off my gym shorts now that my much slimmer mid-section no longer needed to be stuffed into my waistband, and I realized the other day that I had to wear my belt two holes looser than before.

A few of the boys who heard Mr. Peterson were staring at me while they pulled their sweat-drenched gym shirts over their heads. In that moment, I didn't feel the need to run away to that bathroom stall I spent months changing in. I no longer felt the shame of my body burning in my chest. For once, I didn't feel self-conscious. So I looked away from the staring boys and took my shirt off right there in the locker room for the first time.

In the corner of my eye, I saw a few kids still glancing at me, but I didn't avert my gaze when our eyes met. Nope, I just looked over at them and held eye contact with whoever locked eyes with me. Eventually, they just looked away. They didn't whisper anything to their friends, they didn't laugh at me—they just carried on with changing out of their gym clothes. I smiled to myself as I finished changing, basking in the realization that the days of hiding away in a piss-stained stall to change clothes would be in my rearview for the rest of my days.

Once I was done changing, I grabbed the apple and water from my backpack and headed to lunch. As I munched on my apple on the way to my usual spot by the track, I saw Johnny, Kylie, and Travis coming from the parking lot with bloodshot eyes, and they were laughing like a pack of hyenas…

"Have you seen Johnny lately?" Glenn asked as he pulled out of Mom's neighborhood. Most days on our evening drive to the gym, we'd end up talking about our estranged brother.

"Yup, I did today, actually. He was coming from the parking lot with Travis and Kylie when I was going to lunch. They were high and giggling all weird."

"They were probably hot boxing," he said, shaking his head. "That Travis kid… It's that fucking Travis kid's fault… I knew he was bad news the second I met him." He turned to me, squinting. "Wasn't he your friend first?"

"Yeah, but he barely talks to me anymore. Neither of them do. They basically spend every single break getting high so I just figure they're probably too stoned to talk when they see me."

Glenn shook his head again. "Johnny's gonna get expelled. And he's gonna end up going to one of those schools where there are a hundred fuck-ups just like Travis." He took a deep breath and then sighed. "Also, that Kylie girl that picks him up from Dad's sometimes… what's her deal? She his girlfriend?"

"I think so? They're always together whenever I see him."

"So that means she's probably another bad influence on him."

"Probably," I muttered, watching the rain roll down my window. "Travis and Kylie… I don't think either of them are bad people… I think they've just had rough lives."

Glenn glanced over at me. "So has everybody else…"

Chapter 17

"Yo," this kid beside me whispered while I was in the middle of working on my algebra classwork.

I looked over at him. He was this stout kid with broad shoulders, muscular arms, a pudgy belly, and chubby cheeks who sat next to me the whole year thus far. "Yeah?" I whispered.

"Yo, what's your secret?" he asked in a hushed voice.

I glanced at the teacher to make sure he was still grading papers then turned back to the boy. "Secret for what?"

"You know, for losing all that weight so fast. What's your secret?"

Two months and 15 pounds later, people weren't just starting to take notice of my weight loss, some of the heavier kids who I never spoke to before would approach me from time to time and ask for weight loss advice.

"I need to cut 10 pounds by next Friday, and I'm fucking stressing," he continued.

I squinted at him. "For what? Your parents making you do it?"

"No, for wrestling."

Mr. Martinez cleared his throat. "Are we in a fish market, boys?"

We shook our heads.

"Then don't make it sound like one," Martinez said, looking back down at his papers.

What was my secret? Well, I started skipping breakfast most days, and if I did eat anything it was just an apple or a single piece of untoasted wheat bread. The gnawing ache and the constantly

The Haystack

growling stomach that came with being hung
to deal with, but I knew I had to keep it up so ɪ
continue feeding off of my remaining fat I had yɔ
either that or put back on the weight.

As I began to nod off in my second period that ɔ
reminded of the other drawback of my secret weight lo
regimen—the unrelenting fatigue. Trying to keep from falling
asleep during my teachers' lectures all day was another exercise in
itself. To keep myself awake, I'd bite down on my tongue, shake
my head as subtly as possible, and I'd dig my fingernails into my
forearm so hard that I'd sometimes break the skin. Hell, even
walking in the sun between classes and after school was super
draining, so I'd stick to the shade as much as possible.

By lunchtime, I was borderline catatonic, so I started buying a
microwaved burrito from the cafeteria every day. I'd wind up
devouring it within 30 seconds, like I'd been adrift at sea for a week
and that was the first piece of food I'd seen since the shipwreck.

When I finished my burrito that day, a wave of guilt swept
over me from knowing the hunger stole control from me, so I did
what I did every day—I went to the track and ran until the bell
rang for my fifth period class.

That night at dinner, I was so weak after the gym that I couldn't
even get myself to eat. I just sat there poking at my chicken breast,
watching the juices bleed out of it onto the plate. When I finally
got the strength to pick up my knife and cut the meat, I looked up
and saw Mom smiling at me.

"What?" I asked.

"I'm really proud of you, honey," she said.

"Oh… For what."

"For getting healthier and exercising! You're doing it all on
your own, and that's awesome."

attempted a half-hearted smile that I think she bought, then I took a bite of chicken.

Upon swallowing it, I imagined the emaciated, rapid dog that was my hunger watching the chewed bits of meat hitting my stomach. I imagined he'd burst out of the cage I had him trapped in all day and feverishly run out to devour the meal, only to growl at me after being unsatisfied by the amount I'd fed him that day, then he'd rebel by thrashing in my gut all night. That's what it felt like, anyway. And it was the same during the day.

But I knew if I ignored it long enough, if I didn't give in, eventually the beast inside of me would feast upon my fat instead.

Hunger no longer had control of me. I had taken control of the leash.

Chapter 18

"Can you believe it's going to be June tomorrow?" I asked Glenn as he pulled up to the gym that Friday evening.

Glenn sighed. "Dude, please don't remind me. Graduation's in three weeks. Three fucking weeks! Then I'm done! Like *done,* done. I'm not ready for that yet..."

"I don't blame you," I said mid-yawn.

"What's been up with you? You always seem so tired?"

I shrugged. "Oh, haven't really been sleeping lately."

"They have energy drinks at the gym. If you want one, check with Oscar."

"Alright. Lemma try the elliptical first. Maybe it'll wake me up."

When we got to the stairs, Glenn and I fist-bumped each other, then he went to the weight room while I headed upstairs to the cardio area.

An hour on the elliptical at my normal pace was all I could take before it felt like I was about to blackout. So, I hopped off the machine and pretty much dragged my feet all the way to Oscar's office with my eyes barely open.

"Hey, Oscar," I said sleepily from the doorway. "Glenn said you might have something to help me get through my workout?"

"Say no more, Brody, I gotchu!" he said, flashing me a phony smile before heading to the fridge. He pulled out some red bottle with black lighting all over the label then handed it to me.

"Warrior Rush?" I muttered.

"This stuff? This'll put a bonfire under your ass for sure!"

When I saw the bracketed text near the nutrition label that read: "EQUIVALENT TO FOUR CUPS OF COFFEE," I pointed at it with a cocked brow. "Isn't that a lot?"

He shook his head. "Just sip it slowly, my dude! Also, don't worry about paying, that one's on me!"

Oscar swaggered back to his seat the way all cocky meatheads seemed to do, greeting the gym patrons he passed with that same manic tone he used with me.

I sat on the bench near the locker rooms sipping that extremely sweet drink for a while, waiting to get the jolt of energy that the label and Oscar promised me. By the time I got back to the cardio area, it was already 7:30. *Glenn said that we had to be out by 8:00 sharp so he could finish his senior project.*

Frustrated that the drink hadn't kicked in yet, I started chugging it in hopes it would kick in quicker. About halfway through, that's when I felt it. My heart began palpitating, and it felt like electricity was surging through me and making my hairs stand on end. And, as I climbed on the treadmill, my stomach churned. I stepped right back down off of the machine and stumbled over to a nearby counter, setting the bottle down as my other hand clutched my stomach like that'd make the queasiness go away. It didn't. With each second that passed, I got more nauseous. Suddenly, my mouth filled with salty saliva and I started booking it down the stairs.

"What's wrong?" Glenn yelled as I sprinted past him and his friend.

I didn't say anything. I couldn't, because it felt like I'd puke right there if I dared open my mouth. So I kept running. I stormed into the locker room, hooked right into the bathroom, and started tugging at the first stall door like a madman.

"Occupied, asshole," a man inside said.

I ran down the row of occupied stalls until I finally yanked open an empty one at the end. My knees had just barely hit the ground when a rush of acidic, fruity liquid came rushing out of my mouth and somehow went right into the toilet without splashing the seat. After heaving three times, I felt so dizzy and lightheaded that I just sat right there on the floor, slumped against the stall wall, and closed my eyes, listening to the rapid drumroll in my chest.

"Jesus," someone said.

When I opened my eyes, I found Glenn and his friend standing over me.

"What the fuck…" Glenn said, his jaw hanging and eyes wide. I'd never seen him so freaked out.

"Dude, he should go to the hospital," his friend said very nonchalantly.

"It's fine," I groaned, rubbing my stomach. "It's not blood, it's pre-workout. Drank it too fast, that's all."

"Oh, good… Shit… Maybe you should rest until I'm done," Glenn said, looking at his watch. "We only got 20 minutes left."

I rose from the floor and staggered past them towards the exit.

"Dude!" Glenn shouted.

"I'm fine!" I barked. "I'll meet you at the car in 20!"

The caffeine that I managed to absorb before puking eroded my exhaustion and had me feeling jittery and clear headed, so I raced back to the cardio room to take advantage of the buzz before it faded.

My stomach roared and churned while I ran on the treadmill, but I just kept taking deep breaths and powered through. About ten minutes in, all the TVs cut away from their usual programming and flashed a BREAKING NEWS bulletin. There was a shooting in Arkansas where a guy wearing a gas mask burst through the doors of a mall with a shotgun, then shot and killed 15 people and wounded 20 others before turning the gun on himself. Everyone on the row of treadmills before me was staring up at the screens, some with their hands on their mouths in shock, others watching unaffected as though it were just a shampoo commercial.

Two photos of the shooter appeared on screen, a current one and one of him when he was about my age. He was a white man with brown hair and a thin face and, as a teen, he looked like just another kid in my school. Nothing about him was remarkable—he didn't look crazy or evil, just average. Someone just like him could be standing beside me and I wouldn't know he was a mass murderer. Even his family didn't know he was capable of something like that, because the relative they interviewed described him as "quiet, shy, and socially awkward," and emphasized that she "never thought he'd do something so horrendous." I found it odd the focus was so much on the shooter and didn't acknowledge the victims at all. The news almost seemed like they were worshiping him...

As the story came to an end, my gaze wandered to the bottom corner of the screen and I saw it was 7:58, so I stopped the treadmill and raced downstairs.

That weekend, we were staying at Dad's. Like most nights at our father's apartment, we sat on the couch that Sunday evening and watched TV while we ate dinner. I held my plate up to my chest, forked a small piece of steak, and scraped the tiny piece into my mouth. Slowly, I chewed the meat, savoring it while I pushed the refried beans and rice around my plate. Even after I finished chewing, I just sat there scooping up food and dumping it off of my fork.

"Eat your food," Dad grumbled, staring at me like a prison guard.

"I'm not feeling good, so I don't have much of an appetite." I shoveled a forkful of food into my mouth to appease my father.

"You never have much of an appetite anymore," he said with a scowl. "How much weight have you lost since the last time I asked?"

For some reason, I glanced over at Glenn, who was staring worriedly back at me. My eyes snapped right back to the TV. "I dunno. Last time I checked it was, like… 20 pounds?" It was actually 30 pounds. I didn't know why I'd lied.

"Twenty pounds…" Dad said. "Another 20 pounds in four months?"

"There something wrong with that, Dad?" Glenn asked.

"Isn't that a good thing?" Johnny chimed in. If he hadn't spoken, I probably would've forgotten he was there. Like me, he was out of it, barely touching his food as he nodded off at the other end of the couch. Those dark circles he had around his eyes made him look way worse than I felt.

Dad glared at Glenn, then pointed at Johnny. "That one over there," he said, redirecting his finger to me, "looks about as healthy as this one right here. And I hope *this one* doesn't look like death because he's hanging with Johnny's junkie friends and doing God knows what."

Johnny's eyes widened, but he didn't look away from the TV.

"Yeah, you!" Dad yelled. "You don't have me fooled, you little shit! I know you haven't changed since your mother kicked your ass out! Now I have to be the one to watch you destroy yourself!" Dad turned his glare on me. "Destroy *both* of you!"

That's when it clicked. "Wait!" I blurted out. "What're you talking about? I'm not doing what Johnny's—"

"I'm not doing anything!" Johnny interrupted.

"You really think I'm an idiot, don't you, Johnny?" Dad yelled. "You think I don't know what you and that junkie whore of yours get into?"

Johnny sprang up from the couch and ran to his room, slamming the door behind him. There was some rustling around, then a drawer was dragged open only to slam shut immediately after.

That's when Dad raced towards the bedroom and banged on the door.

"I know what you're doing in there!" Dad's voice boomed with a rage I'd never heard from him before. "Open the door right this second or pack your shit and get out of my house!"

Glenn and I raced to the hallway and peeked around the corner right as Dad grabbed the doorknob, twisting and turning it with a violent rattle. He banged on the door again so hard that the pictures on the wall almost fell off. Then he lowered his fist and took a couple of deep breaths.

A few seconds later, the door flew open. "Oh, what?" Johnny shouted, getting right in Dad's face. "You want me to leave *your house*? Well, I'm looking around, Dad, and I don't see a house. All I see is a shitty little apartment meant for one person even though you try to cram all of four us in this shithole with you!"

Dad stood there with clenched fists, his unblinking eyes furiously scanning Johnny's face.

"Lemme ask you something, Dad," Johnny continued. "Is this really what you wanted for your kids, or did you dream of something better? I really hope you did, because if having them sleep in a closet is your idea of the American Dream, you better wake the fuck—"

A clap echoed through the apartment when Dad slapped Johnny across the face and grabbed him by the shirt in the same beat. "Let me tell you what I didn't dream," he said, each word seething as it slowly came out. "I didn't dream of having an ungrateful leech for a son—a drugged out, disrespectful shit who doesn't know a fucking thing about hard work or what it means to be a man."

Johnny just stared at him all wide-eyed, his jaw trembling with fear.

Dad released Johnny's shirt then stepped back, staring at our petrified brother who was shaking like a cold, starving coyote.

All of the sudden, Johnny bolted by Dad, bumped past Glenn, then ran out of the apartment. He slammed the front door so hard behind him, one of the pictures on the wall fell and shattered.

I turned back to Dad just in time to see him wiping away a tear as he stared at the carpeted floor. With a sniffle, he marched past us, picked up the picture, and stared at it for a moment before hanging the broken thing back on the wall. Then he opened the door, wiping another tear away as he left the apartment.

Me and Glenn followed after him but, when I got to the door, I stopped and stared at the shattered picture. It was a photo I remembered well, one of a much younger version of our dad holding his three kids lovingly at the park. Five-year-old me was standing there clutching a bag of bread that we were about to feed the ducks in the lake behind us. The way we were all smiling, we all looked so happy back then.

"Johnny!" Dad called as I stepped outside.

All I heard was the echo of his voice and the crickets chirping throughout the neighborhood.

Dad fished the phone out of his pocket, dialed Johnny's number with shaky hands, then held it to his ear. "Fuck!" Dad exclaimed shortly after. He covered his mouth with a hand and just stared at the ground. "Come on, boys," he said, jogging towards the parking lot.

As soon as the last car door slammed shut, Dad peeled out of his parking spot like he'd just heard the starting gun of a street race. Unlike where Mom lived, the town of Corona always looked so menacing and dangerous after the sun set. And you always knew something bad was happening nearby because there seemed to be a helicopter circling every ten minutes with police sirens blaring in the distance and, whenever you left the complex, you'd see a cop car cruise down the block shining their spotlights on the homeless people sleeping on the sidewalks.

"Can you boys call him?"

We did, and he didn't answer any of our dozen calls in the twenty minutes we spent spamming his phone.

"I doubt he got this far," Glenn said, scanning the block. "Maybe he's back at the apartment?"

Dad didn't respond.

"Should we call Mom?" I asked. "Maybe if *she* calls John—"

"No!" Dad barked. "Keep your mother out of this."

"We should call the cops," Glenn said. "Fill out a missing person's case."

"No," Dad said. "No cops."

"Well, how else are we gonna find—"

"If cops find him and he's got drugs on him, he'll go to jail. And the last thing I want is one of my boys having a record…"

The longer we drove around, the more homeless and shady people I saw walking the streets, the more I began to worry that something horrible happened to my brother. I imagined him getting kidnapped by people in a sketch van. I pictured him getting robbed and stabbed by a crackhead. I visualized a world where he just ran away and never came back.

What the hell are we going to tell Mom when we go back to her place Monday if we don't find him?

Even though Mom didn't speak to Johnny for months after kicking him out, she asked me pretty much every day how he was doing and what he was up to. Of course, I told her half-truths, because I knew about as much about his life as she did, and what I did know would only devastate her if I told her. And I knew if we didn't find Johnny that night, she'd have a breakdown and blame herself for everything.

By the time I snapped out of my nightmarish trance, Dad was pulling back into his apartment complex. As we walked across the lot to the stairs, Dad stopped abruptly, stared at something across the lot, then just ran towards whatever it was without saying anything. By the time we'd caught up to him, he ran around to the passenger side of a car parked in farthest corner of the lot then yanked open the door.

"Stop! Dad, stop!" Johnny yelled as Dad dragged him out of the car toward Glenn and me.

"Keep your eye on him," Dad said, shoving him into Glenn. He whipped back around and charged back to the car.

"Dad, calm down! Stop it!" Johnny yelled. He tried running after Dad but Glenn grabbed him by the arm.

The driver's side door opened and a very disheveled-looking Travis stumbled out. There wasn't even a glimmer of fear in his eyes as my burly father marched toward him. His expression was deadpan, empty.

"Listen, Mr. Castillo," Travis said, raising his hands. "I know you're upset but lemme explain—"

Dad slapped Travis across the face so hard, he stumbled back. "You have 10 seconds to get back in your car and get the fuck out of here before I whoop your skinny little ass up and down this parking lot for everyone to see."

I expected Travis to give Dad that smug grin he always gave people when he wanted to get a rise out of them. I expected Travis to calmly tell him that he was going to press charges for assaulting a minor, following up with some racist remark about how Dad better hope he had a valid green card. But Travis did none of those things. Instead, he stared back at Dad with something like remorse then flashed Johnny a sympathetic look as he climbed back into the car.

"I don't want you hanging around that boy anymore," Dad said, still watching Travis drive off as he walked towards us.

"You didn't have to hit him!" Johnny said. "We weren't even doing anything…"

When Dad stopped in front of Johnny, he flinched. But he didn't hit our brother, just hugged him tightly. "I'm just glad you're okay…" he whispered.

Johnny didn't hug him back. He didn't say anything. He just looked over at me and Glenn until Dad let him go and started back towards the stairs.

Glenn patted Johnny's shoulder then followed behind Dad, leaving the two of us standing side by side in the cool night air.

Part of me wanted to hug him too, but I couldn't bring myself to do it. "I'm glad you're alright too," I said softly before leaving him behind to sort through his thoughts.

Chapter 19

"Here you go," Mom said, startling me awake just as I was nodding off.

Dozing off at the dinner table became a nightly occurrence in the days following the whole Johnny running away debacle. Usually, hearing Mom walking towards the table or some noise from the kitchen would snap me out of it, but this time she caught me.

"Thanks," I groaned, looking down at the insane amount of food she placed before me. There were two thick chicken thighs, a mountain of extra buttery mashed potatoes, and five long asparaguses drenched in oil and salt. Compared to what she and Glenn had on their plates, my plate had more than both their servings combined. "Uh, why'd you give me so much?"

Mom gave Glenn a weird look before meeting my gaze. "Well, I just figured you've been going to the gym so much that maybe you deserve a little extra, that's all," she replied.

"Oh…" I looked back down at the intimidating pile of food before me.

My head was throbbing so bad that the scraping of their utensils against their plates, the sound of them chewing, and the air conditioner's hum left me clenching my teeth. Somehow, the noise grew louder and louder with each passing second until it sounded like a slaughter house in my head.

Stop… Please make it stop! I'll do anything.

My body ached, I felt cold, my eyelids too heavy to keep open—my body wanted that food but all I wanted was to crawl in bed and rest while the hungry beast growling in my gut feasted upon the remains of my fat, fat that I knew was there even though I couldn't see it.

While I sat there playing with my food and trying to block out the sounds, I kept catching Mom and Glenn glancing up at me. And, as I locked eyes with my brother, my stomach roared so loud that it made both of them perk up and stare at me.

"I'm feeling kind of sick," I said, my chair screeching as I pushed away from the table. "I think I'm gonna go to bed.

"Wait!" Mom said, staring at me with worried, sad eyes. "Just try and eat a little bit? At least have some mashed potatoes!"

My stomach groaned, like it was agreeing with her request.

"No, I'm okay. Really." I turned and started walking.

"Dude!" Glenn barked. "You *need* to eat something. You haven't eaten all day."

"Yeah I did. I had an—"

"An apple and some bread is not enough for a boy your age," he retorted. "You need to start eating more. You're starting to look thin. And not the healthy kind of thin, dude."

The level of concern on their faces made me feel compelled to sit back down, not because I agreed with them but because I felt guilty. But what did I have to feel guilty about? I'd been ridiculed for my weight and the insane amount of food I ate for as long as I could remember, and now that I was finally doing something about it, everyone was trying to get me to eat more?

What do you people want from me? Nothing I do is ever good enough! That's what I wanted to scream, but I didn't. I just stormed off.

"Brad!" Glenn called out. "Brad! Brad!"

I kept running up the stairs. Then, when I got to my room, I slammed the door as hard as I could to send them a message.

On the way to my bed, I turned to the figure in the mirror to my left. Standing before me was a fifteen-year-old boy who was around five-feet-eight-inches tall with greasy brown hair, and bags under his bloodshot eyes. His cheeks were so sunken in that you could almost see the outline of his teeth through the skin. His shoulders poked through the top of his shirt like daggers, and his arms were merely bones wrapped tightly in dry skin.

The boy in the mirror removed his shirt when I took off mine. One by one, I dragged my finger down my ribs like keys on a grand piano, and the gaunt boy in the mirror mimicked me. Then I looked into the boy's brown eyes.

That's when the world suddenly stopped.

His eyes looked like mine, some of his features resembled mine, but he didn't look anything like the image of myself that I had in my head. Suddenly, I felt detached from my body, as though I was floating outside of myself like an astral body who was staring at his physical form.

I get it now… I see what Glenn meant… This is what my family has been seeing for the last few months…

And despite that realization, I didn't go back downstairs like I knew I should. Instead, I turned off the light, crawled into bed, and closed my eyes.

Once again, I began dragging a finger up and down my protruding ribcage and, this time, a smile crept across my face.

Chapter 20

The First Monday of June

The following Monday morning, it was even more of a struggle to get out of bed than it was the previous weeks. I was so weak that I barely had the strength to reach over and swat my blaring alarm clock. Had it not been for the headache still throbbing in my skull, I probably wouldn't have moved at all—I probably would've laid there and suffered for a bit longer.

From the moment that I got out of the bed until I got dressed after my shower, everything felt like a hazy dream. If I didn't have wet hair clung to my forehead and neck on the way downstairs, I wouldn't have been sure if I even showered or not.

Halfway down the stairs, I got dizzy and had to quickly grab the banister. *I can barely stand, so how the hell am I going to walk to school?*

"Morning!" Mom said right as I entered the kitchen. "You want a lift today?"

"Uh, sure," I replied hesitantly. "But don't you have work?"

"Took the day off."

"Oh… For what?"

She shrugged. "No reason. Just felt like it."

In all of my fifteen years, Mom had never taken a day off work without a valid reason. She could be vomiting blood and she'd still go in. I didn't have the energy to interrogate her anymore, so I just followed her out the door.

She and I talked the entire way to school, but I was so out of it, I had already forgotten what we were even talking about.

"Thanks for the ride," I said, opening the passenger door.

"Wait!" Mom blurted out.

I froze with one foot out the door and turned to her.

She didn't say anything. She just stared at me with her mouth agape and her jaw quivering like she was scared to speak. "Shut the door," she finally said.

I did as instructed. "Is something wrong?"

Mom gave me that halfhearted smile she tended to do when she was on the verge of tears but wanted to pretend that everything was okay—the smile she'd give us whenever her and Dad finished arguing and she came to our rooms to say goodnight. "So… I've been doing a lot of thinking, and I feel like it would be good for you to talk to someone. Jodie's daughter has been seeing someone—"

"Who's Jodie?"

"You know, *Jodie*."

I shrugged.

"The Jodie I've been friends with since Glenn was born. She would come with us when we used to all go to Tri City Park and you guys would run around catching beetles. Remember?"

I could barely remember the car ride, let alone memories from a decade ago, so I shook my head.

Mom looked down at her hands and scratched one thumb nail against another, something she did whenever she was anxious. "Anyway, Jodie's daughter Naomi… I'm guessing you don't remember her either…"

I shook my head again.

Mom sighed. "Well, Naomi talks to someone once a week."

"What do you mean? Who does she talk to?"

"A therapist named Dr. Royce. Jodie tells me Naomi was… struggling for a while, and after two months' worth of sessions with him, she's starting to feel like her old self again."

I squinted at her. "So… you want me to see a therapist?" I asked.

Mom seemed frightened in that moment. "I just think it would be good for you. That's all."

That wasn't all. I knew what this was all about, and so did she. She was concerned about my health. Everyone was. And after seeing myself in the mirror the night before, after feeling like I was about to faint all morning, I understood their concern. But I didn't care. I felt too far gone, too withered, too whittled down to make an effort to do anything about it.

When I felt my stomach gearing up for another growl, I grabbed the handle and opened the door. "Can we talk about this later, Mom?"

She tried to smile, but it came off more like a wince than anything. "Okay," she said softly with a nod. "I love you, Brad."

"I love you too." I climbed out of the car and shut the door.

As I walked away from the car, this horrible feeling came over me. It wasn't malaise. It wasn't fatigue. It was something like dread. *Why did she say I love you like she thought she was never going to see you again?* I didn't have the energy to try and decipher her tone or motives, so I tried to push the thought out of my mind while I walked to class.

Then all of these intrusive thoughts started popping up in my head.

You'll never see her again.

Because something bad's going to happen.

Maybe today's the day you collapse and crack your head open on the pavement.

Maybe you stressed out Mom so much she's going to get into a car accident.

Maybe after the divorce and all the crap with Johnny, you starving yourself to death is the straw that breaks the camel's back—what drives her to a heart attack or something...

Something horrible is going to happen. I don't know to who, but one of you is going to find out...

You just had to leave Mom feeling like shit, didn't you? Why can't you make people happy for once? Why do you always leave people feeling like shit?

"Hey, Brad!" a familiar voice called out to me as I passed the library.

When I turned around, there was this lanky, broad-shouldered guy with slicked back hair striding towards me. At first, I thought he was one of the teachers, but as he stepped out of the shade, I recognized him.

"Michael?" I asked in disbelief.

He smirked. "What, we go a year without seeing each other and you forget me?" He chuckled. "How you been, man?"

"I'm good." I sized him up. "Dude, you look…"

"Different? Yeah, I grew up a bit." He dramatically stroked the scruff on his jaw.

I snickered. "I mean, sure, but, dude, you look like a *totally* different person."

"That's what happens when you eat like a sumo wrestler and hit weights twice a day. I usually get in a quick workout at lunch, then hit it again at around 6 or 7." He looked me up and down. The look on his face quickly went from delighted to concerned. "You look different too. How are you doing?" His tone matched the worried look in his eyes.

"I'm … good," I said.

An awkward pause followed.

"Lost a lot of weight, I see," he finally said.

"Yeah."

"Are you… like, um…" He waggled his finger at me while he pondered the right word. "Are you… sick?"

"What? What do you mean?"

The bell rang, and all the students in the area began migrating past us like a flock of sheep.

"Can you meet me at break?" Michael asked. "In the theater?"

"Are we even allowed to go in there?" I asked.

"If you're in drama you can, which I am."

"Yeah, sure thing."

"Cool! See ya then, dude!"

Sick? The word rattled around in my head the entire walk to class. *Does he think I'm dying? Does he think I have cancer or something? Wait… does everyone think I have cancer? Mom, Dad, Glenn, all of them— they think you're dying. But wait, if they all think that, then what if you are?*

I walked out of my algebra test fairly confident. It was a cumulative final with a bunch of basic questions, so it wasn't difficult at all. The only hard part was trying to focus when all I could think about was if I was dying and how badly I wanted to sleep.

To my surprise there were quite a few kids scattered about in the theater during break. Oddly enough, all of them were dressed more eccentrically than the kids who frequented the bleachers in the courtyard. And they all seemed to be grinning genuinely and laughing often.

"Brad!" Mike called. He was sitting on the main stage and eating potato chips.

"Hey!" I said with a wave. I tried to climb up on the stage beside him, but I didn't have the strength to even lift my feet off the ground.

Michael grabbed me by the arm, cupped a hand under my armpit then hoisted me up like it was nothing. "Jesus," he said. "You're light as a fucking feather."

I smirked as I sat beside him.

He extended the bag of chips to me. "Want some?"

"No, thanks…"

He frowned.

"So, what's up?" I asked.

"How're Johnny and Travis?"

"I dunno…" I broke eye contact. "Haven't seen either of them for a while."

"What? How do you not see your own brother? You *live* together…"

I shook my head. "He got kicked out of my mom's place so he's staying at my dad's now. He's usually never there when I visit every other weekend. And when he is there, he's like a zombie."

"Oh… shit… What about Travis?"

"Travis… Travis changed…"

"Weren't you guys best friends at one poin—"

"Yeah, and now we're not," I snapped, looking down at the nail I'd been chipping away at since he brought up Johnny and Travis.

"Do you hate them or something?" Michael asked.

That was a loaded question and I wasn't sure how to answer it. "Do you hate them after what happened after Kylie's party?"

"Honestly? I did. For a while."

"And you don't anymore?"

He shook his head.

"If you don't mind me asking—"

"How'd I get over it?" he asked.

I nodded.

He turned away and pondered it for a while. Then he looked back at me with those genuine green eyes of his. "You know, it's funny… I don't remember. I wish I could say there was some moment or thought that made me get over it—like an epiphany or whatever—but there wasn't. I spent so many days thinking about how fucked up it all was—thinking about how I lost two people I cared for because of their selfish bullshit. Then, boom. After a while, I just stopped thinking about it. What happened back then just didn't matter anymore. It wasn't like they were improving my life when I was hanging out with them. So, I just carried on with my life and focused on myself. On my own happiness. And here's the thing, dude—I have no fucking clue what Travis is going through. Or what Johnny's going through. And I may never know. And if I don't know the whole story, how can I really judge or hate them, you know?"

That nugget of truth really made me think. And the longer I digested it, the more envious of Michael I felt. Somehow, he was still able to believe there was good inside even the vilest of people. It was admirable, and I wanted to be able to live like that, but I knew I could never get out of my own way to see shitty people in a different light once I made my mind up about them. Deep down, I still resented those who had hurt me, and that bitterness seemed to grow daily like a fire someone kept dumping gasoline and tinder on each morning. Part of me always felt like if I didn't hold onto that resentment, I'd only have myself to hate. So I had to keep redirecting the wildfire outwards, because that was the easy thing to do, the thing that brought me the most comfort.

How does Michael chose to face it all head on? What a heavy load it must be to have faith in people. In yourself. In anything at all.

Before I had a chance to think of a reply, the bell rang.

"It's that time," Michael said with a sigh, hopping down from the stage and tossing his empty chip bag into the trash. "Let's hang again at lunch if you're down," he said.

"What about the gym?" I asked.

"What about it?" he said with a grin.

I smiled. "Sure, I'm down."

"Awesome, meet me back here then."

With that, he took a right out of the theater and I took a left. And seconds after I merged with the flock of students, the intercom blared overhead, bringing everyone to a dead stop.

"Lockdown! Lockdown! Lockdown!" a panicked women shouted over and over.

The kids surrounding me looked around at each other. Some had amused smirks, the rest just seemed confused like me.

"This is not a drill!" the woman screamed. "I repeat, this is not a drill! All students, please seek shelter in the nearest classroom immediately!"

In the blink of an eye, everyone went from frozen in place to suddenly stampeding in different directions. Screams and cusses filled the halls. Sneakers squeaked across the linoleum floors as kids pushed one another during their mad-dash to whatever classroom their eyes fell on first. It was pure chaos. There was so much going on, there was so many massive kids barreling by, I couldn't figure out when to move without getting trampled—I didn't know which class to run to. While I stood there paralyzed by fear and indecision, several kids bumped into me from several directions. Then one stocky asshole hit me so hard, I toppled over like I was nothing more than a carboard cutout.

Someone tripped over my backpack. Another person stepped on my foot. As I laid there on the floor in fetal position with my arms shielding my head, all I could think about were those news stories from the last few months of mass shootings, wondering if I'd be the first victim if I couldn't get off that floor fast enough and scramble into a class room.

This isn't happening, I thought. *This can't be happening.*

Something bad is going to happen today, another voice in my head reminded me. *Not to Mom, to you.*

The stomping around me suddenly faded into distant footfalls that were quickly replaced by slamming class doors. That's when I unshielded my head and began to sit up, frantically looking around for an open class to run to.

"Hey!" a man's voice shouted from behind me.

Assuming it was the shooter, I froze. My heart was beating so hard and fast, I began feeling dizzy. A cold sweat broke out across my body.

"Young man, come on!" he said urgently. "Get up and get inside!"

It's a teacher! Go!

"Where are you?" a gruff voice echoed from somewhere in the distance as I scrambled to my feet.

I booked it to that classroom faster than I've ever moved in all my months of running, and as soon as I made it inside, the teacher slammed the door behind me.

"Get under one of the desks and stay down," the teacher whispered, his voice cracking.

The lights were off inside so it was hard to find a desk without someone under it since I was basically blind after having just left the bright hallway. And when my eyes began to acclimate to the darkness, I realized there was a kid under every desk.

I turned to the teacher who was pressed against the wall beside the door holding a fire extinguisher. "There's no space," I whispered.

"Over here!" some girl near the front of the class whispered. When I spun around, I saw her waving at me.

"Thanks," I said, crawling under the desk beside her.

"I want my mom!" a girl sobbed.

"Shhhhh!" someone hissed.

"Oh lord Jesus please!" another girl behind me pleaded. "Please help us! Please help us! Please!"

"Shhhhhh!"

"Shut the fuck up, Tara!" a guy barked. "You're gonna get us all killed!"

"Does anyone know what's happening?" I whispered. "Is it another bomb threat?"

"No," the girl beside me whispered back. "Someone said there was a guy with a gun looking for someone."

"No, I said *two* guys, Cassie," a boy behind me said in a hushed voice. "Mexican kids. My friend texted me about them right before all this. Said one had a pistol tucked in his jeans, so he reported it."

"My brother just texted me that there were these two Hispanic kids he's never seen around school who were asking around about a guy named Jarvis or Trevor or some shit like that," a girl a few desks down whispered a bit louder.

"Dude, some shady guy asked me about a guy named Travis earlier!" another guy chimed in.

Travis? There's no way they're talking about the Travis I know…

Suddenly, there was loud knocking coming from the hallway. "Nora!" a deep voice yelled.

All the whispers stopped in an instant. The only sounds in the room were heavy breathing and quiet whimpers.

"Nora, where are you?" the raspy voice wailed again, sounding much closer that time.

A shadowy figure appeared in the window of the classroom door then three loud knocks followed, triggering a cacophony of screams and yelps from almost every kid in that room.

One girl screamed bloody murder.

"Nora?" the man outside boomed, peeking through the window with bulging red eyes. The knob rattled as he began aggressively trying to open the door.

There were muffled screams from the front of the class. Kids behind me sounded like they were hyperventilating. Several kids, including me, began whimpering quietly.

"Nora? Nora, are you in there?" the man outside asked in a desperate, raspy voice. "Nora? Nora, please open the door. Let's just talk this out."

That voice… Why do I recognize that gravelly, deep voice? I was too terrified to remember.

"Nora!" The man pounded on the door again while jiggling the doorknob. "Nora, let me see my daughter! I'm better now, I promise. The doctor gave me new medicine and said I'm better now. Please, I just wanna see my daughter! Please, Nora, I'm begging you!"

The banging and doorknob jiggling stopped, then all I heard was the man in the hall whimpering. Like a kettle of boiling water, the sobbing crescendoed into a growl and then into a roar. That's when he stared punching and kicking the door. "Nora! I know she's in there! Open the goddamn door!" the fury in his voice was blood curdling, like a monster had replaced the man from a few seconds before. "I want to see my daughter! You can't keep her from me! *Nora!*"

Screams filled the room. The teacher grabbed the knob and leaned his shoulder into the door to stop the man from bursting through.

"Gracie," the man said into the glass in a drastically softer tone. "Gracie, are you in there?"

The room fell silent.

"Gracie, honey, it's Daddy," the man continued. There was a thump and the sound of something sliding against the door, like he had just slumped against it "It's Daddy, sweetie. Don't be afraid! The voices are gone, sweetie, trust me. Daddy's not scary anymore, the demons are gone. Please, sweetie, open the door."

The demons are gone? That's when the memory came rushing back—the memory of a younger, fatter, and equally terrified version of me in the alley behind school listening to a homeless man tell me about the demons in his head who were trying to kill him.

"Police! Put your hands where I can see them!" a different voice barked.

The man at the door moaned and sobbed like a ghost.

"Put your hands where I can see them!" the cop ordered. *"Now!"*

The man stopped crying, then it sounded like a weight lifted off from the bottom of the door, then I saw the side of the man's head pop up in the tiny window, illuminated by the hall lights. That long, greasy, gray hair, that bushy beard that covered most of his leathery face.

That's Leonard... the homeless man I used to write notes to back in middle school...

"Get away from me," Leonard growled. "You're not real! I know you're not real. You took everything from me!"

"Put your hands behind your head! Final warning!"

Then the man looked down. "Don't let them hurt her again, Leonard," he said to himself, looking back at the cop and moving towards him.

Two gunshots thundered outside and I watched in horror as Leonard fell backwards past the window. Everyone in class screamed while the teacher dropped to the ground and went prone.

"It's okay!" the teacher shouted. "Everything is okay, kids."

The screams transitioned into a collective sobbing that went on for a long while, only to begin again when someone knocked on the door.

"This is Officer Matthew Becker with the Placentia Police Department," the man announced. "Everything is safe now. Let's get these kids out of the school."

The teacher rose and clicked on the lights before opening the door. "Come on, kids," he said, his voice all shaky.

"On your way out, please do not look down," the officer instructed as everyone began gathering in the front of the class. He pointed at something down the hall. "Just keep your heads up and your eyes on the other end of the hall."

The class formed a line and, one by one, they filed out of the class. I was near the back of the line, so I got to see the reactions of the students at the front of the line as they left. Some kids left with their hands covering their eyes. Others looked up at the ceiling. A few guys looked down at the scene.

"Hey!" the cop shouted. "I said eyes up! You don't need to see this!"

When it was my turn to leave the class, I tried to avoid seeing whatever horrific thing the cop tried to protect us from, but I couldn't. I had to see Leonard. The cop was busy talking to another officer, so I glanced down and stared right at the scene. Leonard's body was covered with a black tarp, but his old, ragged boots and one wrinkly hand were sticking out from underneath it. And that wasn't the worst part. The worst part was the pool of dark, crimson blood that was spreading outwards from the edges of the tarp—that's what made my eyes widen in horror, that's what made me retch. I probably would've puked right on the kid in front of me if there was anything in me to throw up.

With one hand covering my mouth and one hand on my queasy stomach, I turned around and stared blankly at the lines of kids merging ahead from the different classes.

A girl from a class across the hall stepped out and looked back at the murder scene. "You didn't have to kill him!" she screamed at the cop. "You didn't have to do that!" One of her friends grabbed her then pulled her into the crowd ahead.

Like all the students from the classroom where I sheltered, I walked out of the building in a wide-eyed trance. It wasn't until I saw all of the flashing lights from the police cars parked outside that I snapped out of it. There were cops everywhere. To my right, there was a SWAT team with assault rifles coming out from a door on the other end of our building. Up ahead, there was a news team interviewing faculty. Behind them, there was a crowd of scared-looking people, presumably parents and people from the neighborhood.

"You're not listening to me," some tall kid shouted at a cop. "I'm telling you that the homeless guy who was wandering around wasn't the guy with the gun! It was some Mexican dude in a white shirt and baggy jeans!"

"And I'm telling you that SWAT checked the entire school and didn't find anyone who matched that description. The only person ID'd with a weapon was the suspect that our officers neutralized."

The rest of the conversation was drowned out by the commotion around me.

"No students were harmed this morning during the incident here at El Dorado High School," a reporter said as we reached the edge of campus.

As the teachers led us past the news crews to the army of frantic parents screaming their kids' names, I looked around for Johnny, Travis, or Michael. And, when I couldn't find them, I searched the crowd for my parents.

For maybe two or three minutes, I walked along the wall looking around like a lost child.

"Brad!" my mother called from somewhere in the crowd.

"Mom?"

"Brad! Over here!" At that moment, she burst through the crowd and ran at me with open arms. When we collided, she squeezed me so hard that I could barely breathe. But I didn't care. I didn't need to breathe in that moment. I just needed to be held, I just needed to hug her back just as hard.

"I'm so glad you're okay!" she said as we parted, tears rolling down her cheeks. "Where's your brother? Have you seen him anywhere?"

"No," I said. "But it's okay, I heard the reporter say that no students were harmed."

She searched my eyes for a moment then hugged me tightly, sniffling as she sobbed silently against me.

While we held each other, I looked around at all of the crying kids on their phones who were trying to get in touch with their loved ones, at all of the boys and girls embracing their parents like they hadn't for a decade.

"Let me through!" an angry parent shouted at the cops standing between them and campus. "I need to find my son!"

As soon as he burst past the barricade, a bald cop charged him and started shoving him back to the crowd. That's when a bunch of people started freaking out.

Everything was just so emotionally chaotic, like Leonard's tortured spirit had begun possessing everyone in the area.

"I'm going to try and call Johnny again," Mom said, pulling away from me.

As I stood there watching her dialing up my brother with trembling hands, I looked at her face, like *really* looked at her face. In that moment, it was like I could see past the mask she always wore in front of us, the one she used to make us seem like she had it all together even when we knew things were bad. All I saw in her eyes was heartbreak, not just from this madness at school, but also heartbreak from all the worrying Johnny and I put her through. She was like a sculpture whose face was re-sculpted from a beautiful smiling woman to a tortured maiden. And Dad and Johnny weren't the only ones holding the chisels responsible, I held one too.

I'm tired of seeing her like this. I can't keep being one of the reasons she's stressing out every day.

"Mom," I muttered, taking a deep breath afterwards.

"Yes, honey?" she said, closing her flip phone.

I exhaled slowly. "That doctor your friend's daughter has been seeing… I was thinking meeting with them might not be such a bad idea."

In that moment, all the pain left my mother's eyes and she smiled in a way I'd never seen her smile before.

Kylie's Story

Chapter 21

The beginning of the school year
The night of Kylie's first week of school party...

"Kylie?" a girl spoke in a muffled voice.

Not only was I too out of it to open my eyes, but I wasn't even sure if the voice I'd heard was real or something I dreamt, so I rolled over and drifted back off.

"Kylie, wake up!"

A slap to the face startled me awake, and the second I opened my eyes and stared at the figure standing over me, the room began spinning. "Morgan?" I groaned, scrunching my face from the taste of beer and vomit in my mouth. "What's happening?"

"The cops are here!" Morgan said in a panicked voice.

"Wait... what? What the hell happened?"

"These kids from Esperanza showed up, a fight broke out, then everyone ran for it when they saw flashing lights. The cops have your mom on the phone so they need you to come downstairs."

That's when my heart stopped and my stomach twisted into a knot. That's when the dread made me go catatonic.

"Come on," Morgan whispered as she pulled me up off Mom's bed. She then wrapped an arm around my waist and escorted me all the way downstairs.

At the bottom of the steps, red and blue flashing lights caught my eye, drawing my trance-like gaze to the front window. There were a few cops breathalyzing kids on the sidewalk while another officer cuffed a tall guy I'd never seen before. It wasn't until a police radio squawked from inside the living room that I faced front and realized exactly how much trouble I was in.

"Oh no…" I gasped, staring at the mess.

There were red Solo cups and puddles all over the place. Shards of amber glass glimmered on the floor near the couch. One of the dining room chairs was smashed into pieces on the floor in front of the two cracked living room windows. And if all that wasn't bad enough, there was blood splattered all over the fucking floor. It looked like a warzone…

"Are you Kylie?" an officer by the couch asked.

I nodded.

He extended a phone to me. "Your mother."

I put the phone to my ear and waited for the screaming to start, but there was just silence. "Hello?" I muttered. "Mom?"

She sighed a gust of air into the mic. "How bad is it, Kylie?" she asked with a bit of a slur. She didn't sound disappointed, just annoyed. And, of course, she didn't even ask if I was okay.

"Honestly? Not great," I said, surveying the carnage. "But I can get it all cleaned up."

"It's not good, Malik," she whispered to my step-father, more annoyed than disappointed.

"Of course…" Malik grumbled in the background. A cork popped right after. "Seriously, is *one* weekend without trouble too much to ask from your daughter, Dana?"

There was rustling on her end. "Malik, not now…" Her voice sounded muffled, like she was trying to cover the microphone. "You know, the officers asked if I could come back tonight, but I told them you could keep out of trouble until we get back tomorrow afternoon. Can you manage that *at least*?" Mom asked.

"Yeah…"

"Good. Now, the officer wants to know if there is someone who I need to press charges against. Is there?"

"There better be!" Malik shouted. "Someone needs to pay for the damage!"

"You're not helping, Malik!" she spoke with that quiet rage that she only reserved for him.

"You're right," Malik said. "*Your* daughter, *your* problem." There was some thrashing, then a door slammed right after that. A long bout of silence followed.

"Kylie?" Mom finally said. "You going to answer me?"

"Oh... I don't know who's responsible for any of this. I was sleeping upstairs."

"Christ..."

I looked over at the bloody-faced Mexican kid who was sitting on a dining room chair with his hands cuffed behind his back. "But there's someone I didn't invite that the cops have cuffed in the dining room."

"You're no help. Just put the cop back on..." she snarled.

After I handed the officer the phone, he filled her in on the fight that broke out and how they arrested one of the three perpetrators from Esperanza. "Several of the witnesses say that this kid and his friends started the fight," the cop explained to Mom. "So, if you want to press charges..."

The Mexican kid looked at the cop, eyes wide with panic.

"Okay, ma'am," the officer said, handing the phone to me.

"Mom," I whimpered, "I'm so sorry—"

"*Sure* you are..." Mom sneered. In the background, I heard her pouring something into a glass—probably wine per usual. "Do me a favor? Try not to fuck up anything else until I get back. Jesus, I don't know how much longer I can deal with this."

The call ended before I could respond.

With tears welling in my eyes, I followed the officers as they escorted the suspect and the last witness out of the house. The second Morgan shut the door behind them, I started bawling.

"It's going to be alright," she said as she embraced me.

I stood there crying in her arms until I started sobbing hard enough to make myself sick. That's when I pushed her away and ran for the bathroom.

The entire time I had my head buried in the toilet, Morgan knelt beside me, holding my hair up and patting my back. And when there was nothing left to puke, she helped me up, led me to my room and crawled in bed with me.

I laid there for a while staring at my ceiling, thinking to myself how dumb of an idea it was throwing that party, thinking of how much trouble I was going to be in when Mom got home.

"What am I going to do?" I asked.

"No point in worrying about it now," Morgan whispered. "Just rest. We'll figure it out in the morning."

With a nod, I rolled onto my side and shut my eyes.

The next morning, I awoke to the buzzing of my phone in my pocket and was instantly greeted by the worst headache ever. There was a cool breeze blowing in through the cracked window, but I still felt nice and toasty despite not being under my covers. It wasn't until I tried rolling over that I realized Morgan was all snuggled up to me with an arm draped around my torso. I always thought she was pretty but, when she was asleep, she looked borderline angelic. Part of me wished I could tell her that, but I knew how weird it'd sound, so I kept it to myself.

Trying my best not to wake her up, I rolled over as gently as possible then fished my cell phone out of my pocket. Of course, the text was from Mom and not from Johnny like I'd hoped.

Mom: Leaving now. Be home in 3-4 hours.

Reading that made the pounding in my head worse. "Morgan," I whispered, squirming out from her embrace.

"Hmm?" she groaned sleepily.

"My mom will be home in, like, three hours." I sprang out of bed only to plop right back down onto the mattress with a hand planted against my forehead. "Ugh… my head…"

"You're too hungover," she said as she sat up. "And even if you weren't, there's no way you and I could clean this entire house in three hours."

"So, what the hell are we going to do?"

"I'm going to call a few people from the party and ask if they can help." She flipped open her phone and got to texting.

"You're going to *ask* them? It's Saturday morning, you know everyone is going to say no…"

"Well, if they don't want to help out of the kindness of their hearts, then I'll blackmail them into coming by threatening to tell their parents about them drinking and all the other debauchery they did here last night." She smirked fiendishly. "Perks of being sober is a perfect memory."

I sat there massaging my temples for a moment, trying to recall what happened during that party. A bunch of hazy, vague memories started pouring in, then Brad Castillo's face popped up in my mind.

"Wait, Brad was here, wasn't he?"

"Johnny's brother? Yeah."

"What happened to him?" I asked.

"You tell me… You're the one that took him to your mom's bedroom."

"I did?"

"Yeah, didn't think you'd remember that…"

"I kinda remember him walking out of the room."

"Yeah, when the fight broke out downstairs, I sent Michael and Johnny to come get you, but you were in here all out of it and crying from whatever happened, so they just ran downstairs to help Travis fight those Mexican kids. Brad went down with them."

"Wait, Johnny was in the fight?"

"Yup. He was pretty pissed about you running off with Brad, and then he was even more pissed when he saw you crying. I'm, like, 99% sure that's the reason he jumped in the fight." Morgan's phone vibrated. "Oh! Zoey said she'll help."

"Well, that's at least one person," I muttered.

"Yup!" Morgan looked me in the eyes. "So… what's up with you and Brad? Were you trying to hook up with him?"

"No," I said quickly, "I mean, I don't think so?"

"Aren't you and Johnny—"

"I don't know."

"C'mon, that's bullshit. I see you guys together."

"Like I said, I don't know. Two months ago, I would've said yes, but lately… I dunno, he just seems so detached. And he's a different person when Travis is around."

Morgan stared at me for a moment before going back to texting. "So, you were trying to piss him off by hooking up with his little brother?"

"That's not it at all!"

"What is it then?"

I blanked because I truly didn't know. I thought Brad was cute in an awkward sort of way. He seemed sweet and shy, the total opposite of his brother. Maybe I was attracted to that? And if drunk me took him to my mom's room to do who knows what, I guess there must be a part of me that likes him.

In that moment, though, all I could think about was Johnny and how what I'd done must have seriously hurt him. *I have to text him and apologize,* I thought, flipping open my phone.

Me: Hey just woke up. Sorry, I was super fucked up last night, don't remember anything. Did you get home OK?

Morgan's phone chimed as soon as I closed mine. "Michael said he can help!" She turned to me. "Hey, maybe he can tell you what happened to your *boyfriend…*" For some reason, her words came off bitter. "Come on, let's get started downstairs.

About fifteen minutes later, help arrived with cleaning supplies, trash bags, and rubber gloves. Zoey and Fiona took the upstairs while Michael stayed downstairs to help Morgan and me.

"Here you go!" Morgan said, handing Michael the mop and bucket.

"Uh…" he groaned, reluctantly taking them. "Why am I on mopping duty?"

She pointed at the blood stains. "That's your mess, isn't it?"

Glaring at her, Michael dunked the mop in the bucket of soapy water. "For the record, Brad and I stayed out of the fight. Her boyfriend and Travis are who you can thank for this."

"Oh… What happened after you guys left?" I asked, dropping a bunch of bottles into the trash bag.

Michael stopped mopping. "Travis and Johnny were being assholes so I went home. They all went to Travis's after. Haven't heard from them since."

"You haven't even heard from Johnny at all?" I asked.

He scowled at me. "That's what I *just* said."

Morgan shot him a dirty look. "She just asked a question."

"And I answered it!" he barked. "Look, I had a shitty night, same as you. Now do you want my help or not?"

When three o'clock rolled around, the house was as close to clean as it was going to get, so we pretty much called it quits.

"Zoey and Fiona said they'd give me a ride," Morgan said as the pair carried their supplies out to the car. "You want me to stay? I can explain to Dana what happened so she doesn't freak out…"

"I can handle it," I said.

Morgan looked disappointed. "Alright… Call me later."

"I will," I said as we hugged. "Thanks for everything."

"Don't mention it!" she said on the way out the front door.

Michael emerged from the kitchen with two filled garbage bags. "Sorry for acting like a dick earlier," he said.

"It's cool," I said, holding open the door for him. "I'm sorry Morgan was acting weird."

"That's just Morgan though, isn't it? She's always defensive over you." He smirked, and I cracked a smile too. He started to walk out only to pause in the doorway. "Hey, try and get ahold of Johnny... I don't know what's been going on with him, but I know Travis has something to do with it."

"Yeah, for sure."

After shutting the door, I plopped down on the bottom step and checked my phone. There was no response from Johnny, which was weird because he always responded so quickly.

Something is wrong.

Right as I was about to call him, the door burst open. Mom didn't even look at me, she just ripped the sunglasses off her burnt, leathery face and surveyed the house.

"Not so terrible," she mumbled, marching into the kitchen with her heels clacking against the hardwood. A drawer opened, the familiar rattle of a prescription pill bottle followed, then she stomped back into the hall and stumbled past me on her way upstairs.

"Where's Malik?" I asked.

"Oh, probably galivanting with some whore he met in the casino." There was a slight slur in her words, which means she'd either been drinking on the drive over or she woke up drunk again.

"Mom, I'm sorry about the—"

Her bedroom door slammed shut.

She didn't go off on me like I expected, but at least she gave me some kind of reaction, I thought as my eyes burned and welled with tears.

As crazy as it sounds, part of me wanted her to flip out and scream at me because that would at least be a sign that she could feel—that she wasn't still the numb, empty shell she'd been since Dad died. I was around 9 or 10 when he passed, so I still remember a time when she was capable of being angry whenever she wasn't the sweet, giddy woman who was full of vitality. That person had vanished, and I desperately wanted to see her again.

As I wiped a tear from my cheek, my phone vibrated. It was a text from Johnny.

Johnny: Hey, I'm in Corona. A lot of shit happened.

Me: What do you mean, what happened?

Instead of a text back, I got a phone call.

"Hey," he answered with a sigh. "Basically, my mom found my weed so she kicked me out. Now I have to live with my dad in his shitty apartment for a while."

"My god, that's awful," I said. "Are you okay?"

"I guess," he said with middling conviction. A long pause followed. "What're you doing right now?"

"Nothing. Just got done cleaning the house."

"Could you come over, please? I really need to see you."

"All the way to Corona?"

"Yeah, I'll give you gas money."

"I don't know, that seems pretty far …"

"Kylie… *Please*." There was this childlike desperation in his voice that I couldn't ignore.

"Hold on a second." I snuck up to Mom's room and opened her door as quietly as I could. She was snoring on the bed with her sunglasses still on, so I knew she'd be out like that for a while. "Alright. I'll text you when I get there."

Chapter 22

It was only supposed to take about twenty-five minutes to get to Corona, but thanks to almost five miles of bumper-to-bumper traffic, it took me an hour to get to Johnny's apartment complex. Then it took another two minutes of driving around the neighborhood to find one of the guest spots Johnny told me to park in.

Between the hangover, all the cleaning I'd done, and that long-ass drive, I was so tired that I was basically falling asleep while texting him that I had arrived. Barely ten seconds after messaging him, he texted me back.

Johnny: Apartment 264.

Even though the picture Johnny painted of his dad made him sound like a grumpy hard-ass, he didn't seem all that bad when I met him the night that he dropped Johnny off at the movies to hang with me last year. But considering his dad just found out he'd been smoking weed, I thought it'd be best not to run into him today.

Me: Can you come down instead?

Johnny: Be down in a minute.

After that grueling drive, I desperately needed to stretch, so I climbed out of the car and leaned against the hood while I texted Morgan about what happened when Mom got home.

"Hey!" I heard Johnny call from the stairs.

When I saw Johnny walking towards the car with his eye all swollen and his nose all bruised, my jaw dropped. "Holy shit…" I gasped. "Your face! Are you okay?"

He smirked. "You should see the other guy..."

"The one you knocked out or the one you beat over the head with a bottle?"

He just snickered and hugged me. His embrace was so tight, it was almost as if he thought he'd float away if I wasn't there to keep him on the ground. He held me so close, I could feel his racing heart hammering against my chest. It wasn't until we parted a few moments later that I'd realized he was crying.

Johnny sniffled as he quickly wiped a year away. "Let's get out of here before my dad comes back."

"Okay. You want to get something to eat?"

Johnny squinted at me like I just said the dumbest thing in the world, then he smirked and pulled out small bag of weed from his jacket pocket. "Sure. After, though." He returned the bag to his pocket and started walking around to the passenger door.

I climbed back in the car. "I thought you said your mom flushed your stash..."

"She flushed the stash she found..." He pointed at something on the other end of the neighborhood. "If you drive over to that alley down there, there's a parking lot that's always empty."

"Okay," I said as the engine roared to life.

The alley Johnny had me drive through was filthy, the walls were covered in gang graffiti, and there looked to be makeshift tents nestled between the dumpsters and piles of trash. Thankfully, the private lot that the alleyway led to was free of any crazies and didn't look nearly as sketchy as the route to it.

Even though there was no one around and no windows overlooking the parking lot, Johnny nervously scanned the area several times before finally grabbing the rainbow-colored pipe from the glove compartment. The feverish way he packed the bowl, sparked it up, and took that first hit made it seem like he might die if he didn't smoke ASAP. The massive cloud he coughed out quickly filled the car, sending me into a coughing fit before I could get my window down.

"What are you doing?" he asked.

"I can't get a contact high. Gotta drive back later."

Chuckling, he offered me the pipe. "Don't act like you don't want to."

I stared at it longingly, because I did want to. Desperately. Weed was the only thing that seemed to clear my mind of the darkness and despair that plagued me day in and day out, but I decided to stop for a while because it screwed up my concentration so bad the previous year, my GPA dropped to a 2.5.

"When's the last time you even smoked?" he asked.

"Almost two months…"

"Two months too long… C'mon, don't make me do this alone."

A smile crept across my face as I rolled my window back up.

"And, just like that, there she is," Johnny said with a cute grin.

I snatched the pipe from him and took a nice, long pull, holding the burning smoke in my lungs for as long as I could until the tickle in my throat made me cough it all out. He chuckled as he took the pipe back from me.

There were no spoken words while we passed the pipe back and forth, just a whole lot of coughing, snickering, laughs, and smiling at each other.

After Johnny took his last toke, the smile vanished from his bruised face and he went into this trance as he stared at the pipe in his hand. I didn't say anything, I just watched him curiously, waiting for him to snap out of it. "Hey…" he said after a long bout of silence. "What did—what did you do with Brad last night?"

There it is… I knew the question was coming but I still wasn't prepared.

He looked over at me, and there was something like anger and childlike fear in his eyes.

"Nothing," I said. "Nothing at all." That wasn't entirely a lie since I had no clue what happened.

He squinted his bloodshot eyes at me as if he were trying to peer into my mind, his way of calling "bullshit."

This is why he asked me to come over, I thought. *I should've been the one to bring it up, because now it just looks like I was hiding something.*

"Are you telling me the truth?" he asked.

"Johnny," I said, placing a hand on his arm only for him to pull away from me. "I did absolutely nothing with your brother last night. I can promise you that."

"Then why'd you take him into your mom's bedroom? Why were you so flirty with him? Why were you crying if nothing happened?"

"I don't know… I get flirtatious when I'm drunk sometimes, but that doesn't mean anything." That might have been a lie.

I usually only got flirty with people I genuinely liked. Sure, I thought Brad was a particular kind of cute, but I realized on the ride over to Johnny's that I didn't think that because of how he looked, it was the naive innocence he carried with him everywhere that attracted me and made me curious. That's why I wanted to tease him. His innocence reminded me of how I used to be before life broke me.

"You saw me," I continued. "I was completely shitfaced. I act like a fucking idiot when I get that—"

Johnny leaned over and hugged me. "I'm just so afraid all the time," he whimpered.

"Afraid of what?" I asked.

"Everything. My parents. I don't want to let them down, but I feel like I always do." He rested his head into my shoulder. "And

I'm scared of losing you. You're the only thing that's holding me together."

I pulled away and cupped the side of his face. "You're not going to lose me," I whispered. "I'm not going anywhere. I'm sorry for what I did last night. It was stupid and I'll never do anything like it again, I promise."

He buried his face back into my neck and broke down.

How Johnny was in that car, he was only that way with me. In public he'd walk around with his chest puffed out, deliberately quiet and mysterious like some rugged outlaw walking through a quiet Western town. Then, in our moments alone, he'd reveal the parts of himself that he hid and kept guarded from the world. That's when I'd go from being the girl who pretended she didn't care about anything to being this tender, nurturing presence who'd reassure him everything would be okay.

This was our unspoken arrangement. At first, I enjoyed being the one he came to—I enjoyed being the light for someone for once instead of the burden I was to everyone else. But, as I sat there consoling him, I'd realized that I was beginning to resent our arrangement. Because I always seemed to be the one being the light for him, but he was never that for me. He always had so much going on that he needed to get out, I never really got to vent like I wanted to that day. Nope. Instead, I always just wound up burying my troubles into the dark recesses of my mind while I consumed myself with his troubles. It was starting to feel like I was losing myself in him…

None of that mattered after he lifted his head off of my shoulder and planted his lips against mine. Kissing him in that smoke-filled car reminded me of why I sacrificed myself over and over again.

All I remember after that is a lot of kissing, giddy laughter, some more hotboxing, and then some more kissing. Things went on like that for what felt like an entire day until Johnny finally asked if I was hungry.

"I'm starving. But I can't drive though…" I replied.

"I'll drive. I drive better high, anyway."

"What? No way!"

"What, you wanna walk?" He climbed out of the car. "In this neighborhood?"

I was too high to argue or come up with a better idea, and there was no way I was walking around Corona, so I climbed over the center console to the passenger seat without another word.

The orange sun was sinking towards the horizon by the time we finally left that parking lot. Miraculously, Johnny drove around for nearly 15 minutes before we found a hole-in-the-wall burger joint named Welches Burgers—the only place that didn't look like we'd get murdered on the walk to and from the car. The burgers were greasy and bland, and the fries didn't have enough salt, but that didn't stop us from devouring our meal.

As we were finishing the last of our dry fries, Johnny's phone began buzzing on the table.

"Fuck!" he exclaimed, pounding a fist on the table. "It's my dad. I told him I'd be back soon, and that was four hours ago." He thumbed the down key on his phone. "Holy shit! He called, like, four times the past hour. We need to go! Can you pay? I had to give Brad all my money."

"Uh… yeah…" I muttered, reaching into my pocket.

No matter how many times I told Johnny to slow down on the way back, he insisted on driving like a maniac. If speeding wasn't bad enough, he was also switching lanes so aggressively that cars honked at us on every other block. As if by divine intervention, we somehow made it to his dad's complex without getting stopped.

"Hey," he said as we went over the speedbump. "As soon as I pull up to the apartment, I'm going to hop out and I want you to get out of there as fast as you can, okay? My dad can't see you like this."

"What? I'm too fucking high to drive now!"

"Look, if he thinks you're making me smoke weed, he'll never let me see you again."

"I'm not making you do anything."

"Doesn't matter to him. He's just going to associate you with me being high, and that can't happen. Just trust me, alright?"

"Whatever. Fine."

"Kylie, I'm not trying to..." His words trailed off as he leaned forward and stared at something up ahead. "Ah shit... he's sitting on the stairs..." Right as Johnny began to slow down, Mr. Castillo looked up from his phone and stared right at us. And, when he started walking towards us, Johnny slammed on the breaks, shifted into park, then turned to me with wide eyes. "Quick, switch seats with me!"

I crawled over him then he scrambled out from underneath me, diving into the passenger seat right as his dad popped out from behind a truck and started marching towards us.

"I'll text you later!" Johnny yelped as he climbed out of the car.

The second Mr. Castillo realized it was Johnny, his expression went from confused to extremely pissed. He then began screaming so hard at his son, the veins in his neck and forehead bulged. The last thing I saw before starting my three-point turn was his father standing there glaring at me.

It was after nine o'clock by the time I made it back to the house. Had I not pulled into a random parking lot near Johnny's place to sober up an hour, I don't think I would have been sober enough to make it home alive. Honestly, I'm still not sure how I even made it without getting pulled over because I kept getting honked at for driving ten miles under the speed limit. It took every ounce of focus I had to keep that needle on the 60 mph line those last ten miles.

Given how late it was, I just knew Mom would be waiting for me on the couch with a glass of wine in hand the way she always was when I came home late, so I didn't bother sneaking in. To my surprise, I wasn't greeted by yelling when I walked through the door like I expected, just silence. The house was dead quiet right up until I got to the top of the steps and heard her snoring just as loud as she was when I left.

There's no way she's been sleeping this entire time, I thought, slowly opening her door and peeking into her room.

Just like when I checked earlier, she was still laying in about the same position with her mouth gaped open. Her sunglasses were even still on her face, albeit slightly more crooked than before, which means she must have moved a little bit.

Unbelievable, I thought, shutting her door and shaking my head.

When I got to my room, I flopped onto my bed and laid there staring at the ceiling. For some reason, all I could think about was how Mr. Castillo kept calling and texting Johnny when he didn't come back home on time—I kept picturing that worried, furious look on his face when he started going off on his son.

I threw a party, wrecked the house, and had cops show up to a house full of drunk kids and my mom barely scolded me for it. She didn't even look at me when she came back and saw the damage, she just grabbed her pills then stumbled her drunk ass upstairs and passed out. She didn't even know I was out all this time! I could leave now, do drugs with my friends, and she wouldn't even know I was gone…

Oddly enough, I began feeling envious of Johnny for having two hard-asses as parents. *Sure, he gets in trouble for being out too long and for doing drugs, but at least that means his parents give a shit…*

As that thought crossed my mind, my phone chimed in my pocket. It was a text from Johnny that read: **Hey, it's gonna be** hard for you to come by now cuz dad's really suspicious about you. We'll find a way to sneak around it. Meet me in the parking lot before school Monday. Love u.

Great… as if things weren't shitty enough.

Me: Sounds good. Love you 2.

Chapter 23

The bong bubbled like a pot of violently boiling water as I sucked in a lung-full of smoke. Still holding my breath, I leaned forward then handed off the bong and the lighter to Johnny, who was sitting in the passenger seat of my car. And while he worked on sparking up the weed, I went back to being the paranoid one who couldn't stop scanning the empty dentist's office parking lot for cops or anyone who might rat us out.

Over and over, Johnny thumbed the flint wheel and failed to get the Bic lighter to flame up. "God dammit…" he grumbled.

My high ass found his struggles so funny that I cracked up, spewing plumes of white smoke into the already hazy car.

Travis, who had been relaxing with his eyes closed in the driver's seat, turned his severely bruised face to Johnny and just stared at him with the most unamused expression. Of the two of them, Travis's face was the most bruised. Ever since I saw him that Monday morning, I'd been waiting for him to brag about the fight and how he kicked the shit out of the Esperanza kids, because that's what Travis did—he was a boastful, smug ass who never missed an opportunity to be the loudest, toughest, coolest guy in the room. But, that whole day, he was uncharacteristically quiet, which was great because I couldn't really tolerate him most days. Putting up with him was just the price I paid to be around Johnny.

"Dude, hurry up!" Travis blurted out. "Lunch is over in fifteen. I wanna get something to eat."

"I'm trying! Chill!" Johnny fired back.

With the flame finally lit, Johnny took a nice, long rip. And the second he took his mouth off of it, Travis snatched the bong from him. As soon as he finished taking his last hit, he passed the bong back to me then started the car.

"I think I'm being followed," Travis said as he pulled out of the parking lot.

Johnny looked in the sideview mirror then started looking around in a panic when he didn't see anyone. "By who?"

"Use your brain."

"Those Mexican kids?" Johnny asked. "Dude, they got arrested." Johnny looked back at me. "That's what you said, right? You saw them getting taken away by the cops?"

"Well, I said I saw one of them being arrested."

"That means two of them got away," Travis said.

"Oh c'mon," Johnny said. "Those guys were so fucked up I doubt they're even able to walk."

"I'm not worried about them walking, I'm worried about them *talking*." Travis turned into the school parking lot, which was essentially right across the street from the dentist's office we'd just left.

"So you *are* worried, then?" Johnny asked.

Travis glanced at Johnny with a scowl. "I'm not worried about three limp-dick Mexicans," he said calmly. "I'm considering the possibility that those matching tattoos on their arms mean they have some dangerous friends, and I'm mildly concerned that maybe they told those friends about us."

"What, you think they're a part of a gang?" Johnny asked.

"It's a possibility. And, if I'm right, there could be a group of hypothetical gang members who know our names and what school we go to…"

And they know where I live… That thought made me shiver.

"Why would you say that?" Johnny barked. "You know that's just gonna scare Kylie."

"Well, if someone I cared about was in a situation like this, I'd rather them be scared instead of unprepared."

I shook my head and chuckled. "Right," I said. "Would be awful if this was happening to someone you actually cared about."

Travis just glanced at me in the rearview mirror with dead eyes.

The three of us were so stoned that we walked at a snail's pace to the cafeteria. Somehow, we managed to get our lunches and walk out to the bleachers with time to spare.

"Isn't that your brother," Travis mumbled with a mouth full of calzone.

I followed his finger and spotted Brad sitting all alone at our usual spot.

"Hey! Brad!" Johnny yelled.

The second he turned around, I looked down and started trying to unwrap my burrito. Just like when Brad walked in on us smoking in the bathroom earlier that day, I couldn't look him in the eyes. Not only did I feel awkward and anxious about bringing him into my mom's room, but I also felt super guilty about what I did to Johnny. I knew that the only thing that could make things right with Johnny was to stop talking to Brad altogether. It was a shitty thing to do to one of the few good people I knew, but that was the only way to keep the peace.

"Where you going?" Johnny asked.

"Where've you been?" Brad barked.

By the time I finally got my burrito unwrapped and took a bite, I looked up and realized Travis and Johnny were walking towards the bleachers and Brad was heading towards the gym.

Out of nowhere, Johnny turned around, his red eyes darting all over the direction Brad just went. "Wait, where's he going?" he asked. "I thought he was following us."

"You're so high, you're imagining things," Travis said, chomping into his calzone.

"Shit," Johnny said, setting his lunch down on the bleachers. "I'll be back." He hurried off after his brother.

"There you are!" Morgan said out of nowhere, sitting down beside me with a half-eaten bowl of salad in her hands. "Where'd you guys go? I've been texting you…" Her words trailed off when she looked into my bloodshot eyes, then she looked over and watched Travis eating his food like a feral dog. "Again? Didn't you guys already smoke before school?"

"What's it to you?" Travis mumbled.

"Just seems kind of, I dunno… excessive, I guess."

"Yeah?" Travis said with a smirk. "Well, everything that comes out of your mouth is excessive, but you don't see me bitching about it, do you Morgan?"

Morgan's jaw just dropped.

That's when Johnny returned and sat on the other side of me.

"Couldn't find him?" I asked, reluctantly.

"No, I found him… He was just running," Johnny said, unwrapping his lunch.

"Running where?" Travis asked.

"Around the track," Johnny replied.

"Who?" Morgan asked.

"Brad," Johnny said.

"Well, that's good," Travis said with a smirk. "Little fucker could afford to lose a couple dozen pounds."

I could tell by Johnny's face that he wanted to say something, to stand up for his little brother, but something about Travis made him censor himself.

"The fuck's your problem?" Morgan spat.

"Nothin'," Travis said coolly. "I'm peachy."

"Why're you being such an asshole to everyone, Travis?" Morgan asked.

"I'm just busting balls like I always do. It's not my fault you've got thin skin…"

That's when the bell rang and everyone around us began to rise. Travis remained seated and kept eating his calzone. Johnny, Morgan and I got up then joined the herd of students.

"Why's he being such a cunt?" Morgan asked.

Neither Johnny nor myself could formulate an answer—we were too high. But, even if we were sober, Travis wasn't exactly someone we could make sense of.

By the time school let out, I was beat. So, instead of meeting up with Johnny or Morgan like I normally would after the final bell, I decided to head straight home to take a nap.

As I pulled up to my house, I spotted a van parked alongside the curb with a big CALICO GLASS AND SCREEN logo along the side. Of course, the first person I see when I walk into the house is Malik.

He gave me this dirty look then pointed at the three men in wrinkled white shirts who were hauling out the broken windows. "You wanna know how much your little party is gonna cost your mom and me?" he asked me.

I just blinked at him.

"Hey, gentlemen!" Malik called to the men. "If this little lady didn't throw a rager of a party this past weekend, your company wouldn't be making $2,500 today, so feel free to thank her for today's earnings if you'd like…"

That upset me so much, my body began trembling.

The workers glanced at each other, not knowing what to say.

Malik just looked at me with a shit-eating grin, and that stupid smile of his pissed me off even more. "There you go," he said. "You wanted attention? There's your attention…"

Asshole. That's what I wanted to scream at him. But, instead, I clenched my jaw and raced upstairs, slamming my bedroom door as hard as I could to convey my fury.

That's the kind of bullshit I'd been dealing with ever since Mom and Malik moved in following their engagement two years prior. Scratch that. From the very beginning, he made it very clear that he didn't want anything to do with me, but it definitely got worse after he moved in. Like, if he wasn't making a mockery of me in front of strangers like he did with the window guys, he'd do things like criticizing the way I ate with a fork or he'd make a snide comment about my weight or he'd comment on how poorly I was doing in school like he actually gave a shit.

The worst part was that Mom used to stick up for me when he first started doing things like that, but ever since they got married a year ago, she just let him get away with belittling her teenage daughter.

It's not like I even did anything to him. I've always done my best to stay out of his way, so I couldn't figure out what his problem was with me. I always sort of figured the way he treated me had something to do with the fact that he lost custody of his two kids to his ex-wife after a very messy divorce. Like, he hated me because I wasn't the sweet, brilliant angels his kids were, and he was mad that he was stuck with me instead of his children.

As I laid there with burning eyes, my body jittery with adrenaline, I thought back to the days when my mom used to have my back—back to the days where she was sweet and present. I reminisced about when Dad was still alive. I pictured his smiling face with those thick-rimmed glasses and that bushy goatee of his. For some reason, I remembered the time at that old Champs sports bar when he told the waitress how he used to work there when he was her age. He made a silly joke about how she shouldn't smoke pot in the freezer because that's how he got fired, then Mom smacked his shoulder and all of us laughed. After that, he turned to me with a smile and ordered a banana split for me and him to share.

Like any time I thought back to the good ol' days, the memories I tried to keep buried crept into my head. All I could think about after that was him laying in that hospital bed, unconscious. I could hear the delayed beeps of his heart monitor. I could smell the harsh chemical stench of hospital cleaning solutions. I pictured my mom howling as she pulled her hair and dropped to her knees in the hallway when the doctor told her there was nothing more they could do for Dad.

I laid there crying into my pillow for a while. Eventually, I calmed down enough to grab my phone so I could text Johnny and Morgan, hoping they could help me take my mind off things. To my surprise, they'd both texted me during my drive home.

Morgan: What're you doing right now? You wanna hang at my place?

There was nothing more that I wanted than to spend time with her and vent about the BS that just happened. That is, until I read Johnny's text.

Johnny: Travis and I are smoking for a couple hours, come hang.

That's when I texted Morgan: **Hey! I'd love, but I can't. Got a lot of homework to do. I'll see you tomorrow though?**

Then, to Johnny, I texted: **See you in 20.**

After that, I ran back downstairs, grabbed my keys, and hurried out the door before Malik could ask any questions. Right as I was about to back out of the driveway, I looked in the rearview and spotted a car I'd never seen before parked in front of the house with two people inside. The second I turned around to get a better look at them, their engine roared to life then sped off.

A knot twisted in my belly when I thought back to what Travis said earlier about how Mexican gang members might be watching him and Johnny after the fight.

You're just being paranoid, Kylie, I thought as I pulled out of my driveway.

Chapter 24

The First Saturday of June

After passing the bong back to Johnny, I grabbed my phone and brought it super close to my face so I could see the time through the dense smokescreen filling the car.

Now way it's already after ten o'clock, I thought.

Time flows a lot differently when you're high. Like, while you're stoned, seconds feel like minutes, and minutes start feeling like hours. But then you sober up and, all the sudden, the day that you thought was dragging somehow flew by and it's time to race back to class or get home. Considering that we pretty much smoked weed three times a day during the week and a few times on the weekends, it's no wonder none of us could fathom how it was already June when it felt like the school year had just started.

In the mornings, we'd either smoke in the bathroom or in my car, then we'd go to the dentist's office parking lot before lunch to hit the bong. After school, we'd wind up going to whatever spot Travis picked. There were a few weeks where we'd stopped following yet another blowout with Travis but, on this *particular* Saturday, Johnny talked me into going out with him and that asshole friend of his. That's how we ended up at this parking lot in Tri-City Park that was beside the lake and right outside of a gated community.

While Travis took a long pull on the bong, I stared out the window, thinking back to the times Dad used to bring me to that lake on the weekends and how we used to feed the ducks together. The sweet memory was shattered when the thick smoke filling the car choked me and sent me into a fit of violent coughing. I couldn't catch my breath no matter how hard I tried, so I had no choice but to roll my window down to ventilate the car.

"What're you doing?" Travis snapped. "Roll that back up, dipshit!"

"I can barely breathe," I wheezed, coughing a lung out right after.

Johnny began coughing too. "Me neither, dude," he said, rolling the passenger window down a bit as if he was waiting for me to do it first.

"So," Travis said, turning to me, "are you guys trying to get us caught?" He then glared at Johnny.

"Do you see anyone around?" Johnny croaked, handing me the bong. "This place is a ghost town at night. We're fine."

Just as I was about to blow the smoke through the tiny opening above the window, both my window and Johnny's rolled up on their own, thanks to Travis using the master control. I scowled at him, then rolled my window back down, only for him to roll it back up again.

"Travis!" I yelled.

"Do you happen to have night vision?" he asked. "Unless you do, we're not rolling these windows down. There could be cops or someone else watching us right now. And a lone parked car in an empty lot is already suspicious enough without smoke clouds flowing out of it."

"*Fine*," I said. "Let's just go. The bowl is cashed anyway. Is that okay with you, your majesty?" After about eight or nine months of putting up with his volatility and bullshit, I'd had enough. And I was feeling sassier than normal that night because I didn't even want to be out and about smoking. Me and Johnny had actually tried quitting so we could focus on school, but after Travis made us go to Champs earlier that day, my anxiety had gotten so bad that it was impossible to get through the rest of the day sober.

Travis just glared at me with a clenched jaw.

I glared right back.

"Travis, come on, man. Let's go," Johnny said.

Instead of starting the car, Travis reached into his jacket pocket and pulled out an orange bottle that rattled. "One sec," he said, popping the pill bottle open. He shook two pills into his palm then slapped them into his mouth, swallowing them dry.

"Uhh…" Johnny hummed. "What'd you just take?"

"Don't worry about it," Travis said, starting the car.

"Travis!" Johnny barked.

Travis sighed. "They're Percocets. They're not gonna kick in for like 30 minutes, so don't worry, alright?"

"Where'd you get them?" he asked.

Travis just side-eyed him with that cold, dead stare he always gave people when he was annoyed. "Do you wanna play 21 questions, or do you want me to drive us home?"

"Whatever," Johnny grumbled. "Just go."

Travis shifted into reverse and backed out of the spot. As he approached the exit, he clicked on the blinker and looked both ways as he rolled to a stop. That's when the brightest light I'd ever seen lit up the car.

"Oh shit!" Travis shouted as we all turned to look out the back window.

Beyond the glare of the spotlight, I could just make out the silhouette of a car. "I think that's—" I stopped mid-sentence when the red and blue lights began flashing.

"Cops!" Johnny hollered.

Travis shifted into park, and all I could hear was the rattle of his pills as he shoved the bottle into his jacket. "Just stay calm," he said. "Whatever I say, just go with it. Got it?"

Two silhouettes approached from the left and right of the car. The one on the driver's side blinded us with his flashlight as he peered inside, then he knocked on Travis's window with the flashlight. "Alright, everyone out of the car. Now. Nice and slow."

Travis opened his door and got out first. Johnny and I followed suit right after.

"Line up," the other cop said.

Now that there wasn't a flashlight in my eyes, I got a better look at the officers. The one who knocked on the window was younger, maybe in his late twenties. The other was much older.

"You know why we're here?" the older cop said.

Johnny and I looked over at Travis, who was staring down the older cop.

"No, sir," Travis said. "Can't say we do."

The older cop chuckled. "Okay," he said. "Got a call from a dogwalker that there was a concerning odor coming from this side of the park. And by concerning odor, I mean *illegal*. Becker?"

"Yeah, Sergeant Bohne?" the younger cop responded.

"You smell something illegal wafting out of this here car?"

Becker leaned forward and sniffed dramatically. "I think so…"

Bohne squinted at us. "And just look how bloodshot these kids' eyes are…"

"Redder than a baboon's ass, Bohne," Becker said, shaking his head.

"Now," the older cop continued, "if we search your car, which we have more than enough probable cause to do, we're not going to find anything other than what's giving off that smell, are we?"

"No," Johnny said. "No, there's nothing else in there."

"This one seems a little nervous, huh?" the older cop muttered to his partner.

"A little?" the younger cop chuckled. "Kid looks like he's ready to shit himself."

Johnny looked at the ground with his head hanging.

"Are you going to arrest us or not?" Travis asked.

The cops stopped smiling and scowled at Travis. The older cop then got right in his face, but Travis didn't flinch. "You want that?" Bohne asked. "You want us to arrest you?"

"I want you to just do what you're gonna do and stop torturing my friend."

The older cop kept staring at him with fury in his eyes. "Big man, huh? Not afraid of a couple cops, are you?"

Travis said nothing.

"You probably think you're some badass, huh?" Bohne continued. "Guess what? I see punks like *you* more than I see kids like them—kids terrified of having their lives ruined. Kids scared of consequences, like normal people should. But not you, right? No, you're *sooo* above all this shit. Not afraid of anything because you don't value your life or anyone else's."

Travis maintained his glare, and the older cop stepped back a bit. "Now, seeing as how I'm not in the mood to ruin a few young lives tonight, I'm going to let you all off with a warning. No search. No calls to parents. Pretty good deal, wouldn't you say, Becker?"

"Seems too good to be true," the younger cop said.

"Well," the older cop continued, "steady yourself, because there are a few conditions. I'd like you all to apologize to myself and Becker here for being lawbreaking little shits, and then I'd like you to thank us for letting you off the hook. Oh, and admit that what you were doing was wrong and that you're ashamed of yourselves, then promise that you'll never do anything like this again. Do all that, and you're free to go." He looked at me. "Let's start with you."

"I—" I said in a shaky voice, "I'm sorry for what we did—"

"Sorry to who?"

"Officer Becker and—" I blanked on the last guy's name.

"Officer Bohne," he finished.

"I'm sorry, Officer Becker and Officer Bohne. Thank you for letting us off the hook, and—" I was too scared and high to remember the rest. Bohne fed me the lines and I recited them one after another.

When I was done, Bohne gave me this sweet, grandfatherly smile. "Alright, one down," he said, turning to Johnny. "Go ahead."

With his eyes locked onto the pavement, Johnny began rattling off the lines. "I'm sorry, Officer Becker and Officer Bohne. Thank you for letting us go and—"

"Hey!" Becker shouted, making me and Johnny jump. "Look at us when you talk to us."

Johnny slowly raised his head and met Bohne's gaze with tear-filled eyes. "What we were doing was wrong. And I'm ashamed of myself, and I'll never do it again."

"Jesus," Becker said. "This one's crying. Never seen someone break so easily."

Bohne looked at Travis. "Alright, big man. Your turn."

Travis just stood there staring at Bohne without so much as a twitch of an eyelid.

Becker looked at Bohne, who didn't take his eyes off of Travis.

After a few moments Bohne got in Travis's face once again. "You wanna try that again?" the older man growled.

"Travis…" Johnny said.

Travis still refused to speak.

"Really, kid?" Bohne grumbled "You really think this is worth it?"

Travis said nothing.

"That's fine," Bohne said, retrieving a pair of handcuffs from his duty belt. "I like it better this way."

Bohne spun Travis around then pushed him against the car. And when Bohne heard the pills rattle in his jacket, he began patting Travis down until he found the Percocets. "Huh?" he hummed, squinting at the bottle. "Oxycodone, eh? Damn, this just keeps getting better! Officer Becker, would you kindly read who these belong to." He tossed his partner the bottle.

Becker caught it effortlessly then gave it a once over. "Looks like a Shauna Hackett."

Bohne cuffed Travis and swung him around. "Thought your name was Travis, boy. You been playing tough all this time because your mommy gave you a girl's name?"

Travis's face went beet red, but he continued fuming in silence.

"That's his mom," Johnny said.

"Alright," Bohne said as he flung him back around. "Well, hopefully Mom has the money to bail you out for stealing her meds."

Johnny and I watched in horror as Bohne pushed Travis over to the police car. I expected Travis to try to resist, but he just let Bohne shove him in back of the police cruiser like an obedient child.

While Bohne read Travis his Miranda rights, Becker was just standing there in front of us, grinning like he was enjoying seeing the fear in our eyes.

This guy looks like he's getting off on seeing terrified kids. Who let this sick fuck become a cop?

"Have a nice night, you two," Becker finally said after his partner shut cruiser door on Travis.

Johnny and I were frozen like statues as we watched the cruiser drive off with Travis. And once the cop car was out of ear shot, the only sound in the park was the occasional croak of a frog. That is, until Johnny's phone began ringing.

"Hello?" he answered.

The phone wasn't on speaker, but I could still make out the distant screaming of Mr. Castillo on the other line. "Where the fuck are you? Do you know how many fucking times I've tried calling you?"

"I'm sorry! I lost track of time!" Johnny shouted, walking back to the car.

As I climbed in the driver's side, my phone began vibrating in my pocket. I'd hoped that I'd see **MOM** on the screen. I'd hoped that she'd finally noticed I wasn't home on time and she was finally calling to scold me like a parent who cared was supposed to do. But it wasn't her. It was Morgan. After what had just happened, I didn't want to talk, especially while Johnny was in the car trying to get his dad to calm down.

"Alright, I'm on the way now!" he said, closing his flip phone as he climbed in the car. Then he stared off into the distance like he was in shock.

I reached over the center console and grabbed his hand. "Travis's going to be okay," I said.

He wiped his face and nodded. "I hope so," he said quietly. "Let's go."

Chapter 25

The entire drive to Corona, neither Johnny nor I spoke. We didn't even put on the radio. He just stared out the passenger window the whole time while I focused on driving him home without crashing.

Expecting Johnny's dad to be waiting for him on the steps like the last few times, I pulled into a spot a few apartments down and cut the headlights.

"I can't believe he got arrested," Johnny finally said.

"Don't worry," I whispered. "Those cops were just trying to scare him. His mom'll pick him up at the station and—"

"His mom's nuts!" he blurted out, still looking out the passenger's side window. "Like, clinically nuts! The only sane family member he has is his aunt, and she hates him. She'll probably let him sit in a cell for a few days to teach him a lesson."

"Well, maybe that's not such a bad thing..." I muttered.

The second he turned to me with fury-filled eyes, I regretted uttering those words. "I'm sorry, what?"

"I'm just saying, maybe that'll be good for him."

"Are you out of your fucking mind? How could being arrested for weed and pills be good for him?"

"No, I'm just—"

"You're saying you're okay with what happened to him?"

"No! No that's not what I'm—"

"Then what *are* you saying?"

"I'm saying it was inevitable! Look, I know he's your friend but something's been up with him these past few months, and I know you've seen it too! All he does is ask us to smoke—that's literally all we do! Then he takes us to all of these secluded, public places to smoke like we'd never get caught. Now he's on pills and God knows what else when we're not around. Is that really what you want for him? Because he would've probably kept getting worse until he got this reality check."

Johnny shook his head at me, the rage in his eyes building.

"All I'm saying, is that maybe Travis being there for a little while will help him out in the long run. I mean, fuck, we could've been in that cell with him had we—"

"Wait, why are you making this about us? Our friend is sitting in a fucking cage right now and you're making this out to be some sort of cautionary tale for you and me?"

"No, Johnny, you're not listening to me!"

"Trust me, I'm listening. You've always hated Travis. You're just making it loud and clear now that he's not around."

"What?"

"Give it a rest. You always wanted to get rid of him so you could have me to yourself and now you're fucking ecstatic that something's done just that."

"Johnny…" I reached for his hand, but he snatched it away. "Travis is heading down a bad road, and I don't want you to follow him. I don't want either of us to. I'm terrified that we'll all end up in jail or worse."

Johnny looked away and opened the door. Then he paused like he was going to say something else, but he just got out of the car and slammed the door.

I sat there watching him storm off toward the stairs until the darkness swallowed him. That's when the image of his silhouette disappeared behind a wall of tears.

During the drive back home, I tried my hardest not to break down, but all I kept thinking was: *This is it… this is how I lose Johnny.* And then I started imagining what life would be like without him.

That's when I started bawling so hard that I had to pull over on the shoulder of the freeway.

Johnny… I'm going to lose him too, I thought, sobbing with my forehead against the steering wheel. *I've lost my dad, and I pretty much lost Mom. And now I'm going to lose Johnny. Alone… I'm going to be all alone. Everyone I care for leaves me in one way or another…*

For some reason, I started thinking about the last time Dad took me to the lake in Tri-City Park. That feeling of sitting by that lake with him, a loaf of bread in my hands, feeding the ducks as they waddled up to me, us laughing and having a good time—I wanted to feel like that again. I wanted those days back. And thinking about how I'll never have days like those again made me cry even harder.

Right about the time I started calming down, my phone began ringing in the cupholder. It was Morgan again. The last thing I wanted to do was talk, but I picked up anyway.

"Hello?" I answered.

"Oh, you finally have time for me now?" she said with attitude.

"Morgan—"

"You finally took a long enough break from the bong to pick up, huh?"

"I'm sorry, it's just been—"

"Five days… That's how long I've been trying to get ahold of you. Not that you give a shit. You probably don't even know what fucking day it is."

"Fuck you," I said.

There was a moment of silence. "What?"

"I said *fuck you.* If you just called to tell me what a piece of shit I am instead of asking how I was or what's been going on, then you're just a big piece of shit too." I hung up and tossed the phone onto the passenger seat.

In all our years of friendship, I never talked to her like that. Part of me was glad she called to pick a fight, because I desperately needed a reason to blow up on someone. At the same time, I felt so guilty that my oldest best friend had to be at the receiving end of the venom that was bubbling inside of me all night.

If driving home high and upset wasn't bad enough, a storm rolled through, making those last ten miles even more treacherous. And I suck at driving in the rain.

Thankfully, I somehow made it home right as the rain was turning into a torrential downpour. I ran from the car to the front door, and right as I turned the knob, thunder boomed overhead, scaring me so bad that it made me slam the door behind me.

"Shit," I whispered, turning to the living room, where there was light flickering from the muted TV. I could just barely make out that the lump on the couch was Mom and not Malik. And, for once, she wasn't snoring. "Mom?" I whispered.

No response.

Something felt off about her laying there with her mouth agape and no snores filling the room, so I crept closer, flicking the switch on the way to her. The soft light of the corner lamp bathed the room, and my eyes wandered over to the coffee table, where there was an empty wine bottle, an empty glass, and a pill bottle. That's when I realized Mom's chest didn't look like it was rising and falling.

"Mom!" I shouted. I ran over and put two fingers on her neck. Not only was her pulse insanely fast, but her breaths were so shallow, I could barely hear them. "Mom!" I cried, trying to shake her awake.

She didn't budge.

With trembling hands, I fished the phone from my pocket and dialed 911.

"911," a woman answered, "what's your emergency?"

"My mom! It's my mom! I need you to send an ambulance!"

"Okay. Take a breath and tell me what's wrong with her," the operator spoke calmly.

"She mixed wine with pills and now she's unresponsive and barely breathing! Please, send someone!"

After I gave them the address, I knelt there beside her, freaking out. I didn't know whether to roll her onto her side to keep her from choking on her vomit if she threw up or if I should do CPR or something.

I need someone to be here with me—anyone… Malik, I thought, searching for a second wine glass. *Maybe he's passed out upstairs!*

"Malik!" I screamed, running towards the stairs.

Of course, when I got to her room, the bed was empty. *Shit! I'll call him then.*

I'd never saved his number, so I raced back downstairs and searched the living room for Mom's phone. When I finally found it tucked between the couch cushion, I flipped it open and called him, only for it to go to voicemail.

If I call twice, he'll know it's urgent, I thought, dialing him again while checking Mom's pulse.

He didn't answer the second time either.

I just want my dad right now… I need to hear his voice. I need him to calm me down and tell me everything is going to be alright…

Johnny's face popped into my head and, suddenly, he was the only person I wanted to speak to. Except, when I scrolled down to his name on my phone, I couldn't hit call—not after the way he looked at me earlier, not after the coldness I felt from him before he left my car.

Instead, I kept tapping down until I got to Morgan's number. Against my better judgement, I hit call. *Please pick up… I don't have anyone else left.*

"Kylie?" she groaned sleepily like I'd just woken her up.

"Morgan!" I cried between my heavy panting. "Morgan, I need you to come to my house!"

"It's two in the morning…"

"Mom's dying!"

"What?"

"She mixed wine and some pills! I don't know what to do!"

"Have you called 911?"

"I did! They're on the way!" I began hyperventilating. "But… could you… I need you…"

"Of course. I'll be there as soon as I can."

Right as the call ended, there were three loud bangs on the door. "Paramedics!" a man shouted.

"It's open!"

A man and a woman rushed in with a big bag and a stretcher. One checked her vitals while the other asked me a bunch of questions. The next thing I know, they had her on oxygen and they were hauling her out on a stretcher. The sky rumbled with thunder as I followed them out into the rain.

"Do you want to ride with us or do you have another way to get to the hospital?" the woman EMT asked.

As I was about to answer, a pair of headlights raced down my block and stole my attention. It wasn't until the car was illuminated by the ambulance's flashing lights that I realized it was Morgan's car that was pulling up to my house.

Chapter 26

"I'm sorry," the male EMT said to Morgan right outside the door to the ER, "only family is allowed back with the patient."

"But—" I started to say.

"It's fine, just go," Morgan yelled. "I'll be here in the lobby if you need me."

With a nod, I turned and hurried down the hall to catch up to the paramedics, who were in the middle of filling in the nurse and doctor who had taken over guiding Mom's gurney through the ER.

"What're her vitals?" the doctor asked.

"Her pulse is at 179 bpm. Blood pressure 138/87. Body temperature 99 degrees Fahrenheit."

"Is she responsive?" the doctor asked.

"As of a minute ago, yes," he responded.

I was so focused on listening to what they were saying and trying to read their expressions that I didn't realize Mom's eyes were slightly open. Her eyelids fluttered as she scanned the four strangers looming over her.

Mom's arm flailed like she was trying to get the doctor's attention. "What... happened?" she groaned weakly.

The doctor leaned over her with a reassuring smile. "Ma'am, you've been brought to the hospital because you mixed your antidepressants and alcohol. Your daughter found you unresponsive on your couch," she said, gesturing to me.

When Mom's head lolled in my direction, her eyes went wide. "Kylie..." she said, shaking her head. "No... I don't... I don't want… my daughter seeing me like this. Take her to the lobby. Please."

"Mom!" I cried. "I'm not leaving!"

"Please," Mom begged.

"Are you sure?" the doctor asked.

"Yes, I don't… I don't want her in here."

I froze right in the middle of the hall, then the nurse escorted me back to the waiting room.

Morgan sprung out of her seat when she saw me. "What happened?"

"Mom made me leave," I said, sitting beside her.

"She's just looking out for you," Morgan said, rubbing my back. "If I had a daughter, I couldn't imagine ever letting her see me like that."

"How selfless of her…" I grumbled sarcastically, shaking my head.

As I slouched in my seat, I scanned the room, looking from the little boy crying across from me to his mother who was on the phone ignoring him. Then I glanced over at this old man in a tattered, oversized green coat who was sprawled out across five chairs. The skin not covered by his bushy beard was leathery and sunburnt, and his gray hair was clumped together in jaw-length locks.

Morgan nudged me, snickering quietly. "He looks like us after a few shots," she whispered.

For the first time in what seemed like forever, I smiled.

All of the sudden, the homeless man let out this hoglike snore that made every head in the room turn, including the receptionist's. The woman peeked out into the waiting room then walked away. One of the staff members then walked behind the double doors.

Moments later, a security guard barreled out through the double doors and approached the homeless man. "Excuse me, sir," he said calmly. When the man didn't respond, the guard shook the chair. "*Sir.*"

The hobo's eyes shot open. "Hmm?"

"Who are you here waiting for?" the guard asked.

The homeless man looked around confused like he didn't know where he was.

"Sir?"

"I'm waiting for my daughter and wife," the homeless man said as he sat up.

"Oh. What are their names?"

The hobo zoned out for a moment. "Nora… and my daughter Gracie. Nora and Gracie McTavish," he grumbled.

"Okay, and may I have your first name, Mr. McTavish?"

"Leonard."

The guard walked to the receptionist, and the longer Leonard sat there watching the guard, the more his red eyes bulged with terror. Suddenly, his wide eyes began darting left and right like he heard something no one else did.

"What do you think's wrong with him?" Morgan whispered.

I shrugged, watching the guard walk back to the hobo. "No clue…"

"Sir," the guard said to Leonard, "we searched our records and there don't seem to be any patients here with those names. Are you sure you're at the right hospital?"

The homeless man ignored the guard and continued surveying the lobby with panic in his eyes.

"Mr. McTavish?"

The homeless man jumped up so fast that he almost fell over.

"Sir," the guard said calmly, holding his hands out. "I'm gonna need you to calm down."

"Go away!" the homeless man yelled. "Stop following me!" He looked around at the frightened people in the lobby. "All of you, stop following me! Please! I can't take it anymore!"

My heart began racing at the thought that he was about to attack someone.

"Sir!" the guard said sternly. "I'm sorry, but I'm going to have to ask you to leave, otherwise, I will have to call the police."

The homeless man slowly backed away towards the exit. "Just leave me alone," the homeless man pleaded, not even looking at anyone. "When will you creatures leave me alone?" The automatic doors slid open then Leonard ran out into the rain.

The guard walked over to the exit, looked around, then turned with a wry smile. "Sorry about that, folks. That was pretty whacko, huh?"

Nervous laughter filled lobby.

I turned to Morgan to say something stupid like, *"That was nuts, huh?"* or something to that effect, but then I saw her staring out the window behind us, her unblinking eyes wide with concern.

"What's wrong?" I asked.

She stood up. "I have to help him."

"Help who? The homeless guy?"

"His name is Leonard, and yes.

I cackled. "You're joking."

"I'm not… He's just looking for his wife and kid. The poor guy probably has dementia or something and he's out in that storm without an umbrella or a raincoat… Look, you don't have to come with me. Just wait for your mom, I'll be back in a bit." Just like that, she walked out the exit.

I can't let her be alone with that guy, I thought, springing up from my seat and chasing after her.

The rain was coming down so hard, my hair and clothes were drenched before I caught up to her halfway to her car. "What're you doing?" I shouted.

"I told you, I'm going to find Leonard!" she yelled over the loud rainfall. "There's a homeless shelter not far from here."

"What're you gonna do, pick him up and take him there? He's batshit crazy!"

"He's probably just schizophrenic, but I don't think he's violent. Would you wanna be left out here like that?"

I imaged myself as an old woman who finally lost her sanity after life finally broke me the same way it probably did Leonard. *Of course not,* I thought.

"Look," Morgan yelled, "you don't have to come, I'll be fine. Just go inside and I'll be back in a few minutes." With that, Morgan got in her car and started the engine.

I wanted to go back inside where it was warm and safe, but I didn't want to leave her. *If something happens, she'll stand a better chance if I'm there,* I thought, opening the passenger door.

I slammed the door and pulled down the seatbelt. "Let's try and be quick."

"He couldn't have gotten this far," Morgan said, driving slowly through the parking lot.

"Maybe we should turn around and check the other end of the lot," I muttered.

"Wait!" Morgan said, pulling over. "There he is!"

"Where?" I asked.

She pointed over at the sidewalk where Leonard was just lying on the ground all curled up under a tree that provided a little shelter from the rain. Seeing him like that made me sad, it reminded me that he wasn't just some mentally disturbed man but a human in need of compassion and care.

"Wait here," Morgan said, climbing out of the car.

While I watched her run over to Leonard, I flipped open my phone and clicked my way down my recent calls until 911 was highlighted, then I rolled down my window a bit. *Just in case he flips out…*

"Sir, would you like us to drive you to a shelter?" I heard her shout.

The man said nothing.

"Leonard?" I called from the car.

That made him perk up. "Gracie? Nora?" he called.

"Yes, Leonard," she said. "It's us."

The fear evaporated from his wet face.

"What're you doing out in the rain?" Morgan asked.

"I don't know."

"Well, c'mon then, we're going back home. Okay?"

Leonard nodded then struggled to climb to his feet. As Morgan led him to the car, I got out and climbed in the backseat. That way, if he lost his shit, he wouldn't be behind both of us.

As Morgan drove, Leonard stared at her with this innocent confusion.

"We're almost there, Leonard," Morgan said sweetly.

"I thought you were gone," Leonard said.

"We were," Morgan said, "but we came back."

"I'm sorry, Nora," Leonard sobbed. "I'm so sorry for everything that happened."

Then he squirmed in his seat and turned back to me. "Look at you, Gracie… You've gotten so big… Are you in high school now?"

I simply smiled nervously and nodded.

His face lit up. "Oh my! Which school? El Dorado, right? I live right by there. I knew that's where you'd end up."

I forced a smile. "That's the one!"

That's when his smile faded and tears trickled down his cheeks. "Wow… Gracie… I'm so sorry, honey. I'm sorry I missed out on your life—that I couldn't be there for you when you needed me. But I couldn't shake it. I fought really hard, every day. But it destroyed me, and I'm sorry."

The way those bright blue eyes of his felt like they were peering into my soul, the sweet way he spoke to me—for one reason or another, I had a flashback to the last time Dad spoke to me before he died. He sat beside me on the couch and told me he loved me more than I'd ever know, then he kissed me on the cheek and said good night. Then I thought back to the last time I saw him, the evening I sat at his bedside in the hospital. I sat there all day, waiting for him to open his eyes and say anything at all, hoping for a miracle. But they never opened.

As though Leonard saw the pain in my eyes, he gave me this pitiful look and placed his rough hand on mine, giving it a gentle squeeze. "It's okay, sweetie," he said in this soothing tone. "Everything is going to be okay…"

As my eyes welled with tears, the car came to a stop.

"We're here," Morgan said.

We walked Leonard into the shelter and told the woman behind the counter the situation.

"I understand," she said. "We'll take care of him."

"Leonard?" Morgan said as the woman held the door open for him. "We'll be back, okay? Just go with this lady and she'll take care of you, okay?"

Leonard nodded. "Okay. When will you be back?"

"Soon," she said with a smile.

Me and Morgan stood there smiling and waving until the door closed behind him.

Morgan didn't drive off right away after we got back in the car, she just gave me a little smile then sat there with her hands on the wheel, tapping her thumbs on it. She looked lost in thought, but I couldn't tell if she was reflecting on her good deed or waiting for me to say something. And I did want to say something—I wanted to apologize so badly. Witnessing her act of selflessness that night hit me like a bucket of ice water to the face, reminding me how incredible she was and how undeserving I was of her friendship after how badly I treated her the last few months. For that reason, I couldn't get myself to just say what was in my heart.

"We should get back to the hospital," she said after a long bout of silence.

"I've been a shitty friend," I blurted out, staring at the glove compartment.

She and I stared at each other for a few beats, then her look of shock melted into a warm smile.

"Well, that's an understatement…" she said with a smirk.

We both laughed.

"So, how're the guys?" she asked with an exasperated breath, like she'd been holding her breath all night waiting to ask me about my life.

"Not great."

"Oh… How're things with Johnny?"

I let out a long sigh. "Let's just say he's probably better off without me."

"What do you mean? What happened?"

"Too much. He's a good person, I know that, he's just… pulled in too many directions. I'm starting to realize that maybe we're just not good for each other."

"I'm sorry." She rubbed my shoulder.

"Don't be, it was my fault. All this shit's been my fault."

"What do you mean? What shit?"

My eyes began burning and the tears quickly pooled in my eyes.

"Hey…" Morgan embraced me. "It's okay."

"I fuck everything up!" I croaked mid-sob. "I always fuck everything up. I'm just so tired of myself!"

She didn't say anything for a while, and I couldn't help but think it was because she couldn't think of a lie to soothe me. "You've gotta give yourself a break, Kylie," she finally whispered. "For as long as I've known you, you've always thought so poorly of yourself. Whatever negative thing you think about yourself, however awful you might think you are, you're the only one who really thinks that."

"Then… then why does everyone end up walking out of my life?"

"Because that's what happens with people. No one will be in your life forever. Some people are only meant to be with you for a short while. You can't blame yourself for it. You can't carry all that on your shoulders. But you'll never have to worry about that with me. Unfortunately, you're gonna have to put up with me for a long, long time."

A childish giggle escaped me as we released each other. As I pulled away and wiped the tears from my cheeks, I wound up getting lost in those beautiful green eyes of hers.

She smiled at me with this look that I'd never seen before. It was something like longing. And, as we held each other's gaze, her smile faded and the longing intensified. The way she looked at me in that moment made my heart race—it made my palms sweaty. This intense, giddy passion washed over me and, the next thing I knew, I was inching my face closer to hers.

Then our mouths met. Her lips hesitantly puckered against mine, and it felt like I got shot through the sky into outer space, floating amongst the stars.

Then, when the realization of what I'd just done hit me, I pulled away. The bliss I felt evaporated in an instant when I saw worry in her eyes, like we'd done something wrong.

"I'm sorry," I said.

Morgan smiled. "For what?"

I smiled back then leaned back in for another kiss only to freeze when my phone started ringing. "Shit," I said, looking down at it. "It's a random 714 number…"

"It's probably the hospital," she whispered breathlessly.

"Hello?" I answered.

"Hi, this is Peggy, the nurse from Placentia-Linda Hospital. I'm just calling to let you know that your mom has been stabilized—"

"Is she going to be okay?" I blurted out.

"Yes, but we're going to keep her the rest of the night to keep an eye on her."

"Is she awake?"

"Yes, she is."

I moved the phone from my mouth. "My Mom is stabilized," I said to Morgan with a smile. "Can we head back now?"

"Of course," she said, starting the engine.

Chapter 27

Morgan slowed to a stop right in front of the ER entrance, turning to me with a smile as she shifted into park. "Go ahead inside, I'll go find a spot."

I shook my head. "That's okay, just head home. They're not going to let you in anyway."

"You sure?" Morgan asked. "I don't mind."

"No, it's fine. I'll probably stay with Mom until she's discharged, so you'll just end up sitting around by yourself for who knows how long."

"Yeah… true…" Her words trailed off, and we sat there staring at each other for a while, smiling for no reason.

"Thanks for everything," I said, wrapping my arms around her.

She squeezed me tightly. "Anytime. Text me in the morning. Or call me if you need anything."

We parted and, with one last smile, I climbed out of the car and hurried to the entrance.

A receptionist opened the double doors for me then a nurse led me down a series of hallways to the emergency department, where walls of blue privacy curtains concealed the patients hooked up to the beeping machines beyond them.

At the far end of the room on the right, the nurse pulled open a curtain. "Dana," he said to my mom, who was laying there in a daze, staring at the wall, "you have a visitor."

Mom looked at me, but she didn't smile.

"Do you need anything?" the nurse asked.

"No," Mom said.

"Okay, I'll be back in a little while to check on you." He left, pulling the curtain closed behind him.

Mom turned back to the wall, paying me no mind as I sat on the chair beside her bed.

"How are you feeling?" I asked.

"I've been better," she said, still not looking at me.

"What happened?"

"Malik left me."

"What?" I exclaimed.

"I was looking for something in his car and found nude pictures of some girl in his trunk. When I asked about it, he freaked out and called me crazy, then he threatened to call the police for invasion of privacy. After a while he admitted it was one of his college students—some 21-year-old." She started tearing up. "He threw away *six* years for a girl who's four years older than you."

"I'm sorry, Mom," I said, rubbing her cold hand. "Is that why you… you know…"

She sniffled, curling her lips into her mouth like she was trying to keep words from slipping out.

"Did you… Were you trying to…" I couldn't bring myself to ask if suicide was her goal.

That's when she broke down, sobbing in a way I haven't seen her do in years. Eventually, she looked at me with bloodshot eyes, her face full of so much pain. "I'm so sorry, Kylie. I wish you didn't have to go through all of this. I hate myself for putting you through this. I wish I could go back…. I wish I didn't—" She sniffled hard. "I'm just… so, so sorry, honey."

I held her hand tightly. "It's okay, Mom."

She sat up a bit and opened her arms, and I didn't hesitate to embrace her. For the first time in so long, we just held each other. And when we finally stopped crying, I was so exhausted that I fell asleep in my chair beside her shortly after she drifted off.

The next morning, I woke up to nurses rustling around and talking to Mom while they checked her vitals. She got the all clear shortly after that, so she signed her release papers. That's when I texted Morgan asking if she could pick us up.

By the time the nurse wheeled Mom outside, Morgan was parked right out front, standing outside of the car. She greeted us with a smile and an energetic wave. "Hey, Dana! How are you feeling?"

"I'm good, sweetie, thank you," Mom said, rising from the wheelchair. "And thank you for keeping Kylie company last night. Lord knows it was a… well, I'm just glad she had someone to help her through it."

Morgan smiled. "Anytime."

The whole ride back, Mom was super talkative. She spent most of the trip asking Morgan about how her father was and how she's been since she hadn't seen her in a while.

"Here we are," Morgan said as she pulled into the driveway.

"You want to come inside for breakfast?" Mom asked.

Morgan looked over at me in shock. I was as stunned as she was because Mom hadn't invited Morgan in for anything since we were in middle school, before she'd lost herself.

"C'mon," Mom said, nodding towards the house. "How do pancakes sound? You used to love my pancakes back in the day!"

Morgan smiled, cutting off the engine. "Well, I'd be an idiot if I turned that down, wouldn't I?"

Morgan and I sat in the kitchen chatting with Mom while she worked on breakfast. Seeing my mother moving around so full of life that morning warmed my heart. For the life of me, I couldn't stop smiling.

"So?" Mom asked after Morgan and I took our first bite of cinnamon pancakes topped with bananas. "I haven't lost my touch, have I?"

Morgan and I glanced at each other.

"Actually, Dana," Morgan said, taking another bite, "they're even better than I remember!"

Mom smiled and gave Morgan a kiss on the side of her head like she used to when we were younger, when things were better.

That entire meal, we sat there laughing and reminiscing on the good old days when we were young and carefree. As I looked over to the empty fourth chair, I imagined Dad sitting there laughing with us. That's when a wave of sorrow rippled through me and my eyes started burning. At that exact moment, Morgan's hand found mine under the table. I smiled at her and turned to Mom, who was beaming at me from across the table.

Suddenly, everything felt okay, and I had this insane feeling that things were going to be that way for a long time.

Travis's Story

Chapter 28

June
Shortly after getting arrested at Tri-City...

Sergeant Bohne brought the cruiser to a stop on a desolate road somewhere on the outskirts of town. As far as I could tell, he took us up north near Carbon Canyon, the complete opposite direction of the police department.

"So, Travis *Hackett*..." Officer Becker said from the passenger seat, turning to look at me through the plexiglass partition. "Hackett... What is that, Dutch?" Like an annoying little kid, he waved my ID around until I made eye contact. "Is it or is it not Dutch?"

I just went back to looking out the driver's side window, wincing from the cuffs that felt like they were cutting off my circulation.

Bohne, the older cop, rapped a knuckle against the glass. "Young man, Officer Becker asked you a question."

"I don't know, *Officer Becker*," I snapped.

The young cop chuckled like an asshole. "Kid doesn't even know his own lineage. Damn shame..."

"Lemme see that," Bohne said, taking the ID. He adjusted his glasses, squinted at it, then looked back at me, studying my face.

"Definitely Dutch," Bohne said, handing the ID back to Becker.

"Shit," Becker said, shaking his head at me, smirking. "These are the kinds of things you're supposed to know at this age... Can't say I'm surprised though. Your folks clearly didn't teach you to respect your elders, so why would they go over family history, right?" He smirked smugly at me.

As bad as I wanted to blow up for him bringing up my parents, I didn't. I just clenched my jaw. I know Becker's type because I go to school with a hundred assholes just like him. He was the bully in high school who probably peaked too soon and failed to go pro as a football player or some shit. And because he needed an outlet to exert power over others, he became a cop. Judging by how young he looked, he couldn't have been on the force for more than a year. So I said nothing, knowing the less of a reaction I gave them, the less fun they'd have.

"You know, son," Bohne said, looking back at me through the glass, "If I were you, I'd start thinking of people to call when we get to the station. The boys we got sittin' in the cells at this hour ain't exactly hospitable."

"Yeah, I'd be shitting myself if I were you," Becker said. "Like those little friends of yours were shitting their pants a few minutes ago. At least they were smart enough to comply, huh, Bohne? Unlike fuckhead over here."

"Some people understand compliance early on," Bohne said. "Suppose for others, it has to be learned."

Becker snickered. "Well, nothing teaches a lesson better than getting stuck in a cell all night with some lunatics!" With that, he faced front and stared at me in the rearview mirror with those soulless brown eyes, smirking like a douchebag.

He looked like such an idiot trying to be intimidating, I just started laughing.

"What's so funny?" Becker asked.

"Nothing," I said with a strained voice, trying to stifle my laugh and put on my serious face. Unfortunately, the more I tried to stop laughing, the harder I cracked up. I was laughing so hard that I couldn't even open my damn eyes.

A car door opened.

"Becker!" Bohne shouted. "He's not worth it, son! The pills are probably just kicking in."

He wasn't wrong, I felt super spaced out and euphoric at that point. I was so out of it that, when the door beside me opened, it sounded all muffled.

"Don't worry, Becker," I said breathlessly between the laughter, my eyes still shut. "I'm seriously terrified. Honestly. I'm not laughing at you…"

Suddenly, I felt my body jerk forward then my head smacked against the glass partition.

"Becker!" Bohne shouted. "Becker, stop!"

I didn't understand how I hit my head until I realized Becker had me gripped by the shirt and the back of the neck. And, by the time it clicked, he was already dragging me out of the backseat.

"You wanna laugh?" Becker snarled, spinning me around and shoving me back first into the hood of the car. His eyes were wide and deranged. "You want to fucking laugh at me, you little shit?"

"Get off him," Bohne shouted, running around to our side of the cruiser. "Becker, stand down!"

"I'll give you something to fucking laugh at!" Becker drew his gun and rammed the muzzle right against the middle of my forehead, his finger on the trigger.

I leaned back against the hood completely petrified, because the last thing I wanted to do was give him a reason to pull the trigger. The only sounds I could hear in that moment were my racing heart and his heavy breathing.

"How's that feel, Travis?" he snarled through gritted teeth, spit leaving his mouth with each exhale. "Not so fucking funny now, huh, big man?"

Normally, that would be about the time I'd call someone like him out for being full of shit, but the fear I felt in that moment left me too terrified to even breathe.

He's going to fucking kill me, I thought, staring at his finger on the trigger. *I won't even hear the shot, everything will just go black, and that'll be it for me.*

"Becker!" Bohne shouted. "*Stand. Down. Now!*"

Becker stared at me a little while longer, smiling like a psychopath, his left eye twitching.

"Becker!" Bohne repeated.

He exhaled, slowly lowered his pistol, then took a step back.

"You stupid son of a bitch," Bohne said as Becker holstered his weapon. "Do you have any clue what you just did?"

Becker said nothing, he just maintained his death glare.

Bohne looked over at me with panicked, worried eyes. "Uncuff the kid," he said.

"What?" Becker asked, arching a brow. "You crazy?"

"Crazy?" Bohne said. "You just abused a minor and put a gun to his head for Christ's sake! Now, uncuff him!"

"Why? You think anyone would believe some kid high on oxy over two officers?"

Bohne got in Becker's face. "Did you forget that they just installed dash cameras in the car," Bohne whispered, like I couldn't hear him. "What, you think that if we get rid of those tapes no one would start asking questions about what happened? That's not something I want to deal with. Your bullshit isn't worth losing my badge over. Now, uncuff him…" He took a step back.

With a sigh, Becker pulled me off of the car then began fiddling with his belt.

"Now," Bohne said, walking up to me, "what Officer Becker just did was highly unethical and illegal, and, for that I apologize."

Becker grunted as he unlocked my cuffs. The pressure finally faded as I moved my arms from behind my back. Pain flared from my wrists when I rubbed the red indentations.

"And because what he did was completely out of line," Bohne continued, "you're free to go."

"Are you fucking kidding me—" Becker said.

Bohne raised a hand to his subordinate, silencing him.

"Let me guess," I finally spoke up. "There's a catch?"

Bohne nodded.

"What," I said before he could speak, "I agree to forget that your partner went psycho and you both forget why you arrested me?"

Bohne smiled faintly. "See, I knew you were a bright kid… No one finds out about this, and I mean no one. Not even your friends. Understood?"

I nodded.

"Then I guess you're free to go," Bohne said.

I looked over at Becker, who was shaking his head. "You know what? I'd be more inclined to forget if Officer Becker apologized to me."

"Alright, Becker," Bohne said with an exasperated breath, gesturing to me. "Whenever you're ready."

"If you think I'm going to apologize to this little—"

"I think you've got suspension without pay if you don't shut the fuck up and follow orders," Bohne said.

Becker looked down at the ground, his fists clenched. "I'm sorry," Becker muttered.

I smirked. "Officer Bohne, I'd like it if he looked at me."

Bohne snapped his fingers and Becker slowly looked up, scowling. There was murder in his eyes, and it made me so very happy. "I'm. Sorry," Becker grumbled.

"For what?" I asked.

Becker's left eye twitched. "For acting aggressively and stepping out of line as an officer," he said.

I stood face to face with him, breathing in his words like clean summer air. Then I looked over at Bohne. "Okay," I said. "We're good."

Becker stomped off and climbed in the passenger seat, slamming the door. Right as I was walking towards the car, Bohne slammed the back door.

"Wait, you're not planning on leaving me here, are you?" I asked with a confused smile.

"I said I'd let you go," Bohne said as Becker dropped my phone out of the window. "Never said I'd give you a ride. You still broke the law. Consider this your punishment. Have a safe night, Travis." He slammed his car door then drove off towards town.

"Unbelievable…" I muttered, shaking my head as I watched their taillights disappear around the bend.

I surveyed my surroundings. There was nothing around but trees and an open field. Aside from the chirping of crickets, it was dead quiet out there. If things weren't bad enough, I flipped open my phone only to find it had zero bars of service.

"Great…" I sighed, walking in the direction the cops drove.
How the fuck did I even get here?

Chapter 29

The beginning of the school year
The Monday after Kylie's first week of school party...

Everything started going sideways for me that Monday after Kylie's shitshow of a party. Well, technically the Saturday right before that. There I was, hungover and taking bong rips to smoke the pain away when Joan walked in looking pissed as all hell. But she didn't yell, she just dropped the bombshell on me:

"I got a call from Newport Academy," my aunt told me. *"Your mom's done with her treatment... I'm picking her up on Monday."*

Every minute after that, I felt myself spiraling deeper and deeper into an abyss. *Mom's being released from the hospital. She's coming back... for good...* Those were the only thoughts in my mind the rest of that weekend while I laid around stone sober recovering from the fight. And, as down as I was feeling, what I felt during those two days was nothing compared to when I woke up to get ready for school.

On Sunday evening, Joan told me she'd be back home with Mom around 5:00 P.M. on Monday. The dread I felt when I got up that morning worsened with each passing hour. The only times I didn't feel like I was drowning in it was when I was getting stoned with Johnny and Kylie, not that I particularly enjoyed having Kylie around, but her annoying ass didn't bother me nearly as much when I was high. The crazy thing is, things had been so terrible that I'd rather bicker with her than deal with the shit in my head. So at least she's useful for something, even if that something is being a necessary antagonist.

Following our last smoke session of the day in the dentist's office parking lot behind school, I dropped off Johnny at Kylie's house then headed home. I figured that, since I was still high, I better use the time to lay around and mentally prepare for Mom's arrival.

No way, I thought, staring at Joan's car in the driveway from four houses down. I glanced at the clock. *It's 3:55… What the hell is she doing home already?*

Thinking about Mom wandering out all wide-eyed and out of it while screaming at the top of her lungs sent me into a bout of heavy sweating. I wanted to turn around and speed off, but the panic made it impossible to drive. I was hyperventilating and overheating, and I needed to take off my jacket immediately, so I parked four houses away and started squirming out of it. Right as I got the jacket off, my phone buzzed in my pocket.

Fuck, it's Joan, I thought, pressing the answer button on the Sidekick. "Hello?" I said hesitantly.

"Where are you?" Joan asked. "We're at the house."

I didn't talk—I just listened to see if I could hear Mom in the background. "Where's my room? What happened to my room?" I heard Mom say. A pit formed in my stomach.

"It's upstairs, Shauna," Joan said. "Hey, guess who I got on the phone?"

As though every nerve in my body stopped working, my body froze. I didn't even breathe.

"Shauna?" Joan asked when Mom didn't respond. I heard the staircase creak. "Shauna, you're not supposed to walk off by yourself! I gotta go, Travis. When will you get home?"

I zoned out, my gaze affixed on the house.

"Travis?" Joan said.

"Uh, I had to drop Johnny off at his dad's, so it'll be another hour…"

Joan sighed on the other line. "Dammit, I told you—"

"I *know* what you told me, but I didn't expect you back an hour early," I snapped. "Look, I'll be there as soon as I can." I ended the call, holding the phone tightly in my hand.

I'm going to have to face Mom eventually, I thought. *I'm going to have to look her in those vacant eyes and treat her like everything is like it used to be before Dad died... But not yet. Right now, I need an escape.*

That's when I started going through my contact list, stopping on Pierce's number. He'd been the guy I bought all my weed from for close to a year.

"Yo," he said with that always raspy voice of his. That guy always sounded like he'd either just woken up or like he just blew out a lung-full of smoke.

"Yo, I need a 20," I said.

He let out a long, obnoxious yawn. "When you getting here?"

"Fifteen minutes."

"Make it 10." With that, the call ended.

I put the car in reverse and head back to the main road.

On the drive to Pierce's, all I could think about was the last time I saw Mom. It was five years ago, when we went to visit her at the psych ward.

Joan and I used to go see her at least once a month until I couldn't take it anymore. Each visit was basically us sitting with Mom in a giant white room while she just stared out of the window like we weren't even there. Like every other time I went, I just sat there, staring in horror at the woman she'd become. Meanwhile, Joan would ask her how the orderlies were treating her and if she'd made any new friends, like she was in a goddamn summer camp. Except, Mom wouldn't answer any of those questions, because she was either too drugged up or her mind was just too far gone.

And that's why I stopped going. It just hurt too much.

The last time I remembered Mom making eye contact with me was when Joan took me to see her on Christmas Eve back when I was 12—the Christmas after Dad died trying to save lives on 9/11. I'd painted a picture of her, Dad, and me holding hands with Santa Claus flying his sleigh above us, and when I handed it to her, she stared at it blankly.

"Is that Noah?" Mom asked.

Joan rubbed my head and smiled at me. "Yes, that's him, Shauna," she said to Mom. "Travis made that all by himself. Isn't that nice?"

That's when Mom looked down at me with vacant eyes and a smile—the first smile I'd seen on her face since before Dad's passing. "His skin isn't burnt in this." The smile I was so happy to see on her face suddenly seemed twisted.

Joan gasped and cupped her hands over my ears like that'd somehow block what I'd already heard.

The rest of that night, Mom didn't speak. She didn't move. She just kept staring at that photo with that deranged, broken smile stretched across her face.

After that visit, Joan stopped taking me to see her. When I asked why, she simply told me, "Your mom needs some time alone for a little while. And while we're away the doctors are going to work extra hard to make her better so she can come home again."

"So, Mom's crazy, right?" I asked bluntly.

Joan's jaw dropped. "What? No! What makes you think that?"

"That's what the kids at school told me. They said that losing Dad made her go crazy."

"What? Kids at school said that to you? What're their names?! I'll make sure they never—"

"Is she?" I interrupted.

Even though I was only 12, Joan's hesitation in that moment confirmed that the rumors were true. "Listen, sweetie," Joan said

softly, "your mom's just… sick. But not like when you get a cough
or a cold—her sickness is in her head, and it makes it impossible
for her to do a lot of the things you and I can do, like go to school
or go to work."

"Because of what happened to Dad?" I asked.

"It's for a lot of reasons, honey."

"Is it—is it because of me?"

Joan held me tightly and rubbed my back. "No, no, not at all. I
never want you to think that again! Sometimes things like this just
happen to people. All we can do right now is wait for the doctors
to make your mom better."

"How long will it take?"

"Not long, sweetie… Not long…"

As months turned into years, my suspicion that Joan was
nothing more than a liar was proven correct, and my resentment
for her began to grow. Joan did everything a good guardian should
do for a kid. She tried to make birthdays and holidays special for
me, she took me on camping trips, she tucked me into bed, she
picked me up from school, helped me with homework—but none
of that was enough to keep me from hating her for giving me false
hope. How could I be grateful when I thought her acts of kindness
were a part of an elaborate ploy to claim me as her child because
she was incapable of having her own?

And then she had the nerve to make me go to church—a place
where some old man in a white robe told me more lies, like how
God watched over all of us and how he'd take care of us because
we were all his children. The priest said that if we prayed, God
would help us. I rejected all of that, because none of it made sense.
If there was a God who loved us, then why would he let those men
hijack those planes and kill all those innocent people in New York?
And when Dad tried his hardest to save as many lives as he could
out of selflessness, then why would he be punished by having

500,000 tons of burning steel collapse on top of him? It seemed to me that shitty people got to live long lives while the good people were burdened with things like dementia, cancer, and freak accidents. It all seemed like one cruel joke to me.

That's why when I was 13, I told Joan I was done going to church forever. And, eventually, she stopped going too.

It wasn't long after that when I found true salvation from the darkness: weed and booze. Only by frying my brain with anything I could get my hands on was I able to cope with this shit. Getting fucked up just made everything so much better, because it was easier to live when I was too messed up to even remember who I was.

Chapter 30

Right as I knocked on my dealer's door, there was a loud crash one apartment down. Shortly after, a woman screamed, then some guy in there with her started yelling.

Pierce opened the door a moment later, shaking his head, sizing me up with those steely blue eyes of his. "Those fuckers are at it again, huh??" he muttered. "Watch out." He bumped past me.

"What're you doing?" I asked.

Pierce pounded on his neighbor's door three times like a damn cop. The screaming and shouting stopped, then the door swung open and out walked this stout, 40-year-old dude.

"The hell do you want?" the man yelled.

"Would you mind keeping the noise down, please?" Pierce asked. "I think everyone in the complex would appreciate that. Or I can call the cops. Up to you."

"Fuck off," the man snarled, stepping back inside and slamming the door in Pierce's face.

I snickered. "You can't call the cops, dude, they'd smell your place from the parking lot."

"Ha," he chuckled. "No shit. Just needed to make him think I would." He gestured for me to follow him.

Pierce's apartment was never clean—far from it. On that day, it was particularly filthy. The floor was blanketed in dirty clothes, from the sink rose a tower of dishes, and there was molding food sitting on his kitchen table like he forgot it existed. The only clean item was the tea cup he always had steaming with freshly brewed tea whenever I came by.

"Wait here," he said when we got to the living room. He then ducked into his room. "You know, Travis, these last-minute get-togethers gotta stop," he said, walking out of the room with a wooden box in hand. "From now on, schedule in advance. Got a new influx of clientele the last few months, and with bigger business comes…" He looked at me and gestured for me to finish.

"Am I supposed to know?" I asked.

Pierce sighed. "Better business models. And better business models require…?"

I rolled my eyes. "Scheduling."

"Exactly. So, going forward, give me a 24-hour notice when you need something." He looked down at the box and flipped through the bags of weed. "If I remember correctly, you wanted a 20. Right?"

I nodded, grabbing my wallet and pulling out the last of the gas money Joan gave me.

Pierce took it with a nod then put the bag in my palm. Then he took a sip of his tea, and lit a Marlboro. "You know—" He took a long drag from the cigarette. "You've been coming to me for like a year now, and you're still buying the same shit."

I stared blankly at him. "Yeah? What else am I supposed to buy?"

"People change it up after a while, you know? Branch out. Try new things."

"I mean, I buy different strains—"

"Not talking about weed strains."

"Oh. Well, I'm alright for now," I said.

"Alright… You get tired of strolling down the same street over and over, just let me know."

When my phone began vibrating in my pocket, I took one look at the clock, realized it was two minutes after I'd said I'd be home, and knew without checking that it was Joan. *I told her I'd be home in an hour and it's already 5:02 P.M.* "Would you mind if I smoked here?"

"Uhhh…" Pierce looked at his watch. "I got another client coming in 10 minutes," he said.

"I'll be quick," I almost yelped.

Pierce sighed. "Alright." He nodded towards the kitchen counter. "Pretty sure there's a pipe over there somewhere."

I'd just started packing the bowl when the commotion from next door started up again, this time even louder than before.

Pierce's eyes went dead, then he took a deep breath and exhaled slowly. "Okay." He stubbed out the cigarette in the ashtray, swaggered past me, then yanked open his door.

I followed him then peeked outside right as he began pounding on the door with even more fury than last time.

The woman screamed.

"Go away!" the man yelled.

Pierce kicked the guy's door so hard, I heard wood split as it swung inward. And when he stormed inside, I hurried over to the neighbor's apartment to spectate, because I loved a good fight.

"What the fuck are you doing in—" the neighbor shouted.

In a blur, Pierce's fist crushed the man's nose, sending the stubby bastard stumbling back into the dresser. The man howled, holding his face as blood flowed down his chin and dripped onto the floor. He looked up at Pierce with unbridled terror.

Pierce took a deep breath and smirked as though he was getting high off the man's fear. "Ah shit," he said, looking at his own fist, "I got blood on my hands. You guys have paper towel?"

The trembling woman by the sink pulled a knife from the drawer beside her, never taking her eyes off Pierce for a second.

"Ma'am?" Pierce said calmly. "Don't worry, I'm not going to hurt ya. I'd just like a paper towel."

The woman grabbed the paper towels from behind her and tossed them down by Pierce's feet.

Pierce picked it up and tore a piece off as he turned back to the man. "As I was saying," he said to the man while wiping the blood from his knuckles, "I would really appreciate it if you kept it down." He balled up the bloodied sheet and tossed it on the floor beside the terrified man. "Otherwise, I'm going to have to come back here and be a little less restrained. Do we understand each other?"

The man said nothing, until Pierce took a step towards him. "Yes! Yes, I understand!" he shrieked.

Pierce smiled. "Thank you." After that, he left their apartment.

In the two years I'd known Pierce, I'd never seen him do anything like that. Honestly, I was impressed.

Right when we walked back into his apartment, his phone went off in his pocket. "Sorry, bud," he said, reading the message, "but you're gonna have to smoke out in your car. Client's early."

I nodded, staring at the pipe I was about to light.

"Just take it with ya, I won't miss it."

Chapter 31

The third call from Joan came just as I was finishing up my smoke session behind the Blockbuster near the house. Just like with the last call, I ignored it and just kept smoking until there was nothing left in my newly acquired pipe but ash.

It was 5:31 P.M. by the time I pulled up to the house. Part of me wanted to wait a little longer before going in, then I thought, *it might be better to face Mom before this high starts wearing off.*

With a deep sigh, I climbed out of the car. My stomach churned and I began hyperventilating as I approached the front door. As soon as I walked in, Joan came out from the kitchen and glared at me with her arms crossed over her stomach—the exact reaction I'd expected.

"I know," I said before she could go off on me. "I know."

The ceiling cracked right above me, and my heart raced as I imagined Mom pacing her room like a zombie.

"Go say hi to your mom and tell her dinner's almost ready," Joan said, retreating into the kitchen.

I crept up the stairs as slowly as possible, not just to delay the inevitable, but also to make sure Mom didn't hear me coming, because I didn't want her to surprise me, I wanted to see her first. When I got to her room, I knocked on the door softly.

No response.

"Mom?" I croaked, sounding like a scared little boy. "Mom, can I come in?"

Still nothing.

It wasn't until I gripped the doorknob and looked down at my hand that I realized how bad I was trembling. I used to joke how my hands were so steady that I could be a surgeon. Even with all of that adrenaline pumping through me before I jumped into the brawl with the Esperanza kids, I wasn't trembling. But there I was, shaking like a cold, wet dog because I was afraid to face my own mother.

You can do this, I thought, huffing as I pushed the door open.

Mom was just standing on the other side of the room with her back to me, her gaze transfixed on something beyond the tiny circular window. Her wild, stringy hair lay on her shoulders in a fuzzy messy.

"Mom," I said softly as not to startle her.

She didn't move an inch.

"Mom," I repeated, a bit louder.

Still nothing.

I crept up to her and followed her gaze to this dead hummingbird lying on the roof right below the window. That's when I put my hand on her shoulder. "Mom—"

Her head snapped towards me so suddenly, I jumped back and almost fell into the closet behind me. She just stared at me with those same lifeless eyes she had when she was in the psych ward. It was like she wasn't fully gone but also not fully here—like she was trapped in a perpetual state of limbo.

I mustered a smile. "Hi, Mom."

Her expression totally changed. Her eyes brightened with a partial glimmer of the light that I hadn't seen in her since before Dad passed away. "Travis?" she asked.

I nodded.

Smiling, she cupped both her hands on my cheeks. "Look at you! Look. At. You."

"Yeah, I know… It's been a long time," I managed to say.

She didn't say anything more, she just held my face, her eyes scanning me like she was trying to figure out if what she was seeing was real.

"Uh, Joan asked me to bring you down for dinner," I said softly. "C'mon, take my arm."

She did without hesitation, and I escorted her down to the kitchen.

"Hey, there you are," Joan said, setting the last plate of RAGÚ drenched noodles on the table. She motioned towards one of the chairs. "Shauna, why don't you sit over there?"

"Here," I said, pulling the chair out for Mom.

"Travis?" Joan said. "Get some soda from the fridge please."

With a 2-liter bottle of Sprite in hand, I headed back to the table, where Mom was just sitting staring curiously at her meal.

"It's spaghetti, Shauna," Joan said. "Your favorite!"

Mom didn't respond. Her vacant eyes wandered over to her spoon before she glanced over at me. She watched me twirl my noodles around my fork then she looked back to her spoon. And when Joan started slurping noodles, Mom's head snapped towards her direction. That's when Mom picked up her spoon and held it out to her sister.

"What's this?" Mom asked. "I can't eat with this!"

"Sure, you can," Joan said. "Just use it to scoop the noodles up."

Mom poked around at the spaghetti and attempted to twirl it around like we did.

Joan scooted over and grabbed the spoon. "Here, like this…" She demonstrated the technique.

"Why can't I just use a fork?" Mom asked, annoyed.

"Because your doctor said so," Joan said.

"That I couldn't use a fork?"

"That you couldn't use any sharp objects for a while."

Mom's face scrunched up like it hurt trying to make sense of the situation. A few seconds later, her expression softened, her posture relaxed, and she replicated the technique Joan showed her.

During the meal, Joan attempted to strike up small talk with Mom several times only to wind up being ignored. After the sixth or seventh attempt, she gave up altogether, so we wound up eating to the sounds of metal utensils scraping plates and cringeworthy slurping from both Mom and Joan.

"Travis…" Mom said out of nowhere without looking up at me. "Are you still seeing that Greta girl?"

"Uh…" I groaned.

It took a moment, but the memory of Greta came back to me. She was this girl in my fourth-grade class back when we lived in Brooklyn. I was new to school and she was one of the first people I'd met that spring. I had told Dad that I liked her, then he went and told Mom who thought it was so adorable that she wouldn't stop asking me about Greta every day during dinner.

"Oh yeah… her," I muttered. "I haven't talked to her in a long time."

"Oh…" she said, disappointed. "That's too bad, she was such a sweet girl."

I cocked a brow. *Wait… you never even met her…*

Joan and I finished eating before Mom did, so she made me help clean up. And when Mom finally finished, my always demanding aunt asked me to take Mom back up to her room.

"Used to be my favorite …" Mom muttered halfway up the stairs.

"Hmm?" I hummed. "What used to be your favorite?"

"Spaghetti. Your grandpa used to make it a special way, you remember that?"

Surprisingly, I did remember. "Oh yeah! He used to put garlic or something in it, right?"

"And better tomatoes. Sweet ones. Not that horrible stuff from a jar."

I let out a genuine laugh. *Even in her state of mind, she can still see how shit Joan's cooking is*, I thought, leading her to bed.

"Alright, Mom, I gotta go…" I said, heading for the door.

"Where are you going?"

"I just have homework."

"Oh, alright then."

I turned to her with a half-smile. "But if you need anything, I'm right down the hall."

"You know," she said, "the older you get, the more you look like your father." The pain that appeared on her face in that moment mirrored the sorrow that washed over me. Her bottom lip quivered and her eyes quickly welled with tears. "Can you hand me my medicine, please?" She wiped her tears away with one hand while pointing at her dresser with the other.

The only bottle on the table was Percocet, prescribed in her name.

"What's this for?" I asked, handing it to her.

"Pain." She popped the pill back and dry-swallowed it. "Doctors gave it to me after my accident."

"What accident?"

"When I jumped. I broke both my legs, and they still hurt." Mom handed the bottle back to me.

As I returned it to the dresser, all I could hear was this rustling behind me. By the time I turned around, she was already in bed with the blanket over her.

"Can you turn the light off?" she asked, yawning afterwards.

"Sure," I said, flicking the switch down.

"Love you, honey," she said from the shadows.

Those words hit me like a freight train, and they left me standing in the doorway completely stunned and blinking like something just blew into my eyes. I guess that's what happens when it's been almost five years since you've heard your mother say those words to you.

"Love you too," I choked out after a long pause, pulling the door behind me as I left.

I stood outside her room in a trance, thinking about what she said. Not the '*I love you*' part, but about her accident.

Why did she jump? And where did she jump from? Was it a suicide attempt? Even if it wasn't and she seriously injured herself, I'd have to know about that. Either me or—

I basically broke into a jog towards the stairs, and then I ran down them so hard and fast that Joan called out to me.

"Travis? Is everything o—"

"What happened to Mom in the hospital?" I asked, storming into the kitchen and glaring at my aunt.

Joan stopped drying the plate in her hand. "Uh, she was in there a long time... Are you referring to something specific?"

"When she jumped..." I snarled.

Joan sighed. "Are you sure you want to know?"

I let my death stare do the talking.

"Around eight years ago, she jumped out of a window and they found her down in the bushes. Her legs were broken, along with a few ribs. She spent about a year in bed recovering after that. Had she not been on the third floor, she probably wouldn't have survived, so thank the Lord for that."

"Why'd she do it?" I asked through gritted teeth.

"For the same reason she was in there in the first place..."

"And you just decided to keep this from me?" I shouted.

"Travis—"

"Why didn't you tell me?"

"I didn't want you to worry—"

"Didn't want me to worry?! She's my fucking *mom*, Joan!"

"Yes, and you're my nephew. It was my job to take care of you. Christ, you were just a kid, what was I supposed to tell you? Trust me, it was incredibly hard for me to—"

"Oh, so this is about *you* then…"

"No, Travis. Everything I did was for you. I get that you're upset, but one day, you'll understand that—"

"Oh, *fuck off* with that!"

"Sometimes it's better to keep people you love from the truth. When you were old enough to hear it, I was going to tell you."

Hate and anger have plagued me every second of every day since Dad died, but what I felt as I stood there across from Joan was something much darker. All I could do was visualize myself slapping her across the face as hard as I could, and it took everything in me to keep my body from acting out that malicious thought. What I envisioned was so vivid, I could already feel the sting in my palm and the feeling of her cheekbone banging into my finger bones. The thought frightened me so bad, it startled me out of my dark fantasy.

I was so scared of what I might do that I turned away and ran—out of the kitchen, up the stairs, and into my room. I slammed my door so hard, the closet mirror rattled, and the picture of me and Dad on the dresser fell over.

As though I was drunk, the room spun as I staggered to my bed. My heart felt like it was beating too fast and too slow at the same time. The air felt too thick to breathe. So many thoughts were going through my head at once. I shut my eyes and cringed as if there were blaring fire alarms pressed right against my ears.

I didn't want to think. I didn't want to feel. I just wanted to be numb. As I was just beginning to quiet my mind and dissociate from my body, this familiar sound began permeating my room—

those low, distant moans that used to haunt me as a kid and wake me up in the middle of the night.

It's Mom… Whatever horrors that have been haunting her since Dad died still have her wailing in her sleep… Why now? Why does she have to do this right now?!

Just when I thought I couldn't feel any more hate, I felt more of it bubbling up inside of me than I ever had before.

I hated Joan.

I hated those ghastly moans.

I hated myself.

I hated that this was my life.

For a while, I laid there breathing hard into my pillow until I began to drift off to sleep. My last thought before passing out was *maybe the dead are far better off than the living.*

Chapter 32

The second half of freshman year

Something about the sound of bubbling bong water always soothed me. Whenever I'd take a nice long rip, I'd just focus on sound and the rest of the world would just fade away for a few seconds. Then I'd sit there with my eyes closed, holding the smoke in my lungs as I slouched in my seat after handing off the bong to whoever was next. Like most days where we smoked in the car outside the dentist's office, the person I passed it to was Johnny.

"Mom's been kind of worried," Johnny said as he took the bong.

"Why?" Kylie asked. "He looks like he's dropped another, like, 30 pounds. Isn't that a good thing?"

"Yeah, but have you seen how much weight he's lost in the last seven or eight months? Seems kinda drastic, no?"

As dramatically and loudly as possible, I blew the smoke out of my lungs and the haze in the car thickened. "Who are we talking about?" I groaned, coughing after.

"Brad," Johnny said.

"Oh yeah, Brady Boy. What's he been up to? I barely see him around anymore."

"No clue," Johnny said, exhaling smoke. "He doesn't talk to me. Or Dad. He only really talks to Mom and Glenn."

"Is Glenn your mom's boyfriend?" I asked.

"What? No! Glenn's my older brother," Johnny said.

"Oh yeah, him…" I said with an eye roll. "Never liked that guy."

Johnny looked offended.

"What?" I asked. "You don't like him either."

"He's still his brother," Kylie chimed in. "How would you feel if he insulted someone in your family?"

"I wouldn't give even half a fuck."

"Well, he's not you. I know that's a hard concept to grasp."

Johnny sat there staring at me like he was expecting an apology or something.

"Okay, I'm *sorry* I insulted your brother that you hate," I said.

"*Great* apology, Travis," Kylie said sarcastically.

Shaking his head, Johnny sparked up and took a nice, long bong hit. He barely held it in for half a second before he started coughing like a pneumonia patient.

"Are you okay?" she asked, rubbing his back.

"I'm fine," he choked out, passing her the bong.

"So, did I miss something?" I said, turning to Johnny. "What's the issue? What's wrong with Brad?"

"He's been losing a crazy amount of weight in a short amount of time," Kylie said. "If you ever paid attention, you'd know that."

I just glared at her in the rearview mirror the way I always did when she pissed me off. And she always seemed to piss me off. I had no idea how Johnny put up with all of her complaining and whining. I mean, sure, she was pretty, but there were plenty of pretty girls who were far more tolerable and not nearly as bland personality wise.

A second after her bong-rip, Kylie broke into a fit of violent, lung-rattling coughs. Not gonna lie, seeing her almost hack up a lung made me snicker.

Johnny bumped my arm with his elbow. "That's not funny, dude," he muttered.

There he goes again, jumping to defend her... I couldn't believe what a ball-less bitch he's become these last few months.

"Oh my god," she croaked. More coughs followed. "What is this stuff?"

"Some new strain my dealer gave me," I said. "Kinda forgot to warn you guys that it's pretty strong. Might wanna go easy on it."

Kylie coughed so hard that she choked, prompting Johnny to turn and shift onto his knees like he was about to crawl back there with her. "Babe? Are you okay?" he asked.

She didn't say a thing. Her eyes just went all spaced out like there wasn't a thought in that empty head of hers.

"What the hell's in this shit, dude?" he shouted.

"Nothing," I said. "It's just weed."

"Is it laced with something?"

"No, of course not... Then again..." I stroked my chin.

Johnny went from looking concerned to terrified.

A grin stretched across my face. "Dude, relax. I'm kidding!"

"You think this is funny?" He gestured to Kylie. "You turned my girlfriend into a fucking vegetable!"

"I mean, it's *kinda* funny. Just look at her."

"She's not gonna be able to go to class now!"

"Then take her home."

"Lunch is almost over!"

"Well," I said, looking at the radio's clock, "looks like you got 10 minutes." I opened the car door.

"Hey!" Johnny shouted as I climbed out of the car. "Where are you going?"

"To take a piss before class. She's your problem, not mine."

"Fucking asshole," Johnny grumbled, crawling into the driver's seat and slamming the door.

His overreaction to literally nothing had me cracking up from the time he drove off until about the time I got back to campus. *Damn. As sad as it is, this is the happiest I've felt since Mom came back home...*

On the walk over to the courtyard, I caught a glimpse of a kid booking it around the track by himself.

Who the hell runs during lunch? That's when I vaguely recalled Johnny saying something earlier about how Brad had pretty much been skipping lunch every day to run since that second week of school. *Is he trying out for the track team or some shit?* I thought, detouring to the track.

It was crazy how he and I went to the same school and never really saw each other. I mean, that's probably because I was always off getting high during lunch and breaks, or maybe I was just too stoned to notice him if we did pass each other. And the few times I did see him in passing, he was always powerwalking through campus with his head down, lost in thought, and I didn't want to bother him because I could tell by his face that he had a lot going on up in his head.

Not gonna lie, I missed talking to that dude. Brad was pretty much the only person I spoke to back in eighth grade. Hell, I'd go as far to call him my best friend during that time, even a brother. Before I met him, I'd gotten comfortable just keeping to myself. But after we became friends, I'd tell Brad things I never confessed to anyone before—things I still haven't told anyone else till this day. That's probably because I connected with him in a way I didn't with Johnny or anyone else and I saw a lot of myself in him. Like me, he was a loner who'd built an entire world in his head to help him cope with the shitty hand life dealt him. Then, for whatever reason, we got to high school and he became more withdrawn while I burst out of my shell and sought out new friends and parties to hit up.

That's when I started hanging out with Johnny. Sure, he didn't seem as smart as Brad, but what he lacked in wit he made up for in bravado. I'd expected the three of us—or four before Michael became a little sensitive pissant—to hang out and get shitfaced every weekend to make the next four years tolerable.

Unfortunately, we lost both Michael and Brady Boy pretty much in one week, and Kylie filled the void. Scratch that. I sort of lost Johnny too, because he'd become half the guy he was before Kylie ruined him.

As I approached the track, Brad had just finished his run and was heading towards his backpack. "Hey, dude," I said with a smile and a wave, genuinely happy to see him.

Brad glanced at me, panting like crazy as he wiped away the sweat pouring down his face. Without saying anything, he just picked up his bookbag and grabbed his water bottle.

"You look… Fuck, dude, you look like a totally different person. In a good way," I said, nodding. It wasn't an exaggeration. Those chubby cheeks of his were gone, leaving behind a slim profile with pronounced cheekbones. His potbelly flattened in line with his chest. He almost didn't look healthy, like he'd had some sort of disease or a tapeworm, but I didn't want to say that since this was my first time talking to him in months.

Without a word, Brad slung his backpack over his shoulder and started up the hill towards the basketball courts.

"Hey!" I shouted, trotting up behind him.

Still no response.

"Brad!"

Still nothing.

"Dude, can you stop and talk for a second, please?"

Brad whirled around. "What do you want?" he asked coldly.

I grinned. "What do I want? What're you talking about? It's me."

He stared at me blankly.

My smile faded. "I, uh… heard you came out here most lunches."

"I do."

"You training for something?"

"No."

"Is something wrong?

"No." He walked off. "I gotta get to class…"

"No you don't," I chuckled, hurrying after him. "Class doesn't start for another—"

The bell rang, and Brad picked up speed.

"Fine, I'll walk with you then," I said, walking alongside him.

"That's alright."

"What do you mean that's alright? C'mon."

Brad glared at me. "*Travis.* It's *alright*," he snapped through gritted teeth.

That stopped me dead in my tracks. *Brad never talked to me like that before*, I thought, watching him storm off. *He'd never talked to anyone like that before… He treated me like I was a nuisance or something… What the hell did I do to deserve that?*

Part of me wanted to chase after him and say, "*Fuck you, dude, no one talks to me like that*," and then write him off for good, but all those fond memories we forged in eighth grade reminded me that he didn't deserve my wrath. Besides, not only had he gone from chubby to ghoulish in a few months, but he'd also gone from chill and quiet to as volatile as me. Clearly, there was something serious going on with him, something Johnny couldn't even fathom.

Maybe he needs help… Not sure what I can do though, I thought, finally making my way to class. *Maybe no one can help him. He's just going to have to figure it out on his own like everyone else…*

I got to bio class right before the bell rang and, as expected, Johnny's seat was empty.

"Afternoon, class," Mr. Lefferts groaned. "If you all could please take out your textbooks and turn to page 145."

Heavy books smacked onto desks and the sound of pages flipping filled the room. Right as Mr. Lefferts began writing on the board, the door flung open and everyone in the room looked over as Johnny walked in panting like his brother was post-run.

Mr. Lefferts flashed him an annoyed look. "Nice of you to join us, Castillo."

"Sorry, had an emergency," Johnny said, glaring at me on the way to his desk. "What page are we on—" he whispered to the student sitting next to him.

"Page 145," Lefferts said.

I couldn't help but snicker at how red his face was. And when he heard me, he glanced over and gave me the finger.

After the bell rang, Johnny booked it out of class without me, something he never did. Clearly, he was pissed at me, but that didn't stop me from tracking him down though.

When I finally caught up to him at the end of the hall, I bumped his arm with my elbow. "How's Hellen Keller doing?"

He just side-eyed me.

"Ah, c'mon, you got to admit, that was funny," I said.

Johnny maintained his poker face.

"Okay, what do you want me to say, I'm sorry? Cuz I'll say it if it makes you feel better."

Without looking at me, he picked up speed.

His hissy fits never lasted this long before, I thought, basically jogging to catch up to him.

"Dude, alright… I'm sorry."

"No you're not," he grumbled, still avoiding eye contact.

"You're right, I'm not. I just want you to stop acting like a girlfriend who's mad at me for not noticing her new haircut, that's all."

Out of nowhere, Johnny whirled around and got right in my face. "Could you stop acting like a smartass for once in your fucking life?" he shouted. "Shit, man. She was so sick when I got her home that she ran straight to the toilet and puked for five minutes straight! And when I finally got her in bed, she was shaking and begging me not to leave her because she thought she'd die from whatever it is you gave her. Does that sound fucking funny to you?"

Johnny was getting so loud that everyone walking by had begun stopping and spectating.

"You wanna talk about this somewhere else?" I asked.

"Oh, what?" He gestured at the audience, "I thought you weren't afraid of anything? I thought you loved attention!"

"No, I don't give a fuck about them, but I'd prefer it if we went into the bathroom or something to—"

"What? Get me to smoke myself into a coma so I can forget what a fucking asshole you are?" The fury in his eyes reminded me of how he looked before the fight with the Esperanza kids. Usually, I enjoyed seeing that side of him, but it's different being at the receiving end of his rage this time.

I looked around at the bloodthirsty crowd who were recording us with their phones like a fight was about to break out. *Why do I feel like I'm about to get sucker punched?*

"Do we have a problem here, boys?" a man's voice boomed from behind me.

"Nope," I said, turning to campus security. "No problem here."

The cop eyed me suspiciously as Johnny stormed off.

"Hey!" someone hollered seconds after the security guard left.

I looked over my shoulder and found this pimply-faced kid and a blonde dude walking up to me. "Yeah?"

Pizza Face looked around all paranoid. "You sell weed?" he whispered, getting so close I could smell the lunch on his breath.

"Why do you ask?"

"Because that guy you almost fought said you had weed that can put you into a coma!" the blonde guy said with a grin.

"Oh. Well, I just smoke it. I don't sell it."

"God damnit," the blonde said as they walked away.

"Told you he wouldn't sell us any," the other muttered.

After the final bell, I headed to the parking lot and waited by my car for Johnny and Kylie the way I always did. And when they didn't show after a few minutes, I called up Johnny—because that's what I always did to reel him back in after he got mad at me for something. As the call went to voicemail, I happened to look to my right and see Kylie's car driving by with Johnny at the wheel.

I snapped my phone shut. "Fuck it," I said, climbing into my car and slamming the door.

As if I wasn't already annoyed with Johnny's bullshit on top of what happened with Brad, I got to the God damn parking lot of the dentist's office where we normally did our post-school smoke only to pull out an empty baggy of weed from the glove box.

Great, Pierce is going to bitch at me again, I thought, dialing him up.

"Travis," he answered, sounding annoyed per usual.

"I know, I know…" I said.

"Apparently you don't."

"I can be there in 10 minutes. In and out, I promise."

He sighed. "This is the *last* time."

Chapter 33

"So, how'd you like the new strain?" Pierce asked. He opened the wooden box and sifted through the little baggies inside.

"Didn't really do anything for me," I said.

He looked up with an amazed expression.

"You're kidding," he said.

I shrugged. "Turned one of my friends into a vegetable though."

"That stuff was straight from Australia. It's about as potent as it gets."

"If you say so…"

"Well, if that didn't fuck you up to your liking, then I'm not sure I've got anything else that will. Least not weed, anyway."

There weren't many things that could make me panic, but realizing that there wasn't a strain strong enough to make me as numb as I wanted to feel was one of them. Seriously, I thought I was going to have a panic attack.

"I'm gonna go out on a limb here and assume you've heard of Percocet?" he asked.

"No," I said firmly.

"You *haven't* heard of it?"

"I have. I'm saying no to buying it."

"What do you think it is?"

"Something I'm not buying."

"Okay, okay, suit yourself."

Pierce started rummaging through the box of weed baggies again. "So, what do you want? Most of these will get you about as high as a shot of NyQuil. But," he said, shaking a finger at me, "let's say you take a few hits of this Plushberry." He placed the baggy on the table. "It's an indica that'll give you a nice body high, but it's not gonna make you catatonic. However," he said, pulling out an orange bottle of pills from the box on the end table next to him, "if you take a few hits of plush and then take one of these oxies that they give to old ladies with bad hips—"

"Dude, my mom takes those," I said. "She's been on them for the last five years."

"For what?"

"She jumped out of a window…"

"Oh… shit… Sorry, dude. But, see. That's good! Not that she jumped out of a window, but that you have proof that they're not dangerous. That's your fear, right? That it'll be a gateway to something harder?"

I nodded.

"Well, you ever seen your mom shooting smack at the dinner table? That was rhetorical, I already know the answer's no. Now…" He pushed the small bag of Plushberry and the bottle over to me. "These two, combined, are gonna complement each other very nicely. The best effects of each will be enhanced by the other—and, lemme preface this by saying I'm not a man of hyperbole—but it's 10 times better than any high you've had before."

I picked up the bottle and examined the scratched off label. "Whose are those?" I asked.

"Mine," he said.

"Let me rephrase. Whose *were* they?"

"Does that matter?"

"Not really… Just curious."

"Exactly." He slouched against the armrest. "How about this? Just pay what you usually would for the weed and I'll throw in this bottle for free. Then, when you come back, you can just pay for the next one."

"Who says I'm gonna want more?"

"Call it a hunch."

"Fine, I'll try them," I muttered, pulling two crinkled tens out of my pocket.

Right as he swapped me the weed for the money, there was a knock at the door.

"Yeah?" Pierce shouted.

"It's me, man," a voice said.

"Refresh my memory… Who is *me*?"

"It's Luis, man."

He pointed at the door. "You mind getting that, Travis?"

The moment I opened the door, my eyes widened and my jaw hung. Standing before me was the Mexican kid from Esperanza that Johnny knocked out at Kylie's party. Judging by the fury in his eyes, it was obvious he remembered me too. And based on how his hand balled up into a fist, I thought he was going to deck me right there and then.

"Yo!" Pierce called out from the couch. "Something wrong?"

"Nah," I said.

"Well, would you mind letting my guest in, please?"

Luis shoved past me, limping as he glared at me over his shoulder with murder in his eyes.

"Luis, is there a problem?" Pierce asked.

"What the fuck's *he* doing here?" Luis shouted.

"You boys know each other?"

"We've met," I said, not taking my eyes off of Luis.

"Something tells me that first encounter didn't go well," Pierce said.

I chuckled. "For him? Not at all. Did he happen to come to you a few months ago with his face all beat to shit?" As soon as those words left my mouth, I preemptively prepared for a rematch.

Like clockwork, Luis charged back towards the door and shoved me against the wall. My arms shot up to block before he even cocked his fist back. Because I saw this shit coming a mile away.

"Luis!" Pierce shouted, springing up from the couch.

Luis stopped mid-punch like the obedient dog he was.

"Let go of him," Pierce said sternly.

When I smirked at him, the muscles in Luis's face twitched as though it took every ounce of will he had to restrain himself. After a moment, he lowered his fist, but he didn't let go of my jacket.

"Luis…" Pierce said. "It wouldn't be wise to disrespect me in my own house…"

Luis snatched his hand off my chest and backed off in a huff.

"Jesus Christ," Pierce grumbled, shaking his head, "I know you're both in high school but can you try and act *somewhat* adult while you're here? Now, whatever discrepancies you two have is your own business, but settle it somewhere other than my home, understand?"

I nodded.

The Mexican didn't react at all.

"I said, do you *understand,* Luis?" Pierce repeated.

"Stop treating me like a kid," Luis muttered.

"Well, stop acting like one! Now tell me you understand…"

"Yes."

"Good boy." Pierce looked at me. "Now, you can go ahead and apologize to my employee for insulting him during work hours. Speaking of…" He snapped his fingers at Luis.

"Employee?" I asked as Luis tossed him his backpack.

"Yes…" Pierce said, unzipping the bag and pulling out a wad of twenties, "and a profitable one at that." He began counting the money. "Still waiting on that apology, Travis…"

"I'm not apologizing to him," I said.

"Yeah, you are," Pierce said.

"*He* came at me."

"After you provoked him. So…" he gestured for me to speak. I hesitated.

"Apologize. Or give those drugs back and never come here again."

I gritted my teeth. "I'm sorry," I snarled.

"That wasn't so hard, was it?" Pierce said with a smirk, still looking down at the money he was counting.

I didn't say anything. I just left the apartment and slammed the door behind me.

I shouldn't have apologized like a little bitch, I thought as I drove away. *That shit was embarrassing, and I hate being embarrassed… All I have is my pride and I let Pierce tarnish it, for what? A few pills and some weed? That's all it takes to become someone's obedient little pet? I should've knocked Luis out like Johnny did and then left. Not like I couldn't find myself a new dealer before the end of the day…*

It wasn't until I took a few hits of the Plushberry in my usual spot in the dentist's office parking lot that I started to chill and feel alright again. But alright wasn't good enough. It was time to finally feel great for once.

Pierce neglected to tell me how many Percocets I should take, but thankfully the portion of the label he didn't peel off still had the instructions.

TWO PILLS EVERY SIX HOURS FOR PAIN.

After accidentally shaking four pills into my hand, I thought of swallowing all of them just to see what would happen, but I didn't want to OD, so I dropped two back into the bottle and popped the rest into my mouth. After that, I cracked the window to let a bit of fresh air in, reclined my seat and waited for the euphoria Pierce promised me.

Did Pierce give me expired pills? I thought, checking the time on the dash. *It's been over ten minutes and I don't feel shit… And I'm starting to lose my high.*

I was smart enough to know that I probably shouldn't take more pills to speed up the process, but smoking some more weed was a must. So, I sparked up the pipe and took two big hits.

I should probably get back home before this shit kicks in. The last thing I want to do is have Joan yelling at me for being home late again while I'm out of my mind…

After dumping the ash out of the window, I shoved the bowl and the pills into the glove box then started the car.

Right as I turned into my neighborhood a few minutes later, things began feeling… funny. Like, I could see my hands on the steering wheel, but I couldn't feel them anymore. It was almost like that hard plastic wrapped in leather had suddenly turned into a cloud that my hands couldn't pass through for some reason. A fuzzy warmth and this weightlessness spread across my body shortly afterwards, making me feel like I'd just gone from the freezer aisle of a supermarket to floating in a heated pool.

Holy shit, this feels great, I thought, basking in the breeze gusting in through the open window.

The houses in my peripheries began to blur by even though I wasn't driving that fast. No matter how hard I tried to focus, I couldn't differentiate them from one another—I couldn't pick out my house even if I tried. All of the sudden, I went from seeing the road to having a bunch of trashcans pop up in front of me. Right as I cut the wheel to swerve around them, my eyelids got really heavy then everything went black for a second until a gentle breeze rushed past my ears and washed over my face.

Every second after that was a struggle to keep my fluttering eyelids from slamming shut.

Stop fighting it, a voice whispered. *Give in.*

No… Gotta stay awake… Gotta make it home…

Go home later. Rest now.

Everything went black.

Then, *BOOM!* There was a loud crash that yanked me back to consciousness. I reflexively slammed on the breaks seconds before hitting something out of sight with so much force that my head whipped right into the steering wheel. Smoke plumed from the hood and the stench of burnt rubber wafted in through the window.

"What the shit," I groaned, rubbing my forehead. Not that my head hurt. Instead of throbbing pain, I just felt this weird, numb pressure.

When I got around to the hood of the car, I saw that my front tires were up on the sidewalk and that there were two trash cans knocked over—one on the yard ahead and the other on the sidewalk, trash littering both the grass and the pavement. It wasn't until I turned around that I saw the scratches on the driver's side door and the skid marks trailing behind the car.

For whatever reason, I started cracking up like I was in some comedic lucid dream.

"Hey!" a man called out from towards the house I crashed in front of.

I turned just as this old guy was hurrying across the lawn towards me. "Shit. Not a dream," I muttered, grabbing the car door.

"Where the fuck do you think you're going?" the man said, the whites of his eyes reddening with rage.

"I gotta get home," I slurred, climbing behind the wheel and shutting the door.

"Wait a second. Are you drunk?"

"No," I slurred, "I don' drink. I'm just tired. Have a nice day." I backed away.

"Hey!" he hollered, slapping the hood of the car. "Get back here or I'm calling the cops!"

As I sped off, I had no idea where I was, but when I got to the stop sign, something in me told me to turn left. After driving a bit further, I saw a house on the right that looked just like mine with a car in the driveway the color of Joan's.

Finally, I thought, pulling into the driveway.

My body felt like it was floating the whole way to the front door, and when I grabbed the doorknob, I couldn't feel anything but the coldness of the metal.

Wait, I thought as I turned the knob. *He said he was going to call the cops... I can't leave the drugs in the car...* It took everything for me to drag my feet back to the driveway. Right as I shoved the pills and weed into my jacket pocket, I heard what sounded like muffled sirens in the distance. *Shit... Just be cool, they don't know where you live...*

One minute I was staggering through the front door, the next I was stumbling into my bedroom.

"Travis?" Joan's confused voice called from downstairs as I shut my door.

I didn't know if she saw me walk into the house like a zombie, but if she did, I knew I had to hide my stash in the usual closet spot.

As I buried the drugs under my boxers, a flash of clarity hit me. *Joan knows where you hide your weed, dumbass... Let her find the weed, it's not like she doesn't know you smoke. Just don't let her find the pills. Let the weed be the decoy.* I retrieved the Percocets then tossed them in the far corner of the closet. *There you go. Everything's safe now. Rest.*

When I belly flopped onto my bed, I heard the springs groan, but I didn't feel the mattress beneath me, it just felt like I'd fallen onto a bed of fluffy cotton. Darkness consumed me pretty much right after that.

Sometime later, I awoke to the sound of the doorbell. As I began to drift back into the blissful unconscious, I heard Joan's muffled voice followed by some deeper, manlier voices—and there were hardly ever any men other than me at that house.

Thinking nothing of it, I shut my eyes and let the blackness swallow me back into that peaceful nothingness.

Chapter 34

"Travis," Joan's muffled voice echoed from some far-off place.

There was this numb pressure on my shoulder, and it felt like my body was being shaken.

"Travis!" Joan yelled, startling me awake.

"What?" I groaned, rolling onto my side to face her, squinting against the hallway light behind her.

"The police and one of our neighbors are downstairs," she said sternly with this serious look in her eyes.

"For what?" I asked, genuinely confused.

"Just come downstairs."

For no other reason than the fact that I felt really, *really* good, I found myself smiling from the time I got out of bed until I neared the bottom of the stairs.

Standing in the doorway were two cops—an older black woman and a younger white guy—and, behind them, some random old guy.

"Son," the lady cop asked, "were you driving that car parked out front?"

I felt so spaced out that I couldn't do anything but smile at her.

"Travis," Joan said, nudging me, "she's talking to you."

I swallowed hard and tried to suppress my smile. "If you mean my car, then yes, I was driving it."

"And did you happen to hit the trash cans on Terrence Reiner's property?" the white cop asked, gesturing to the old man who I could barely see.

"Ugh… I don't know who that is, but maybe?" I said mid-yawn.

The old man barged into the house. "You don't recognize my face, you little shit?" he yelled.

Now that I could see his face, I smiled. "Oh, hey. What's up, man?"

"Don't you fucking smile at me!" Mr. Reiner barked.

"Sir," the female cop said, "please calm down. We'll handle it from here."

"What? Are you serious? Little shit damaged my property and now I gotta—"

Joan raised her hand. "I'd actually feel better if you left, sir."

The old man scowled at her for a few beats. "You know, this is just as much your fault as it is his—"

"I understand that," Joan snapped. "And you can rest assured that I'll take care of it. Now, if you don't mind…" she gestured for him to walk out.

The second his gaze snapped back onto me, I grinned. "Keep it up, you little prick!" he shouted, backing away from the door. "You won't be smiling when you find out how much shit you're in!"

The white cop sighed. "You seem pretty out of it, son, are you sure you're not on something?"

I shook my head.

"No narcotics? No marijuana?"

"I don't do either of those, officer."

"You wouldn't happen to be lying, would you?" the woman asked. "Because Mr. Reiner said you seemed disoriented when he saw you after the crash. Said you were slurring your words."

I yawned. "Long day at school. Haven't been sleeping well lately either."

The cops exchanged a glance then they turned to Joan.

"Ma'am," the lady cop said, "does your nephew have a history of drug use?"

Joan turned to me with this disappointed, annoyed look in her eyes that made my blood run cold—it made my heart race.

This is it… Joan's gonna rat me out, the cops are going to search my room and arrest me for possession of narcotics, then they're going to run my blood at the lab and I'm going to get locked up for driving under the influence… That thought was more sobering than being questioned by the cops while high as a kite.

"No," Joan said to the cops, "he doesn't."

Am I hallucinating or did Joan just cover for me? I couldn't believe my ears. Joan was a liar, that was something I knew well. But never in a million years did I think that she'd ever lie to help me.

"You're sure?" the male cop asked.

Joan nodded. "He has been going through some pretty bad insomnia recently. Went to a doctor for it and they can't figure out the cause, so I'm positive this whole incident was caused by his lack of sleep."

The cops exchanged another look. The lady cop's face was hard to read, but the guy didn't look like he was buying it at all.

The woman huffed as she looked back to my aunt. "I suppose we have no further questions then, ma'am. As I'm sure you're aware, any damages resulting from your nephew's negligence that Mr. Reiner chooses to claim will fall onto you and your insurance."

"I'm aware," Joan said flatly. "I'll work that out with him later on."

"Very well then, ma'am," the male officer said with a nod, leaving with his partner at his heels.

Joan shut the door with more force than usual, then she stood there scowling at me for a while. Never in all my years of pissing her off did she ever look at me with so much anger. The crazy thing was, she didn't yell at me, she just marched past me like I wasn't even there and started up the stairs.

"Where are you going?" I asked, a pit forming in my stomach from her bizarre reaction. "Joan!" When she didn't respond, I moved my numbed legs as fast as I could to chase after her.

By the time I caught up to her, she was kneeling before my closet, tossing clothes over her shoulder until I heard the rustling of plastic in her hand. Just like that, she stood up and stormed past me without making eye contact. I didn't have to follow her to know that the slamming of the toilet lid and the subsequent flush meant she'd flushed my weed.

Before the toilet even finished flushing, her heavy footfalls stomped their way back to my room then she walked straight to my dresser and looked around. When she didn't find what she was looking for, she grabbed my jacket, shook it until it jingled. That's when she reached in and pulled out my keys.

"Joan, come on... Just relax..."

"You're *never* driving that car again," she said. "And you're not getting another fucking dime from me. That's it. I'm done."

In a blur, she pushed past me and left the room.

"Joan," I said calmly. By the time I got to the stairs, she was on her way out the front door. "Wait, where are you going?"

"To clean up *your* fucking mess like I always do." With that, she slammed the door.

I just stood there in the middle of the staircase, completely stunned. When Joan caught me smoking weed those first few times, she used to flip out, search my room for my stash, flush it, then lecture me after. But, after a few months of that, after realizing that I'd never stop, she basically went numb to it all and pretended like I wasn't still smoking. But what happened that day? That was a level of rage I didn't even know she was capable of.

And, despite not knowing what kind of wrath awaited me in the near future, the only things I could seem to worry about in that moment were: *how am I going to afford to buy weed if she cut me off* and *where the hell am I going to smoke without a car?*

In an instant, I went from feeling amazing from the high to spiraling into a dizzying panic that made it hard to stand. All I wanted to do was get as far away from that house as I could and smoke the stress away, but I couldn't. Going to bed while I was still drugged up was the next best means of escape.

I'm not sure if it was the growling of my stomach and the hunger from sleeping through dinner or if it was the ghastly moaning and groaning from Mom on the other side of the wall, but one of those damn things woke me up in the middle of the night. And, just like every other night that I awoke to what sounded like the haunting of a ghost in constant agony, the heart palpitations and shortness of breath immediately ensued, turning each second that I couldn't fall back to sleep into hellish torture that felt like it went on for an eternity.

On the nights that I woke up to Mom's nocturnal lamentation episodes and couldn't fall back to sleep right away, I'd usually grab my weed, sneak out to my car and smoke until I got too high to keep my eyes open, then I'd head back to bed. Being as out of it as I was from waking up at damn near 3:00 A.M., it wasn't until I sat up and swung my legs over the bed that I remembered Joan flushed my stash.

God damnit... What am I going to do now? I can't stay up all night listing to this shit. I can't! I mulled over my options. *I can go sleep in my car...*

Joan took your keys, remember?

Shit... That's when the events that led to me crashing into some trash cans came back to me. *The pills... I still have the pills... I* hurried over to my closet like I was going to die if I didn't get those pills ASAP. Well, maybe not die, but I was definitely going to lose my sanity if I didn't find something to rob me of my consciousness sooner rather than later.

When I finally found the pills in the corner of my closet, I shook two into my hand, swallowed them dry just like Mom does, then I crawled back into bed and waited for the blissful, numb euphoria to make the anguish stop.

Chapter 35

For some reason, I thought losing my car, having my weed flushed, and getting cut off from my only source of money all in one day was going to be the worst part of my week. As it turns out, that was only the start.

Not only did I have to wake up early as hell to walk to school for the first time since eighth grade, but I still got to class five minutes late and had to deal with Mr. Bexley's bullshit just like I did every other day. Except on that day, I was sober but also foggy headed from those pills, so I couldn't even think of a wisecrack to fire back to get a laugh from my classmates.

From the end of first period until fourth period, I kept an eye out for Johnny and even checked all of our usual spots, like the bathroom we smoked at and the bleachers, but he was nowhere to be found.

Okay, it's obvious he's avoiding me now, I thought as I walked to my last class before lunch.

When lunch finally rolled around, I headed straight to the parking lot to see if I could catch Johnny on his walk with Kylie to her car. And, sure enough, I found him a few rows down from where Kylie usually parked.

"Johnny!" I yelled.

They both turned around at the same time, Johnny shaking his head and his pain-in-the-ass girlfriend rolling her eyes as soon as they saw me. But that didn't stop me from pursuing them. Because I needed them.

"Wait!" I shouted as they urgently climbed into her car. "Johnny, just wait a second! Dude, please, hold on. Can we just talk for a second?"

Johnny shook his head then lowered the driver's side window. "What do you want?"

"Look," I said, squatting to lean against the open window, "I understand that you're upset, and I'm sorry about what happened yesterday." I looked over at Kylie. "And I'm sorry to you too. It was fucked up of me not to tell you how strong that weed was. I should have let you know."

Judging by her blank stare, she didn't buy it. "And you're sorry for being an asshole when I thought I was dying?" she asked.

I looked back at Johnny. His brows were raised like he was waiting for me to swallow my pride and admit it. *Say it*, I thought. *You don't have to mean it.*

"Yeah… I'm sorry for that too," I finally said, my stomach twisting from how nauseating that was.

Johnny looked over at Kylie, and when her expression went from resting-bitch-face to something between shocked and mildly satisfied, he turned back to me and gestured for me to get in with a tilt of his head.

When Johnny turned into the dentist's office parking lot, the anticipation of smoking filled me with glee and a tinge of hope— hope that I'd finally be able to temporarily escape the punishment that was enduring my miserable life sober.

After pulling into our usual spot, Johnny got out and walked around to the trunk to get the bong. Kylie watched him the entire time until he disappeared behind the popped trunk. That's when I caught her glaring at me in the rearview as I'd done to her many times.

Don't say anything. All you have to do is tolerate her, then Johnny won't get pissed, I reminded myself. *You need him and you need Kylie for her car.*

When Johnny climbed back into the driver's seat, he unwrapped the protective blanket from around the bong then got to filling it with water from his bottle. "Alright," he said, turning and handing it to me, "here you go."

I snickered. "The bowl's not packed…"

"No shit, that's why I'm handing it to you to pack it…"

"Ugh… hold on… You don't have anything?" I asked.

He squinted at me. "Travis, when do I ever have anything? Everything we ever smoked is whatever you gave us…"

"Right…" I groaned. "Well, we got a bit of a problem then."

"What do you mean?" he said.

"Joan found my shit yesterday and flushed it down the toilet."

"Oh…" He dumped the water out of the window and started wrapping the bong back up.

"What're you doing?" I asked.

"Putting it back in the trunk…"

"No, wait—just—just hold on," I stammered. "I can get some. I just gotta call my guy."

"Does your guy go to school with us?" Johnny asked.

"Uh… No, he lives in Santa Ana."

Johnny squinted at me. "Dude, you wanna drive all the way out to Santa Ana right now?"

"We can make it there in 15 if we take the freeway. You know there's no traffic this time of day."

"Lunch is gonna be over in 15," Kylie chimed in. "Let's just head back and eat."

"Guys, lemme just call him!" I pleaded. "I'm telling you, we—"

"Travis," Kylie hissed as she turned to me. "I don't want to go to a drug dealer's house." She then faced Johnny. "And I don't want you to, either. Let's just head back… I don't even feel like smoking anyway."

"Sorry, man," Johnny said, starting the car. "Just buy some after school and we can smoke tomorrow."

Fuck you, Kylie, I thought, glaring at the back of her head as he pulled out of the spot, hoping that if I concentrated hard enough, she'd blip out of existence. *Now I'm going to have to think of another way to score something from Pierce with no money and no car...*

At the sound of the fifth period bell, I packed up as fast as I could and headed over to Johnny's desk so I could hatch the plan I'd been mulling over since lunch.

"Dude, I forgot to ask you earlier, but could you give me a ride home after school?"

"Uh, maybe? I'd have to ask Kylie," he said, slinging his pack over his shoulder. "Wait, what happened to your car?"

"Holy shit! That's right, I didn't tell you what happened yesterday, did I?"

"Nope..." he said as we headed for the door.

"Oh, dude, it was fucking nuts. So, I'm driving home when I get a text from some girl I met at the party last week—"

"Which girl?"

"Uhhh... I forget... I think it was Danielle or some shit. Anyway, I'm cruising through my neighborhood and reading her text, then bam! Something smacks against the side of my car."

"No shit?" he said, approaching the vending machine. "What was it? Coyote or something?"

"Nah, some guy's fucking trash cans! He had them crazy far from the curb in the middle of the street." I paused when I saw him rummage through his wallet, staring longingly at the 20-dollar bill right in front—my ticket to paradise.

"And then what happened?" he asked, feeding a five into the machine.

"Oh, uh, the dude lost his shit and told Joan he was going to sue over nothing. Then she basically went off on me thinking I crashed because I was high. That's why she flushed my stuff and banned me from driving my car…"

"Fuck, man, that's brutal," Johnny said, opening his chips.

"It's alright. It'll probably be less than a hundred bucks to replace the cans, so whatever. I just hope I get my car back eventually."

"Well, shit. I'm sorry, man."

"It's cool," I said. "I mean, my legs are sore from walking basically two fucking miles to school, but hey, it's good exercise."

"It's all good, dude, I'll give you a lift today."

"You don't have to do that," I said with a smile.

"I mean, you live like right next to Kylie, so it's no problem."

"Thanks, man. I appreciate that."

"Don't mention it. See you in an hour," he said, heading off down the opposite hall that I had to turn down.

"Hey!" I shouted.

He turned around. "What's up?"

"I really am sorry, man. About everything."

He nodded. "I know. It's okay."

"We're brothers, right?"

He hesitated a moment. "Yeah, man, we're brothers."

As I walked away smirking, there was this weird tightness in my chest—a brief flash of guilt that melted away just as quickly as it came on.

Chapter 36

"Wait, I thought he didn't have anything to smoke?" Kylie asked as soon as she saw me reaching for the rear passenger's side door.

"I'm not coming for that," I said. "Long story short, Joan won't let me drive my car anymore and Johnny said he'd drop me off at my place."

"That's why I asked if I could borrow your car until my dad came to pick me up, babe," Johnny finished.

She sighed dramatically. "Fine, whatever. Get in."

An awkward vibe hung in the air during the ride to Kylie's, the kind where one person clearly doesn't want a member of the group around so no one really knows what to say and everyone just stays quiet.

"Alrighty, see you in a few minutes," Kylie said, planting a kiss on Johnny's cheek, smiling for the first time in forever.

Johnny smiled back. "See ya in a bit."

"Bye, Kylie!" I said cheerily as she and I climbed out of the car at the same time.

"Bye, *Travis*," she muttered, somewhat coldly.

"Don't worry," Johnny said as I flopped down onto the passenger seat, "she'll warm up to you before you know it." He smirked.

It wasn't until Johnny reached the last intersection before my subdivision that I decided to pull the trigger on my plan.

"Actually," I said, looking at my phone like I was reading something, "can we make a stop real quick?"

Johnny looked over at me with an arched brow. "Where?"

I let my silent stare do the talking.

When his expression went from confused to scowling, I knew he'd figured it out. "Dude," he grumbled, pinching the bridge of his nose.

"Look, Kylie doesn't have to know," I said. "And it'll only take 20 minutes to get there."

"At 3:00 P.M.?"

"Okay, 30 minutes. Traffic's not that bad right now."

"Thirty minutes there and thirty minutes back? That's an hour detour, I told her that I'd be right back!"

"Dude, just stop somewhere for food on the way back and tell her there was a long line or something."

Johnny just shook his head. Right as he turned to me to say something, this old lady in a Volkswagen Beetle behind us honked and threw her hands up.

"Please, dude," I said.

"Fine. Just this one time. And if she finds out—"

"I'll tell her it was my fault," I finished, flipping open my phone to call Pierce.

Even with the traffic, we pulled up to Pierce's apartment just shy of 30 minutes later. It wasn't until I got out of the car, slammed the door, and started walking away that I'd realized Johnny was still sitting behind the wheel with the engine running.

"Dude, what're you doing?" I asked on my way back to the car.

"Staying here," he said. "I said I'd drive, that's it."

But I also need you to pay, and since you'll certainly say no now, I need you to come with me, because I know you won't say no when Pierce asks for payment...

"I might be up there a while," I said.

"I thought this was only gonna take five minutes," he said, scowling.

"Pierce is a talker, and when he starts, he can just go on and on."

"As soon as you walk in, tell him you can't stay long. Problem solved."

Shit…

"Okay," I said, turning and heading towards Pierce's apartment.

Maybe he'll let me pay later, I said, knocking on his door. *Or maybe he'll deck me in the face for wasting his time and tell me to never come back.* The thought had my heart racing.

I was freaking out so bad over the debacle that I jumped when Pierce ripped open the door, then I just stood there staring at him like a dipshit.

He shielded his eyes from the sun with one hand and pulled the blunt from his mouth with the other. "The fuck's wrong with you?" He looked at me like I was an idiot. "Come in."

"Sorry, I'm super out of it today," I said, walking past him towards the couch.

"So," he said, shutting the door behind me, "how's that new stuff treating you?"

"Good."

"See? The combo was so good you went and smoked all the Plushberry in a night, huh?"

I nodded.

Pierce let out a raspy laugh as he flipped through the baggies in the box of weed. "What'd I tell you? You gotta start trusting me more, man. I'm just trying to look out for you." He pulled out another bag of Plushberry and extended it to me. "Alright. Gonna be another 20."

I didn't take it. I didn't even blink. I just stared at the small bag, trying to think of something other than, "*I'm out of cash, but I can pay you double when I come back next time.*"

Pierce raised his eyebrows and smirked. "You high right now, Travis?"

"Yeah." A nervous laugh escaped me. "Can I, uh… can I use your bathroom real quick?"

The smile vanished from his face as he gestured toward the direction of his room. "First door on the right."

After shutting the door behind me, I flipped the piss-stained toilet seat up then pulled out my phone.

Me to Johnny: Hey, can you come up real quick? It's Apartment 215.

Instead of texting back, he called like a dumb ass, and my ringtone was so loud that I almost dropped my phone while I fumbled to reject the call.

Me: I can't talk, that's why I'm texting. Just get up here.

A second after I hit send, he called back. I rejected the call again then flushed the toilet to make it sound like I'd actually used the bathroom.

Johnny: WTF. Why can't you talk? You in trouble?
Me: No. Just come to the apartment.

Right as I hit send, a knock at the door spooked me. "Hey!" Pierce said. "What's going on in there?"

"One sec," I said, turning on the faucet while I shoved my phone back into my pocket. After quickly washing my hands, I opened the door then dried my hands on my pants.

"You taking calls in there?" he asked.

"Oh, no. My friend kept calling so I just had to text him."

"You know I don't like people coming in here with their phones on."

"I'm sorry, man," I said, pulling my phone out and holding down the power button.

"Look into the Patriot Act and you'll know why I'm so paranoid about that shit," he spoke through gritted teeth as he turned the flame on under his tea kettle. "Now," he said, rummaging through the assortment of teas in his cabinet, "can you please pay me and get outta here before my next client shows."

My body tensed up. "Alright, sooo…" I dragged. "Here's the thing. I don't have any money."

"I'm sorry, say that again?"

"I don't have any money… Not on me anyway."

Pierce looked at me like I'd just pissed all over his floor right in front of him. "So let me get this straight. You make a last-minute appointment once again and I generously squeeze you in during an already hectic day all so you could tell me you don't have any money?"

"Okay, what if I—what if I got you the money later?"

"So, you wanna start a tab?"

"Sure, whatever you wanna call me paying you back next time I see you. I swear to whatever God you pray to—"

"I'm an atheist."

"Pierce, I'm gonna pay you back. Trust me, I wouldn't fuck you over like that."

His annoyed eyes studied my face for a long while. "What if you didn't have to pay me at all?" he asked.

"I don't follow," I said.

Pierce walked past me into the living room. "What if there was a way for you to never have to pay me again?" He nodded at his box of weed. "And you get whatever you want out of here whenever you want…"

Before I could make sense of what he was proposing, there was a knock on the apartment door.

Pierce checked his watch. "Why's he here so early today?" he muttered on the way to the door.

"Pierce, hold on—" I said, stopping mid-sentence when he opened the door.

"Who the fuck are you?" Pierce asked Johnny.

"I'm looking for Travis…" Johnny said confidently, looking over Pierce's shoulder at me.

"You know him?" Pierce asked, turning to me.

"C'mon, Travis, are we going or what?" Johnny asked.

Pierce spun around and grabbed Johnny's shoulder. "Hang on, hang on. No one is going anywhere until you tell me who you are and what you're doing at my place."

Johnny swatted his hand away. "I don't have to tell you shit. Travis, let's go!"

"Johnny, calm down," I said as I walked up to them.

Pierce glared at me then gave Johnny this stare that reminded of me of the look in his eyes before he decked his neighbor for being loud. "Travis, who is this?"

"He's my friend," I said. "He drove me here."

"And now it's time to drive back," Johnny said. "Right now. So, let's go." He started walking away.

"Gimme a sec," I said to Pierce, standing between him and the door. "My buddy's just pissed because I told him I wouldn't be long. Lemme talk to him."

"Make it quick…" he snarled.

I had to jog to catch up to Johnny. "Look," I said quietly, "I was gonna ask you this back in the car, but I thought he'd let me pay him later…"

"Don't tell me you called me up here to ask for money," he grumbled.

"I spent the last of mine yesterday before Joan cut me off. I just need to borrow 20 and I'll pay you back, I promise."

"Travis, for fuck's sake…"

"Dude, this is for both of us. And for Kylie. And you know I'm going to pay you back. As soon as Joan—"

"Why did you even make you drive me all the way here if you knew you couldn't afford to buy—" That's when his expression soured into a scowl. "Because you knew I wouldn't give you a ride if I also had to pay for it."

"Look, I'm sorry, I should've been upfront, but we're here now, so let's pay this guy so I don't piss him off."

He stared blankly at me.

"Dude, I *promise* I'll pay you back."

"How? You just said Joan cut you off…"

"C'mon, you know me, I always figure out a way. Trust me on that. I won't screw you over."

Johnny looked from me to Pierce, who was still watching us from the doorway. Then, with a sigh, he pulled out his wallet and handed me a crinkled twenty. "Just hurry up," he said.

I ran back to Pierce then, without a word, I slapped the money into his palm with a handshake.

He glared at me for a moment before nodding towards the apartment. "Come on." When we got to the kitchen counter, he picked up the baggie then handed it to me. As soon as I reached for it, he snatched it away. "*Never* bring him back here," he said in a deep growl. The tone sent a shiver down my spine. "Understand?"

I nodded.

"Good." He handed me the Plushberry. "And don't come back here without money again…" he said as I was shutting the door behind me.

Right when we were about to get off the freeway, Kylie called Johnny, and even though she wasn't on speaker phone, I could hear her bitching that he was taking too long to come back. Then, pretty much after I took my first bong rip in the dentist's office parking lot, Johnny got another call, this time from his dad.

"Alright, alright, I'm on the way," Johnny said, starting the car and snapping his flip phone shut.

I exhaled a thick cloud of smoke. "What're you doing?" I croaked, coughing afterwards.

"Dad's pissed," he said through a sigh. "I need to drop you off so Kylie can drive me home. Empty the bong so we can go."

"You can't smoke with me real quick?"

"Had we not wasted an hour getting the stuff, I would've had plenty of time for that." He shot me a look.

"Fair enough," I said, salvaging what weed I could from the bowl before dumping out the bong water.

A few minutes later, we pulled up to Kylie's place.

"You good to walk from here?" he asked.

"Yup, I'm good," I said, unbuckling my seatbelt. "Sorry again for today man, I—"

He waved me off. "It's fine." His words said one thing but his tone said the opposite.

"Alright, I guess I'll see ya tomorrow."

"Hold on," he blurted out right as I opened the passenger door. "Take this." He handed me a tiny bottle with a label that read Clear Eyes. "Use that before you walk in the house."

"Why? I've never needed this—"

"That was before Joan was on your ass. You need to cover your tracks better."

"Thanks, dude," I said. "I appreciate it."

I waited until I was one block away to put the eyedrops in. It's a good thing I did too, because as soon as I opened the door, Joan was in the living room staring right at me. And if I could see the whites of her eyes from where I was, she could certainly tell if mine were red from her seat.

"You're late," she said with frustration in her tone, scanning my face. "Where have you been?"

"Sorry, I don't have a fucking car anymore so it takes a bit longer to walk home…" I fired back.

She just chuckled and shook her head. That's when I stomped my way upstairs.

As soon as I got to my room, I locked the door, grabbed the pills from the closet, then downed two before crawling in bed.

While I laid there waiting for the high to kick in, I tried brainstorming a way to come up with the funds to keep the self-medication going. But, before I could think something up, the pills started doing their thing, submerging me in that thick molasses I'd been dreaming of all day. So I pulled the covers up over me and let myself go in the beauty of that feeling, unafraid of its inevitable end or the fact that I had no way to sustain it in the future.

Chapter 37

As soon as Johnny shifted into park in front of my neighbor's house, I reclined the passenger seat as far back as it could go, then I applied my Clear Eyes drops the way I'd been doing every day this last month following our after-school smoke sessions—or, in this case, following one of our post–Pierce visit smoke trips.

"Alright, dude," I said, turning to Johnny as I returned the seat to its upright position. "See you tomorrow. And I promise I won't be late coming down this time." I let out a chuckle.

He went from smiling to getting this weird look on his face, like there was something he wanted to say but didn't know how. "Look, I got no problem picking you up in the morning or taking you back home, but I can't keep driving you to Santa Ana anymore. And I can't lend you money anymore either."

And there it is, I thought, wincing from the words that hit like a kick in the balls. I'd been waiting for him to tell me that ever since our third trip to Pierce's place, but I still wasn't prepared for it.

"Is this because I haven't paid you back? Because I'm telling you, I should be hearing back about that cashier job soon!" That was a lie. Applying was on my list of things to do because it was the only thing that I could think of to solve my drug fund issue. But since Johnny kept letting me borrow money, I never actually went through with it. I couldn't. The thought of standing behind a register all day pressing buttons and pretending to be all enthusiastic and chipper for customers I didn't give a fuck about made me nauseous.

"Travis, I just can't do it anymore, alright?"

"What're you gonna do for weed then?"

"Nothing," he said.

My eyes widened. "So, what, you're just gonna quit?"

"Dude, I haven't talked to my mom since she kicked me out, and if I keep this up, it's only a matter of time until my dad catches me and kicks me out too."

"He's not gonna kick you out—"

"You don't know that!" he shouted. "You don't know my dad…" he said more calmly. A long silence followed. "Look, I'm sorry… But things have been so shitty for so long, man. I gotta try and do *something* different, you know? Kylie told me that maybe I should—"

"Oh, I get it," I said. "Anything to please your little princess, huh? She doesn't want you hanging out with me anymore, is that it?"

"What? No, that's not it at all!"

"Well, you know what? Go on ahead and let her control your fucking life more than she already does."

"Dude… Chill… She just thinks I need to stop getting high!"

"Because she knows if you stop smoking, we'd see each other less. She wants me out of your life entirely because she fucking hates me."

"That's not true!"

"Oh, bullshit! It's as clear as day. You're either oblivious or too pussy-whipped to see it." That's when I got out, slammed the door shut, and marched to my house without looking back.

There wasn't anyone on the first floor when I walked in the house, so I closed the door quietly then snuck up to my room.

This is it, I thought, retrieving the orange bottle from under the pile of clothes in the far corner of my closet. I shook the last two pills into my palm and stared at them with longing, like I was about to say goodbye to an old friend forever.

I popped the pills into my mouth and washed them down with what little water was left in my bottle. I don't know if it was the anxiety of knowing these were my last pills or if it was the cotton mouth and dry throat from smoking, but it felt like the pills were just stuck in the middle of my esophagus. So, instead of crawling into bed and waiting for the oxy to kick in, I ventured down to the kitchen to get some more water.

"Hi, sweetie," Mom said from behind me just as I reached the bottom of the stairs.

My head snapped towards the living room where she was smiling at me from the couch. "Hi, Mom," I said, trying to sound like she didn't just startle me.

Her sleepy eyes studied me, then her smile faded a bit. "What's wrong?"

I cleared my throat. "Nothing."

She arched a brow and smirked. "Oh, honey, you haven't changed a bit."

"Hmm?"

"Ever since you were five, you'd always clear your throat before lying."

Usually, an accusation like that would've sent me into a panic, but since she said it more like a fond recollection rather than a malicious conviction, I couldn't fend off a smile.

Mom picked up the remote and held it out to me. "Come. Put on anything you want."

I took the remote from her as I sat down. Since I had no idea what was on TV that time of day, I just left it on whatever channel it was on, which happened to be CBS. A news story about the homeless crisis in the county was running with footage of sunburnt bums dressed in clothes that looked so filthy I could almost smell them through the screen.

Mom shook her head. "Those poor people," she said softly.

"Eh, I dunno," I said.

She looked over at me. "You don't know what?"

"I mean, no one just *ends up* like that. You have to either seriously fuck up or—"

Mom lightly slapped my arm. "Don't swear!"

I grinned at how genuinely offended she was. "Okay, sorry, sorry. What I meant was, you have to seriously mess up your life to end up like that. That doesn't just happen out of nowhere. Who knows, maybe they hurt a lot of people and that's why no one wants them around anymore. Maybe some of them deserve to be where they're at."

Mom stared at me. "Travis, no one is rotten enough to deserve that life. No one. Even if some of those people did bad things, that doesn't mean they're bad people, and it doesn't make their situation fair. Everyone deserves a second chance. Everyone deserves the opportunity to change."

Had anyone else made that argument to me, I would've annihilated each and every claim by carefully explaining to them why that was bullshit before telling them that they should feel stupid for believing in something so naïve. But, instead, I nodded and smiled. Because the last thing I wanted was to shatter her optimism with the truth.

"Yeah, I guess you're right," I said.

Not wanting to debate that topic any longer, I started flicking channels until Mom blurted out, "Ooh, I used to love that show!"

So I left it there and watched it with her until the pills kicked in. Sitting there with Mom, listening to her laugh at that old sitcom while the euphoria swept me away—in that moment, things were good. I didn't have a care in the world. I wasn't even worried anymore about what I'd do the next day now that I was out of Percocets and didn't have a cent to my name.

In that moment, I was at peace.

Chapter 38

It occurred to me on the walk to school the next day that, as well-liked as I was among the acquaintances I partied with and those I chatted with in class, there had to be a few kids that'd let me borrow a couple of bucks. As long as I told them something like "*I don't have money for lunch*," there was no way they could say no.

So that's what I spent all day doing. Between classes, during breaks, and at lunch, I tracked down every kid I'd ever talked to or smoked with at a party, even if I didn't know their names, and I asked them for five bucks. I figured if 50 of them said no, there'd be at least ten that'd say yes, and that had to be enough to score maybe half a bottle of Percocets and hopefully some more Plushberry too. Despite all the people I'd asked, I only had $25 by the time last period rolled around.

Is this enough? I wondered, counting the money at my desk. *There's no way that's enough if the Plushberry costs $20…*

After the last bell, I ran around in a panic asking anyone I'd recognized who I didn't already ask if I could borrow money. Every single one of them said they didn't have any.

Liars… Each and every one of them…

The bus squealed as it came to a halt. A few passengers limped off only for twice as many dead-eyed, miserable-looking hollowed souls to board and crowd the bus. It felt like a moving purgatory of sorts. Or maybe this was hell. It had to be, because, somehow, I could smell the funk on one of the people who stood beside me through the pissy, musty stench that had already been hanging in the air since I boarded a few blocks from school.

The bus stop was right outside of Pierce's place, so at least I didn't have a far trek ahead of me on top of what I'd just endured. Almost as soon as I knocked on his door, he yanked it open.

"Why you look like someone shat in your oatmeal this morning?" he asked, stepping aside so I could pass.

"Had to ride the bus because my aunt took my car key…"

"Speaking of which, I've always wondered… how the fuck do you even have a license? Didn't you say you were a freshman?"

"Oh," I laughed. "People ask me that all the time. Basically, I started school kind of late because my birthday is later in the year. Then I got such shit grades in the months after my dad died, I got held back a year. So now I'm older than most kids in my class by, like, two years."

"Ah… I see," he said, pulling a bag of Plushberry from his box. "So, it seems like you're smoking through your supply faster and faster each week,"

"I guess so…" I swapped him four fives for the baggie. "But I was actually hoping to buy some more pills too."

"No shit? Thought those would last you a bit longer." He got up and made his way into the room. "You know, I don't blame ya. Back in the day, I'd burn through a bottle in less than a week!"

"Geez."

He emerged from the room shaking a full bottle of pills like a maraca. "That'll be $200," he said, dangling it in front of my face.

"Shit… I barely have enough for the weed," I muttered.

Pierce's face muscles relaxed as he lowered the bottle.

"Can I start a tab? I'm getting a job soon and I can—"

"Sorry, I don't do payment plans." He started walking back to his room.

"Wait!" I said, running after him. "Pierce, please, can I have, like a quarter of the bottle? How much can $20 get me?"

"Not enough."

"Please, you got to work with me, here. You don't understand, I… I need those."

"Oh, no, I understand. But like I said—"

"I'll do whatever you want! *Anything!* Here—" I held the weed back out to him. "Take this back! That's 20 dollars off. Now all I need is 180, right? Uh, you like jewelry? My aunt's got a diamond necklace. Must be worth at least $250!"

"You got it on ya?"

"Well, no… But if you gimme the pills today, I can bring it tomorrow right after school. Hell, I can skip school and bring it to you in the morning, if you want!"

Pierce held the bottle over the open drawer with two fingers, staring at me with a smirk while he shook it like he was trying to taunt me. "Tell you what," he said, dropping the pills in the drawer and shutting it slowly. "What if we worked out another deal? One that doesn't involve you stealing from your poor aunt."

"Okay…"

"You remember when I said you could have whatever you want and you wouldn't have to pay a dime?"

"Yeah…"

"You remember Luis?"

I shook my head.

"That Mexican fella you almost fought with here a few months ago?"

"What about him?"

"He's one of the privileged few who doesn't have to pay. All he's gotta do is take some of my stuff around town, sell it to some of his friends or friends of friends, and come back every week with the profits. And, in return, everything I have that a man can smoke, snort, shoot up or pop is his for the taking. Within reason, of course."

I stared in horror at the dresser like the pills trapped inside were my own children. "Okay," I said. "When do I start?"

With a smirk, Pierce walked over to his closet and pulled down a blue backpack from the top shelf.

"You can start whenever you wanna start. You just can't come back here until you've sold everything." He unzipped the backpack and shoved it into my chest, sending the sweet smell of skunk blowing up into my nostrils. "I'd say about five of the bags are eighths, but the rest are grams."

"Oh… okay."

"Now, I doubt the kids at your school give two shits or even know about different strains, but in case they ask, tell them it's *Northern Lights*. Clear?"

I nodded.

"Sell the grams for $10 and the eighths for $25. Altogether, there should be about 300 bucks' worth of product in that bag. So, when you come back here, I expect not a cent less than that. Understand?"

I nodded.

"Here," he said, grabbing some white T-shirts from a drawer, "shove a couple of these in there. Should help keep some of the smell down. But, just in case, take a few drier sheets." He handed me a box of Bounce sheets.

"Thanks," I said, layering a few of them on top of the shirts I'd just crammed in on top of the weed.

"I shouldn't have to say this, but don't let anyone take that bag from you. And don't smoke any of it."

"Of course not."

"Cool. Heads up." He chucked the bottle of pills over.

The bottle hit my palm with a rattle, only for me to fumble it.

Pierce snickered. "Look at us, huh? Finally working together." He draped an arm around my shoulders as we left the room. "You know, my father always used to say, *'Never hire your friends because, in the end, you'll wind up becoming enemies.'* But what the fuck did he know? My old man died without a penny to his name and didn't have any friends to lend him one, never mind show up to the funeral."

At that moment, there was a knock on the door.

"Who is it?" Pierce hollered.

"It's Luis, man!"

"Ah, got it. One second." He turned to me and patted me on the back before opening the door.

Luis grimaced the second he saw me, adjusting the black backpack he had slung over one shoulder.

"Now, boys," Pierce said, stepping between us. "You're coworkers now, so let's try and act professional from this day forward, got it?"

Luis looked at him all confused. "Mm-hm," he grunted.

I nodded reluctantly then pushed past him.

When I got to the bus stop, a red Honda Civic hatchback across the street caught my eye. There were two Mexican dudes inside, both about Luis's age. When the guy in the driver's seat looked at me, I immediately recognized him to be one of the guys me and Johnny fought at Kylie's party. And when the guy he tapped on the shoulder turned and looked at me, I realized he was also one of the guys we fought. And based on how they were staring back at me with wide-eyed death glares, it was safe to assume they remembered where they recognized me from.

That's when the bus pulled up. After I paid the fare, I grabbed a seat on the side of the bus facing their car and watched them. Right when the bus's doors shut, Luis came walking up to their car with a bit of a limp. A second later, the asshole in the driver's seat pointed in my direction. Luis scowled as the bus pulled off, and I took the opportunity to flash him a shit-eating grin.

As I turned back around, the smell of weed and dryer sheets wafted into my nose. That's when it hit me. *Where the hell am I going to hide this much weed? If Joan walked into my room, she'd definitely smell this...*

Maybe one of the trash cans?

No, I can't sell shit from a bag that smells like trash.

Maybe Johnny can hold it?

Fuck that. Even if he accepted my apology, even if he were to hold this shit for me, he'd probably screw up and his dad would eventually find it...

It wasn't until I was walking through my neighborhood and saw some old lady working in her flower garden that an idea came to me.

Joan's car wasn't in the driveway when I got home, so I went through the side gate and hurried across the backyard to the garden shed. The paint on the door was chipping away, the doorhandle was rusty, and, if that wasn't indicative enough that she never came in this shed, there were also cobwebs all over the place.

She'll never think to look here, I thought, moving aside the large, unopened soil bags and stuffing the backpack in the far corner. After that, I rested a sack of soil on top of the gap that I crammed the backpack into, then I shut the door. A smirk crept across my face when I felt that the pills I popped on the walk home from the bus stop had finally started kicking in.

Chapter 39

In order to grab the stuff from the shed without getting caught, I had to wake up and head to school before Joan got up to get ready for work. That meant waking to my alarm an hour earlier than usual, around 5:00 A.M.

Tiptoeing down the stairs wasn't a problem. I've done it many times before, so I knew where to step to avoid making the wood creak. The problem was getting the shed door open without the hinges screeching like a banshee. Slowly, I opened the door inch by inch until it was just wide enough to squeeze through. Once I retrieved the backpack, I slipped back out of the shed, shut it stealthily behind me, then made my way to the side gate, checking the upstairs windows to make sure no one was watching.

Campus was basically a ghost town when I arrived. Aside from the janitors and a few teachers, the only kids there were some band and choir kids stumbling like braindead ghouls on their way to who knows where. Not that I was any livelier than them. My eyes were fighting to stay open the entire walk to the courtyard.

Alright, I thought, plopping down onto the cold bleachers and looking up at the rising sun. *Now… who the hell am I going to sell to?*

Thirty minutes passed before students began trickling in to the courtyard. None of them were people I recognized, but part of me thought maybe it was a good time to try and sell to a stranger first, someone who'd only know me as a dealer, like the way I only knew Pierce as one.

All I have to do is find someone who looks trustworthy…

That was easier said than done because, as more students swarmed the campus, I couldn't spot one kid who remotely fit that bill.

It wasn't until the bell rang and I started walking to class that I realized there was no way I could bring that bag in with me without someone catching a whiff of what was inside. Figuring the only place to hide it was somewhere that smelled even stronger than the skunky contents of the bag, I hustled over to the locker room.

Even in the morning before the first gym class it smells like funk and musty ass in here, I thought as I walked towards my locker. *There's no way anyone would be able to sniff this out.*

By the time lunch rolled around, I wasn't only stressing out from not having made any sales, but I was also super on edge from being sober all day. I was tempted to smoke during one of the breaks in the bathroom, but I couldn't risk doing that on campus anymore, not when I ran the risk of getting caught and losing Pierce's product. Basically, Johnny and Kiley's car were the only options, as they always seemed to be. So, I gritted my teeth and ran over to the parking lot.

Unfortunately, Kylie's car wasn't in its usual spot when I got out there. "God damnit!" I shouted, clenching my jaw as I turned back towards campus. "Can one fucking thing go right today? Just one?"

On the way to the lunch room, I spotted two kids walking out who looked familiar—a pimply-faced guy and a blonde dude. *Wait, those are the guys who asked if I sold weed when Johnny blew up on me a few months ago...*

"Hey," I yelled, jogging up to them. "You two still looking to buy?"

Pizza Face grinned. "Depends what you're selling!"

I smirked back. "Meet me by the bathrooms outside of the gym in five."

The two boys were loitering outside of the restrooms looking paranoid as hell as I strolled out the gym entrance. With a nod, they followed me inside to the handicap stall where me, Kylie, and Johnny used to smoke in the beginning of the year.

"Okay," I said, unzipping the backpack. I pulled out the two different sized baggies of herb and showed it to them. "This here is Northern Lights—better than anything you've ever smoked. A gram is $15 and an eighth is $30."

The dirty blonde looked to Pizza Face then turned to me with a blank stare. "Uh, which one has more weed?"

"The eighth. The one that's more expensive," I said without sounding too condescending. The last thing I needed was to mock my only customers.

"Get a gram," Pizza Face said to his friend.

Nodding, the dirty-blonde reached into his pocket, pulled out a ten and five from his wallet, then swapped me for the product.

I shoved the money into my backpack. "You trying to smoke now?"

The two looked at each other, confused.

"Uh, in here?" Pizza Face asked.

"No," I said. "You guys got a car?"

"I do," blondie said.

"Alright, let's go," I said, slinging the pack over my shoulder. "I know a spot."

After blazing in the dentist's office parking lot, blondie drove us back to campus with a few minutes to spare—an impressive feat because he, like his friend, was baked out of his mind.

"Holy shit," the blonde kid said, staring up at the clouds as he climbed out of the driver's seat, "I've never seen a sky so pretty!"

Zit Face chuckled. "That's the gayest thing I ever heard you say, dude."

"Fuck off!" he said, shoving his buddy.

The bell rang right as we got to the courtyard. "Yo, gimme your phone," I said.

The blonde kid did as instructed.

"You guys call me if you want some more," I said while putting my number in his contact list. "Name's Travis, by the way." I handed the phone back to him.

"I'm Greg," blondie replied.

"Nigel," Zit Face said.

"Feel free to send any friends my way if you know anyone looking to buy, alright?" I said.

They nodded.

"But don't just hand out my number to anyone, only people you know are cool. Understand?" I said sternly, hardening my gaze.

They both went all wide-eyed as they nodded.

"You got it, Travis," Greg choked out.

As soon as the fifth period bell rang, I got up and headed for the door without looking at Johnny, just like I avoided looking his way when I walked into class. Since my phone had buzzed a few times right before the bell, I fished the T-Mobile Sidekick out of my pocket and woke the screen on the way out of class.

Unknown Number: Hi. Nigel told me to text you. Looking to buy. Could you meet me in the parking lot after school? Space number 68.

I smirked as I replied: **Sure thing.**

"Travis!" Johnny called right as I slipped my phone back in my pocket and started walking to my next class.

"Yeah?" I asked, turning around.

"Can we talk for a second?"

"About what?"

"Look... Travis... Kylie didn't—"

"It's fine, dude. I get it."

"But you don't understand. She—"

"I know, I know. It's fine. Just drop it." I said, somewhat coldly.

My response and tone left Johnny looking all confused, and seeing him squirm with uncertainty was oddly rewarding. "Okay..." he finally said after a long pause. "Look, if you want to meet up after class and smoke in my—"

"Nah," I said cutting him off.

He looked totally dumbfounded. "You sure?"

"Yeah."

"Okay... Need me to give you a lift home then?"

"Nope. Won't be necessary. I'll walk."

"But—"

"Look, man, I gotta go, alright? Don't worry about me. Have fun with your girl."

I turned and walked off, a swelling feeling of bittersweet victory in my heart. *I don't need him anymore,* I thought. *I'm done trying to appease Kylie to keep myself in Johnny's good graces. I don't need him, just like I don't need Joan and her money. I don't need anyone. I can make it on my own. That's the way it should be.*

Never rely on anyone, you'll only wind up disappointed...

Chapter 40

In the days following my first two sales, tons of buyers started hitting me up. Sometimes, as many as five new numbers a day would text me about how they heard I had some good stuff and asked me when and where to meet. The funny thing was, the weed wasn't even *good*, it was adequate at best. That's the week that I learned that quality didn't matter to most people; what mattered was word of mouth. Hell, I'm pretty sure if I started selling oregano to those dumbasses, they'd still keep sending me referrals.

What's crazy is, I had so many customers flowing in that I'd started getting selective with who I sold to. Just like I did with Greg and Nigel, whenever a new customer texted me, I'd ask them if they had a car. And if they did, I'd tell them to meet me in the parking lot at lunch or immediately after school. Once they paid me, I pocketed their money, and handed them the stuff. Then I'd ask them if we could smoke together. Almost all of them said yes. As for the assholes who said no? Well, I gave them back their money and took back the weed, telling them to never text me again. That was my test to gauge their respect for me and to see how trustworthy they were.

With the last bag sold during lunch that Monday, I headed to the handicap stall in the gym bathroom to count my earnings. *$350... holy shit... That's $50 over what Pierce told me to bring back to him. Maybe I should just pocket the extra $50... He won't miss it if he wasn't expecting it in the first place.*

No, another voice said. *On the off chance he told me the wrong amount on purpose as a test, give him everything. Even if it isn't a test, this could be* *your way of showing him what you're capable of. Besides, there's no amount of money in the world that could buy the respect of someone you admire, and I'd rather have Pierce's respect than an extra $50.*

All I could think about during those last two classes was how much money I had in that bag. It felt like everyone knew how much I was toting around and someone was just waiting to jump me and steal it. That's why as soon as the last bell rang, I headed right to the bus stop and didn't stop to talk to anyone. I didn't even pull out my phone to text Pierce—I just sat on the bus bound for Santa Ana clutching the bag to my chest, keeping my eye on the shady dudes sitting around me.

When the bus dropped me off, I hurried across Pierce's complex faster than I ever have before.

"Who is it?" he shouted cautiously after I knocked on his door.

"It's Travis," I said.

Moments later, he opened the door with a blunt between his lips. He glanced down at the backpack in my hands then back up at me. "I don't remember you scheduling an appointment."

"You make your employees do that too?"

"I make everyone do that."

"Oh. Well, I sold everything, so…" I said in a hushed voice.

He looked impressed. "Come on in. I got a few minutes."

I unzipped the backpack as I walked past him. "$350," I said, turning the bag upside down and dumping the cash onto the table.

"You're shitting me," he said, squinting at me as he sat down.

"Nope. Counted it twice."

Pierce stubbed out his blunt in the ashtray then got to counting the money. When he was done, he looked up at me in awe. "You sold everything in *three* days?"

I smiled smugly.

Pierce chuckled, nodding in approval. "Okay, okay."

Like every other time I came over, there was a knock on the door. *Let me guess, it's Luis...*

"Yeah?" Pierce shouted.

"Luis," the voice replied.

Of course it is... Seems like he comes by right after school like I do...

Pierce nodded towards the door, so I walked over and opened it. As soon as I saw that Luis had a black eye, I cracked a smile.

Luis, who already looked pissed before he saw me, scowled even harder as he stomped by.

Pierce smirked. "You boys get into another little powwow recently?"

Luis just chucked his backpack at Pierce's feet without a word.

Pierce looked down at it before glancing back up at him, no longer smiling. "You wanna try that again?" he asked, condescendingly.

"Sorry..." Luis said, looking all embarrassed as he picked up the backpack.

"You see what Travis brought me, Luis?" Pierce said, pointing to my earnings. "This tenacious son of a bitch sold 30 grams in three days! Three days and he's already operating like Pablo-fucking-Escobar."

Luis just side-eyed me.

Pierce pulled out a gym bag from somewhere on the other side of the couch and scrapped all of my money into it with the exception of a few bills. "And because he exceeded my expectations...." He grabbed the remaining money and handed it to me. "Travis, that's all yours."

"You sure?" I asked.

Pierce nodded, giving me this proud, fatherly look. "Consider it your bonus." He smiled, then turned to Luis. "Now, let's see how much you brought."

"It's all there," Luis snapped, storming off towards the exit.

"Hey! Whoa, where you going?" Pierce asked.

Luis froze with his hand on the knob. "Home."

"Not before I count this, you're not."

Luis turned back around

Pierce quickly counted the money. When he was done, he got this confused look on his face then recounted it. As he slammed the last twenty on the stack, he looked up at Luis with rage in his eyes. "One hundred and seventy bucks? Did I or did I not give you $400 worth of product?"

"I—I got jumped last week," Luis stuttered. "They took everything in the bag!"

"Bullshit."

He pointed at his black eye. "How'd you think I got this, huh? The only reason I have anything at all is because I kept the money I'd already made under my bed."

Pierce let out this long, seething sigh.

"Pierce, I swear on my father's fucking grave that's what happened."

"You want to know what I think happened?" Pierce said, rising from his seat. "You know what sounds more likely?" He walked towards Luis slowly. "I think that you and those spic friends of yours snorted and shot up everything left in that bag. Then you sobered up, realized how much shit you were in, and you came up with some bullshit story, asking one of your friends to punch you in the face to make it all seem believable."

In an instant, Luis had gone from a smug wannabe badass to a trembling little bitch who looked like he was about to cry. "Pierce... please," he said, his voice cracking. "I promise you, that's not what happened!"

Pierce studied Luis for a moment then got right in his face. A smile tugged at the corner of my mouth from the anticipation of

Pierce fucking him up the way he did to his neighbor that one time. Unfortunately, that's not what happened.

Instead, Pierce just grabbed the doorknob and flung the door open. "Don't come back here. Ever."

His eyes went wide and his jaw hung. "What?"

"You heard me. Delete my number from your phone. You're done. Get the fuck out."

"Pierce, please! This wasn't my fault! I need that money. My mom's—"

Pierce backhanded Luis and a loud clap echoed through the apartment. Luis just held his cheek and stared at him in horror.

Pierce got in his face. "Be a fucking man and get out!"

As if what just went down wasn't already embarrassing enough, Luis wiped away a tear on his way out of the apartment.

Pierce shut the door, closed his eyes, and took a deep breath. "There's nothing I hate more than excuses," he said, sighing after. "If you can't take responsibility for anything, you're nothing."

I nodded in agreement.

"Grab your bag, go to my room, and fill it up with whatever you find in the bottom drawer of the dresser."

"Uh, okay," I said, picking up the backpack. "How much do I take?"

"Just grab all of it."

I kneeled before the dresser and opened the drawer. "Holy shit…" I whispered. Not only was there small bags of weed like I'd sold before, but there were even tinier baggies filled with what looked like sugar. "Uh… there's coke in here too…"

"Yeah…"

"Am I supposed to take that?" I asked.

"Did I or did I not say to fill your bag with everything in the bottom drawer?" he shouted calmly from the kitchen.

"Just making sure," I said with nervousness in my voice, my heart racing as I scooped up handfuls of baggies and dumped them into my pack.

As I was walking back into the kitchen, Pierce was just setting two mugs with teabags in them on the counter. "So," he said as the teakettle began whistling, "you're gonna sell the eighths and the grams for the same price as last time. The dime bags, you're gonna sell for $40 each. Altogether there was around 20 bags, right?"

I nodded, wincing as soon as doubt crept into my mind.

He shook his head at me and gestured to the bag. "Lemme see…" he groaned. When I handed it to him, he rummaged through the bag then silently counted the contents. "Yeah, there's 20. Alright, so I expect a take of $400. Should you come back with any more than that, it's yours, same as today."

I nodded. Then, for a moment, I stared at the pack.

"Something wrong?" he asked.

"So… I'm selling coke now?"

The teapot began whistling as Pierce stared me down. "Is that an issue?"

"No… it's just… that's just a bigger load to carry, is all."

"And?" he asked.

And coke is a whole 'nother level! I can get away with having weed on me if Joan or a teacher finds it. Like, twenty kids already got busted for weed this year and they're still at school. But if they find coke on me? If a cop were to catch me with coke… That's it.

"I don't know… Won't I get in more trouble if I get caught?"

The whistling teakettle crescendoed into an ear-piercing scream as Pierce stared at me from across the counter, not blinking as he scanned my face. "First of all," he finally said as he turned around and removed the kettle from the stove, "don't get caught and it won't be a problem. Second…" he filled both cups with steaming water, "You're a minor. So, if you're dumb enough to get caught, you'll probably get in as much trouble as you would for selling weed. So," he slammed the kettle back on the stove, "circling back to my first point, just don't get caught…"

"Fine, then I want another five bags of Plushberry for the extra effort and risk."

Pierce smirked.

"You don't have to worry, I'll earn it. I'll sell everything faster than that spineless little bitch Luis ever could."

His smirk widened into a gracious smile, then he nodded at the box of weed. "Help yourself," he said. Right as I finished tucking the five baggies of Plushberry into the backpack beside the coke, Pierce walked over with both mugs in hand then offered one to me.

"Thanks," I said, taking it.

He looked like he wanted to say something to me, but no words came out. Instead, he simply extended his mug to me then I clinked mine against his.

After shooting the shit with Pierce over tea like a couple of classy English gents, I left his apartment almost thirty minutes later than usual. And because I'd left so late, I knew something was off when I spotted Luis and the rest of his Mexican posse chilling in the usual spot further up the block. Two of them were leaning against the red Civic hatchback while Luis stood in front of them freaking out about something.

I need to get to the bus stop without being seen, I thought, keeping my head down and taking a left instead of a right so I could cross the street from the corner opposite of them. *The last thing I need is them jacking all this product from me.*

Somehow, I made it across the street and all the way to the bus stop before one of them pointed my way. That's when all three of them turned and looked at me with fervid scowls.

"Hey!" the tallest one shouted as they walked around the car and stepped down onto the street. The only thing keeping them from getting to me was the traffic racing by.

Ah shit… What do I do? Run? Call Pierce and tell him his ex-employee is trying to jack my shit?

No, you can't come off like a weak little bitch to Pierce now. Think of something else.

As I stood up and looked for the best direction to run before the light changed, I heard the squeal of a bus's breaks from my left. At the same time, the *whoop-whoop* of a police siren from the right stole my attention. I turned just in time to see the cops pull up behind the Mexicans' car right as the street cleared up. That's when the cop called out to them, stopping them dead in their tracks.

The officers had just approached the three goons when the bus pulled up and obscured my view. By the time I paid my fare and found a seat near the window facing the scene, one of the officers was in the middle of searching their car.

The bus screech as it pulled off, prompting Luis to look up and glare at me as he leaned against the hood of the car.

Looks like the universe is on my side for once, I thought, smirking as I gave that asshole a two-finger salute.

Chapter 41

"Before we go," I said as Greg dumped the ashes from the pipe out of the driver's side window, "you boys ready to branch out a little?"

Nigel turned to me, squinting with a curious smirk. "What're you even talking about?"

I pulled out a dime bag from my backpack then held it out between them.

Nigel's bloodshot eyes widened with horror. "Put that away!"

"Dude, chill," I said calmly.

"Is that coke?" Greg asked.

I nodded.

"How much?"

"Bro, we're *not* buying that!" Nigel shouted.

Greg held up a hand to him. "How much, Travis?"

"Forty," I said.

Greg stared at the bag for a moment. "Fuck it," he said, pulling out his wallet.

Nigel's eyes bulged as he watched his buddy swap two twenties for the coke. "Have you lost your fucking mind?" he blurted out.

"Dude, relax," Greg said, tucking the coke into his pocket.

"Relax?!" Nigel almost yelped. "Do you know how royally screwed you are if you get caught with that?"

"I'm not gonna get caught, just like I never get caught with weed. Besides, I'm not going to snort this shit at school. It's just for Kim's party. I'll keep it at my house till then."

"That's not till Friday! You don't think your dad's gonna find it before then?"

Greg put his pipe in the glove compartment and started the car. "If I don't give him a reason to ransack my room, he's not going to find it. Just chill, dude."

The two of them went tit for tat like that all the way back to the school parking lot while I sat in the back snickering and shaking my head. A second after Greg pulled into his spot, Nigel opened the door and bolted towards campus like he saw a SWAT team coming at us.

"What a pussy," Greg said to me as we started walking.

I laughed. "The weed's just got him paranoid."

"Nah, he's always like that."

"I was trying to give him the benefit of the doubt." I chuckled. "Hey, did you say you were going to Kim's party on Friday?"

"Yeah," he said.

"Which Kim?"

"Griswold. You know her?"

"Yeah, yeah," I said, nodding. "We go way back. She and I don't talk much now, but I've been to a couple of her parties." Those were all lies.

"Oh, then you should come through. Gonna be fucking crazy! She invited, like, half the school."

"Okay, cool," I said. "I'll swing by. Just send me the address."

"Will do."

A house party, I thought, smiling to myself as Greg and I parted ways in the courtyard. *If I go there with a bag full of drugs and sell to a bunch of drunks, I can make a killing. Money is going to be bursting through the seams by the end of the night! But there's no way Pierce will let me grab more product unless I sell what I've got first. That means I have four days to sell all this shit… Easy.*

Three days. That's how much time it took to offload the rest of my haul. Once my customers caught word that I was selling coke, my number was going around like the clap at an orgy. Seriously, my phone was vibrating every other period after I sold that dime bag to Greg. And, with the increase of new clients came an increase in diversity. Like, I had buyers from every corner of every clique. I'm talking goth kids, preppy theater kids, swim team kids, jocks, punks, hipsters, cheerleaders, nerds, and even members of student council.

That just goes to show, drugs were the great equalizer. No matter how rich or poor, or happy or sad—every person from every walk of life got bored and needed an escape from the mundane eventually. And when that happened, they came to people like me and Pierce.

Whoever said money doesn't buy happiness obviously wasn't high when they said it.

Pierce finished counting the money on the table then glanced up at me from the couch, looking impressed as all hell.

"Five hundred?" he said in disbelief, "*five-fucking* hundred?"

I smirked.

He chuckled. "Travis my man, if you keep this up, pretty soon I'm gonna start expecting this from you. But for now, bra-*fucking*-vo!" He patted me on the back then start brushing all the money off of the table and into the collection bag. "I'm gonna have to get bigger shipments to keep up with you. You've got serious potential to be one of my best guys."

"I'm glad you said that, because I want a grand's worth this time," I said.

Pierce froze for a moment, then he burst into laughter. When he finally settled down, he scanned my face. That's when his smile faded. "Shit… you're serious?"

"Damn right."

"You've only been doing this for a couple weeks."

"Why does that matter? You said it yourself, I'm one of your best guys."

"No, no… I said you've got the *potential* to be. Look, you're hungry. That's good, I respect that. That's what I want. But I just can't risk that much product on you yet. Let's just give it a couple more months, then you'll get what you want. I promise." He picked up his mug and sipped his tea.

"No," I said. "There's a huge party tomorrow night and I know I can flip a grand's worth. Trust me, by Saturday night, I'll have well over a thousand dollars to dump out on your table. That's a Travis Hackett guarantee."

Pierce stopped mid drink and stared at me with the rim of his mug pressed to his lips. After swallowing what was in his mouth, he put the mug back down on the table. "Okay." He handed me my backpack. "Come with me."

I followed Pierce into the room and, after he tossed the bag of money into the closet, he opened the third dresser drawer from the top, and started filling my *work* backpack with weed and dime bags. I could see the gears turning as he ran the numbers in his head, calculating his way to $1,000 worth of product.

"Alright," he said, zipping up the bag and handing it to me.

"Thanks. You won't regret this."

"I know I won't," he said, nodding and smiling. For some reason, he stood there staring at me, smirking.

"What?" I asked.

"Nothing, just… Fuck, man, it's like looking back in time." After that, he just patted me on the shoulder and left the room.

I didn't know what he meant by that. And as bad as I wanted to ask him to elaborate, I just followed silently behind him then headed for the door when stepped into the kitchen to light a cigarette. Unsure of whether it was okay to leave, I looked back at Pierce and found him in a daze as he took a long pull of his cig.

"Alright, see ya soon, Pierce," I said, reaching for the doorknob.

"Saturday," he said, blowing out a cloud of smoke.

I nodded. "Saturday."

"Wait," he said, just as I turned the knob. "Don't forget that." Still in a Zenlike trance, he nodded towards the four twenties on the table.

I shoved my earnings in my pocket then left the apartment, wondering the entire walk to the bus stop if what he said about looking back in time was a compliment. I hoped it was.

Since Joan's car wasn't in the driveway when I got back home, I headed straight to the shed to stash the goods the way I'd done every day since I started working for Pierce. The house was dead quiet when I walked in, except for the clunking of the grandfather clock.

Mom is always cooped up in her room, I thought, creeping up the stairs.

Instead of heading right to my room, I stopped in to check on Mom. Her door was cracked a bit, so I didn't have to worry about disturbing her with that noisy doorknob. All I had to do was push it open nice and slow. Per usual, her room was dark and she was curled up in bed facing the wall.

She needs to get out this damn house, I thought, pulling the door closed.

When I got to my room, I sat on the edge of my bed staring at the eighty bucks that I'd just gotten paid. It didn't make me happy, nor did it make me sad. I just felt... indifferent. It's funny, a few weeks prior to that, I was so desperate to make money, but now that I had it, I had nothing to spend it on since Pierce was also paying me with the drugs that I originally needed cash to buy.

What good is money if I don't have anything to spend it on? That's when the image of Mom popped into my head.

I laid around in bed until I heard Joan come bumbling through the front door with what sounded like a bunch of rustling bags.

"Hey, Joan?" I asked as I trotted down the stairs.

"Yes, Travis?" she replied unsurely as she unpacked groceries.

"Can I use the car?" I asked.

"For what?" she snapped.

"I… I want to take Mom out for a little bit."

She stared at me, holding a head of lettuce in her hand like the question was so ridiculous that it robbed her of her motor function. "Take her where?"

"I don't know. I just want to get her outta here for a little bit. Maybe drive around or go get ice cream? I don't know. Either way, I'd be back in an hour."

"No," she said, placing the lettuce in the fridge.

"C'mon, Joan!" I pleaded. "How long's she been cooped up in this house? She could use a little—"

"I'm not letting you drive the car."

"I'm not going to do anything stupid. I'll be with Mom. I'm asking for her, not for me."

Joan snorted and shook her head.

"So, what, I'm never going to be allowed to drive a car again?"

With a sigh, Joan closed the fridge and looked up at the ceiling, shaking her head.

"Look," I said. "Joan, I'm sorry for what I did—"

Her head snapped to me and she met my gaze. "Why?"

"Because it was wrong."

"Why was it wrong?"

I gritted my teeth, preparing for the pain I was about to inflict on myself with what I was about to say. "Because, not only did I go against your wishes, but what I did was dangerous and dumb, and I betrayed your trust. Time and time again, I've screwed up and I haven't gotten any better. And that's why I'm not mad at you for doing this, because you were justified in punishing me after giving me so many chances."

It looks like she's buying it, I thought, searching her face. *The fish is on the hook, now all I have to do is wrangle her in.*

"With that said, I've spent the last few weeks thinking about my actions and I know I was wrong, so I am so sorry for everything I've put you guys through. And I don't know what else to say other than I'm genuinely, *genuinely* sorry."

I could tell by the look in Joan's eyes that her defenses were down. But, as quickly as the appreciation and glimmer of joy in her eyes appeared, they vanished, twisting back into wary disdain.

"That's nice, Travis. But you're still not driving that car." She turned back around and resumed unpacking bags.

It took everything in me not to blow up on her. Without grunting or growling, or saying another word, I turned and ran back upstairs.

What an absolute cunt, I thought, shutting my door and heading right to the closet to grab my Percocets. *What was the point of taking Mom out of the mental ward if she was just going to keep her locked in the house all day? Fuck her. Who made her our fucking warden?* I popped two pills in my mouth.

Minutes later, right as the pills kicked in, I thought about the money I'd earned. Then I thought about Mom and how to get her out the house. That's when an idea came to me.

Fuck you, Joan, I thought as I changed my alarm. *I don't care what you say, I'm taking Mom out whether you like it or not.*

Chapter 42

While I didn't have to wake up at 5:00 A.M. to sneak out to the shed the next morning, I did still have to beat Joan out of the house, which meant getting up closer to 6:00. So, as soon as my alarm went off, I got dressed then waited until I heard Joan get in the shower before sneaking out of the house.

School wasn't my destination that morning, the neighbor's yard across the street was where I skulked over to after leaving the house. I hid behind their bushes for nearly fifteen minutes until I finally heard Joan's car start up, then I watched through the gap in the bushes as she backed out and sped off down our street.

Finally, I thought, emerging from behind my cover and jogging back to the house, checking the neighbor's windows to make sure no one was watching.

Since Mom was home, I still had to maintain some semblance of stealth, so I snuck in through the front door and crept up the stairs the way I did pretty much every day. As expected, Mom was still asleep when I peeked into her room, somehow in the same position she was in when I checked in on her the day before. I shut her door softly behind me then headed down the hall to Joan's room.

Of course. It's locked, I thought after trying her knob.

After grabbing a pair of paperclips from the junk drawer in the kitchen, I headed back up to Joan's room.

You picked your own lock once just to see if you could, so you can do it again, I thought, kneeling before her door and straightening the paperclips. It took a few minutes of fiddling, but eventually I felt the makeshift lockpicks bump against the lock's grooves and I heard that sweet click.

Joan's room was sorely undecorated, save for a few imitation Jackson Pollock paintings and a wool rug by her bed—exactly what one would expect from someone with the personality of a sandbag. With that said, her lack of furniture meant there weren't many places she could hide my car key. And since she'd never expect me to break in, I knew she didn't go out of her way to hide them. That's why I checked the dresser first.

As I reached for the top drawer, I spotted a bottle of prescription pills beside a picture of her and Mom. *Zoloft,* I thought, examining the bottle. *Hypocrite...*

I rummaged through her drawers from top to bottom, making sure to keep things neat so she didn't know I was in here. It was in the very last drawer on the bottom under her jeans where I found it. With the key clutched in my hand, I headed out, making sure to lock her door behind me.

It was around 7:30 when I heard the toilet flush, my cue to get out of bed.

Right as I opened my door, Mom was exiting the bathroom.

"Morning, Mom," I said.

Her head snapped in my direction. "Travis? Aren't you supposed to be in school? Is it already the weekend?"

"Nope, it's Thursday," I said, following her into her room. "I guess some upperclassmen released a bunch of crickets all over campus, so they canceled school so the exterminators can fumigate the place." That was a story someone told me about what happened at their old school, so I figured it was a pretty believable tale to tell her.

"Are you serious?" she asked with a curious smile. "Why would someone do something like that?"

I shrugged. "It's almost June, so maybe it was a senior prank or something."

She shook her head. "Kids…"

"Yeah… So… uh… I was thinking that, since I'm free, maybe we could go out and get some breakfast? I've got some money saved, so I want to treat you."

"Is Joan here?" she asked.

"Nope. She left for work an hour ago."

Mom stared into her dark room.

"But if you're tired, we don't have to…"

"No, I'd like that a lot, Travis," she said with a smile. "Just let me change first. Could you hand me that pill bottle and the glass of water over there?" She pointed at something that said GEODON. I remember Googling that after the first time I saw them next to her Percocet. Pretty sure they were for schizophrenia and bipolar disorder.

"Here you go." I handed it to her. "See ya downstairs in a bit."

As soon as I pulled out of the garage, Mom groaned and shielded her eyes from the sun like that was her first time being in the daylight in decades.

"So," I asked, reaching over and flipping down the sun visor for her, "what're you feeling for breakfast?"

She didn't respond, she was too busy staring out the window at nothing but the desolate neighborhood.

"I was thinking Champs—" I continued.

"Where the hell is everyone?" she asked.

"Probably at their jobs."

"What about your classmates? They have the day off."

"Oh, kids my age tend to sleep in when there's no school."

"Hm…" She looked up at the sky. "But it's a beautiful day."

Champs was one of those old diners nestled in a strip mall surrounded by corporate chain restaurants, one of the few older establishments left in this area. Joan used to take me there a lot as a kid. Back then, it was almost always packed around breakfast time, even on a weekday. But when Mom and I walked in, I was shocked to find the only other customer there was this lone elderly man who sat in a corner booth by the door. He wasn't even eating or anything, he was just staring at his steaming cup of coffee.

There was a sign that said "SEAT YOURSELF," so I led Mom to a booth across from the counter hoping that it'd result in faster service if we needed it. Not long after we sat down, a freckled-faced girl with long brown hair rushed over to our table, a bright smile stretched across her face.

"Hi, y'all, welcome to Champs," she said, handing us menus. "Can I get you two started with something to drink?"

"Just waters, please," I said, smiling as I admired her beauty. She seemed to be about 18, which begged the question: *What the hell is she doing working here this early on a school day?*

"Alrighty!" she said chipperly. "I'll be right back with those for ya."

I couldn't help but check her out as she walked away. That's when a balled-up napkin hit me in the chest.

"Travis…" Mom said, dragging my name out. "Behave…" She smirked.

Laughing, I grabbed my menu and brought it up to my face to hide from Mom's gaze.

"You like her, don't you?" Mom asked.

In an instant, my cheeks flushed with warmth. "No!" I buried my face back into the menu.

A minute later, I heard rapid footfalls approaching the table. "Ohhh-kay," the waitress said, setting the waters down before us.

"So, y'all made up your minds yet or would you like a little more time?"

Mom looked at me then chuckled. "Yeah, I'll have a blueberry muffin and scrambled eggs."

She scribbled down the order. "And you?"

Between how pretty she was and how embarrassed Mom had me feeling, my face was red hot. I cleared my throat and dropped the menu. "Uh, just a stack of pancakes, please," I said as quickly as possible without making eye contact.

In the corner of my eye, I caught her smiling at me. "Okay! I'll have that out for you folks as soon as I can!"

As soon as she left, I shot a dirty look at my grinning mother. "That wasn't funny," I said through gritted teeth.

"I'm pretty sure seeing you all blushing and nervous made her morning!" Mom said, taking a sip from her water after. "She likes you, by the way."

"No way! My face must've been beet red. If anything, she was probably embarrassed for me."

"No, she thought it was cute. Trust me, I know the eyes."

I took a sip from my water and sighed.

"You should ask for her number," Mom continued.

"No way."

"C'mon, just do it! You two would make a cute couple. And she knows you're out to breakfast with your mom, she's probably—"

"I said no. That's not happening."

"Fine…" Mom said, raising her hands in surrender.

Maybe ten minutes later, the waitress emerged from the kitchen with a tray of food. The second I saw her, it took everything in me to keep my face from lighting up. Then she had to go and flash the prettiest smile I'd ever seen as she set my pancakes down in front of me. As I flashed her a smile back, there was this funny feeling in my chest, like I'd inhaled a cloud of smoke from a burning weed field.

"Is there anything else I can get you two?" she said, looking from me to Mom.

"I think we're good," I croaked.

"Alrighty, just wave if—"

"Question for you," Mom interrupted.

For fuck's sake...

"Ask away!"

"How old are you, dear?" Mom asked. "You look like you should be in school, not working this early on a weekday."

She giggled. "I'm seventeen, ma'am. I do home school, so I work in the mornings to help my mom with bills then I do school stuff in the afternoon so I can take care of my siblings while she's at work."

"I see. It's very admirable that you're helping your mom like that!" Mom said, glancing at me.

"Thanks! Anything for my momma!" she said.

"My Travis here knows all about taking care of his momma!" she smiled at me, as did the waitress.

At the end of the meal, the waitress came by to drop off the receipt and take our plates away.

"Go on," Mom said. "It's now or never." She smirked.

Shaking my head, I pulled two twenties out of my pocket and slapped them on top of the receipt. "Maybe next time," I said, standing up.

"Thanks for stopping in!" the waitress said when we were a few feet from the door, flashing me another dizzying smile from behind the counter. "Hope y'all have a good rest of your day."

"You too!" I replied.

As I walked past the lonely old guy in the corner booth who was still staring at his coffee, something took over me.

"I... uh... forgot something," I said to Mom before hurrying back to the table.

Using the pen the waitress left on the table, I wrote my number on the receipt. I thought of writing a message next to it, something like "*call me*," but I opted to just write my name. As I set the money back on the bottom half of the receipt, I looked up and saw her smiling at me. Blushing, I gave her a thumbs-up like an idiot then hurried out the exit.

When I got outside, Mom was standing by the passenger door with this all-knowing, smug little smirk.

I laughed. "Shut up..."

While I drove, Mom had her window down with her arm out the window, playing like her hand was swimming through the gust of warm air. Mom seemed so captivated by every building and store we drove by that I didn't want to take her home yet, so I wound up cruising aimlessly around town for a while.

My phone was buzzing in my pocket the entire time, so, at every red light, I pulled it out to check and see if the waitress had texted me yet. She hadn't, but I did have a bunch of texts from my customers asking if I was at school and if I'd be able to meet them at lunch so they could buy some weed.

"Is that Tri-City?" she asked as I turned onto Kramer Boulevard.

"I think so," I said, looking through the trees at the big lake in the center of all the greenery.

"Let's go there!" she said excitedly.

After finding a place to park, Mom and I did a lap around the lake, stopping every so often to look at all the ducks out on the water and the honking geese waddling along the shore. On the opposite end of the lake where we started, there was this old guy sitting by the water with a fishing rod in hand, looking just as entranced as the old man from Champs.

Maybe that's just what lonely old men do… They just stare off into nothing, probably thinking about the days when they were young, I thought, staring at him.

"You catch anything good today?" Mom asked the man as she approached him.

The man looked at her surprised, like he hadn't been talked to by anyone for years. "I've only caught two fish since dawn," he said, smiling at us.

Mom looked around. "Where are the fish?"

"This lake is catch and release only, so I put them back in the water after reeling them in."

Mom seemed perplexed by this.

At that moment, the rod jerked in the man's hand. "Looks like I got a bite!" the man said, sitting up straight while reeling it in, yanking the rod in the opposite direction the fish was tugging in. After almost a minute of struggling, the line went limp. "Ah damn… I lost 'em…"

"It's okay!" Mom said. "It was exciting to watch, nonetheless!"

The old man beamed.

I was stunned by how perceptive and chatty Mom was acting that day. It was a complete 180 from the manic-depressive daze she was trapped in when she first came home. Between how she was back at Champs with the whole waitress thing and what'd just happened at the park, it felt like I was starting to see glimpses of her old personality return.

Shortly after saying goodbye to the old fisherman who introduced himself as Albert, we continued the last half of our hike around the lake. Right around the time we were a few yards from the parking lot, Mom halted abruptly. I looked up from my phone and saw that she was squinting hard, massaging her temples.

"You okay, Mom?" I asked.

"Mm-hmm. Just a headache. Can we go home now?" she asked with a groan.

"Yeah, let's go." I took her hand and led her back to the car.

Back at home, I helped Mom to the couch then ran upstairs to get the pills she asked me to grab for her. It wasn't until I saw the Percocet bottle beside the Geodon pills that I realized I hadn't taken any all day. Not only did I not pop any oxy, I also didn't smoke, which made no sense because I'd felt perfectly fine since I woke up.

I can't remember the last time I felt this good sober, I thought, grabbing her meds.

Back downstairs, I popped in the kitchen to get Mom a glass of water then hurried into the living room. "Here you go."

"Thank you, sweetie," she said, taking the water and pills from me. She quickly popped the top off the bottle, took two pills, then washed them down with a big gulp of water. With her eyes closed, she inhaled deeply then let out a nice slow breath. It seemed ritualistic to me, almost as though she were praying for relief as her medication made its way down her throat. After a few moments, she opened her eyes the flashed me a tired smile. "You know... I don't think I've had that much fun since back home."

"Yeah..." I sighed. As great as that outing with Mom was, a wave of melancholy washed over me as I thought about all the other good times Mom and I shared together—memories that involved Dad, fragmented evocations that I'd either suppressed or made myself forget to cope with the loss of my father.

Mom put her hands on her stomach and winced, letting out a little groan. "I'll be right back," she said, rising from the couch.

"Are you okay?" I asked.

"Yeah, it's just the medication." She started up the stairs.

I waited at the base of the stairs until I heard the bathroom door shut. That was my cue to run out to the garden shed. *Can't risk Joan finding the car key in my room or on me if she happens to notice it's missing,* I thought, hiding the key underneath the backpack.

I made it back into the house right as the pipes in the ceiling rattled with the flush of the upstairs toilet. At that same time, the house phone started to ring. Of course, I didn't answer it, I just ignored it the way I always did and headed over to the fridge to grab a soda.

As I chugged my Sprite on the way out of the kitchen, the answering machine beeped and Joan's voicemail response played.

"Hi, this is Gwen Dawson from El Dorado High School," the caller said.

"Shit," I whispered, freezing in the middle of the staircase.

"I'm calling in regard to Travis Hackett," the woman continued. "Apparently, he was absent from all of his morning classes and we have yet to receive a call from a guardian excusing him today. If you could give us a call back—" That's when I shut the machine off.

"Travis?" Mom said from behind me a second later.

I winced before turning around. "Yeah?"

"Was that the school?" she asked.

All I could do was stare at her.

She squinted at me. "There wasn't a senior prank, was there?"

No words came out. I couldn't think of anything to get me out of this now that she'd heard the voicemail.

With a sigh, she looked down at the floor, nodding as though the situation was just starting to make sense. When she finally looked back up at me with disappointment etched on her face, she didn't say anything. She simply walked over to the answering machine and pressed the button to replay the voicemail. And when the woman rattled off the number to call at the end of the message, Mom dialed it. I just stood there like a guilty toddler, watching it happen.

"Yes, El Dorado High School," the woman on the other end answered.

"Mom—" I finally piped up.

She raised her hand to me. "Yes, hi," Mom said. "This is Shauna Hackett. I'm calling about my son, Travis Hackett." She paused. "Yes, I understand… Mm-hmm… I'm sorry. We had a bit of a family emergency and I forgot to call to let you all know he wasn't going to be able to make it in today…" There was another pause. "No, no, everything's fine now, but Travis isn't going to be in for the rest of the day… Okay, thanks for understanding. Bye now." Mom hung up and looked at me with a mix of sadness and anger. "You know, I don't even care that you skipped school, Travis, it's the lying I can't take…"

Her words stung so badly that I couldn't even speak the words she needed to hear. I just stood there and watched her shake her head at me before she walked out of the kitchen. In that moment, I was filled with so much guilt that it felt as though my body deflated. The darkness that had been absent all day returned in a flash, hanging over me like a cloak.

Just as I started towards the stairs, my phone vibrated. Part of me didn't want to be bothered with anyone, but I hated leaving my customers waiting, so I pulled it out to see who it was.

Unknown Number: Hi, Travis! It's Ashley, the waitress from Champs :)

At last, the text I'd spent all morning waiting for had come through, but now that it was here, I didn't want to respond.

What's the point? I wondered, staring at her message. *If I give this girl a shot and things happen to work out, it'd only be a matter of time until I wind up letting her down.* I slipped the phone back into my pocket. *It'd only be a matter of time until she ends up giving me that same look Mom just did, the one that everyone seems to give me eventually…*

Chapter 43

Last Day of May

On the night of Kim Griswold's party, Joan didn't go to bed until 10:30ish. Like every other night that I snuck out for a shindig, I waited until about 30 minutes after hearing my aunt's bed springs groan before sneaking out, just to make sure she was in a deep sleep.

Never in my life was I more paranoid than I was during that walk to Kim's place. Seriously, I must've checked over my shoulder every thirty seconds to make sure I wasn't being followed. With all the product I was hauling, how could I not be paranoid?

Relax, Travis, no one knows what's in the bag other than you, I reminded myself.

That reassurance did nothing to calm my nerves, because another voice quickly contradicted it. *Everyone knows me and what I sell. I'm sure they know I'm going to the party. Maybe they're waiting to ambush me before I get there...*

Maybe I should take some Percs to help me to relax... No, can't do that. I need to be clear headed so I can sell everything and get the hell out of there.

When I arrived at the address that Greg texted me, I found myself standing before a pale gray, three-story house with expertly trimmed shrubbery adorning the front lawn and a fancy stone path leading to the door, adding to the fact that this girl's parents were loaded. Through the open windows, I saw dozens of silhouettes, some standing around while others danced.

It was the usual scene when I walked in—about 30 kids scattered between the living room and kitchen, some sitting around chugging booze or chatting while others texted away on their phones. As I slinked through the crowd, I noticed a bunch of the kids I passed glancing at me only to stare at my backpack like it was the weirdest thing in the world.

As I gripped the bag's straps tighter, someone tapped my shoulder, prompting me to spin around ready to fight. The shocked look on my face melted into a smile when I saw it was just Greg, who was standing there with two girls beside him.

"Hey!" he yelled over the cacophony of chatter and music, "You made it!"

"Damn right I did," I said with a smirk, dapping him up.

"This is Skyler," he said, gesturing to the brunette. Then he pointed to the blonde. "And this is Kim…" He squinted, looking up to the left. "Wait… you guys already know each other."

The blonde cocked her head. "No, I don't think so… Hi, I'm Kim!"

I nodded. "Travis."

Greg looked back and forth between us with his face scrunched in confusion. "Wait, Travis, I thought you said you knew—"

"What's in the backpack? Liquor?" Kim asked.

"Let's go somewhere private and I'll show you."

Kim led us upstairs to her room, then Greg shut and locked the door behind us. As soon as I unzipped the bag and grabbed a handful of weed baggies, Skyler winced from the smell that wafted out.

"Wait," Kim said to Greg, "is this the guy you bought that coke from? The guy you said's been selling weed to everyone?"

"Yeah," Greg said, "but I thought you already knew him—"

"Yeah, that's me," I said, grabbing two dime bags from the small pocket and showing her.

Kim squinted at me. "What're you doing here?"

"I told Greg I knew you so he'd invite me to your party. Figured it'd be a good place to make some sales while making things a bit more fun for your guests," I said, figuring the truth would give me better rapport with her.

Kim glared at me. "My boyfriend's downstairs—a six-foot-two linebacker with lots of scholarship offers. If I wanted to, I could call him up here and he'd throw your ass out."

I smirked. "Yeah, I guess you could. But something tells me if he actually existed, he'd be up here with us already."

She and I stared each other down. The longer we held each other's gaze, the more attracted to her I became. It wasn't just her beauty, it was the fiery feistiness she exuded. Judging by the look in her eyes, something told me she was intrigued by me too.

Eventually, she looked from my eyes to the dime bags in my hand. As soon as she reached for them, I pulled them back.

"Easy," I said. "Money first."

She scowled at me with a little smirk then she turned to Skyler. "How much money do you have?"

"Twenty," Skyler said.

Kim looked at Greg.

"Same. Twenty," he said.

Kim collected the money then handed it to me.

I placed one bag in her palm. "It's 60 for two," I said.

"You're fucking kidding," she said.

I didn't say anything.

Sighing, she grabbed her purse off her dresser, pulled out a crisp 20-dollar bill then handed it to me.

"Pleasure doing business with you," I said, giving her the coke.

"Humph," she grunted, pulling out a little straw from her purse. She then sauntered over to her desk, dumped out a bit of coke, then started cutting the powder into lines with her license.

With a loud sniff, she inhaled one of the lines then rubbed her nose afterwards. "Fuck!" She looked at me, impressed. "Not bad."

I gave her a nod then started towards the door.

"Where are you going?" Kim asked as Greg snorted a line. "You're not gonna do a rail with us?"

"Nope. I'm on the clock." I smirked.

"What, are you scared?" she asked, grinning, her pupils dilated.

Greg eyed me curiously, smiling as fiendishly as she was. And when Skyler finished doing her line, she did the same, extending the straw to me.

Honestly? I was afraid of cocaine, but I didn't want her to know that, so I took the straw from Skyler while maintaining eye contact with Kim.

The remaining line of coke seemed thicker and longer than the ones they all did. I didn't hesitate, I just snorted it as fast as I could. And, when it was over, I winced from the burning in my nostril, relaxing my face before turning back around. "Enjoy the rest," I said, planting the straw in Kim's palm before leaving the room.

From what I saw in movies, I thought coke hit right away. So, when I didn't feel anything on my way downstairs, I thought maybe it was a bad batch or something.

Never mind, I thought as a numbness spread outward from my nose to the rest of my face, then down to my throat. My arms and legs felt tense and relaxed at the same time. My heart felt like it was replaced with a caffeinated hummingbird on... well... coke. *Ah shit... Don't freak out. Just breathe and focus. And keep a grip on these backpack straps.*

The room started to spin. As I stumbled through the living room to the distorted tune of Fall Out Boy's "Dance, Dance," I kept catching people staring at me curiously while others pointed at me before whispering something to their friends. At one point, I almost fell over and had to grab onto some dude's shoulder to keep my balance.

"Travis?" the guy said.

I didn't even look to see who he was, I just kept moving towards the empty spot on the couch. When I finally flopped down on the sofa, I went from staring at my tingling fingers to my eyes darting all around the room, scanning the faces of all the people gawking at me. Having so many eyes on me sent my heart rate from a flutter to what felt like having a crazed prisoner trying to punch his way out of my chest. The next thing I knew, everything went black.

It was a slap to the cheek that snapped me back to consciousness. "What the shit," I groaned, looking up at the person looming above me. "Nigel?" I looked from him to the ten people behind him who were all staring at me, some of whom were recording me with their phones.

"Oh, thank god," he said. "I thought you were dead!"

"How long was I out?" I asked.

"A few minutes," he said.

A flash of panic struck like lightning. *The backpack,* I thought, springing up. When I found the bag wedged between me and the arm rest, a wave of relief washed over me.

Greg appeared to my right, a coke-fueled grin stretched across his face. "Yo, you alright?"

"I'm good," I said, slumping back against the couch.

"Good." Greg waved to someone then a skinny kid wearing a V-neck walked up beside him, followed by a redhead chick who had on so much eyeshadow that she looked like a raccoon. "My friends here are wondering if you've got any more coke?"

The word "coke" made a few people look over.

That's when I sprung up from the sofa and slung the backpack over my shoulder. "Upstairs," I said, gesturing for them to follow me.

After I sold a dime bag to both the raccoon and V-neck, two more girls came into the room and they each bought an eighth of weed. By the time I left the room, there were a bunch of kids in the hall and on the stairs, all of them clamoring to buy some of my *party favors*.

That room became my place of business for the rest of the night. I swear, every time someone left, another person knocked and asked if I still had stuff to sell. Maybe an hour into setting up shop in the room, the backpack was 75% money, 25% drugs. Then, a few customers later, all I had left was a single dime bag of coke.

Just as I was about to leave the room with the skaters who I'd just sold the last of the weed to, Kim appeared in the doorway. "Oh, you're finally done using my room as your pharmacy?" she asked with a smirk.

"Yup," I said, winking at her.

"It seems you're pretty famous downstairs," she said.

"Probably because I sold to half the party."

"And half the school, apparently."

"And that." I grinned.

"Apparently that's not all you're famous for. I just heard you started a fight at a party the first week of school. That true?"

"It is."

"Did you also send one of the kids to the hospital?"

I shrugged. "Maybe. Who knows?"

"Hmm… You're not going to do something like that here tonight, are you?"

"Not unless someone tries to kick my ass," I said, walking up to her. "Now, if you'll excuse me."

She put a hand on my chest. "Where are you going?"

"I got one more sale to make."

"Why leave if you've got a perfectly good customer standing right in front of you?" Smiling naughtily, she held up a twenty and a ten. Right as I reached for the money, she yanked her hand back. "Easy there," she said. "Coke first."

Without breaking eye contact, I unzipped the small pocket and pulled out the last dime bag. "Same time," I said.

"Same time," she whispered back.

Something about the way she looked at me had my heart racing. And I knew she was the reason since I had pretty much come down from the coke by then.

During the swap, my fingers caressed hers as I took the money from her.

Her face lit up. "Now that you've made you're final sale, how about you celebrate with your last customer of the night?" she said in this seductive voice.

The way my heart started thumping, it was like I'd done another line of coke. "As much as I'd like to, I should really go—"

"Where?" she asked, cutting me off.

I didn't answer.

"Exactly." She pushed me back then shut the door behind her.

Kim opened the tiny baggie, dumped some powder out onto her pinky nail then snorted it. Without missing a beat, she tapped out another bump onto her nail then held it out to my face.

Unlike last time, I hesitated, staring at it unsurely.

"So, tonight *was* your first time doing coke?" she asked.

"No. I've done it a bunch of times."

She smirked as if to call me out on my bullshit. "Well, what are you waiting for?" She inched her finger a bit closer to my nose. "Since you're such a *man* and all."

After that first line, I never want to do coke again, I thought, trying to keep my face from showing her how panicked I was.

Kim cocked her head. "Unless you're not one in which case I can just find someone else to—" She stopped mid-sentence when I leaned in and snorted the powder from her pinky nail.

I sniffled, brushing my burning nose. "Happy?"

She shook her head. "You know what else a real man would do? Kiss me."

At the exact second that I pressed my lips against hers, the coke kicked in. While we made out, she steered me back to her bed. That's when I took off my backpack and tossed it towards her desk. After the back of my legs collided with the mattress, I toppled over and she fell on top of me.

She pulled away abruptly just as I started caressing her back. "Did you hear that?"

"Hear wha—" I started to say, my words trailing off when I heard the commotion downstairs. It was a mix of kids hollering coupled with what sounded like a stampede of gazelles running up the stairs and down the hallway.

Out of nowhere, the door burst open and this dude ran into the room all wide-eyed. "Cops!" he yelled, sprinting for the window beside her bed.

Another kid raced in right behind him. "Cops!" he parroted more breathlessly.

Kim scrambled off of me then I sprung up and raced over to the window.

"C'mon, let's go!" I yelled when I saw she was still in bed.

"Where?" she shouted. "This is my house!"

"Police! Everyone stay right where you are," a cop's voice boomed from downstairs.

By the time I looked back over to the window, the first guy was helping his friend climb out onto the roof. In my coke-fueled frenzy, I didn't even take the time to look down and check to see how far down the roof was, I just climbed out legs first like the second guy did. The instant I felt the shingles beneath my sneakers, I turned towards the direction of the two roof-runner's footfalls and bolted after them. As I ran across the slanted surface towards' the part of the roof that extended over the backyard, I looked down at all the kids racing across the yard and those scrambling over the fence.

Suddenly, a bright light shone past me. "Get back inside!" a cop shouted from Kim's window.

That's when I jumped off the roof. Pain flared in my ankles and knees when I hit the grass, then I went into a tumble as kids trampled by me. After that, I ran—over the fence and through the back yards of a couple of houses until I eventually hopped over one last fence and landed on the sidewalk. Red and blue lights flashed behind me as a pack of kids sprinted by, followed by the sweeping light of a cop's flashlight as he ran towards us.

It wasn't until I stopped to hide in some shrubs two blocks later that I realized I had forgotten something.

Shit… the backpack. I don't have the backpack…

Chapter 44

June 1ˢᵗ

Please tell me last night was just a nightmare. That was the first thought that crossed my mind when I woke up the following Saturday. It wasn't until I took my first deep breath that I noticed how irritated my right nostril and sinuses were. *That's right, my nose burns because I snorted cocaine last night… twice…* Then I rolled over and noticed how sore my thighs were and how badly my knees ached. *You're in pain because you jumped off a ten-foot-high roof and ran almost a mile from cops last night. You ran all the way back home without the bag full of Pierce's money…*

"Shit…" I whispered, staring at my ceiling, my heart racing from the panic that ensued.

For a while, I laid there on my back listening to the birds chirping outside my window, my body paralyzed by the uncertainty that awaited me when I showed up to Pierce's apartment later without what I imagine was close to $1,100.

A knock at my door startled me so bad that I sprung out of bed. *It's Pierce! He's coming to collect,* I thought. But then the door opened and, for the first time in my life, I was relieved to see Joan.

"Travis?" she asked, eyeing me curiously. Her face was all done up like she was about to hit the town. "It's three o'clock in the afternoon. What are you still doing in bed?"

"Didn't sleep too well last night."

"Oh… Well… I was thinking maybe me, you, and Shauna could go out today. You said you wanted to take her to the park or a diner or something, right? We could do that."

"Maybe tomorrow… I'm not feeling so good right now."

"Oh, okay," she said. She looked like she was about to leave, but she ended up lingering in the doorway. "Are you sure?"

I nodded, avoiding eye contact.

"Well, we're gonna go out for a little while. Feel better, okay?" She shut the door.

A minute or so later, there was another knock.

"Honey?" Mom said. "Can I come in?"

"Yeah," I said.

Mom gave me this pitiful smile as she walked towards me. Then, just like she used to when I wasn't feeling well as a kid, she sat on the edge of my bed and put her hand on my forehead. "You don't have a fever… What's wrong, sweetie?"

"I'm just not feeling good, is all," I said.

"Well, maybe some fresh air will make you feel better."

"I think I just need some sleep. You guys have fun though."

"Okay…" she said disappointedly. "If you need anything, call Joan." She rose from the edge of the bed.

"Will do," I groaned.

She flashed me one last smile then walked out, shutting the door behind her.

When Mom and Joan left the house a few minutes later, I headed to the bathroom to grab some Advil for my pounding headache only to find out there was only one pill left. *Percocets it is,* I thought, heading back to my room.

"Shit," I said, stopping in the middle of the hall, remembering I was out of pills. That's when my eyes wandered over to Mom's door.

I didn't even hesitate to walk in there and grab the Percocet bottle from her dresser. *No… I don't want to waste her pills if I'm not going to smoke too,* I thought, setting the pills back down. *And I can't really smoke all the Plushberry that Pierce gave me considering I left all five baggies in the goddamn backpack.*

After fishing my phone out of my pocket, I sat on the edge of her bed then dialed up Johnny.

To my surprise, he answered after a few rings. "Travis?"

"Hey," I said. "What're you up to?"

"Nothing. I'm at my dad's. Why?"

"You, uh… you want to hang out?"

"Now?"

"Yeah, the sooner the better."

"Kylie's over so…"

"That's fine. Bring her too."

"Is that Travis?" I heard Kylie say in the background.

"Yup," he said. "He wants to hang out. Hold on, Travis." There was some rustling, then everything sounded all muffled for a bit like he covered the mic with his hand. "Okay, we're down, but it'll be a few hours before we get there."

"That's fine," I said, strolling over to the window to make sure Mom and Joan didn't come back for something.

"What do you wanna do?" he asked.

"Right now, all I want to do is get out of the house. We can figure out the plan when you get here."

"Okay. We'll be at your place around five or six."

"Sounds good."

As I was sliding the phone back into my pocket, I looked down and saw that the dead bird that mom was looking at the day she came home was still there. Its rotting body was swarming with an army of ants. They were crawling on its bones, scavenging whatever decayed flesh remained. The ants trailed in and out of its empty eye sockets and along its cracked spine, feasting without remorse or respect for what the thing was before it had cracked its head on the glass and died.

The sun was setting when Johnny texted that he was outside. Before I left, I popped into Mom's room again and pocketed her bottle of Oxycodone. With each step I took after that, the damn pills rattled like crazy, so I stopped in the bathroom and grabbed some toilet paper, stuffing it into the bottle on the way down the stairs.

Johnny was leaning against the car when I walked outside. As I approached him, we stared at one another for a moment before we both smiled and hugged each other.

"How you doing, man?" Johnny asked. "You good?"

"I've been better," I said, looking at Kylie, who was in the passenger seat giving me the dirtiest fucking look. "Guessing she's not happy to be hanging out with me today?" I whispered.

"Meh, we talked about it on the way over and she's cool. It's not like we were really doing anything anyway."

"Gotcha. Well, I'll try not to be a dick today."

He chuckled. "Good to hear. So, where are we going?"

"Let's just get as far away from here as we can."

"Copy that."

"Hi, Kylie," I said as I climbed in the back seat.

She waited a beat before responding. "Hi, Travis." She looked to Johnny. "So, now that we drove all this way, what's the plan?"

"Not sure," I said. "I didn't really have one."

"Shocking…" she sassed.

"Kylie," Johnny said sternly.

"You guys hungry?" I asked.

"Yeah, I could eat," Johnny said. "Babe?"

Kylie let out a long-winded sigh. "Sure."

"You guys ever been to Champs?" I asked.

"Yeah," Johnny said. "Not since I was a kid though. *That's* where you wanna go?"

"Yeah," I said bluntly.

Johnny looked at Kylie for approval.

She just sat there for a moment before nodding slowly.

"Champs it is," Johnny said, starting the car and backing out of the driveway.

From the time we left the house until we made it to the light outside my neighborhood, an awkward silence permeated the car. That is, until Johnny cleared his throat and looked at me in the rearview mirror.

"So," he said, "you hear about that party last night?"

My heart skipped a beat. "Yeah."

"Kylie saw on Myspace that the fucking cops swarmed the place and arrested a bunch of kids for having weed and shit. Someone said something about coke. You hear anything about that?"

"Yep."

"Were you there?"

"Nope."

"Really," Kylie said, turning to me. "Cuz my friend Fiona was there, and she told me she saw you."

That got my blood boiling, but I was able to suppress the urge to snap at her. "Well, she must've been messed up because I wasn't there," I said calmly.

"Well, she doesn't drink or do drugs, so…"

"Babe," Johnny said, "if he said he wasn't there, he wasn't there. Just stop, okay?"

Smirking at the fact that Johnny finally took my side for once, I looked out the window. *Now how the hell am I going to buy weed with her in the car?* I wondered, my smile fading. *Better question: Who the hell am I going to buy weed from since there's no way I can go to Pierce's…*

By the time Johnny pulled into the Champs parking lot, there was only a sliver of the burnt orange sun peeking up over the horizon.

"Holy shit," Johnny said, pulling into a spot near the door. "I haven't been here since I was like five."

"On second thought," Kylie said, turning to Johnny. "I can't do this. Can we just go somewhere else, please?" There was panic in her voice.

"Why? What's wrong with this place?" Johnny asked.

"I just can't, okay?" she shouted.

Jesus, what the hell happened to her here, a bad case of food poisoning?

Johnny placed a hand on her shoulder. "Hey, look at me…"

She looked up at him like a traumatized little girl.

"Just breathe," he said calmly. "I'll take us somewhere else." He turned to me. "Travis—"

I raised a hand. "It's cool, we can go wherever."

With a nod, Johnny shifted into reverse.

As we cruised down the street looking for another eatery, Kylie started hyperventilating.

"Kylie?" Johnny said, glancing over at her. "Are you okay?"

She pointed at something ahead. "Can you stop in that alley?" She then opened the glove compartment and pulled out a baggie of weed.

Wait, what? I thought. *Who the hell did she buy that from? You know what? I don't even care…*

"Maybe we should find a better spot to smoke," Johnny said as he pulled over and peered down the alley.

"Yeah," I chimed in. "Let's go somewhere we know is safe. What about the usual spot?"

"What usual spot? You mean that parking lot at the dentist's office?" Johnny asked.

"Yup," I said.

"Fine, whatever," Kylie muttered.

"I didn't even know you guys were still smoking," I said, looking at Johnny. "I thought she made you quit."

Kylie twisted in her seat to face me. "I didn't *make* him do anything. Believe it or not, he's able to make his own decisions."

Once again, it took everything in me not to explode. "Whoa," I said with a smirk, raising my hands in surrender. "Didn't mean to piss you off. I was just confused why you had weed if you quit, that's all."

"I started keeping some for emergencies, and that's all you need to know," she snapped.

"Fair enough," I said, slouching back in my seat.

With Kylie dealing with whatever got her all freaked out back at Champs and with me busy brainstorming a way to keep Pierce from killing me, the car was nice and quiet during our night-time parking lot smoke session. That is, until my phone started ringing.

In an instant, I went from relaxed to freaking the hell out thinking that Pierce was calling to ask about his money. Thankfully it wasn't him, it was Joan. Not that her calling was much better.

"Shit," I said to myself.

"What?" Johnny asked.

"Hold on. I gotta take this." I got out of the car and walked a little bit away before answering. "Hello?"

"Are you serious, Travis?!" Joan yelled.

"Joan, just calm down—"

"Don't you fucking *dare* tell me to calm down!"

"I'm just hanging out with my friends. I'll be back soon."

"Let me guess, you're with your little stoner buddies, right? You'll hang out with them at the drop of a hat, but you won't hang out with your mom? By the way, she's been worried sick about you since we left."

My stomach twisted into a knot and I felt sick to my stomach. "Joan, I just—"

"What? You just *what*? Go ahead. What bullshit are you going to tell me this time?"

Nothing came to me. Even if I had a good lie to tell her, the second I walked in, she'd smell the stench of weed on me.

"You know what? Fuck it. Don't come home tonight."

"What?" I asked.

"Yeah, just spend all night getting high with your friends. Don't worry about me or your mom! Just do whatever the hell you want since that's all you ever do anyways!" The call ended.

Johnny gave me this concerned look as I walked back to the car. "Everything alright?" he asked.

"Yeah," I said through a sigh. "Let's finish up and get some food. My stomach feels weird."

The Taco Bell down the street is where we ended up. Kylie and Johnny chatted during the meal, but I was quiet the entire time. All I could think about was Mom worrying about me all day only to come home and find out that I lied to her yet again so I could hang out with friends instead of her. Thinking about how hurt she must've been made me so nauseous that, halfway through my second taco, it was getting hard to eat. When salty bile rushed up my throat, I stopped mid-bite, dropped my food, and raced to the bathroom. I just barely made it to the toilet when everything I'd eaten came rushing out of my mouth like a geyser.

"Holy shit," Johnny said to me when he saw me walking back to the table. "Did you just throw up?"

"No. I'm fine," I said.

"You don't look fine. You look pale as hell."

I took a few sips of Sprite hoping it'd settle my stomach, then I looked out the window. "Let's go to Tri-City."

"And do what?" Kylie asked.

"Finish smoking."

"I don't know," Johnny said. "It's getting late. I told my dad I'd be home in half an hour."

"So, you'll be a little late. He'll get over it. C'mon," I said. That's when I got up and started putting on my jacket.

"I should probably get home too," Kylie said.

"Why don't we just go tomorrow?" Johnny asked.

I threw my hands in the air. "Fuck it. I'll just go myself." I stormed off towards the exit.

"Travis, what's going on?" Johnny asked as he ran outside after me.

"Don't worry about it," I said over my shoulder. "Just go with Kylie."

"Dude, just let me drive you home! You're being ridiculous."

I didn't turn around. I didn't say anything. I just kept marching towards the road. *Home is the last place I want to be. All I want to do is go back to the last place I felt happy—the last place everything felt okay.*

Maybe a minute later, a car pulled up alongside the curb next to me. "Get in," Johnny yelled.

I ignored him again.

"Let's just go," Kylie said.

"Do what she says, Johnny," I shouted back.

"Alright," Johnny said. "We'll go to Tri-City. Just get in."

"Johnny, I can't—" Kylie whined.

"Kylie, we'll just smoke a bowl and leave, okay?" he said.

"Fine. Whatever."

"You hear that, Travis?" he shouted. "Will you get in now?"

"Fine," I said, climbing in the back seat.

"Alright, how do we get there?" Johnny asked.

"You know what," I said, opening the door I just slammed shut, "just let me drive."

Chapter 45

June
Minutes after the arrest...

And that's how I got arrested, I thought after reflecting on everything that led me to walking down that dark, desolate road in the middle of who the hell knows where.

I guess being stranded out here is better than being in a jail cell all night. At that exact moment, there was yipping and howling somewhere not too far behind me. *Actually, I think a night in a cell would be better than getting mauled by coyotes...*

Twenty minutes into my walk in what I hoped was the right direction, I heard the faint rumble of a car engine up ahead. Not long after, the glow of headlights crested over the hilly road before me. As soon as the dull yellow light bathed me, I started flailing my arms in a panic.

"Oh, thank god," I said to myself as the beat-up truck pulled to a stop. When I walked over to the passenger door, the driver clicked on their dome lights, and my jaw dropped. It was the old man from my neighborhood whose trash cans I hit—the neighbor who called the cops on me over nothing.

It was clear by how his eyes widened that he recognized me. Then his shock twisted into a wicked smirk as he began to laugh.

I rolled my eyes. "Look, I get it, alright?"

The old man cackled at the horrible irony of the situation.

"I know I don't have the right to ask this of you, but can you just drive me home? Please?"

"Sure, I'll give you a ride if you can answer *one* question..."

"Okay…"

"What's my name, boy?"

My body went rigid as my eyes widened. *Ah shit… I have no idea…*

"That's what I thought!" He laughed hysterically as he sped off down the road, honking his horn wildly to taunt me.

"Dick…" I said, shaking my head as I continued in the direction he drove, hoping home was where he was heading.

The longer I walked, the harder it got to keep myself from collapsing. It wasn't just fatigue from the trek, but the combination of the pills that I popped before getting arrested and the weed had my legs feeling super wobbly and had me drowsy as all hell.

Right as I was about to take a break, another pair of headlights appeared ahead. Thankfully, the driver pulled over as soon as they saw me flagging them down.

The middle-aged Mexican woman rolled down her window. "Oh my god!" she said with a slight accent. "What are you doing out here by yourself?"

"Someone thought it'd be funny to abandon me out here."

"Oh my…" she gasped.

"Is there any way you can you drive me into town? Please?"

"Which town?"

"I live in Placentia, about two miles from El Dorado High School. Anywhere near there would be fine."

She studied me for a moment. "Okay," she said, leaning over and unlocking her passenger door. "Get in."

"Thanks," I said, climbing in.

As she pulled back onto the road, she looked over at me. "You poor thing, you're shivering. Here, let me put on the heat for you."

As she was fiddling with the knob, something big jumped out onto the road in front of us. When it turned to face us, its eyes glinted from her headlights, but the thing didn't move.

"Brake! Brake! Brake!" I yelled.

The woman gasped as her gaze snapped back to the road, then our bodies jerked forward when she slammed on the breaks. The car screeched to a stop a few feet from this large coyote that was twice the size of the dogs in my neighborhood. The thing just stood frozen in the middle of the road, staring at me through the windshield.

Is that what I heard howling a little while ago? Shit… If I was still walking, I would've run right into him… As that thought crossed my mind, three more coyotes emerged from the trees and brush, all smaller than the first one.

That's when the woman shouted something in Spanish and honked the horn, scaring them off back into the shadows.

Chapter 46

"Which house is it?" the Mexican lady asked as she cruised down my street.

"Right here's good," I said, pointing at the corner home four houses down from mine.

"Alright," she said, pulling over.

I unbuckled my seatbelt. "Well, thank you for the ride."

"You're welcome," she said with a warm smile.

I opened the door and started to climb out only to stop and turn back to her. "I'm sorry, I didn't get your name. I'm Travis."

"Gloria," she said.

"Thank you, Gloria," I said with a nod, climbing out of the car after.

"Don't worry about it, Travis. Try not to get yourself in any more trouble."

"I'll do my best," I said, shutting the door.

As I dragged my feet towards the silhouette of my house, Joan's words from earlier echoed in my mind. *Don't come home tonight… Yeah, just spend all night getting high with your friends. Don't worry about me or your mom! Just do whatever the hell you want since that's all you ever do anyways!'*

When I passed my mailbox, I halted at the edge of the driveway and stared at the house with the same disdain everyone tends to look at me with eventually. *Maybe I shouldn't go home. Ever. If I do, whether it's today or tomorrow, it'll just be the same bullshit day after day after day. I'm just going to get yelled at then I'm going to lock myself in my room until it's time to sneak out to get high like usual. Then I'll do something to piss off Joan or hurt Mom and go through the same cycle all over again. I can't keep putting Mom through that, but I can't change who I am… Maybe I should just run away and leave this town for good.*

That's when I remembered that my car key was still stashed in the shed under the soil bags where I used to keep the backpack.

Without missing a beat, I bolted over to the side gate, sprinted across the backyard, then opened the noisy shed door as slowly and quietly as possible. *All I got to do is get my car out of the garage without waking Joan and I'm free,* I thought, slipping the key into my pocket as I closed the shed door stealthily behind me.

Thankfully, our garage didn't have one of those automatic openers, which was nice because it meant I could lift it open as slowly as I needed to in order to keep from making noise. I was so hellbent on getting out of there as quickly and quietly as possible that I didn't even stop to go back and close the garage after I pulled out onto the street. I did, however, stop on the way out of the neighborhood when I saw the beat-up truck belonging to the old man who chose to leave me stranded in the middle of nowhere out of spite. And, because I was feeling equally spiteful, I got out, grabbed a rock from his front yard and chucked it at his windshield, shattering it. The last thing I saw before I peeled out was his downstairs lights coming on.

My first thought when I pulled onto the main road was to just head east. There was no other reason for picking that direction other than the fact that it was the quickest way to get out of California—the best way to go to get me as far away from that town as possible.

Am I really going to do this? It's not like anyone would care if I was gone. I mean, I guess Mom would, but that's only because she hasn't fully realized that me being in her life would only end in heartache. If I stay, it'd probably take two or three more of my screw-ups to realize that having me was the worst thing that's ever happened to her. If I stay, she'll only end up looking at me with the same vitriol and disgust as Joan and everyone else does.

"Fuck it," I said, taking a sharp right onto CA-91 East, my eyes wandering down to the gas gauge.

How far do you think you're going to get on a little under a half tank of gas with no money, dipshit?

When I looked back up, I saw a sign for Corona. *Maybe Johnny can spot me some money. Yeah… worth a shot. And it would be nice to have one last goodbye before I skipped town.*

Right as I fished the phone from my pocket to call him, it started buzzing in my hand. I'd expected to see Joan's name when I looked down but, instead, I found it was Pierce who was calling me.

"Shit!" I shouted.

Should I answer?

You might as well. He's your friend, so maybe he'll understand what happened when I explain it to him. Maybe he'll let me crash at his place until I can work off what I owe him, then I can leave town when I have enough money saved. I've got nothing else to lose.

"Hello?" I answered.

"Travis," Pierce answered sternly, "Saturday's almost come and gone. You know I don't like people who don't keep their promises…"

"I know. It's just… these last 48 hours have been crazy, dude."

Pierce paused for a moment. "Crazy how?"

"I honestly don't think I can tell you everything over the phone before it dies."

"Then why don't you come on over, drop off the money, and we'll talk about it?

My heart started racing so fast that my vision pulsed with each beat.

"Hello?" Pierce said after my long pause.

"Sorry," I said. "Reception out here's awful."

"Where are you?"

"About halfway to Corona."

"The fuck you doing all the way out there?"

"Gotta see a friend about something then I'll head over to your place."

"Alright. Give me a time."

During my pause, I gripped the wheel so tight that my bones hurt. *What can I tell him that won't piss him off?*

"God damn it, you still there, Travis?"

"Sorry… Uh… I'm probably going to be at my friend's for a while, so maybe in the morning?" I said, staring at the raindrops that had just hit my windshield.

"Give me a *time*," he sneered.

"How about between nine or ten o'clock?"

He sighed. "You're killing me, Travis. Alright, that's fine. Don't be late, got it?"

"Yeah. Got it."

The drizzle had turned into a goddamn monsoon by the time I got to Corona. Since I had no clue where Johnny even lived, I drove through town until I found a place to pull over that didn't look like somewhere I'd get murdered. What I eventually settled on was the well-lit parking lot for the hospital on Main Street that was a quarter mile or so from the freeway exit. Unfortunately, when I finally got around to calling Johnny, it went straight to voicemail.

"You've got to be kidding me," I grumbled, slumping into a slouch.

Now that I was no longer driving, my lids started getting heavy. *I guess I can sleep here until morning,* I thought, scanning the parking lot. In a matter of minutes, I fell asleep to the sound of rain beating against my hood.

The sun woke me up around nine the next morning. Still half asleep, I felt around for my phone, squinted at the screen and redialed Johnny.

"Travis?" Johnny answered, sounding more excited than I'd ever heard him. "Holy shit!"

"Yeah, I know. Listen, what's your dad's address?"

"Wait, why?"

"Because I'm in Corona."

"What are you doing here this early? And how are you not in jail right now?"

"Long story. I'll tell you everything when I see you."

"Okay. You can't come over now though. It's Sunday. Dad's here."

"Well, is he going out at all today?"

"I don't think so, and I probably won't be able to get out of the house until he goes to bed tonight."

"Shit… are you kidding? What time does he go to bed?"

"After dinner—around eight probably."

"The hell am I supposed to do all day in this shithole town?"

"Dude, you're the one who showed up out of nowhere without calling first."

"I did call. Last night around eleven. Your phone was off."

"Oh… yeah…" he said. "After what happened last night, I didn't want to talk to anyone."

"You mean after I got arrested?"

"No, after that."

His dad started yelling in background.

"Listen, I gotta go, Travis. I'll tell you everything tonight, alright?"

"Fine," I said, shaking my head. "Call me when you're ready."

As soon as I hung up the phone, it started buzzing again. *Shit, it's Joan… There's no way I can deal with her right now.*

I waited for the call to end before texting Pierce that I wouldn't be able to meet up with him until later that night. After that, I rolled the windows down, crawled into the backseat, and laid there until I fell back asleep.

"Holy shit," I groaned when I woke up and saw it was dark out. My eyes then wandered to the phone I just grabbed from the floor of the car. "7:32... How did I sleep almost eleven hours?"

Ignoring the 20 missed calls from Joan, I opened my messages and wound up clicking on the 10 texts from her instead.

Joan text 1: YOU DID NOT TAKE YOUR CAR AND LEAVE THE GARAGE DOOR OPEN ALL NIGHT... PICK UP YOUR PHONE!

Joan text 2: PICK UP YOUR GOD DAMN PHONE, TRAVIS!

Joan text 3: TRAVIS ANSWER THE PHONE OR IM CALLING THE FUCKING COPS!!!

The rest of the texts were about the same, so I backed out after reading that third one and clicked my way down to the text from Johnny that had directions to his place from the Main Street exit. Right before I could hit send on my text to Johnny, he called.

"Hey," I said groggily.

"Come over now," he said breathlessly, like he was running. "Hurry!"

"Is everything alright?"

"Just hurry! I already sent you directions. Just look for an apartment complex called Cinnamon Tree. When you get there, flash your lights and I'll come down."

It took about six minutes to get to the complex. Not long after I parked and flashed my lights, the bushes near the far end of the building shook then Johnny popped out of the brush all wide-eyed like a damn prairie dog. After looking both ways, he sprinted to the car.

"Drive," he said before he even got in.

"Shit, alright!" I said, shifting into reverse as soon as he slammed the door. "Where we going?"

"I don't give a shit," he snapped. "Just drive."

"Dude, what happened?"

He didn't answer. All I heard was him sniffling. By the time I turned around, his jaw was trembling and there was a tear rolling down his cheek.

"Johnny, what's wrong?"

He just started full-on crying. "I hate it here! I fucking hate everything!"

"Holy shit... Alright, I'm pulling over," I said, turning down the first alley I saw.

"I can't fucking take it anymore."

"Talk to me. Tell me what happened." That's all I could think to say because consoling crying people was never something I was good at.

He shook his head, snorted really hard then sighed. The crying stopped after that.

"Did something happen with Kylie?" I asked.

"That's part of it," he muttered. "We broke up."

"Ah shit," I said, fighting off the urge to smile. "What happened?"

"Doesn't matter," he said.

I patted his shoulder. "You'll be alright, man. It's her loss."

With a grunt, Johnny wiped his tears then looked out the window.

"So..." I said, breaking the silence. "What happened back at home that had you hiding in the bushes?"

"Me and my dad got in a big fight. Pretty sure he's going to kick me out."

"Damn, so… what are you going to do—"

"I don't want to talk about my shit anymore," he interrupted, turning to me with rage in his eyes that slowly melted away. "How'd you get out?"

"From where?"

"That cop car."

"Oh, yeah… Long story."

"What do you mean? Are you on the run or something?"

"No, no. Let's just say they fucked up big time and I worked out a deal with them."

He sat there blinking at me. "Seriously? That's all you're gonna tell me?"

"Yeah. I promised not to talk, and I'd rather not risk it."

"So you drove all the way down here to tell me that?" he asked.

"Not exactly."

"Then why?"

I zoned out and tried to put together the right words to tell him that I was running away and why I had to skip town.

"Also," he said, snapping me out of my trance, "I thought Joan wasn't letting you drive this car anymore…"

"Yeah…" I said, looking down at my ringing phone. When I saw Joan's name on the screen, I dismissed the call, took the battery out of my phone, then dropped it and the cell in the cup holder.

"What's going on?" Johnny asked.

I started the car and drove it through the alleyway, picking up speed the further I went.

"Travis, where are we going, man?"

"I need you to trust me, alright? Do you trust me?"

His eyes went wide. "Sure, I trust you."

"Good." When I saw what looked like a cop car behind me, I started staring at the rearview mirror all paranoid, worrying that they were hunting me down after Joan reported me missing or whatever. "Alright, look. Here's the situation," I said. "I've been selling drugs the past few months, mainly to kids at school."

"Wait… what?"

"Remember that guy Pierce you met?"

"Yeah…"

"Well, we've been working together and, uh, long story short, I lost about a grand of his money at a party. On top of all that, I really fucked up with Mom and Joan. So now, I'm going somewhere… I don't know where, but I want you to come with me."

"Where?"

"Somewhere in the Midwest maybe? Somewhere far away from all this shit."

"And how the hell are we going to survive on our own?"

"We'll figure it out," I said.

"How?" he asked.

"You said you trusted me, didn't you?"

"Yeah… but—"

"Didn't you just say you hated it here? Then come with me so we can get away from all this shit. Your dad, your mom, Kylie, anyone who's ever pissed you off—we can leave it all behind. But I need you to be with me on this. I need you to trust me." When we stopped at a red light, I turned to him and extended my hand, staring deep into his blue eyes. "We're brothers, right?"

"Yeah," he said, looking down at my hand before meeting my gaze again. "But I can't run away. As bad as I want to, I can't."

"But—"

"Just take me home," he said.

I could tell by the serious look on his face that there was no convincing him, so I turned down the next road, bound for his apartment.

Johnny and I didn't talk during that short drive back to his place. He was off in his own world and I was off in mine, trying to figure out what I was going to do next.

"So," I said, pulling into a spot by the bushes he hid in earlier, "this is it, huh?"

"Travis," he said, turning to me with a partial smile. "Why don't you just stay?"

"Stay and do what?"

He shrugged. "I don't know, but I know you'll figure that out. Kids get in trouble all the time and they all figure it out eventually, right?"

"Right… and all the bums, prisoners, and drug addicts of the world have it all figured out, right?"

"You don't have to be one of those people, Travis. You're a smart guy, you're resourceful as hell, and I've seen you talk your way out of tons of situations," he said with a smirk. "If there's anyone who can get themselves out of a shitty situation, it's you, so there's no reason to run away. Make things right with your aunt and mom, figure out shit with that Pierce guy, and try to make some serious changes then things will work out."

"You say that like I'm not someone people are destined to hate eventually."

Johnny just stared at me. Probably because deep down he knew it was true. And, right as he opened his mouth to speak, something behind me made his eyes go wide. "Oh shit!" he blurted out.

My head snapped to the left and I saw his dad charging towards the car.

"Lock the doors!" Johnny shouted.

Before I could, Mr. Castillo pulled open Johnny's door, grabbed him, then yanked him out of the passenger seat.

"Stop! Dad, stop!" Johnny yelled as his dad dragged him towards the two silhouettes standing near the stairs.

Mr. Castillo basically threw Johnny into the towering silhouette that was his brother Glenn before turning around and stalking back towards my car.

That's when I opened my door and climbed out. "Listen, Mr. Castillo," I said, raising my hands in surrender, "I know you're upset but lemme explain—"

In a blur, his massive hand went from hanging at his side to slapping me across the face. All I could feel was this burning and throbbing in my cheek as I stumbled back into the rear driver's side door.

"You have 10 seconds to get back in your car and get the fuck out of here before I whoop your skinny little ass up and down this parking lot for everyone to see."

As I stood there staring at the fuming man before me, something about the look in his eyes and the anger etched on his face reminded me of the look Joan had given me countless times over the years. My gaze wandered from Mr. Castillo to Johnny, who seemed to be in shock at what his father just did to me. Then I glanced over at the slender figure behind him—some skin and bones kid with a gaunt face I just barely recognized. It was Brad. He looked totally unrecognizable to the kid I'd met over a year ago. His face was sunken in and looked just like mine had the past few days—tired and pillaged of all emotion.

While Glenn and their dad glared at me with malice, the way Brad looked at me reminded me of the disappointed look Mom gave me after I lied to her about why I wasn't at school. The faint connection I felt between us was tainted by regret. I couldn't help but feel that maybe if I'd acted differently things would've turned out better for the both of us. But it was what it was. And things were the way they were because of me.

When my eyes snapped back to Johnny, I flashed him a sympathetic look then climbed back in the car. After that, I sped off. The last thing I saw in the rearview was Mr. Castillo hugging Johnny. For some reason, the image of his dad embracing him after what had just went down haunted my thoughts the entire time I was on the freeway. And that image of them didn't leave my mind until my car began making this annoying-ass beeping sound.

Shit, I thought, looking at the low fuel indicator light flashing on my dash. *I forgot to ask Johnny for some cash before his dad showed up… How the hell am I going to make it out of town now?*

Chapter 47

What am I even doing here? I wondered as I pulled up to Pierce's apartment just after 10:20 P.M. My eyes wandered down to the gas gauge needle hovering over **E**. *And what the hell am I going to do if he decides not to help me?*

As I walked to his apartment, I wasn't entirely sure if I was stupid, a glutton for punishment, or if I was just really hopeful for no reason. My guess was all three.

Here we go, I thought, taking a deep breath before knocking on his door.

Pierce opened the door, smiling like he was impressed about something.

"What?" I asked after being stared at for a few seconds.

"Two minutes early," Pierce said, stepping aside so I could enter. "That's a first." As I walked past him, he looked behind me and his smile faded. "Uh… where's the bag, Trav—"

"That's what I wanted to talk to you about," I interrupted.

Pierce slammed the door and got closer. "Where. Is. The. Bag?"

"Okay, here's the thing…" My words trailed off as my heart beat thumped loudly in my ears. "I, uh…I lost the backpack…"

The way Pierce didn't breathe, blink, or move, it was like he turned into a wax sculpture.

"That party I went to," I continued. "Cops stormed the place and I accidentally left it when I was trying to get out of there."

"The cops took it?" Pierce said.

I nodded.

"The cops have my drugs," he said calmly, which somehow made it even more threatening.

"No! I sold everything before they showed up!"

Pierce slowly nodded as he walked over to the counter and grabbed his steaming mug. "Get out."

"Pierce, listen to me. I know I fucked up but it wasn't my fault!"

"I said get out."

"Pierce—"

Pierce threw his mug so fast that I didn't even know what was happening until hot tea splashed my arm a second before the mug shattered against the wall behind me.

"Travis," he said, his eyes bulging from the rage building up inside of him. "I'm trying to make this easy for the both of us, so please. Get. Out."

"I can't!" I said. "I've got nowhere to go! Pierce, everything around me has gone to shit. And I know that I fucked up, but please, I just... I just really need a friend right now."

Pierce's narrowed gaze burned into my eyes. "Travis, I *really* need you to walk through that door and never come back."

"Wait... Why?"

"Because you made a promise to me and you broke it. And, if you do that, that's it. It's over between us. That's a rule I don't break for family or for friends. So I need you to understand that, if you don't leave in the next 10 seconds, something very, *very* bad is going to happen to you..." he said through gritted teeth.

"Pierce..." I said, trembling. "I'm your friend."

"And that's why I'm giving you ten seconds."

I stood there for a moment before bolting out the door, tears trickling down my cheek as I raced back to my car.

"Please start," I thought, turning the key. The car stalled and wined. "Come on, come on!" I said, giving it another try. Thankfully, the engine roared to life.

Considering there was no way I'd be able to make it too far without gas, I decided to head back to Placentia. The plan wasn't to go home. The plan was to park in my favorite smoke spot then go to school in the morning and ask around for cash until I had enough to fill my tank. Unfortunately, as though the universe were playing a cruel joke on me, the fumes my car was running on took me the 12 miles back to Placentia only for the damn thing to die half a block away from the turn to the dentist's office parking lot.

"God damnit," I roared, punching my steering wheel as I rolled to a stop alongside the curb.

Right as I shifted into park, a pair of headlights in my rearview stole my attention. *Pretty sure that car is red, so it's probably not a cop car,* I thought, turning around to get a better look at it. That's when the headlights cut off. *Definitely not cops. Just a piece of shit Honda Civic.*

Satisfied that I wasn't about to be nabbed by the police and hauled off back home, I climbed out of the car to check and see how far I was from the curb. A second later, I heard the Honda's doors opening behind me. As I was turning to look and see who was getting out, something that sounded like an empty can clattered to the ground in the alley beside me, stealing my attention.

It's just a bum, I thought, eyeing the man in the ripped-up green military coat who was staring at me from maybe ten or fifteen feet away.

"Nora?" he spoke in a gravelly voice. "Gracie?"

That's when I heard it—the sound of three or four sets of footfalls racing towards me from down the block. I spun around as fast as I could only to see a fist hurtling towards my face. Then… pain flared from my nose and left cheek.

The next thing I knew, I was on the ground looking up at three guys in all black who were wearing ski masks.

"Pick his ass up," a familiar voice barked.

As soon as the guys on my left and right lifted me off the ground, the ringleader kicked me right in the stomach. I folded, coughing my lungs out as I tried to breathe in against the pain in my diaphragm.

The leader grabbed me by the hair and forced me to look up at him. "Not so tough without your friends, huh, Travis?"

"Luis?" I croaked, wincing when I felt blood trickling from my nose to my lip.

He ripped his ski mask off and grinned at me, the dull streetlights just barely illuminating his face. "What, you thought I forgot about you?"

"How did you…" I paused to gasp for air. "How did you… even… find me?"

"Been following you since you left Pierce's place," Luis said.

"Told you he didn't make us," the taller goon spoke.

"If you're looking for money or drugs, I don't have either," I groaned.

"That's too bad, but that's not what this is about," he said, reaching into his pocket. Instead of pulling out a knife like I expected, he took out his wallet and pulled out something small and square. "You see this woman?" he barked, shoving a picture in my face. It was a photo of a smiling Mexican woman who was hugging a much younger Luis. "That's my mom! Look at her! Look!"

"I see her!" I shouted, flinching from how hard he was pulling my hair. "I've never seen that woman in my life… I didn't do anything to her."

"Oh, but you did. You see… She had lung cancer. The doctor said that, without chemo, she wouldn't last a year. And since she was unable to work, the only way to afford the treatments she needed was for me to start slinging. That's why I started working for Pierce. And things were good for a while, until some kids rolled up on me in the middle of a deal."

"I had nothing to do with that!" I said.

Luis shrugged. "Maybe not directly. But… you see… *usually*, I'm able to outrun fools when shit like that happens, but ever since you and that other pussy-ass white boy jumped me and my friends at that party, I've been having these knee problems that make it hard to run… You know, because you decided to stomp on my fucking leg. So, because I couldn't run from those guys who rolled up on me, they beat my ass and jacked me for Pierce's shit. And you know what happened when I showed up to the hospital without the money my mom needed for treatment?" he asked, his voice trembling.

I didn't respond.

"They didn't give her the treatment. She died a few weeks after Pierce cut me loose. And guess who I blame for that?"

I said nothing. I just braced myself for the punch I knew was coming.

Luis cracked me right in the jaw then the two other Mexicans threw me to the ground and started kicking me. So many kicks hit me from so many directions that, eventually, the pain just stopped. It was like my body had just gone numb to help me survive.

Or maybe this is what it feels like right before you die, I thought.

"Hey!" a raspy voice hollered. "Leave that boy alone!"

"Vete al auto," Luis said as he and the goons ran down the block. "This isn't over, Travis! We know where you go to school, puto!"

Groaning and wincing, I rolled over onto my hands and knees and tried to push myself up from the concrete, my arms trembling in my peripheries as blood from my nose and mouth dotted the pavement. That's when a pair of weathered old boots stopped before me.

"You alright?" the gravelly voice above me spoke.

I looked up to find the homeless man from earlier kneeling before me with the most piercing green eyes I'd ever seen. The way they stood out against his filthy, leathery face, they looked like two prized emeralds surrounded by ash. "I think so," I croaked.

"Here," he offered me his hand and, when I took it, he helped me up very carefully.

"What's your name?" the bum asked.

"Travis," I was able to muster. "Yours?"

"Leonard. Do you know my daughter Gracie? Gracie McTavish?"

The dim yellow light illuminating his face was suddenly replaced by red and blue flashing lights. Leonard looked up at the approaching car and jumped when the siren blared.

"What's going on here?" one of the cops asked, shining his flashlight on me and the bum.

Leonard just stared at them with frightened eyes.

"Sir," the same cop said, reaching for his gun, "please step away from the boy."

Leonard shuffled back, looking back and forth between the cops in a panic. That's when the second cop pulled out his cuffs and grabbed his arm.

"Hey!" I yelled. "Let him go! He didn't do anything!"

The cop with the cuffs froze.

"He saved me from the guys who did this to me," I continued.

"Alright, what's your name, son?" the lead cop asked.

"Travis."

"And your name, sir?" he asked the bum.

"His name is Leonard," I answered since the man seemed to be in a trance. "Leonard McTavish or something like that."

"Okay. And can you describe the assailants for me and tell us which way they went."

"It was three guys about my age. They were dressed in all black and drove off that way in a red Honda Civic hatchback," I said, pointing down the street.

"Can you tell us anything else?"

Something told me telling them Luis's name could somehow lead to Pierce getting arrested which could lead to me getting in more trouble. So I shook my head no.

The lead cop turned to the hobo. "Mr. McTavish, would you like us to take you to a shelter?"

"No," Leonard said.

"Alright, well you're free to go then," the lead cop said.

And, with that, Leonard looked over at me. I gave the man a nod as a means of thanking him, then he nodded back before disappearing into the shadows of the alley.

"Son, do you need us to call an ambulance?" the lead cop asked me.

"No, sir," I groaned, rising to my feet. "Just a lift home, if that's alright."

Almost as soon as my finger left the doorbell, the door swung open and Joan walked out in her nightgown. When she saw my battered face, her expression went from furious to concerned in an instant, her eyes widening in horror.

"What happened?" she gasped, looking to the officers.

"Are you Joan Hackett?" the cop asked.

"I am. What happened?" she repeated, more sternly.

"Your nephew here was the victim of an assault earlier tonight," he replied.

"Jesus," she gasped, glancing back at me. As our gazes met, she looked at me in this raw, sorrowful, caring maternal way—a look that filled me with warmth and guilt all at the same time.

Seeing her look at me that way made me feel so damn guilty, I had to look down at the HOME SWEET HOME mat that was now speckled with my blood.

"Ma'am," the lead cop asked, "is it alright if we came in?"

"Of course," she said, stepping aside. When I walked past her, her hand fell on my back and she gave me a little rub.

The rest of that night was a blur. After the cops left, Joan bandaged me up in my room, asked me if I needed anything, then left me to rest.

The next thing I remember was waking up to the sun in my face followed by a cool morning breeze. I peeked against the light and saw three hummingbirds perched at the window. After a few moments, one flew off and then another followed right after. The last thing I saw before drifting back off to sleep was the last bird peering through the window at me before turning and flying off, chasing after its friends.

Epilogue
The Haystack

Part 1: Brad

Even after three weeks of me adhering to Dr. Frederick Royce's meal plan, the relatively small serving sizes of food Mom gave me for dinner that Friday night had me feeling too stuffed to even lay down. So I did what I'd been doing since school let out last week—I sat up in bed playing Xbox with the intent of gaming until either my meal digested or my eyes bled. And, now that I was combating what my doctor called anorexia by consistently eating two to three meals a day, I actually had the energy to stay awake until midnight or later.

It was a little after 9:00 that night when my cell phone chimed with a text. *No one ever texts me this late,* I thought, pausing Halo and grabbing my phone from the other side of the bed. When I saw it was a message from Michael, I wasn't surprised. Ever since we reconnected the day the cops killed Leonard, we've been hanging out and texting each other pretty regularly.

Michael: Yo, dude! Didn't you tell me that Johnny got in so much trouble for running away that he wasn't allowed to even walk to the corner store by himself?

Me: Yeah… Why do you ask?

His response didn't come until three minutes later.

Michael: Because my friend Noah dragged me to the Haystack memorial party for that dead homeless guy and Johnny just showed up with a bunch of stoner kids…

Ah crap… If that party gets busted and Johnny gets caught, Dad's definitely going to kick him out this time. If that happens, that's it… he'll have no choice but to live on the streets like Leonard. I can't let that happen to my brother. I can't.

Me: Where's the party again?

After hitting send, I hopped out of bed and got dressed faster than I had in my entire life. By the time I was done getting ready, my phone chimed with another text.

Michael: It's a place called Kirby Farm. It's like 2 miles from your place. Out near Carbon Canyon. If you take North Rose Drive straight down, you can't miss it. Why, you coming to get him or something?

Me: Yeah. Gonna ask Glenn to take me if he's still home.

Michael: Dude, don't tell him you're coming here! Ever since this place was abandoned, pretty much every high schooler in town knows kids only come here now to get wasted.

Michael again: I got an idea. There's a pretty nice neighborhood across the street. Just tell him you're meeting me there to do some gaming or something. Text me when you're on the way and I'll meet you near a random house near the entrance of the community.

Just as I was stepping out of my room, I heard the familiar jingle of Glenn's keys downstairs followed by the clunk of the front door lock.

"Glenn, wait up!" I shouted through a whisper as to not wake Mom.

He spun around, eyeing me curiously. "What's up?" He looked me up and down. "You going out?"

"Yeah… I was actually going to ask if you could drop me off somewhere on your way to the theater."

"Uh… depends which direction you're going. The movie starts in, like, thirty, and it's at the theater in Yorba Linda."

"Michael invited me to hang at his friend's house across the street from the old Kirby Farm."

"Wait, is that the old farm Mom and Dad used to take us to? The one with that giant hay maze we used to play in?"

"Yeah, I think so."

"The abandoned one near Redwood Grove, right?"

I nodded, maintaining my poker face.

"Okay… I think that's only, like, five minutes out of the way… I can take you. You gonna need a ride back, or you staying the night?"

"Uh. I'll let you know."

He nodded towards the door. "Alright, let's go."

I felt bad lying to Glenn, but I knew telling him the truth would've probably ended with him snitching on Johnny to Dad, and I couldn't risk that happening.

Glenn pulled into the neighborhood that was right across the street from the dirt road leading to Kirby Farm then he dropped me off at this random house that Michael texted me the address to. Thankfully, my brother was in such a rush to get to the movies that he didn't even wait to make sure I made it inside okay, he just did a three-point turn and sped off. As soon as he disappeared around the bend, me and Mike bolted across the street.

Other than the dirt road leading into Kirby Farm, all the land between it and North Road Drive was heavily wooded, making it impossible to see the barn until you were right up on it. That level of seclusion was probably the main reason kids decided to start partying there the second they heard it was abandoned.

The further down the road we trekked, the louder all the music and voices became. And around the time I started smelling cigarettes and weed, the old barn came into view, illuminated by the warm glow of a small bonfire and the headlights of a few cars that were parked facing the building.

"Fuck, this place fell apart," I said, surveying the graffiti-covered building with blotches of brown, splintered wood peeking through the chips in the dull red paint.

"Yeah, nothing like it used to be when I last came here, like, six or seven years ago," Michael said. "Graffiti aside, I'm pretty sure it's been this rundown for years. My dad said that this place hasn't been profitable since the nineties."

"Yeah, you're probably…" My words trailed off when we walked around to the back of the barn. There were probably a hundred kids scattered across the property. A bunch were huddled around a bonfire in the old horse pen near the stables, others were scattered across the field, and there was another cluster near a keg beside this giant, cube-shaped tower of hay—the structure all the kids in school called The Haystack. "Holy shit, man. All of these people are here for Leonard?"

Michael snickered. "I'm pretty sure the girls who organized this thing and the kids they invited are here to honor that Leonard guy, but everyone else just came because they heard secondhand whispers of a party being thrown at The Haystack. What was supposed to be a way to pay tribute to the man who was gunned down for no reason has essentially become a start of the summer shitshow," he said, gesturing to the drunken revelry before us.

"You're probably right," I muttered.

"No, I'm *definitely* right," he said with a grin. "You've heard the rumors around school… Despite everything that's come out, everyone but a handful of kids still talk like the crazy homeless guy who lived behind our school decided to break in and kill some girls named Gracie and Nora, and it's fucking ridiculous."

As much as it sucked to admit, he was right. Most kids were too ignorant to actually listen to the facts. But I wasn't.

Ever since the shooting, I'd been obsessed with the story—checking online and watching the nightly news to keep up with new developments. Because, unlike most kids, I actually spoke to the troubled man once. And, just like all the kids who either saw Leonard that day or those who were in the hallway of the shooting said, every single report confirmed that there was zero evidence that man came to our school to hurt anyone. But no matter what the facts were, there were idiots spreading rumors that the man who kids spent years spinning urban legends about suddenly decided to evolve from the homeless guy who lived behind our school to becoming some psycho who hunted teenage girls.

So, what was the evidence that supported that he was nothing more than a harmless, troubled man who was just confused and looking for his family? Well, for one, he didn't even have a gun on him like Officer Becker—the cop who shot him—claimed during the press conference outside the school. It was revealed later that all Leonard had on him was a pocketknife that wasn't even in his hand when he was shot. Also, the day after the shooting, it came out that the only Gracie and Nora at El Dorado High School told the cops that neither of them had ever seen or heard of Leonard McTavish before, debunking the rumor that they were his targets.

A week later, an investigation into Leonard's past led the cops to a woman in Arizona named Nora Wilson. Apparently, she'd changed her last name from McTavish years after divorcing Leonard. When questioned, Nora told police that, shortly after the birth of their daughter, Leonard had a psychotic break and started having daily hallucinations. Medical reports confirmed that he was diagnosed with a rare case of sudden onset schizophrenia. No matter what meds they gave him, his situation worsened. And after he began acting hostile around their young daughter Gracie, Nora left him and ended up marrying some cook named Nathan Wilson years later.

Still, even after all of that evidence proving he was harmless, people were still saying that he was there to kill those two girls. It made no sense, as things rarely do.

"Alright," Michael said, bumping my arm with his elbow, "let's split up. I'll head over to the kegs, and you check by the barn. The reception sucks out here, so if we can't find him—or if one of us does—let's meet up by The Haystack in ten."

I nodded. "Sounds good."

After searching every cluster of drunk, red-eyed kids partying near the parking area outside the building, I worked my way through the barn and followed the smell of weed to a group of upperclassmen who were sitting around in one of the horse stalls taking bong rips.

If I keep following the smell, I'm bound to find him eventually, I thought, dodging a group of swerving girls on my way out of the barn's front door.

On my way to The Haystack, I caught a glimpse of a familiar face in the corner of my eye. "Kylie?" I called out, stopping abruptly and turning to her. It was then that I saw she was walking hand in hand with Morgan, heading in the direction of where all the parked cars were.

"Brad!" she said with a confused smile. "I didn't think you were coming. Wait, did Johnny send you here to look for me or something?"

"Huh? No. I'm actually here looking for him. Have you seen him around anywhere?"

"Oh," she said, glancing at Morgan. She then turned back to me. "Yeah… Me and your brother haven't exactly been talking much since the breakup."

"Oh… yeah," I said. "Heard about that."

Kylie averted her gaze, looking down at the ground.

Morgan snorted at whatever she saw off in the distance. "Have you checked The Haystack yet? Pretty sure I saw him climbing up there with the other junkies, like, twenty minutes ago."

"Why would he climb that?" I asked, looking up at the top of the tower to see if I could spot him on the roof of the thing.

"Because there's a room up there," Kylie answered.

I turned to her with a cocked brow. "What do you mean?" It was only after I turned back and looked a little lower that I saw a faint glow coming from a small gap near the top of the tower.

"Supposedly," Kylie said, turning to the Haystack, "a bunch of creative-ass stoners came here a few weeks after it shut down and decided they wanted to play *architects* after seeing that the Kirby family left the bales that they used to use for the hay maze all stacked in a giant cube—"

"So they built a staircase to the top then they hollowed out a little room for scum-fucks to drink and get loaded in private," Morgan chimed in.

"I see," I said, turning back to the girls.

When Kylie met my gaze, she stared at me for a moment before she got this really guilty look on her face. Then, out of nowhere, her eyes got all watery. That's when she turned to Morgan. "Can we go?" she asked, her voice sounding all choked up.

Morgan nodded. "Good luck with your brother, Brad. You both better get out of here before this place gets busted."

"Thanks," I said with a nod.

"See ya," Kylie said, giving me a little wave.

"Bye, Kylie," I said, turning towards The Haystack.

"Hey, Brad?" she called out a few seconds later.

When I turned around, I found her over by her car, one hand on the top of the driver's side door, the other on the roof. "Yeah?"

"I'm… I'm sorry." After that, she flashed me a pitiful smile then climbed in the car and shut the door.

I was so confused, I wound up standing there watching them drive down the dirt road until her taillights disappeared. *Sorry for what?*

I worked my way around the side of the barn then weaved through the mob of kids scattered between the big red building and The Haystack. Right as I was finally about to slip through a gap in the crowd, a hand fell on my shoulder. Expecting to see either Johnny or Michael, I twirled around in a flash only to find the bruised face of Travis smiling at me.

"Travis?" I blurted out, my eyes darting from one black and blue patch to the next. Though his face was bruised, there wasn't any swelling like he had following the fight at Kylie's, leading me to believe he was beat up more than a week or two earlier.

"Brady boy!" he cheered. "I thought that was you walking around in the barn!"

"What the hell happened to you?" I asked.

Travis's smile faded. "I got into a bit of trouble, that's all."

"You always get into a bit of trouble, Travis," I said, turning and starting towards The Haystack.

"Wait! Wait!" Travis called out in a desperate tone. "Where are you going?"

"To look for my brother." I started walking again.

"Johnny's here?"

"Yup."

"Wait!" Travis said, grabbing my jacket. "Just wait for a second!"

"What?"

"Look, I know I fucked up. I get that. You have no idea how much I get that. And I'm sorry. I'm truly, truly fucking sorry. For everything. I want to try and make things right, with both you and Johnny, in any way I can."

"Good to know…" I turned away.

"Please, Brad! Please give me that chance!" He sounded even more desperate than before.

I stared at him for a few beats. "You want to make things right?" I asked sternly.

He nodded.

"Then stay the fuck away from me and my family. Understand?"

Travis didn't say anything. He just stood there staring at me. Before he could say anything else, I turned and continued moving through the crowd.

As I crossed the dirt field, I looked up at the two-story-high Haystack and saw the moonlit heads of two kids poke up from the top of the cube.

When I was about halfway up the hay staircase, the pair of kids were making their way down past me, the stench of weed radiating off of them like skunky cologne.

"I'll smoke, I'd even try shrooms," the chubbier guy said as he jumped down onto the haybale step below the one I was on. "But I'd never mess with *that* shit."

"Same," his friend said. "I don't even like being around that stuff."

When I got to the top of the hay tower, I crawled over to the entrance and poked my head into the "doorway." Amid all the coughing and talking, I heard Johnny's voice say something along the lines of, "Just let me use it real quick and I'll give the lighter back to you."

After taking a deep breath to prepare myself for the confrontation ahead, I crawled through the hole and dropped down into the tiny, lantern-lit room. Since the ceiling was only about four-feet high, I had to crawl over to where Johnny and the four other kids with bloodshot, half-open eyes were sitting. Johnny didn't see me coming since he was too busy looking down at the bong, sucking smoke out of it with desperate urgency, but everyone else was staring at me. Well, everyone except this skinny guy with long hair who was holding a lighter underneath a spoon that was filled with this bubbling brown gunk. On his lap, there was a needle.

Johnny erupted into a coughing fit, spewing clouds of smoke into the room as he passed the bong to the weird-looking guy beside him. When my brother looked over at the kid to see why he wasn't taking it, he followed the guy's gaze to me.

"Brad?" Johnny said. "What're you doing here?" His head snapped towards the boy heating up the spoonful of sludge then he snapped his fingers. "Put that shit away."

"Why?" the boy groaned.

"Just do it!" Johnny barked.

The boy seemed too out of it to ask any more questions, so he just set it down beside him reluctantly.

The girl across from him removed the joint from her mouth and blew out a smoke cloud. "Wait, why are we hiding shit? Who's the stick figure, Johnny?" she asked.

"He's my little brother."

"Oh." She extended the joint to me, but I just stared at it. "What? You don't want any?"

"No, he doesn't want any," Johnny said, his eyes filled with scorn.

The girl turned to him. "Oh… kay… Sorry?" She snickered. "I was just trying to be nice. Didn't know he couldn't make decisions for himself."

Johnny sighed. "Alright, everybody out. Now," he said.

"Wait," the girl said, "why do we have to leave?"

"Because I paid for what you're smoking. That's why…" he snarled.

The boy beside him held up his spoon and needle. "Where are we supposed to do this at?"

Johnny cocked a thumb over his shoulder. "There's a whole forest surrounding this place. I'm sure you'll find a spot."

"Fine," the spoon guy grumbled, crawling for the exit.

The others got on all fours and followed him, muttering all sorts of cusses and pissy remarks on their way to the hole. While the girl waited for the guys to climb out, she took a long pull of her blunt, giving Johnny a dirty look the entire time. Then, when it was her turn to go, she chucked the tiny joint over at the ashtray near where she was sitting. That's when I turned and looked at the syringe on the blanket beside Johnny.

"I'm not doing that shit, Brad," Johnny said. "I swear to God, I've never touched that stuff. I don't even know that kid! He just walked in with one of my other friends and—"

"Why do you keep doing this, Johnny?" I asked.

"Doing what?"

"Sneaking out at night. Hanging with people like that. Doing shit like this. Why do you do it? What's the point?"

Johnny looked away then stared off into nothing for a moment. "I don't know," he finally said. "Why did you nearly starve yourself to death?"

I sat there quietly like I didn't know how to respond to that. But I did. Because, deep down, I already knew the answer. *Coping*, I thought. *It's all I've been doing for years. And, at this point, it's all I knew how to do. Starving myself turned out to be the way that worked the best.*

"It's just been bad ever since Kylie left me, man," Johnny continued. "I mean, since Mom wants fucking nothing to do with me, and since Dad's on his way there, Kylie was all I had. Now she's gone, and I just… I don't know what to do, except this." He gestured to the bong.

I stared at him a while then sat beside him against the wall of hay. "You remember that brown house we used to live at? The one that looked haunted with the orange tree in the backyard?"

Johnny squinted at me unsurely, nodding.

"Remember when we tried making the backyard into a swimming pool?"

Johnny snickered. "Oh yeah! When Dad didn't want to take us to the water park, right? We dug that big-ass hole and tried to fill it up with the garden hose."

"Yeah. Remember how pissed Dad was when he got home and saw what we did to the lawn?"

"He was about as mad as he was when he thought I ran away," Johnny joked.

I chuckled. "If Mom didn't stop him from giving us the belt, none of us would've been able to sit for weeks."

Johnny and I laughed.

"I think about that all the time," I said after settling down. "About the three of us having fun, getting into trouble like that."

"Those were the good old days," he mumbled.

"I think that memory is the only one I have," I said with a lump in my throat. "I can't remember any more of the three of us—any good ones, anyway."

"Yeah… me neither," he said solemnly.

"I hate that. I wish I had more memories like that. Not just memories of us, but ones with Mom and Dad too. I don't know why that all had to end. But just because it did, that doesn't have to be the end of the good memories. I think that's our problem. The reason I almost starved myself to death, the reason you started smoking, the reason Glenn drifted away from everyone—that didn't happen because our parents got divorced, it happened because the three of us shut each other out and stopped being there for each other, like brothers should be." It took everything in me to fight off the tears pooling in my eyes, but they rolled down my cheeks anyway. "I don't think I would've gotten the help I needed if I kept shutting myself off from everyone—if I didn't open up to Glenn and Mom, if I didn't give myself that chance. The chance to be happy. Everyone needs someone, Johnny. Someone to care—to help you through all the bullshit. And that's us. Your family. And we want you to stop this. Please. We need… we need you back in our lives."

Johnny turned to me with this look on his face like he was about to say something profound or sentimental, but when he opened his mouth to speak, he started coughing. A second later, I inhaled a lungful of acrid smoke and started hacking too. I didn't notice it before because it was already smokey in there from all the weed, but everything had become significantly hazier since we started talking.

"Holy shit!" Johnny shouted, pointing at something across from us.

Squinting against the smokey haze burning my eyes, I followed his finger to the orange glow flickering near where the girl was sitting earlier. "Oh my god! It's on fire!"

Part 2: Travis

Just go home, I thought. *Just turn the other way and start walking. Hitchhike if you have to. Just get out of here. Brad's done with you. Johnny's on the same train. Accept that and get over it. Move the fuck on and start walking.*

But I didn't. As much as the voice in my head tried convincing me otherwise, some other part of me knew that I couldn't just let that be it for the three of us. After everything Johnny, Brad, and I went through together—I knew they were the only true friends I ever had.

That couldn't have all been for nothing. If you want to make amends, do it tonight.

So, when I saw Brad climbing up to the top of The Haystack, I ran after him. Except, when I got there, I didn't climb the staircase of hay, I just sat on the bottom step, trying to come up with the right words to say to make things right.

A few minutes later, I heard some girl scream, "Holy shit!"

When I looked up in the direction of her voice, I saw everyone between me and the barn looking up at The Haystack, eyes wide with horror as they gravitated towards my direction.

Something that smelled like burning grass wafted into my nose as I sprung up from the bale.

"The Haystack's on fire!" some dude behind me shouted right as I set my sights on the angry flames dancing against the night sky.

"Do you think anyone's in there?" another guy asked.

For a moment, I watched the top of the hay cube, waiting for Brad and Johnny's heads to peek over the edge. Through all the clamoring behind me and through the crackling inferno above, I heard screams coming from the top. That's when I knew they were trapped up there.

"Someone call the fire department!" a girl behind me screamed.

Fire department? Please, I thought as I scrambled up the makeshift staircase. *By the time they get here, my friends will be piles of ash!*

"What the hell is that kid doing?" some girl shouted.

I was only a few bales away from the top when the flames had consumed the last few steps. "Shit! Shit! Shit!" I panicked, looking around for another way in.

To my right, I spotted this cube of hay that was sticking out more than the rest, like someone inside had tried pushing the block out only to give up halfway through. Pointy pieces of straw stabbed at my hands as I scaled my way up the hay bale wall. After finding a good foothold, I grabbed the protruding block with one hand then shimmied it side to side until it looked like it was three-quarters of the way out. That's when I pulled it as hard as I could, completely dislodging it and letting it fall to the dirt below. A dark plume of smoke erupted out of the hole and, through all the popping and crackling of the fire, I heard someone coughing.

As soon as I climbed up into the tiny hole, I began hacking and choking on the smoke. "Brad? Johnny?" I hollered, desperately trying to fan away the smoke even though it wasn't going anywhere.

"Help!" Johnny screamed, coughing violently afterwards.

After I fell into the sweltering room, I could barely see him through all the smoke. "Johnny!" I called.

He turned to me, squinting, the flickering flames illuminating his soot-covered face. "Travis?" he asked. "Over here!"

"Where's Brad?"

He pointed down and, through the smokescreen, I saw an unconscious Brad sprawled out on the floor. "He passed out!" Johnny shouted. "Help me get him up!"

"Wait, the hole I came through isn't wide enough to help Brad through if he's passed out. Help me push another block out!"

"Okay!" he said, crawling alongside me.

"On three, we both need to shoulder it!"

He nodded during his coughing fit.

"One!" I shouted.

"Two!" we said in unison. "Three!"

Even with both of us hitting the block, it only budged an inch or so.

"Again!" I yelled. "One! Two! Three!"

Just like last time, it moved a few more inches.

"Last one!" Johnny yelled. "One! Two!"

On three, he and I shouldered that thing with everything we had then the hay bale dislodged and tumbled down to the ground below.

"Johnny, you go first then I'll lower Brad out to you."

With a nod, Johnny scrambled through the hole. "Alright, send him down!" he said a few moments later.

I picked up Brad and carried him to the exit, hoisting him through the hole headfirst.

"I got him," Johnny said, pulling him out the rest of the way.

As Brad's legs slipped through the opening, the heat behind me intensified. When I looked back, I saw the tips of the flames licking the air inches away from my body. "You clear?"

"We're clear!" Johnny yelled back. "Come down! Quick!"

I climbed out legs first, letting go of the straw ledge right as I watched a wall of fire rushing towards me. The fire erupted out of the hole like a flamethrower as I fell down to where the guys were. Then, when my feet hit the hay, I lost my balance and stumbled backwards towards the edge. Right as I felt myself going over, Johnny grabbed me and pulled me back towards him.

"Holy shit!" I shouted. "Thanks."

He just nodded.

"Lower him down, we got him!" some guy down below shouted.

When I looked over the edge, I saw a bunch of kids gathered near the base reaching up to help since the flames below had already engulfed our path to the ground.

"Grab his arm!" Johnny shouted.

I did, and then we lowered Brad's limp body down. Once the two guys on the ground carried him a safe distance away, Johnny and I jumped down, hitting the ground with a roll.

"Brad," Johnny shouted, scrambling over to his brother on all fours. He brought his ear to Brad's nose and listened. Then Johnny put his mouth to his brother's and followed up with chest compressions. "Come on!" Johnny yelled after listening for breathing. He administered another round of mouth-to-mouth. "Wake up! Come on!"

A few compressions later, Brad's eyes shot open and he began coughing violently. "What happened?" he groaned, looking up at me and Johnny before scanning all the people staring down at him.

"You almost died, that's what," I said, offering him a hand as Johnny did the same.

The still coughing Brad took our hands then we hoisted him up. And once he was back on his feet, he looked over at me and gave me a little nod. Smiling, I nodded back.

As the firetruck sirens blared in the distance, the three of us backed away from The Haystack, never taking our eyes off of it as we did. For a while we just stood there, side by side, staring up at the roaring inferno in silence.

Then, as if we all had the same thought at the same time, we looked to one another before turning away from the blaze and headed towards the dirt road together. Right before we rounded the barn, I glanced back at the raging fire and watched as the black smoke trailed up into the never-ending night sky, giving one last dance before evanescing into the stars.

About the Author

Brandon Calvillo is a writer, director, and actor from Anaheim, California. Following his rise to social media fame on Vine, he has gone on to create dark, comedic content that highlights the hypocrisies of American life for his combined 4.8 million followers on YouTube, Instagram, and TikTok. Outside of social media, Brandon has starred in television and film roles, written journalistic pieces for Playboy Magazine, and co-wrote the feature film *FML: A Social Media* Adventure with fellow comedian Jason Nash. His professional portfolio also contains achievements such as having written, directed, and acted in over ten short films, such as *Wild Nothing*, which starred American filmmaker Shane Black in a supporting role.

Made in United States
North Haven, CT
19 November 2021

11295262R00221